T0321830

THE TROUBLE WITH
MRS MONTGOMERY HURST

By the same author

The Secrets of Hartwood Hall

THE TROUBLE WITH MRS MONTGOMERY HURST

Katie Lumsden

MICHAEL  JOSEPH

PENGUIN MICHAEL JOSEPH

UK | USA | Canada | Ireland | Australia
India | New Zealand | South Africa

Penguin Michael Joseph is part of the Penguin Random House group of companies
whose addresses can be found at global.penguinrandomhouse.com

First published 2024
002

Copyright © Katie Lumsden, 2024

The moral right of the author has been asserted

Set in 12/15pt Baskerville MT Pro
Typeset by Jouve (UK), Milton Keynes
Printed and bound in Great Britain by Clays Ltd, Elcograf S.p.A.

The authorized representative in the EEA is Penguin Random House Ireland,
Morrison Chambers, 32 Nassau Street, Dublin D02 YH68

A CIP catalogue record for this book is available from the British Library

HARDBACK ISBN: 978–0–241–55611–5
TRADE PAPERBACK ISBN: 978–0–241–55612–2

www.greenpenguin.co.uk

MIX
Paper | Supporting
responsible forestry
FSC® C018179

Penguin Random House is committed to a
sustainable future for our business, our readers
and our planet. This book is made from Forest
Stewardship Council® certified paper.

For Mary Rose,
who loved books

Contents

Map x

Dramatis Personae xiii

VOLUME ONE: JULY 1841

I. In which the Ashpoint family prepare for a ball 3

II. In which surprising news spreads through the ballroom 16

III. In which gossip brews at Ashpoint Brewery 28

IV. In which Mr Lonsdale entertains thoughts above his station ... 38

V. In which we hear two histories of love 46

VI. In which we cultivate the acquaintance of a very grand family ... 59

VII. In which cards are played and whisky is consumed 69

VIII. In which the Hursts return 81

IX. In which the Hursts do not call 90

X. In which Mrs Elton will not be deterred 100

XI. In which Miss McNeil receives a call and Mrs Elton
     is outmanoeuvred 114

XII. In which Melford shops and Miss McNeil is slighted 125

XIII. In which we are told stories 135

XIV. In which Lord Salbridge collects rent and hearts 142

XV. In which Mrs Elton presides over a dinner of great splendour ... 151

XVI. In which Miss Ashpoint makes a new friend and
     Lord Salbridge makes trouble 160

XVII. In which Miss Elton overhears what she should not 167

VOLUME TWO: AUGUST 1841

I. In which Miss Ashpoint is out in the open and Lady Rose hides 177

II. In which Miss Elton plays a sonata 184

III. In which the Hursts come to tea 191

IV. In which Miss Ashpoint offers some advice 204

V. In which Mr Lonsdale revises his opinion 218

VI. In which cricket is played and tea is drunk 225

VII. In which Miss Elton's fate is discussed 237

VIII. In which calls and plans are made 243

IX. In which new friendships are established 255

X. In which Radcliffe Park is invaded 260

XI. In which Miss Elton is slighted and Lord Salbridge is enlightened 267

VOLUME THREE: SEPTEMBER 1841

I. In which Diggory Ashpoint rides and Mrs Hurst calls 279

II. In which Miss Elton's confidence is shaken 290

III. In which a storm breaks at Wickford Towers 298

IV. In which a new tide of gossip spreads through the county 306

V. In which two young ladies are made uneasy 315

VI. In which Lord Salbridge returns home 326

VII. In which we witness an act of sabotage 332

VIII. In which Melford consumes a feast 340

IX. In which Melford dances 347

X. In which Sir Frederick overcomes his shyness 355

XI. In which an answer is not given 362

VOLUME FOUR: OCTOBER 1841

I. In which Mrs Hurst gives some advice 373

II. In which Mr Ashpoint does his duty 381

III. In which Mr Hurst's tale is told 387

IV. In which Miss McNeil decides 397

V. In which Mr Ashpoint finds his answer 406

VI. In which Miss Elton's fate is sealed 411

VII. In which the tide of gossip changes course 420

CONTENTS

VIII. In which the sun shines for Diggory Ashpoint 425
IX. In which the toasts are made 430
X. In which Miss Elton acts for herself 435
XI. In which Lord Salbridge miscalculates 442
XII. In which the dance goes on 448

Acknowledgements 457

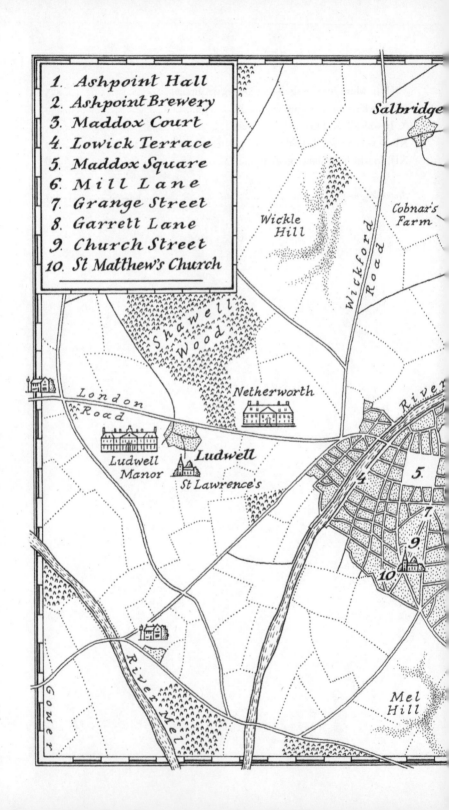

1. Ashpoint Hall
2. Ashpoint Brewery
3. Maddox Court
4. Lowick Terrace
5. Maddox Square
6. Mill Lane
7. Grange Street
8. Garrett Lane
9. Church Street
10. St Matthew's Church

Salbridge

Cobnar's Farm

Wickle Hill

Wickford Road

Shawell Wood

Netherworth

London Road

River

Ludwell Manor

Ludwell

St Lawrence's

4

5

7

9

10

Gower

River Mel

Mel Hill

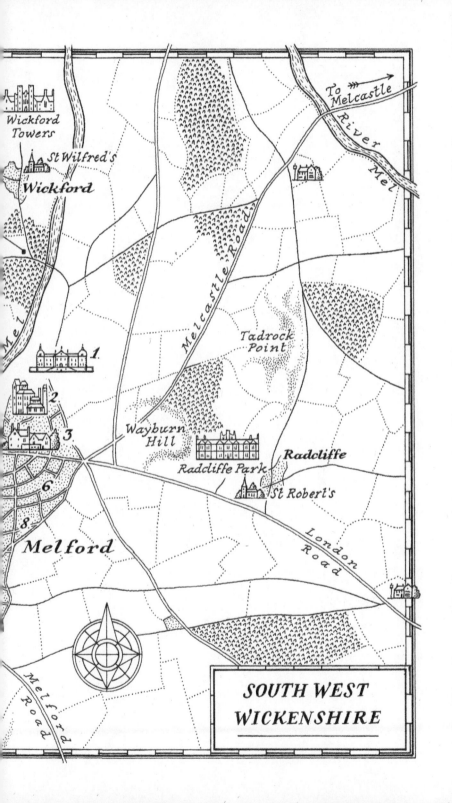

Wickford
Towers

St Wilfred's

Wickford

To Melcastle

River Mel

Melcastle Road

Mel

Tadrock
Point

1

2

3

Wayburn
Hill

Radcliffe

Radcliffe Park

St Robert's

6

8

Melford

London
Road

Melford
Road

SOUTH WEST
WICKENSHIRE

Dramatis Personae

Ashpoint Hall and Brewery

The Ashpoints, residing at Ashpoint Hall, just outside Melford

Mr James Ashpoint, a wealthy brewer, a widower, 52 years old
Mr Diggory Ashpoint, his son, 24 years old
Miss Amelia Ashpoint, his daughter, 23 years old
Miss Ada Ashpoint, his daughter, 15 years old
Master Lawrence Ashpoint, his son, 10 years old
Bella, Amelia's maid, 19 years old
Ellington, Diggory's valet, 28 years old
Miss Thomas, the children's governess, 27 years old
Martha, a nursemaid, 22 years old
William, a footman, 21 years old

The Brewery Staff

Mr Hartley Lonsdale, the foreman, 28 years old,
    residing at 5 Mill Lane in Melford
Oliver Magner, a brewery worker, 41 years old
John Parcels, a brewery worker, 50 years old
Sam Fedmouth, a brewery worker, 33 years old

The County Families of Wickenshire

The Ravensdales, residing at Wickford Towers, 5 miles from Melford

Alexander Ravensdale senior, the Earl of Wickford,
    addressed as Lord Wickford, 58 years old
Minerva Ravensdale, his wife, the Countess of Wickford,
    addressed as Lady Wickford, 52 years old
Alexander Ravensdale, their son, the Viscount of Salbridge,
    addressed as Lord Salbridge, 26 years old
Lady Rose Ravensdale, their daughter, addressed as Lady Rose,
    18 years old
Johnson, the butler, 41 years old
Bertha, the upper housemaid, 20 years old

The Hammersmiths, residing at Maddox Court, in Melford

Lady Rebecca Hammersmith, a baronet's widow, addressed as Lady
    Hammersmith, 53 years old
Sir Frederick Hammersmith, her son, a baronet and the squire of
    Melford, addressed as Sir Frederick, 29 years old
Beth, a housemaid, 26 years old

The Eltons, residing at Ludwell Manor, 4 miles from Melford

Mr Augustus Elton senior, squire of Ludwell, 56 years old
Mrs Sophronia Elton, his wife, 48 years old
Mr Augustus Elton, their son, MP for the constituency of Melford
    and Wickford, 28 years old (residing in London)
Miss Felicia Elton, their daughter, 19 years old
Mrs Jennings, the housekeeper, 45 years old
Mrs Hubbard, Mrs Elton's 'own woman', 43 years old
Sarah, Felicia's maid, 20 years old
Lucy, a parlourmaid, 27 years old
Peter, a footman, 25 years old

**The Hurst Household, residing at Radcliffe Park,
2 miles from Melford**

Mr Montgomery Hurst, squire of Radcliffe, 31 years old
Mrs Alley, the housekeeper, 53 years old
Jenny, a housemaid, 16 years old
Meg, a kitchen maid, 23 years old

**The Alderton Household, residing at Netherworth,
1 ½ miles from Melford**

Major Charles Alderton, a retired military officer of independent
    means and uncertain birth, 32 years old

The Townsfolk of Melford

The Craytons, residing at 3 Church Street

Mr Crayton, a banker, 49 years old
Mrs Crayton, his wife, 46 years old
Mr Edmund Crayton, their son, 22 years old

The Maddon and Waterson household, residing at 24 Garrett Lane

Miss Gertrude Maddon, 63 years old
Miss Arabella Waterson, 61 years old

The McNeils, residing at 9 Garrett Lane

Mr Phineas McNeil, a land agent, a widower, 52 years old
Miss Clara McNeil, his daughter, 23 years old
Hannah, a maid-of-all-work, 26 years old

The Palmers, residing at 1 Lowick Terrace

Captain Theodore Palmer, a retired naval officer, 45 years old
Mrs Lucille Palmer, his wife, 42 years old
Miss Anne Palmer, their daughter, 22 years old
Miss Louisa Palmer, their daughter, 20 years old
Miss Cassandra Palmer, their daughter, 18 years old
Miss Julia Palmer, their daughter, 15 years old
Miss Elizabeth Palmer, their daughter, 11 years old
Maggie, a housemaid, 17 years old

Others

Mr John Duckfield, vicar of Melford, 30 years old,
    residing at the vicarage, 1 Church Street
Monsieur Pierre Brisset, a music teacher, 23 years old,
    residing at 2 Garrett Lane
Miss Honoria Nettlebed, a dressmaker, 37 years old
Mr Graves, waiter at the Lantern, 28 years old
Mrs Grace Abbott, a cottager's widow, 27 years old,
    residing near Wickford
Janey Abbot, her daughter, 5 years old

VOLUME ONE
July 1841

CHAPTER I

In which the Ashpoint family prepare for a ball

THROUGHOUT THE NOBLE COUNTY OF WICKENSHIRE, THERE were many households in which order reigned. There were families who dressed neatly and quickly, who were ready to depart in good time for any social occasion. There were homes where the corridors were free from clutter, where quiet prevailed, where the occupants were capable of assuming their best finery without descending into utter chaos.

The Ashpoint household was not one of these.

They were due to leave for Lady Wickford's ball in twenty minutes, and everything was still in disarray.

Amelia Ashpoint – three-and-twenty, wearing pink muslin with bad grace – was standing in front of the large mirror in her sitting room while her maid redid her hair. It was hard to stay still, hard not to turn her head towards the events unfolding in the corridor.

The door opposite hers led to her brother Diggory's bedroom, and this, too, stood open. Diggory – one year Amelia's senior, rarely acting it – was half out of the room, half in. His shoes were very shiny. His hair was very shiny. His black silk waistcoat was very shiny. He was currently being pelted by a range of shiny cravats, launched as cannonballs from a slingshot by the youngest Ashpoint child. Diggory had clearly made the mistake of asking Laurie – ten years old, bent on mischief – which cravat he ought to wear.

Amelia spluttered with laughter as a striped cravat hit Diggory's carefully combed hair and undid all his hard work. Her maid tutted and made her look straight at the mirror once more. This was Amelia's second outfit of the evening, for she had managed to tear her first gown a quarter of an hour since, and the floor was a sea of rejected dresses and spurned petticoats.

From further down the corridor she could hear the raised voices of the two last members of her family. Her younger sister, Ada – fifteen years old, forever wishing she were older – had thrown herself down on the carpet and was sobbing heartily, while their father attempted ineffectually to comfort her.

'Come, my dear,' Mr Ashpoint was saying. 'Dry your eyes. Do not wish your life away – you will be old enough in time.'

'It's not *fair*!' Ada shouted back. 'Why *can't* I go to the ball, Papa? Some girls of fifteen are out already. To say I must wait until *seventeen* is *torture* and *cruelty* of the *very* worst kind! And there is no use saying it can be earlier if *Amelia* gets married, because you have been talking about Mr Hurst for a year now and Amelia is *still* not engaged.'

'Well now, Ada,' replied her father, 'we are all very hopeful that Mr Hurst—'

He was cut off by a shout from Diggory as one of Laurie's missiles hit him in the face.

'Laurie!' cried Mr Ashpoint, but his youngest child had already armed himself once more. 'Laurie, put that down – no, *Laurie*—'

Back in her sitting room, Amelia rolled her eyes. Her

maid had finished her hair now and stood back, contemplating the result with a mixture of pride and resignation, as though she were quite aware that Amelia would ruin it within the hour.

'Thank you, Bella.'

'Ought I to go and tell the coachman to expect a long wait?'

As Amelia glanced out into the corridor, a balled-up cravat sailed past her door. 'Probably best,' she replied.

The maid headed for the stairs, avoiding the mess of strewn clothing and stepping gingerly over Ada's prone form. Amelia followed her. She stood in the corridor, watching Laurie giggle as he threw socks at Diggory (he had now run out of cravats), watching Ada weep, watching her father rub her back and make faint soothing noises.

This was all a great deal more entertaining than a ball.

Then her father glanced up at her with anxious, helpless eyes, and Amelia sighed. Something must be done.

She stepped quickly forwards, grabbed Laurie's slingshot and tossed it into her bedroom, then lifted her little brother up under the armpits and carried him bodily down the corridor. She was vaguely aware that such a proceeding might result in the tearing of another gown, but frankly, she did not care. Laurie seemed to think this all part of the fun and put his arms out as if he were flying. Amelia lifted him over Ada and their father and marched down the hall, past the great staircase and into the nursery, where she deposited him in a chair.

The nursemaid looked up from her sewing and smiled. 'Did you enjoy seeing everyone all dressed up for the ball?' she asked.

'Oh, ever so much,' said Laurie eagerly, as Amelia shut the door behind her.

Back in the corridor, Diggory was standing in front of the mirror, patting anxiously at his hair in an effort to repair Laurie's damage. Ada was still sprawled on the carpet, declaring again that life was monstrously unfair. Mr Ashpoint sat beside her, leaning back against the wall. He was still only in his shirt and trousers – no waistcoat, no cravat, no tailcoat – and he looked exhausted.

'Ada,' said Amelia gently, sitting down beside her sister, ignoring her father's anxious mutter about creasing her dress. 'Ada, how about we have a little dance here next week? I am sure Clara will come and dance with me if I ask her, and we could get Julia Palmer to come and dance with you. Clara and I shall teach you how to waltz – what do you say to that?'

Ada looked up at her and sniffed very hard. 'But you hate waltzing,' she said.

'Very true,' said Amelia, 'so think just how kind I am being.'

Mr Ashpoint was rising slowly and quietly to his feet, stepping carefully over the cravats on his way back to his dressing room.

Ada pulled herself up into a sitting position, looking at Amelia through her tears. 'It's not fair,' she said, but this time her voice was gentler. '*You* get to go to balls, and you don't even like them.'

'Exactly,' said Amelia. 'It is quite as unfair for me as it is for you, and I am not crying. To be truly grown-up, you must bear your sorrows.'

Her sister looked up at her, rubbed her eyes, nodded. 'Will you tell me all about it when you come home?' she asked.

'Diggory will at any rate,' said Amelia, 'for he loves balls.'

Diggory turned towards them with a smile and a shrug. 'Free punch,' he said.

Ada gave a watery laugh. 'Who are you going to dance with?' she asked Amelia, her voice a little steadier now.

'Oh,' said Amelia, 'I hardly know.'

'Mr Hurst?'

'Perhaps.'

'I do hope you marry him, Amy, and then Papa will let me go to *all* the balls.'

Amelia hesitated. She frowned, and she was about to refute the likelihood of this event when she saw the look of tearful hope on her sister's face. 'We shall see, Ada.'

'Who are you going to dance with, Diggory?' Ada asked, as her brother gave his hair one last comb with his fingers, then turned from the mirror.

'I bet you a shilling that Diggory will dance with Lady Rose,' said Amelia, 'if he does not blind her with his overly shiny shoes.'

Diggory looked down at his feet. 'There is nothing wrong,' he muttered, 'with shining one's shoes. Just because *you* do not care about your appearance, Amy—'

At that moment, the door of their father's room burst open, and out he came, cravat, waistcoat and tails now firmly in place. 'We must make haste,' he declared, 'or we shall miss the first dance!'

'God forbid,' said Amelia, with a laugh.

'God forbid indeed!' replied Mr Ashpoint, for whom a ball was a terribly serious affair. He had long given up on maintaining etiquette within Ashpoint Hall itself, but he tried very hard to keep up the appearance of dignity beyond the walls of their home, much to Amelia's annoyance. He was hurrying down the corridor so fast he almost tripped on Amelia's dress. 'Diggory, Amelia – the carriage is waiting. Ada, my dear, bear up.'

'Yes, do,' said Amelia, rising to her feet. 'If nothing else, think how you will be able to laud it over Laurie when you are old enough for balls and he is still too little. Imagine what things he will throw at us all then!'

Ada gave a hearty sniff and managed a smile, no doubt to show how grown-up she was – but Amelia still heard her give a little sob as she and Diggory followed their father down the stairs.

Half an hour later, Amelia was gazing out of the window as the family carriage finally jolted through the grand gates of Wickford Towers. She watched the orchard and the rose garden and the great glasshouses roll by, spotted other carriages in the red glow of the summer evening sun. The sound of the wheels changed as they moved from path to drawbridge to gravel, as they crossed the moat and neared the house. From somewhere out on the lawn she could hear the muffled, excited voices of the kinds of young ladies who liked balls.

If guests were still arriving, then they were clearly going to make the first dance after all. Amelia glanced across at her father and brother, wondering if she might be able to avoid it, but Mr Ashpoint was looking back at her with a hopeful, eager smile, as though there were nothing more important in life than a ball, and Amelia knew she would have to dance.

There was a flurry of activity from the coachman outside, and then everything slowed to a halt and the carriage door was pulled open. Amelia climbed out first – probably not as gracefully as Mr Ashpoint would have liked – thanked the coachman and looked around as her father and brother alighted behind her. The vast lawns of Wickford Towers were bustling with people – a mass of tailcoats, muslin and silk. Footmen in livery weaved between the clusters of guests to usher them towards the doors.

Amelia spotted familiar faces amongst the jostling crowd: Captain Palmer and his family, Mr Crayton from the bank, the vicar, the doctor, the miller. It seemed that everyone with even the faintest claim to respectability was here tonight, for she spotted Hartley Lonsdale, her father's foreman from the brewery, somewhere up ahead.

The Earl and Countess of Wickford could invite anyone they chose, of course; title and pedigree brought such luxuries. Amelia's father was very wealthy – he was probably the wealthiest man at the ball – but he was still only a brewer. If Mr Ashpoint invited the butcher to tea, Wickenshire would be scandalized, but if Lord Wickford asked a farmhand to dinner, no one would dare raise an eyebrow.

As Amelia and Diggory followed their father through the crowd towards the great oak doors, she glanced over her shoulder to see the Elton family alighting from their stately carriage – Mr and Mrs Elton all stiffness and respectability, Miss Elton all elegance and grace and emptiness.

They were ushered into the courtyard, before following the crowd into the great hall in the north wing of the house. The scattered noise of tuning instruments mingled with the hum of conversation. Clusters of guests were already inside – sipping wine or punch, gazing in awe around the vast great hall, greeting the Wickford family – and more people were filing in behind them every moment. Amelia and Diggory stayed close together, but they lost their father somewhere along the way, caught by some acquaintance in a discussion of the latest local news. If there was one thing their father loved as much as a ball, it was *gossip*.

The home of the Wickford family was a very different place to the house where the Ashpoints resided. Where Ashpoint Hall was modern, built barely thirty years ago, Wickford Towers had stood for centuries. Where Ashpoint Hall was full of bright, elegant rooms with the newest furnishings and wallpapers, Wickford Towers was a mess of winding corridors, courtyards, oak panelling and antiques. The great hall was an old, grand room, done up just as it might have been when the house was first built: a stained-glass window, walls encased in ornately styled wood, Gothic carvings in the gabled ceiling. This evening, it was lit with torches, and the tables had been moved to leave space for dancing.

The Wickford family stood in the centre of the assembling crowds: Lord Wickford – neat, greying and aware of his own importance, hand out to greet his guests; Lady Wickford – elegant and graceful, smiling at all who passed her with kind condescension; their son, Lord Salbridge – dressed messily in a bottle-green cravat, silver waistcoat and crimson tailcoat, drinking from a very full glass of punch; and their daughter, Lady Rose – petite and pretty in a red silk gown, looking nervously around, curtseying as more guests approached.

Amelia glanced sideways at Diggory, who was staring very hard at Lady Rose. She watched him gaze at her, watched as Lady Rose looked straight back at him, watched her hesitant smile, the pink come into her cheeks.

Amelia smiled to herself.

Diggory took a step forwards, as though about to cross the room, to speak to Lady Rose – but before he could move,

Lord Salbridge had abandoned his post and was shoving his way through the guests towards them. He caught Diggory up in a tight hug.

'Diggory, my dear chap, I have *missed* you,' he declared. 'London was an eternal bore without you.'

Diggory laughed. 'The London Season always seems a great deal more exciting than Wickenshire to me.'

'Oh, to be sure, the country is dull enough – but you are here, and that is something.' Lord Salbridge released Diggory and took a gulp from his glass of punch, which he had narrowly avoided spilling over his friend. 'Well, and what have you been doing to entertain yourself in my absence?'

'Oh, nothing much,' said Diggory.

Amelia tried to suppress a smile, for that was true enough. Her brother was very skilled at doing nothing much. While his friend had been in London for the Season, Diggory had been passing his time much as he did when Lord Salbridge was present: going to the Lantern every other night to play cards and drink slightly too much; sleeping late in the mornings; reading Gothic novels in corners of the library; and not going into the brewery to help their father, however often he was asked.

Lord Salbridge, who seemed to catch Amelia's smile, turned towards her. 'And how do you do, Miss Ashpoint? Engaged for the first dance yet? Will you have *me*?'

Amelia looked him full in the face. 'I fear I must decline that honour. My feet have only just recovered from our last dance.'

Lord Salbridge looked at her, frowned, swayed, then decided she was joking and laughed heartily.

Diggory laughed, too, giving her one of his don't-be-uncivil looks. Amelia had never understood what her brother saw in Lord Salbridge, unless it was simply that Salbridge's hair stood up more elegantly than Diggory's and that he held his drink better.

'We shall have to ask the Palmer sisters then.' Lord Salbridge took Diggory by the arm. 'Come along, old chap,' he said, and Diggory followed him off into the crowd.

Amelia stood alone for a few moments, scanning the faces of the guests. Too much silk and satin, too many waistcoats and fancily tied cravats, too many extravagant hairstyles. She spotted the three elder Palmer girls just as Diggory and Salbridge found them. She saw Sir Frederick Hammersmith by the fireplace, sipping lemonade – for he never touched wine or punch – dressed in a red-and-white floral waistcoat, a turquoise tailcoat and pantaloons that were inordinately yellow. Amelia tried to stop the laugh that sprung to her lips. Sir Frederick, she thought, was the kind of man who dressed outlandishly in an attempt to hide his lack of personality. Everybody said they liked and admired him, because he was a baronet, but Amelia considered him infernally dull.

Finally, she found the face she was looking for: Clara McNeil, standing with her father by the entrance, dressed in a faded rose-print gown, her dark blonde hair tied up behind her head. It was widely acknowledged that Felicia Elton was the great beauty of Wickenshire, but Amelia did not think her half so handsome as Clara.

Before she could cross the room to speak to her, the music struck up in a great crescendo to signal the beginning of the first dance.

The guests all began to move. Those in the centre of the great hall retreated to the outskirts, and a sea of gentlemen crossed the room to secure their partners. Lady Wickford did not approve of dancing cards at private balls, and although a few young people had no doubt made arrangements beforehand, it was chiefly a matter of every gentleman for himself.

Amelia stood back and watched as half the men present descended upon Felicia Elton. She watched as Sir Frederick finally triumphed and led her to the centre of the room. She saw her brother secure Louisa Palmer, saw Lady Rose led off by the vicar of Melford, saw Clara's gentle nod when she was asked to dance by Mr Lonsdale.

Just as Amelia was beginning to hope that she might have escaped the first dance, she was approached by Mr Hurst.

Montgomery Hurst was, Amelia often thought, one of the least ridiculous of her neighbours. He was one-and-thirty, agreeable and kind. He dressed sensibly, wore his brown hair short, was clean-shaven and passingly handsome. He was a little solemn at times, it was true, but he never seemed to mind Amelia's more lively sense of humour.

She did not know him *well*, exactly. He had grown up nearby, for the Hursts were a very old Wickenshire family, but he had left for Cambridge at eighteen and not returned. He had travelled abroad for a while, before settling in Paris. Although Amelia had seen him from time to time on his brief visits home to see his father and to visit Sir Frederick, his oldest friend, it was only upon the death of Mr Hurst senior, some eighteen months ago, that the present Mr Hurst had returned to the neighbourhood. Now, aside from irregular absences in London on business, he had more or less settled at Radcliffe Park.

Over the past year and a half, Amelia and Mr Hurst had struck up a kind of friendship. She liked to dance with him because he never attempted to flirt with her, and she suspected that he liked to dance with her for much the same reason.

'Miss Ashpoint,' he said now, as he reached her, 'I hope I am not too late to engage you for the first dance?'

'You are not,' she said and put her hand in his with a smile.

As they joined the other couples, she saw her father watching them from across the great hall, his delight plain upon his face. Amelia tried hard not to sigh. It had been the dearest hope of her father's life these last five or six years that she would marry; it had been his dearest hope these last eighteen months that she would marry Mr Hurst.

The dance began. It was a waltz, and so Amelia put her hand on Mr Hurst's shoulder, let him lead her round, turning as the one-two-three of the rhythm pulled them on. Diggory sailed by with his partner, and Amelia managed to exchange a smile with Clara before she spun past.

Amelia and Mr Hurst spoke of the weather, of the books they were reading, of the general election. And then, when conversation lulled, Mr Hurst said, 'Your father sent me a note asking if I would dine with you all on Friday.'

Of course, thought Amelia – *of course* her father had invited him to dinner. He was forever inviting Mr Hurst to something or other at Ashpoint Hall.

'I must ask you to give him my apologies, I am afraid,' Mr Hurst went on, lowering his voice a little, 'for I shall be away. I am riding to London tomorrow.'

'I shall tell him,' said Amelia. 'You are going on business, I suppose?'

Mr Hurst hesitated. He moved his feet a little less quickly, less accurately than usual, and Amelia had to step carefully to compensate. 'Well, no,' said Mr Hurst. 'Not business.'

'Oh?'

Mr Hurst looked at her. His expression was a little uneasy, a little – what, apologetic? And somehow, Amelia knew what he was going to say before the words left his mouth, knew that he wished her to convey his apologies to her father for more than a missed dinner, knew that he felt a little doubtful whether he ought to apologize to her as well.

'You see, Miss Ashpoint,' said Mr Hurst, 'I am going to London to be married.'

CHAPTER II

In which surprising news spreads
through the ballroom

NO CONVERSATION IN A BALLROOM WAS EVER TRULY PRIVATE.
Louisa Palmer and Diggory Ashpoint were passing Amelia
and Mr Hurst at that very moment, and Louisa tripped
over Diggory's feet in surprise. The two other couples
waltzing nearby also overheard. The ladies looked at the
gentlemen, and the gentlemen looked at the ladies – and
when the dance finished, each went off to whisper to
their parents, to their siblings, to their friends, that Mr
Montgomery Hurst was to be *married*. They were not quite
sure to whom, but they did know that his bride was *not* to
be Miss Ashpoint.

Another dance began. Partners were swapped, and the
news spread further. Through the polka, the mazurka and
the gallopade, murmurs were exchanged. As the sun set
beyond the stained-glass windows, everybody began to stare
at Mr Hurst with considerable interest and to look at Miss
Ashpoint with passing pity. Over the card table, in the punch
queue, down in the supper room, everyone whispered about
Mr Hurst.

Montgomery Hurst himself seemed to be endeavouring to
avoid enquiry. He selected his dance partners carefully: those
who did not care for gossip – Amelia Ashpoint, Clara McNeil,

Anne Palmer – and those too polite to engage in it, such as Felicia Elton or Lady Rose. He studiously avoided the younger two Palmer girls, Cassandra and Louisa, although they both tried very hard to catch his eye. When he was not dancing, he spoke to his friend Sir Frederick Hammersmith with such earnestness that none dared interrupt.

~

The news reached Mr Ashpoint as he queued for punch.

'Well, Ashpoint,' said Lord Wickford, turning to face him, 'what do you think of it all?'

He wished Lord Wickford would call him *Mr* Ashpoint. Their acquaintance was longstanding – they had gone to the same dinners and been in the same ballrooms for decades, and the friendship between their sons had of course brought them into frequent contact – but they were not precisely *friends*. Whether Lord Wickford called him Ashpoint simply for ease or because he thought him so far his inferior that he need not bother with *Mr*, Mr Ashpoint could never tell. It irked him; it was the kind of worry that kept him awake at night. No matter how the brewery grew and thrived, no matter how large his house or how extensive his lands, Society would always hold its nose as though Mr Ashpoint carried the smell of hops on his skin.

'All what, my lord?'

'Why, this news that Mr Hurst is to be married, of course.'

Mr Ashpoint stared. He blinked, swallowed, took in the words. 'Married?' he repeated.

'Oh yes. I am not sure to whom, but I suppose it is some London girl.'

Mr Ashpoint looked down at the oak floor and felt

himself crumple. *Married*. Mr Hurst was to be married to somebody else.

'I hope Miss Ashpoint is not disappointed,' said Lord Wickford.

Mr Ashpoint felt his cheeks redden. Had he really been so obvious in his aspirations for Amelia? Lord Wickford probably thought it absurdly presumptuous of him. He and Mr Elton probably laughed about it over cards and whisky.

Then Mr Ashpoint looked up and followed Lord Wickford's gaze across the great hall, to where Amelia currently stood with Diggory, laughing very heartily. She did not look especially disappointed.

Mr Ashpoint hardly knew what troubled him more – that Mr Hurst was to be married, or that Amelia did not appear to care. Lately, he had allowed himself to think that perhaps – just perhaps – Amelia liked the man. She never mocked him as she did the other gentlemen of her acquaintance. She danced with him often. She spoke of him with something nearing respect. And what a match it would have been for her, for them – for who could have doubted Mr Ashpoint's position as a gentleman if his daughter married into one of the county families? Lord Wickford might have started calling him *Mr*.

But now, it had all come to this – the announcement that Mr Hurst was to marry another woman, and Amelia's slow descent into spinsterhood.

He worried about all his children. Of course he did. Since his wife's death ten years ago, Mr Ashpoint had suffered from the constant fear that he was doing something *wrong*, that his wild offspring were the result of some grave parental blunder. Diggory drank too much and had very little interest in the running of the brewery that would one day be his.

Ada was a torrent of emotions, and Laurie was either silent and shy or bent on misbehaviour.

But he worried most about Amelia – unruly, witty, headstrong Amelia. She reminded him sometimes of her mother – how often he had teased Charlotte for her stubbornness! But Amelia had a kind of wildness in her, too, that he did not understand, a firm disregard for the opinion of the world. She was now three-and-twenty. She had been out in Society for six years and had shown no real inclination to marry. Even with Mr Hurst, she had laughed off her father's remarks about their possible alliance, and though he had tried very hard to consider this maidenly modesty, still, looking at her now, much as she ever was, he had to admit that perhaps – just *perhaps* – she had never cared much for Mr Hurst at all.

~

The news reached Miss Felicia Elton when she spoke to her parents at the end of a dance. She had become aware, in the last hour or so, of a subtle shift in the room, of fewer eyes upon herself than usual, of more eyes directed towards Mr Hurst, towards Amelia Ashpoint.

'Well, Mama?' she said simply, as she approached her parents. 'Something has happened, has it not?'

Mrs Elton pursed her lips. 'It appears,' she replied, 'that Mr Hurst is to be married.'

'And not to Miss Ashpoint?' asked Felicia.

'No, indeed, for he is to be married from London – to, I suppose, a *stranger*.' Mrs Elton said this with some distaste, as though the idea of a Wickenshire gentleman marrying someone from beyond the county was a clear mark against him.

Felicia expressed no surprise at this news. It would not be proper to do so, and Felicia was indisputably proper.

'Ashpoint will be disappointed,' said her father. He was standing on her mother's other side, back straight, head up, looking over at the spot where Mr Hurst stood speaking to Sir Frederick.

Felicia said nothing. Despite the neighbourhood's intermittent speculation, she had never really thought Mr Hurst would marry Amelia Ashpoint. To be sure, they had danced together often enough – but what of that? Felicia could see nothing much in Miss Ashpoint to appeal to any man. She talked too much, read too many books, roamed the country lanes by herself as though she were above a chaperone, and she dressed as though she did not care what she looked like. Felicia really could not understand why someone like Miss Ashpoint – who, if she did not exactly have status, certainly did have *wealth* – should waste what little looks she had with such behaviour. If *Felicia* had been the daughter of a jumped-up brewer, rather than the daughter of respected members of the gentry as she was, she thought she could have made a better job of it.

There was a great division in this quarter of Wickenshire, as in all such places, between the county families and the townsfolk. Amongst the respectable society of Melford and its surrounding villages – amongst those of enough significance to be invited to this evening's ball – some were *county* and some were *town*. The Eltons, the Wickfords, the Hammersmiths and the Hursts were *county* – they were old, respectable families with their own estates, far above the likes of the Craytons, the Palmers or the McNeils, all of whom lived within Melford itself. As for the Ashpoints – well, who could say? They had the largest house for miles around, owned a great deal of land and were the wealthiest family in Wickenshire, with an income of twelve thousand pounds a year – but new money was new money, and trade was trade. Felicia's father called the Ashpoints a county family. Her mother considered them *town*.

If Amelia Ashpoint was *spirited* – that was, Felicia thought, the most delicate way to put it – then Felicia Elton was . . . well, perfect. She knew she was perfect. She had been brought up to be perfect. She was tall but not too tall, slim but not too slim. Her hair was golden and glossy, forever styled neatly above her head. She played the pianoforte exquisitely, drew and sung brilliantly, and danced with an elegance that few could match. She was quiet, demure and always appeared sweet-tempered and modest. She was of high birth, from an old family, and since her entrance into Society two years before, she had been the declared beauty of the county. She had triumphed in the London Season these last few months and on her return to Wickenshire found herself as much admired as ever.

'Perhaps,' said Mrs Elton, gazing out upon the dancers, 'we shall have to prove true that old saying that one marriage follows another.' She inclined her head very slightly, just as Sir Frederick Hammersmith left Mr Hurst and crossed the room towards them, no doubt to ask Felicia for another dance.

Felicia allowed herself a small, modest smile. Her mother would expect it.

But her father stiffened. He said quietly but firmly, 'Dance with him by all means, Felicia, but do not give him too much encouragement. No daughter of mine shall marry a man with so scant a fortune, baronet or not.'

Felicia, of course, said nothing, and there was no time for

her mother to respond. Sir Frederick was upon them, all smiles and bright colours. Felicia tried not to think about how his yellow pantaloons would clash with her lilac silk gown.

Sir Frederick said, 'Might I have the honour of this dance, Miss Elton?'

In response, she held out her hand with perfect grace.

~

The news reached Lord Salbridge as he was waltzing with Miss Louisa Palmer. He always liked dancing with the Palmer sisters; they wore muslin because they could not afford satin or silk, and Salbridge appreciated how thin muslin was, especially in the right light. To be sure, not one of them was as beautiful as Miss Elton, but Louisa and Cassandra let one hold them quite as close as one liked, and Anne Palmer, though rather stiff, always looked so amusingly afraid of him.

This evening, though, Louisa was being rather a bore. She would not stop talking about Mr Hurst. 'And it seems he really is to marry a stranger, my lord – nobody from Wickenshire at all. Perhaps *you* will know her, as you have been to London for the Season – I have not heard her name yet, but Cassandra said *she* thought she heard that it begins with an R, and really . . .'

Lord Salbridge stopped listening. He let his gaze wander around the room. Felicia Elton was dancing with Sir Frederick. Diggory was dancing with Rose *again*. His parents were in conversation with Mr and Mrs Elton, and Mr Hurst had disappeared from view. Amelia Ashpoint was dancing with – dear God, with Lonsdale, that foreman from the brewery who sometimes sat in the corner of the Lantern and tried so hard to dress like a gentleman.

Salbridge could not understand his parents. There they were, the Earl and Countess of Wickford, the leading family in the county, with centuries of history and pride behind them, and yet they invited anybody and everybody into their house. He knew they felt it their noble duty to patronize country society, to condescend to their lesser neighbours – but really, this was taking it too far. Amongst the crowd tonight, he had seen his sister's music master, his father's steward, that land agent whose daughter followed Amelia Ashpoint everywhere – McNeil or whatever his name was, something terribly Irish – and several wealthy farmers, not to mention Major Alderton from Netherworth, whom everybody knew was the bastard son of some duke or other. It really was incomprehensible.

'I *am* sad they are not to be married in Wickenshire,' Louisa Palmer was saying, 'for I have been *dying* for a wedding here ever since the Queen was married last year. But a newcomer to the neighbourhood will be so *very* exciting, and . . .'

Lord Salbridge pulled her closer as the music droned on. He hoped the new Mrs Hurst was handsome and liked dancing; he hoped she was a lady of quality. He hoped Mr Hurst had chosen well.

~

By midnight, everybody knew that Mr Montgomery Hurst of Radcliffe Park was to be married before the week was out. The whispers had grown louder; the stares had not ceased. The trickle of information had weaved its way around the great hall as the hours passed, and every guest – young or old, male or female, married or single, wealthy or . . . well, less wealthy – was eager to learn more.

The dam burst at half past twelve, when Miss Waterson and Miss Maddon – Melford's resident gossips, both in their sixties and unmarried – accosted Mr Hurst by the punch table.

'My dear boy,' said Miss Waterson loudly, 'do tell us all who on earth you are going to marry.'

There was a moment's pause. All nearby conversation ceased at once. Several individuals were seized with a sudden need for punch and moved a few steps closer. Everybody pretended very hard not to be listening.

'We are all dying to know,' said Miss Maddon, with a smile.

Mr Hurst had turned a little pink. He cleared his throat, hesitated, and then said distinctly, 'Her name is Matilda Roberts.'

The assembled guests glanced at one another – but nobody had ever heard of any Matilda Roberts.

'One of the Oxford Robertses, I suppose?' asked Miss Waterson.

'Or the Suffolk Robertses?' Miss Maddon put in.

'I – er – no, I do not believe that either—'

'And how long have you been acquainted with Miss Roberts?' asked Miss Waterson.

'A month or two,' replied Mr Hurst. Then he paused, and the assembled guests at Lady Wickford's ball all held their breath at once. 'It is not Miss Roberts,' he said quickly, 'but *Mrs* Roberts – she is a widow.'

Everybody stood aghast. One of the musicians misplaced his bow and broke off halfway through the melody. Captain Palmer raised his eyebrows. Mrs Elton pursed her lips. Louisa Palmer fainted – and was very disappointed that nobody noticed. Mr Ashpoint, halfway through filling up his glass, managed to spill punch everywhere. Miss Waterson and Miss Maddon looked at each other with glee.

A *widow*. Of course it was quite natural that a man such as Mr Hurst should marry – but that he should marry a *widow* was a shock indeed.

A flurry of questions began to rise amongst the crowds, but before anyone dared to raise their voice, Mr Hurst put his punch glass down firmly on the table.

'Do you know,' he said, his cheeks red, his manner a pained show of ease, 'I really think I must be going. I have a long ride to London tomorrow, and I really . . .'

He did not finish his sentence. He smiled at his neighbours and strode determinedly across the room, only pausing to bid a quick goodbye to Sir Frederick before he reached the doors.

∾

All this while, Amelia Ashpoint was sitting outside in the courtyard, on a circular bench beneath a tall, old oak. The cool evening air was a relief after the warmth of the ball, and the moon was bright in the darkness. She leant back against the tree and closed her eyes.

She heard the doors open and close, and the melody from within grew louder for an instant, and then a voice said, 'There you are.'

Amelia looked up to see Clara coming towards her. Her cheeks were flushed and one of the ribbons in her hair was coming loose. Amelia smiled up at her.

'I have barely seen you all evening,' said Clara as she sat down at Amelia's side.

'I have been in hiding.'

'From the eyes of Society?'

Amelia laughed. 'I do not know whether the curiosity or the pity is worse. Anne Palmer will not stop staring at me solemnly, and Mrs Crayton keeps shaking her head.' She grimaced. 'But Papa's sad eyes are the worst. I am mostly hiding from him.'

Clara smiled. She leant back, nudged her shoulder closer to Amelia's. 'Yes, everybody has been telling me definitively that you are *not* to marry Mr Hurst,' she said, 'as though I did not know that already. They are all interrogating him at present as to the identity of his bride. Poor Mr Hurst.'

'And poor Mrs Hurst, too, for they will both be the subject of every conversation in Wickenshire for at least four months.'

Clara laughed. 'Well, I must admit *I* am glad,' she said, 'for I was beginning to fear that he really liked you.'

Amelia was shaking her head before Clara had finished speaking. 'I never thought that. He has been . . . useful to me, I suppose. He has kept Papa at bay this last year or so.' She gave a sigh, looked back over her shoulder at the bright windows of the great hall. 'I hate balls,' she declared. 'I have never enjoyed a ball in my life.'

'What about the Harvest Ball, two years ago?' asked Clara. 'The time gentlemen were scarce and so a few ladies stood up together?'

'I had almost forgotten that,' Amelia replied in a low voice. 'Yes, that was *something*, dancing together before all those people, knowing they did not know.'

She reached up to touch Clara's cheek. She ached to pull her closer, to kiss her, but with the great hall close by it would be more than unwise. Instead, she let her hand drop and threaded her fingers through Clara's in the dark. They smiled at each other.

'You will have to dance with me again next week,' said Amelia, 'for I have promised Ada that we shall teach her how to waltz.'

Just then, the great doors burst open and music came flooding out. Clara dropped Amelia's hand and sat up straight, just as Mr Hurst passed them by. He was walking fast, his strides long and determined, but he stopped at the sound of movement behind him. He turned, and Amelia bowed her head slightly. Clara stood up and curtseyed.

'Ah, goodnight, Miss Ashpoint, Miss McNeil.' Mr Hurst gave a laugh, half bashful, half amused. 'I am afraid you have caught me running away,' he said. 'There were so many *questions*.'

Amelia smiled. 'I hope your bride is prepared, Mr Hurst, for the very great and varied honour of being a newcomer in Wickenshire. We have so little novelty here that nothing new is safe.'

Mr Hurst bit his lip. He put his hands in his pockets, sighed, opened his mouth as if to speak, then changed his mind. He turned away, then looked back. 'I do hope you will like her,' he said, and he sounded so very earnest, so very anxious, that Amelia felt her levity slip away.

'I am sure I shall,' she said. 'I look forward to meeting her.'

'As do I,' said Clara.

Mr Hurst nodded. He looked a little heartened by this, but still, Amelia saw him frown as he turned and walked out into the dark.

CHAPTER III

In which gossip brews at Ashpoint Brewery

THE FOLLOWING DAY, WICKENSHIRE WAS ABUZZ WITH talk of the marriage of Mr Montgomery Hurst. Everybody knew, whether they had been invited to the ball or not, that Mr Hurst was to marry, that he was to marry a *widow* and *stranger* no less. It was whispered in parlours, in bedrooms, around breakfast tables. It was murmured in shops, in the streets, at the brewery. Everybody had something to say about Mr Hurst and his new bride. Quite why one of the most sought-after bachelors in the neighbourhood, with a good position and six thousand a year, would marry a lady who had been married already was a mystery to them all.

The Palmer family – breakfasting at home on Lowick Terrace in Melford – decided that she must be a very handsome widow, if she had caught Mr Hurst. The Crayton family – breakfasting in their house behind Crayton's Bank – thought she must be a very *wealthy* widow. Mr Duckfield, the vicar of Melford, sat alone eating his kippers and toast, wondering why Mr Hurst was getting married in London when there was a perfectly good church in Melford.

Old Miss Waterson and Miss Maddon sat together in their little house on Garrett Lane, debating the intricacies of this new marriage. They wrote up a list of possibilities on a large blackboard left over from the days when Miss Waterson's mother had taught at the Sunday school: was Mr Hurst's bride wealthy or poor, a lady of fashion or an unknown – how long had she been widowed – was she young or old, beautiful or plain? When they ran out of speculations upon the new Mrs Hurst, they turned the blackboard around and spent the rest of the morning drawing lines between young maidens and bachelors, dividing Society into suitable pairs and contemplating the next Wickenshire match.

Towards the end of the afternoon, Mr Ashpoint was sitting at his desk in the brewery counting house. He liked to call it the counting house, for that had a pleasingly business-like sound to it – even though it was simply a few rooms on top of the stables that forever smelt faintly of manure. After last night's ball, he had woken late with a headache – although admittedly not so late, nor with so bad a headache, as Diggory – and he still felt weary and dejected. He had spent the afternoon organizing orders for hops from Surrey and trying to do his accounts, unable to ignore the thought that the only hope for his daughter's future was currently in London, preparing for his marriage to somebody else.

It was nearing six o'clock, and he would be expected home for dinner soon. He stood up, stretched his legs, walked over to his office window and looked out upon his brewery. It was a large, untidy mass of red-brick buildings, but Mr Ashpoint liked it the better for that. The main tower was six storeys high at its tallest point and loomed above the rest, but surrounding it were the offices, the malthouse, the supper-house and an assortment of warehouses of differing ages and heights.

He searched the buildings, the courtyard, the throngs of workers passing to and fro, looking for the familiar figure of Mr Lonsdale. He did not like to leave the works before his foreman. It was preferable to leave just after him, to maintain the belief amongst all (including Mr Ashpoint himself) that he was the harder worker of the two.

Lonsdale was at this moment just leaving the malthouse. It was not hard to spot him, for he was always dressed in such a superior manner. The men bustling around him were all in work clothes, but Lonsdale wore a perfectly correct cravat, shirt and jacket, and a silver watch chain gleamed from his waistcoat pocket. Mr Ashpoint looked down at his own messy cravat, at the faint stain on his shirt cuff where Laurie had spilt his tea at breakfast. He sighed deeply.

Hartley Lonsdale, the foreman and manager of Ashpoint Brewery, was eight-and-twenty years old. He was a farmhand by birth, a brewer by trade, a gentleman by dress and manner, and a talented man by all accounts. He had started work at the brewery when he was ten years old and soon proved himself a resourceful, sensible boy. At fourteen, he was one of their best lads. At twenty, he was a superior worker to men ten years his senior. At two-and-twenty, he was indispensable to the foreman. At four-and-twenty, when the old foreman died, Lonsdale was temporarily promoted to fill the vacant position. Mr Ashpoint had looked for a replacement for months but had not found anybody who could do the job so well, and thus Lonsdale was foreman still.

And then, over the last few years, something terribly strange had occurred. Mr Lonsdale had quietly set himself up as a gentleman. With his savings, he bought a small house on Mill Lane that qualified him for the vote. His manner of dress shifted. His voice mellowed. He began to shine his shoes, to carry a silver castle-top card case in his pocket, to read Milton and Wordsworth. He began to speak of 'friends in London' with an impressive, ambiguous air and spent his holidays with a well-known writer who had once been the curate of Radcliffe.

And now, Lonsdale was reaching towards *Society*. At first, he had been on good terms only with those at the modest end of Wickenshire's social scale – the music master, Pierre Brisset, or the land agent, Phineas McNeil. But last year, he had, to Mr Ashpoint's deep discomfort, joined the Lantern, the closest Melford came to a gentleman's club. And his presence at Lady Wickford's ball last night – not to mention his dancing with Amelia – was a source of some unease.

The idea of a self-made man was by no means new to Mr Ashpoint. His own father had been the son of a shopkeeper, after all, and Mr Ashpoint senior had instilled in his son from an early age the knowledge that they were gentlemen – but only just. Lonsdale was a constant reminder of his own precarious position.

Mr Ashpoint gazed out of the window as Lonsdale moved closer to the gates. Then he turned back to his desk, closed the ledgers, pulled on his jacket and made his way towards the door.

He walked along a thin stretch of corridor, then out into the open air, down a set of stone steps at the edge of the stables and out into the courtyard. He was nearing the gates himself when he realized that Lonsdale was still there, that one of the men had stopped him on his way out. It was Magner – one-and-forty, married, three children, a good worker, had a flair for yeast – and he was speaking quickly, a frown on his face. As Mr Ashpoint approached them, he caught the words 'pipe'.

'Everything all right?' he asked.

Lonsdale and Magner both turned at once. Magner bowed his head, took off his cap; Lonsdale nodded but did not lift his hat.

'I was just telling Mr Lonsdale about the piping, sir,' said Magner. 'I noticed a problem – a crack maybe. I'm not sure, but . . .'

'I'll take a look now,' said Lonsdale to Mr Ashpoint, when Magner trailed off. 'Nothing to concern yourself with, sir.'

Mr Ashpoint did not like that. *Everything* at the brewery was something to concern himself with. 'I had better take a look, too, if there is any kind of fault.'

Lonsdale hesitated. He seemed about to protest that Mr Ashpoint needn't take the trouble, but then he looked back at Magner, who was glancing between his two superiors, as though for permission to leave. Mr Ashpoint was just about to give it when Lonsdale said, 'We needn't keep you, Magner – have a pleasant evening.'

Magner smiled, bowed his head to Lonsdale, put his cap back on and joined the stream of men heading out the gates.

'Well,' said Mr Ashpoint, 'shall we have a look at this fault, then, Lonsdale?' These days, now that Lonsdale dressed so well, he had to continually remind himself not to call him *Mr* Lonsdale.

'Certainly, sir, if you wish it.'

Lonsdale turned and set off, and Mr Ashpoint, having no idea where or what this fault was, had to follow him. As they crossed the courtyard, casks and carts were pulled out of their way, and the bustle of workers parted for them (were they parting for *him*, Mr Ashpoint wondered, or for Lonsdale?). When they reached the main tower, Lonsdale checked his watch quickly before opening the door.

'Have you somewhere to be, Lonsdale? I am sure I can examine the—'

'Oh, it is no matter,' his foreman replied. 'I am dining with Mr McNeil tonight, but I am not due with him until seven.'

'Ah.' Mr Ashpoint sighed. It really was intolerable that Lonsdale dined late. Only *gentlemen* dined late. Why could Lonsdale not eat his main meal at lunchtime like the rest of the men who worked at the brewery? Worse still, Amelia had told him this morning that she, too, was to dine with Clara McNeil and her father tonight. The thought of his daughter and his foreman at one table did not sit right with Mr Ashpoint at all. Still, it was too late to revoke his permission now, and Amelia would probably not listen to him if he did.

As they passed through the engine room, there was a rush of steam and heat that made Mr Ashpoint raise his handkerchief to his forehead, accustomed to it as he was. The men on the second shift turned from their work to nod. Mr Ashpoint followed Lonsdale up the steep wooden staircase to the next floor, past the door to the fermenting room, past the hop store and the strong smell it brought. Some of the men were talking in cheerful voices about the unknown Mrs Hurst and what a to-do there always was when the gentlefolks decided to marry, and their voices carried as Lonsdale and Mr Ashpoint climbed another set of stairs and finally emerged into the mash room.

Now, Lonsdale, Mr Ashpoint thought, as his foreman dismissed the men at work here with a quick signal of his head – Lonsdale was a man who *knew* things. He spoke to Society, and he spoke to the workmen. He spoke to shopkeepers and to servants and to the gentry. Lonsdale was just

the sort of man who might know, for example, more about
Mr Hurst's intended bride.

Last night's news had quite knocked Mr Ashpoint down.
He had hoped so very much that Amelia and Mr Hurst
might make a match of it, that such a marriage would
secure his daughter's lasting happiness and his own position. And now – this. Surely it ought not to be so hard.
Other parents did not appear to find it impossible to secure
suitable matches for their daughters. But there was nobody
else whom Amelia seemed to like – and, indeed, nobody
who seemed to like her. When she had first come out into
Society, a few gentlemen had been drawn in by the thought
of a large dowry, but Amelia had soon scared them away
with her sharp wit and refusals to dance. Mr Hurst was
the only one who seemed not to mind her spirited
conversation.

It was a blow to lose Mr Hurst to a stranger, too. If he
had been to marry from amongst Wickenshire's county
families – if he were to wed Felicia Elton or Lady Rose – Mr
Ashpoint would have at least been unsurprised. But that he
should select some unknown widow over his daughter was
maddening. He wished so very much to know *why*.

He told himself that this was entirely for his daughter's
sake, that it was nothing to do with his passing enjoyment of
gossip. He told himself this several times, until he almost
believed it.

Mr Ashpoint waited as his foreman went to fetch a
wooden ladder from the next room, waited as he neatly
positioned it beside one of the mash-tuns. He wished
Magner had told *him* what the problem was, so that he did
not need to stand uselessly by, staring up at the pipework
above them and wondering which was at fault. Alas, Mr

Ashpoint was forced to wait until Lonsdale signalled with an imperious wave of his hand that he should join him at the foot of the ladder.

'Look,' he said, pointing to the pipework above. 'You cannot quite make it out from down here, but Magner said he thought there was a hairline crack in the copper. It will be trouble to fix if there is. I had better take a closer look.'

And then Lonsdale removed his hat and jacket, rolled up his sleeves and made to ascend the ladder. Mr Ashpoint was pleased to keep both his feet on the ground – but he did have to hold Lonsdale's jacket and hat and the base of the ladder, and this somewhat marred his sense of dignity.

'I say, Lonsdale,' said Mr Ashpoint, as lightly as he could, 'what do you know of this marriage of Mr Hurst's? Some of the men were talking of it just now.'

Lonsdale, who was already halfway up, whistled once. 'I think I can see what Magner meant now. Might simply be a mark or a scratch, but . . .' He trailed off. 'And no, I am afraid I know very little of the matter.'

'I only wondered,' said Mr Ashpoint, 'if you had any acquaintance on the staff of Radcliffe. Nobody has heard a jot about Mr Hurst's bride save her name.'

Lonsdale's figure stiffened. 'I have not had much cause to make acquaintance with the staff of Radcliffe Park,' he said coldly. 'No brewery there, of course.'

There was a short pause. Mr Ashpoint held his foreman's jacket and felt rather foolish.

'However,' said Lonsdale, 'my friend Monsieur Brisset was at Radcliffe yesterday morning, tuning the pianofortes, and Mr Hurst mentioned the matter to him.'

'Oh?'

'Yes,' said Lonsdale. He had reached the top of the ladder

now and was leaning sideways to squint at the pipework above the mash-tun. 'Mr Hurst,' said Lonsdale, 'is marrying a widow named Mrs Roberts. But I suppose you knew that – there was quite enough talk of it at the ball last night.'

'Yes, yes.'

'Dear me.' Lonsdale checked the position of his feet on the ladder, then shifted his weight slightly, reached out an arm and ran two fingers along the pipework. 'Yes, there's a crack, all right.'

Mr Ashpoint frowned. Cracks were not good; cracks were how accidents happened. For a moment, Mr Hurst's marriage dwindled in significance and he had a vision of hot liquid trickling down from above, of injuries, of chaos. 'A crack? What kind? How bad?'

'Very thin, not all the way through yet, but we will have a leak on our hands if we are not careful,' Lonsdale replied. 'I think Mrs Roberts's first husband was a naval officer.' Mr Ashpoint could not see his face, but he had a faint sense that Lonsdale was smiling. 'He died about a year ago, Brisset says . . . Yes, this is beyond any of the men. We'll have to get the blacksmith in, or perhaps an engineer from Melcastle . . .' Lonsdale shifted his weight again on the ladder, and Mr Ashpoint gripped it harder. 'We will have to reroute the system so that the blacksmith can work. Perhaps on Monday?' He paused. 'Brisset tells me that Mrs Roberts has led rather a retiring life. There are children, I believe.'

'Children!' cried Mr Ashpoint – and in his shock he almost let go of the ladder.

He had not thought of there being children. Perhaps he ought to have, when Mr Hurst said he was marrying a widow, but somehow he had assumed she would be a very youthful widow who had lost her husband tragically fast.

The idea of Mr Hurst marrying an older woman who had been married many years and had a family already – why, it was beyond irregular; it was almost unthinkable. Why choose a lady so circumstanced when he might have married an unburdened girl like Amelia?

Mr Ashpoint stared up in astonishment as his foreman began to make his way coolly down the ladder.

'Well, sir,' said Lonsdale, smiling, 'shall I call in the blacksmith?'

CHAPTER IV

In which Mr Lonsdale entertains thoughts above his station

'I HEAR, MR LONSDALE,' SAID CLARA, 'THAT YOU HAVE been spreading rumours. Everybody in the square was talking about how Mr Hurst's new bride has *children*.'

'I only told one person,' Lonsdale replied, a faint smile on his lips.

'And that person being my father,' said Amelia, 'you may as well have told twenty.'

Mr McNeil chuckled.

They were in the dining room of 9 Garrett Lane, where Clara lived with her father. The house stood in the heart of Melford; it was compact but neat, the furniture old but well chosen, the wallpapers a little faded. Mr McNeil was a land agent and surveyor, working for Mr Ashpoint and various other clients. His business was flourishing, and though he employed no clerk, Clara often helped with his letter-writing and architectural drawings. Mr McNeil was not rich, and his Irish blood and accent carried with them some stigma, but he was valued enough for his work to be welcome in everybody's studies, if not in everybody's parlours. It had been a great relief to all when he arrived twenty years ago, a widower with one infant child, that, although he was an Irishman, he went to the parish church like everybody else. (Monsieur Brisset, on the other hand, rode over to the Catholic church in Melcastle each Sunday, which had been a source of great consternation to much of Melford since he took up residence in the neighbourhood three years ago.) But Mr McNeil was still an Irishman, and that was enough to lose him and his daughter a few dinner invitations, to make Mrs Elton ignore them if she passed them in the street, to make Mrs Crayton frown.

Amelia thought little of all this. She loved Clara's father because he was Clara's father. She loved Clara's house because it was Clara's, and because it had none of the imposing grandeur she was used to at home. She preferred small rooms to large, anyhow.

'Come, Mr Lonsdale,' said Amelia, 'face up to your charge. Whatever made you say such a thing?'

Lonsdale's mouth curved into a small smile. He put his wine glass down, lifted his fork, then paused. 'Is it not preferable for Wickenshire to wear out its gossip while Mr Hurst is away? It would cause a far greater uproar if the new Mrs Hurst were to suddenly appear with her unknown children behind her.'

'You mean it is true?'

'I believe so.'

Amelia looked at Lonsdale carefully. She had known him for years, seen him come and go from the brewery, met him from time to time at her own house when he came up to see her father. But it was only during the last year or so, as his friendship with Mr McNeil had grown, as he dined oftener at 9 Garrett Lane, that she had come to know him well. She could never quite decide what to make of him. That he was very ambitious she did not doubt. Whether he were ruthlessly

so was harder to judge. Still, she thought he might be useful
to her.

'I wondered if you were merely spreading falsehoods,'
she said at last.

He looked back at her, a slight frown on his face. 'I have
too much respect for your father to mislead him,' he said
simply, and she could not quite tell if he meant it.

'But,' said Mr McNeil, looking up from his mutton, 'it *is*
a little peculiar that Mr Hurst should choose to marry a
widow who already has children. A man like that, with a
fine fortune and an excellent house!'

'Father thinks only of houses,' said Clara with a smile.

'And why should I not? I have always enjoyed any work
I've done there. There's not a better house in the
neighbourhood – save Ashpoint Hall,' he added, with a
half-smile at Amelia.

Clara laughed, and Amelia looked over at her. The
ribbon in her hair was coming loose again.

'I shall have to ask my friend Browne if he has ever come
across a Matilda Roberts,' said Lonsdale. 'He lives not too
far from Richmond.'

'This is your – literary friend, is it?' asked Amelia.

'Yes, that's him – the former curate of Radcliffe, turned
writer these days. I shall have to lend you one of his books.'

'Certainly. One can never have too many books.'

'Oh, I am not so sure, Amelia,' said Clara, her eyebrows
raised. 'I have seen you buy up half the volumes in the bookseller's every week for years, and I think that you may, at
some point soon, have too many books.'

'Nonsense!' cried Amelia. She laughed and nudged Clara's
foot with her own beneath the table. 'Well, Mr Lonsdale' –
turning now to him – 'I wonder if your Mr Browne will know

anything of our Mrs Roberts. But I pity both Mr Hurst and his new bride, for they won't be left alone from the moment they return.'

'Not until the next Wickenshire marriage,' said Mr McNeil. 'If you girls will hurry up and find yourselves suitors, we shall soon have something new to discuss.'

Amelia rolled her eyes, and Clara gave a faint smile.

'Personally,' said Amelia, 'I place my bet on Sir Frederick and Miss Elton.'

~

'Miss Ashpoint,' said Lonsdale, as the two of them left together in the dusk, 'I hope you did not really think I was inventing stories out of malice.'

'Not *malice*.' Amelia shrugged her shoulders, smiled. 'Mischief, perhaps.'

They were a few houses down from Clara's now, and Lonsdale offered her his arm.

She shook her head instinctively, then smiled to soften her incivility when he looked disappointed. 'I am used to walking alone at this hour, and it is scarcely more than a mile up to the house.'

'I wonder that your father does not send the carriage.'

'He used to,' said Amelia, 'but I sent it back empty too many times, and at last he gave up. I like walking.'

That same smile again from Lonsdale. It was an oddly knowing smile – she could not quite read it. She thought of what he had said over dinner and wondered how far she could trust him.

Then he looked sideways at her, and his smile seemed to slip. 'This marriage of Mr Hurst's – it does not . . . hurt you,

Miss Ashpoint? I have once or twice heard your father suggest that perhaps—'

'Oh, goodness, no,' said Amelia quickly. 'That is all my
father's invention. Mr Hurst is a very agreeable man, but I
am not and have never been in love with him.'

'I am glad it does not affect you.'

Amelia laughed. 'Not in the slightest.'

They had reached Mill Lane, where Lonsdale lived, and
he turned towards her in the dimming light.

'Mr Lonsdale,' said Amelia, 'before you say goodnight, I
have a – well, I have a favour to ask you.'

He looked at her keenly. 'What is it?'

Well, she had started now. She could not turn back. She
swallowed hard. 'It is a – a complicated favour. Or, at least,
not all that complicated, but it is a secret, and—'

'You need not hesitate, Miss Ashpoint. I would be glad to
do anything to serve you.'

Amelia began again, talking quickly, hurrying it out. 'It
is – well, there is something with which I could use your
help. I am afraid it is rather a long story.'

∼

Twenty minutes later, Hartley Lonsdale turned the key in
the door of number 5 Mill Lane. It was a very small house,
for all that it had cost three times his annual salary and was
the result of ten years' saving. He stood for a few moments
in the parlour, the room into which the street door opened.
It was neatly furnished and eminently respectable, with
floral wallpapers, old chairs with embroidered cushions and
a small bookshelf containing various volumes that his writer
friend, Browne, had sent him over the years.

He thought of Amelia Ashpoint, her pale face in the moonlight, this favour she had asked of him. That was something, was it not? That she thought well of him, that she trusted him, that she—

A foolish idea, perhaps. Lonsdale had always thought highly of Amelia Ashpoint, but he was not the kind of man to harbour a foolish, unrequited passion for his employer's daughter. He prided himself on being too prudent, too focused to go falling in love when he had no business to.

And yet—

And yet she had agreed to dance with him at Lady Wickford's ball. She had asked him for his help tonight.

If she did truly admire him, if she had been so quick to reassure him of her indifference to Mr Hurst because she was not indifferent to *him*, then – well, it would change everything.

He shook his head and left the parlour. He did not have time to think about such things tonight.

Nobody save Lonsdale ever ventured into the two other rooms of his house. The kitchen was dingy and damp – stark brick and empty shelves. His bedroom was bare – a low Windsor chair, a straw mattress covered with worn blankets, and a cupboard frame he had made himself to hold his clothes.

In the kitchen, he lit a tallow candle and set to work on his laundry. It would take three or four hours, and it was past eleven at night – but he could not afford the luxury of a laundry woman this week. He had ten shillings to spare, and he intended to go to the Lantern after work tomorrow and play a few hands of cards to see if he could improve on it. He knew that his aunt's health had taken another turn for the worse, and he was keen to send her more than usual. If Lord

Salbridge was at the Lantern tomorrow night, he would probably not be invited to play, but if he were lucky, it would just be Major Alderton and the vicar, who were rather less particular about whom they sat down to cards with.

For now, he had half a night's work ahead of him, and he had to be up in seven hours to start work at the brewery. There was definitely no time to dwell on Miss Ashpoint.

❧

Meanwhile, Amelia let herself into Ashpoint Hall, kicked off her boots and made her way up the grand marble staircase. She went down long, wide corridors, said goodnight to the portrait of her mother on the wall and walked past her siblings' rooms. Laurie's and Diggory's were dark, but she knew from the light spilling out from beneath Ada's door that her sister was still awake, no doubt reading in bed.

When Amelia finally reached her own sitting room, she sat down at her bureau, unlocked it and began to pull out reams of paper, sorting and shifting until she had before her two thick piles, each neatly wrapped in ribbon. Both began with the same words, but the one on the left was filled with crossings out and words above the lines, whereas the right-hand version was – mostly – clean.

Amelia frowned. Was it legible enough, presentable enough? Ought she to write out another fair copy? Ought she to read it all over, one last time, make a few final changes before—

She shook her head. There was no time for dithering now. She had told Lonsdale that she would deliver the manuscript of her novel to him tomorrow, and he had promised faithfully to send it on to Mr Browne in London, who would be willing, Lonsdale was sure, to make enquiries with publishers on her behalf.

It was all agreed. She could not go back if she wanted to – which of course she did not, but—

Amelia's heart was racing. She tucked her first draft back into its nook, followed by the edited copy she had spent weeks writing out. Then she locked up the bureau and threw herself down on one of the settees.

Her mind would not settle. She was thinking through too many outcomes – acceptance, publication, the reward for all her exertion and effort, a life as a *novelist*, her book on the shelves of Melford's bookseller's – and, on the other hand, rejection, despondency, the realization that her talents were not what she had long believed them, the death of all her ambition, and—

She wished Clara were here to comfort her, to calm her. Clara would know what to say, what to think. Clara always knew the best balance to strike, how to be both hopeful and rational, while Amelia was always at extremes.

But this was something, was it not? A start. A beginning. If she did not succeed now, she would write another book and another, and one day, surely . . .

Amelia stared up at the ceiling and bit her lip to stop herself smiling.

CHAPTER V

In which we hear two histories of love

THE FOLLOWING DAY, DIGGORY DRAGGED HIMSELF OUT OF bed as early as he could manage (it was about half past ten in the morning) and rang for his valet to help him dress. There was a large hunt happening over at Montague Hall, near Melcastle, and Lord Salbridge had secured him an invite. Diggory did not like hunting – it always seemed a cruel sport to him – but still, a day spent in his friend's company would be a pleasure, and it was meant to be a privilege to be invited to these things: there would be lots of lords and honourables and not very many plain misters. Besides, Wickford Towers was on the road there, and so he was to call for Salbridge first – and because Salbridge was reliably never ready on time, Diggory might get the chance to see Lady Rose.

He paused in the entrance hall and examined himself in the large mirror above the fireplace. He *thought* he looked rather dashing. He liked the red of his riding coat, and his boots were neatly shined. He hoped Lady Rose would ask about the dahlia in his buttonhole, and then he could tell her where he had picked it, could tell her about his rambles along the River Mel and how he had remembered the names of her favourite flowers and looked them up in the library at Ashpoint Hall and—

The door of the morning room opened, and Amelia stepped out. 'That you, is it, Diggory? Deigned to bless the waking world with your presence at last?'

Diggory pulled a face at her in the mirror. 'It is not so *very* late.'

'Papa waited hours for you. Did you forget you were meant to be at the brewery today?'

He turned around sharply, his chest tightening. '*Today? Was I? I didn't – oh hell! – was Papa very cross?'*

'Very,' said Amelia gravely. 'Threats of disinheritance and cessation of allowance – that sort of thing.'

Diggory felt suddenly sick. He knew his father was not pleased with him, that he wanted him to take more interest in the business, that he thought him unsteady and rash, but this was another matter entirely. This was—

And then he realized that Amelia was laughing.

'You're joking, aren't you?' he said flatly. He loved his sister, but she was, undoubtedly, infuriating.

'Always,' replied Amelia, with a light smile. 'But Papa *was* saying something at breakfast about trying to make you go into the brewery *tomorrow*, so you had best be prepared. Where are you off to, anyway?'

'Wickford Towers, then Montague Hall. Some hunt Lord Salbridge wants to attend.'

Amelia nodded. She looked him up and down, her eyes narrowing as she spotted the flower in his buttonhole. 'Hoping to see Lady Rose, are you?'

Diggory flushed. 'I—'

'You know, you always wear odd-looking flowers whenever you are to see her.'

'Is it so very obvious?' he asked quietly.

'What – that you are in love with her? Yes, very.' His sister grinned at him. 'I do have eyes in my head, Diggory. You have been pining and sulking for months while the Wickfords have been in London, and you spent the majority of the ball staring at her. Any fool can see you are entirely besotted.'

Diggory was now the colour of his riding coat. 'Right.'

'Well, you have my blessing,' Amelia said, with a shrug. 'You have liked many a stupider person. As I recall, you were rather taken with Miss Elton at one point.'

Diggory pulled a face at her. 'I was *not* – well, maybe a little, but only before Rose was out. Miss Elton may be beautiful but she is not Rose – and Rose is *everything*.' He gave a deep sigh. 'I dare say I am not worthy of her.'

'Oh, I don't know,' replied Amelia. 'Lady Rose is cleverer and better than you and all that, but you are more entertaining, and very occasionally you are *nearly* charming.'

Amelia laughed, and Diggory felt a little jolt of fondness for her. If Amelia did not think his aspiring to Lady Rose's hand so very ridiculous, then perhaps—

But her smile was faltering. 'I am not certain her brother will like it.'

'Why ever should he not?' replied Diggory in surprise. 'I am Salbridge's greatest friend. To be sure, I am not a lord or a baronet or anything and the less said about Father's grandfather the better, and I know I shall be in *trade*, but we are *something*, aren't we? A great fortune made from brewing is still a great fortune. I may need Salbridge's help to convince his father, but if Lady Rose – well, I hardly know what to think. It is of no use thinking.' He gave a loud, dramatic sigh. 'She'll never have me.'

'She might,' said Amelia, with a sly smile. 'There really is no accounting for taste.'

~

Diggory had known Lady Rose all his life. She was six years younger than him, and six years was a great deal more to a girl of ten and a boy of sixteen than to a young lady and gentleman of eighteen and four-and-twenty. For years he had skulked in corners with Lord Salbridge, drunk and gambled and ridden with him – and failed to notice his friend's sister. He had at one point, as Amelia said, harboured a vague admiration for Felicia Elton, because Salbridge said she was beautiful and Diggory supposed she was. And then, one day last summer, the Wickfords had come back from the London Season, having brought Lady Rose out, and suddenly she was *there*. Not as a distant presence in the garden, not as a girl shut upstairs with her governess, but as a complete, glorious individual.

Lord Salbridge and his sister were not fast friends as Diggory and Amelia were – Salbridge still thought of Rose as a child – but nonetheless, Diggory's friendship with Salbridge, his regular presence at Wickford Towers, had thrown Diggory and Rose much together this last year.

Salbridge had always said that love was for girls and clergy-men and that real men ought not to think of such things. This rather confused Diggory, because although Salbridge was averse to the idea of love, he was not averse to the idea of *women*. And while Salbridge muttered about pretty faces and pleasing figures, while they drank and played cards and carried on as they always did, Diggory had grown ever more aware of Lady Rose's presence at the dinner table, in the gardens, in the parlour. He forgot Miss Elton. He endeav-oured to speak to Rose in the drawing room, to dance with her at balls. The moment he stepped into the grounds of Wickford Towers, he looked not for her brother but for her.

Once, last winter, on riding over to see his friend, he had found Salbridge not at home. Lady Wickford and Lady Rose had entertained him in his absence, showing him the glasshouses in the grounds. Halfway through their walk, Lady Wickford had stopped to rest on one of the benches – in truth, Diggory feared she had grown bored – and he and Lady Rose had gone on together. She told him the names of all the flowers, both in Latin and in English, and where each one had come from.

'You must be very clever to remember all this,' said Diggory.

'Thank you,' replied Lady Rose. 'Only, you mustn't say so to my family, you know, for they do not think it proper for a young lady to be clever. Still, I am allowed to keep the glasshouses quite as I wish and give all the directions to the gardeners, so long as I say to Papa only how pretty the flowers are and keep my horticultural endeavours quite to myself.'

And really, listening to Lady Rose talk was such a pleasant thing to do that Diggory thought he would like to do it forever.

Back in February, when the earl and his family had departed for the London Season, Diggory had wept heartily. He spent a day shut up in his room on pretence of a headache, thinking that, really, this had gone a lot further than he realized. This was Rose's second Season. What if she met someone – some earl or duke or somebody who was not the son of a brewer? If she came back engaged, Diggory thought he might shoot himself (in the leg, probably, or perhaps the left arm). He had counted the days until Rose's return.

But the family had come back to Wickenshire last week, and the only forthcoming marriage appeared to be Mr Hurst's. And Rose had been at the ball two days ago, still free, still talking, still looking back at him with a bright smile on her face. He had danced with her four times. He had held her in his arms while they waltzed. He did not *think* he had said anything ridiculous, though by their fourth dance he had consumed rather a lot of punch – Salbridge kept topping him up – and the details of their conversation had become a little hazy. He had tried to ask her sensible questions about London and to exchange views about this marriage of Mr Hurst's, but it was very hard when all he wanted to do every time he opened his mouth in Rose's presence was to declare very loudly that he was in love with her.

∼

An hour later, Diggory rode through the grand gates of Wickford Towers, over the drawbridge and up to the front door. He left his horse with one of the stable boys, adjusted his top hat, checked the flower in his buttonhole and brushed down his clothes. Then he swallowed very hard and knocked upon the door.

He had calculated correctly: the footman informed him that Lord Salbridge was not yet down, that Lord and Lady Wickford were out paying calls, but that Lady Rose was in the parlour, if Mr Diggory might wish to wait there?

And so he found himself shown into the bright, sun-filled parlour of Wickford Towers, where Lady Rose sat on one of the settees, dressed in a green print frock. She stood up and curtseyed when he came into the room.

'Good morning, Mr Diggory.'

'Good morning, Lady Rose.'

He came forwards to greet her, but he came a little too far, and suddenly they were standing too close together, and Diggory knew she had already been at work in her glasshouses this morning because he could see bits of leaves and flower petals caught in her hair, and he was just wondering if she had come back into the house on purpose because she knew he was to call for her brother when he heard the footman close the door and realized that they were alone.

He was not often alone with Lady Rose. Lord or Lady Wickford or Lord Salbridge were usually there, or a whole ballroom or dining room of people. This seemed like the sort of good opportunity brave men in books would make use of – but Diggory, who was not very brave, began to feel rather queasy. He wondered how long Salbridge would be, whether he had ten minutes or fifteen or twenty in which to act. He wondered how it would be best to begin – and then he became aware that he had been standing in front of Rose for rather a long time without speaking, that she was aware of it, too, that she was smiling at him, and her smile looked so very lovely that Diggory wanted to kiss her – but he was almost certain that was not the right way to begin at all.

Just when he was starting to think that he would never be able to say anything, Lady Rose spoke instead. 'I hope you have recovered from the ball on Wednesday,' she said.

Diggory blinked. 'Recovered?'

'From the punch,' she replied.

This took Diggory entirely aback. He had not had *that* much to drink. He was sure Lord Salbridge had drunk more. He was *almost* sure that he had only been tipsy, but it was so hard to remember. Lady Rose was smiling, as though she thought it all more amusing than shocking, but Diggory began to feel red and hot.

'Did I behave so badly?' he asked quietly.

Lady Rose laughed. 'No, not at all. Only, we let my brother supervise the punch, and I think he asked Johnson to put rather too much rum in it, for I had a dreadful head-ache the next day and Papa did not rise until twelve.' She stopped, and her manner changed abruptly, became hesi-tant, apologetic. 'Oh, I did not mean to – to tease you, Mr Diggory. I only – well, you barely said a word to me during that last quadrille, so I thought—'

'Oh, it was not *that*,' said Diggory, and in his haste to prove that he was not drunk, he added quickly, 'It is just that, some-times, Lady Rose, I find it hard to speak to you, because I—'

He broke off. This was not how he had intended to begin at all. It was probably rather bad form to propose in defence of drunkenness. But Lady Rose was looking at him, smiling, and he saw that she was almost blushing. He swallowed very hard, made himself speak.

'Lady Rose,' he said, very quietly and very quickly, afraid he might never go on if he stopped for a moment, 'Rose, dear Rose, I know I have no business to even try to be worthy of you, but you must know that—'

And then the door banged open and a voice cried, 'Morning, Diggory!' and Lady Rose took a quick step back.

Diggory turned around to see Lord Salbridge in the door-way, dressed in a green riding coat. He had evidently hurried downstairs to greet him, for his valet was following behind, carrying his hat and boots. Salbridge was smiling heartily, and Diggory cursed his poor timing. It was just his sort of luck. He might not have the opportunity (or the courage) to say something to Lady Rose again for weeks.

'Well, Diggory, I hope my sister hasn't been boring you.'
Salbridge laughed. 'Are you ready? We shall be late if you
don't make haste.'

'Oh – to be sure – yes.' Diggory swallowed hard. He
glanced round at Lady Rose, who had resumed her place on
the settee and taken up her sewing, with only the faintest
trace of red in her cheeks. Diggory thought he was probably scarlet.

If Lord Salbridge noticed, however, he made no comment. He only held the parlour door open wider and said,
'Come along, old chap.'

And so Diggory followed Lord Salbridge out into the corridor, out into the hall, the courtyard and round towards the
stables. When he glanced back at the parlour window, he
saw Lady Rose look up from her sewing and smile.

~

While Diggory made his way towards Melcastle, Amelia
was walking down the lanes that led from Ashpoint Hall to
Melford and to Clara's house. The basket under her arm
was heavy, weighed down by the thick parcel of paper
within. She glanced up at the towering buildings of the
brewery, crossed a stile nestled in the hedgerow, then passed
the small building and bright garden of Maddox Court.
She paused to gaze down the lane at the streets of Melford.

She had been making this journey for as long as she could
remember, just as she had known Clara for as long as she
could remember. Some twenty years ago, when Mr McNeil
first arrived in Wickenshire, Mr Ashpoint, pleased to hear
that his new land agent had a daughter just of an age with
his own, had taken Amelia to meet Clara. From then on,

whenever Mr McNeil was at work on Mr Ashpoint's land, Clara was brought up to the house to play with Amelia – and every day she was not, Amelia would beg to be taken to see her, and her mother or father or one of the servants would walk down this very lane with Amelia's hand in theirs.

Amelia remembered little of this, though her father had told her the story often enough. She did remember, though, at five years old, being presented with her first governess – and screaming and shouting and refusing to work through her lessons until Clara was brought to sit calmly at her side. All this ended in Clara coming up to Ashpoint Hall each day for her lessons, in Mr McNeil reducing his fees in exchange for his daughter's education, and in Clara and Amelia becoming inseparable.

It was impossible to say when Amelia had first begun to love Clara. It must have been creeping upon her all her life. When she read novels as a young girl, the idea of marriage never much appealed to her – but love had always seemed familiar, somehow. And then Amelia turned thirteen, and Laurie was born, and her mother died – and suddenly Mr McNeil, aware that the Ashpoint household was in disarray, was speaking of sending Clara away to school. The sheer impossibility of living without Clara, of not seeing her every day, combined with the fresh pain of her mother's loss, almost felled Amelia. She had gone to her father's study to beg him to speak to Mr McNeil, to tell him that Clara's presence was never anything but a comfort to them all. She found him bent over his desk, cheeks pale, eyes downcast, as low as he always was in those days – and it had come upon her all at once that for her to live without Clara was the same as for her father to live without her mother.

She told Clara of this discovery, because she always told

Clara everything, and Clara had nodded simply and said, 'Yes, I have sometimes thought so, too,' and for a while, that was all – until the following year, when they came across an illustration of a man and woman kissing in a book, and Amelia said they ought to try it.

Years rushed by. Nobody minded that the two of them spent so much time in each other's company, because it was the sort of intimacy everybody expected between girls of their age. When they dined at each other's houses, it was quite natural that they would sleep there instead of walking home. And if Clara more often slept in Amelia's room, where there was a lock on the door and the walls were thicker – well, nobody could be surprised that she preferred the grandeur of Ashpoint Hall to her own small home. Their fathers knew nothing, suspected nothing. Mr Ashpoint was pleased that Amelia had found so sensible a friend, and Mr McNeil was pleased to see Clara made much of by his employer's daughter.

They had wondered sometimes if there were other girls and women like them. It seemed unlikely that they could be so very singular; men were known to do such things, after all. They would pull lines from novels, plays, verses to share with one another. They read Wordsworth's poem to those two ladies at Llangollen and wondered, and Amelia held that Shakespeare knew Olivia was more in love with Viola than Sebastian – but it had seemed unimportant when they were sixteen or seventeen, when to be unique was to be special, when to be different was beautiful.

And then they were coming out into Society, and at first it had felt like almost a game, to deceive the men, to hear their fathers talking of matrimony when they had no intention of marrying, to hear Society speak of suitors and matches when they both knew they were sworn to each other. They snatched kisses when their families left the room, held hands under the dinner table, sneaked away at balls to kiss in shadows and empty corridors.

And then the trial of Mr Pratt and Mr Smith came into the newspapers, and the men were hanged at Newgate, and though Clara did not think either the Bible or the law said anything about connections between *women* – still, they were shaken. Amelia could not get those poor men out of her head. And suddenly, to be different was lonely, frightening, dangerous.

After that, they changed their behaviour. They wrote out rules, grew guarded beyond the privacy of their own rooms. They swore to keep each other safe. Over the past six years, secrecy had become second nature, and although it was frustrating, although it was at times wearying, maddening – still, it was, surely, the only way to be.

Amelia held more tightly to her basket, to the wrapped parcel of paper inside. No, secrets were nothing new to her.

She turned now onto Garrett Lane and glanced up at Clara's house. She could see her silhouette at the upstairs window; she was sitting at her desk, no doubt working on some plan or other for her father. Amelia liked that Clara did this – had always liked to imagine that, whenever she was writing at her bureau, Clara was drawing at hers.

Hannah, the McNeils' maid-of-all-work, answered the door with a smile and inclined her head to the stairs before returning to the kitchen. Amelia climbed the stairs and let herself into Clara's room without knocking, as she always did.

'Good morning,' said Clara, turning from her work. Her smile was wide, and she had a pencil mark on her cheek.

Amelia put her basket down on the floor and leant forwards to wipe the mark away. Then she pulled Clara out of her chair, out of view of the window, to kiss her. 'What do you think I have in my basket?' she asked as she pulled back.

Clara glanced towards it. 'What?'

'Why, nothing more or less than the complete manuscript of *The Life and Times of Eliza Wallace* – to be delivered to Mr Lonsdale later today.'

Clara's face broke into a smile, and she tightened her hold on Amelia. 'You mean you asked him? And he said yes?'

Amelia was nodding. She felt a laugh leave her lips, as though Clara's eagerness had allowed her own to break free. 'He will send it to Mr Browne in London, and . . . well, we shall see what happens.'

'We shall see you become a famous novelist,' declared Clara. 'Or, at least, your *nom de plume* will have the fame and you will write the novels.'

Amelia raised her eyebrows, pulled Clara closer to her. 'And here have I been, relying on you to be rational and quell my hopes.'

Clara shook her head gently, raising a hand to Amelia's cheek. 'There is nothing irrational,' she said, 'about believing in you.'

CHAPTER VI

In which we cultivate the acquaintance of a very grand family

SOME MILES ACROSS WICKENSHIRE, THE SWEET SOUNDS OF an exquisitely performed sonata were drifting through the rooms of Ludwell Manor.

Felicia Elton played perfectly. She did not miss a note; she did not lose time. Her fingers moved swiftly across the ivory keys; her right foot pressed the pedal just when required. Each dynamic was adhered to, each repeat acknowledged. The melody lulled and swayed and swelled, filling the music room, from the polished wood floor to the high, ornate ceiling.

Felicia Elton sat perfectly. She kept her back straight, her arms poised exactly where they ought to be. She held her head positioned half an inch to one side to display her neatly styled golden hair to its fullest advantage.

Felicia Elton was attired perfectly. She wore a pale-blue day dress embroidered with silver thread, delicate white satin shoes, simple blue drop earrings, and a plain silver ornament around her neck.

She had just reached the midpoint of the second movement of the sonata when the door opened and in stepped her mother.

Felicia kept playing. To stop midway through a movement

was impossible to countenance, even if she must bear with the slight incivility of keeping her mother waiting. Her music master, Monsieur Brisset, was adamant that a piece ought always to be played through to the end; one had to respect the music.

When Felicia at last finished, she looked up, assuming an air of polite surprise, and said, 'Good afternoon, Mama.'

'You might have stopped before, Felicia.'

'Really, Mama – how you expect me to develop my accomplishments if you interrupt my practice, I hardly know.'

Mrs Elton ignored this. 'Fetch your shawl,' she said shortly. 'I am going into Melford, and you are coming with me.'

'Indeed, Mama?'

Mrs Elton gave a single nod. 'Your father has heard some news this morning, from the *footman* of all people.' She shuddered. 'Apparently, it is all over Melford that Mr Hurst's new bride has . . . *children*.' She whispered this last word with great significance.

'Goodness.' Felicia raised her eyebrows. 'I suppose it is not unheard of for a widow to be in possession of a child.'

'My dear,' said Mrs Elton, with great gravity, 'you know that I do not in general approve of second attachments. For a lady who has had one husband already to seek *another* offends my sense of delicacy. It is more excusable if the lady has not been so fortunate as to bear issue from her first marriage, for of course we females take seriously our duty of expanding the race – but I cannot think well of our future neighbour if, circumstanced as she is said to be, she has taken it upon herself to marry again.' Mrs Elton pressed her lips together and shook her head. 'And as for Mr Hurst – for a young, respectable country squire with six thousand a year to take *such* a bride . . . it is quite monstrous. I am prepared to believe he is to wed a widow, for I heard it from his own lips, but I do not and cannot believe he is to marry a widow who has children already.'

'And so,' said Felicia, 'I suppose we are going to the dressmaker's.'

There were two great fountains of gossip within Melford. One was the Lantern, where the gentlemen of the neighbourhood collected their scraps of local news. The other was Miss Nettlebed's dressmaker's, where the ladies gathered theirs.

Mrs Elton nodded once.

She was a formidable woman – nay, a formidable lady, for Mrs Elton would have been insulted to be called a mere woman. She had long been the self-appointed leader of Society in Wickenshire, and Felicia knew that, in the glory of this unchallenged power, her mother felt it her duty – indeed, her God-given right – to know everything about anybody of consequence.

'Come, Felicia,' said her mother, as the clock chimed eleven. 'The carriage awaits.'

∽

Felicia sat perfectly upright as the family carriage rolled into Melford. The four-mile journey from the village of Ludwell had passed mostly in silence. Her mother sat beside her, dignified and stern in dark-blue silk, looking out of the window with lips pursed as the town sprang up around them. The carriage jolted as the horses traversed the bridge over the River Mel and rattled onto the cobblestones beyond. Felicia shifted almost imperceptibly to ensure her perfect hair and her perfect dress were not disarranged, for any member of the Elton family would have felt ashamed to be overcome by so slight an inconvenience as an uneven road.

Outside the carriage windows, the beginnings of the town trundled by: wattle-and-daub buildings and cottages of tightly packed stone; window boxes blooming with summer flowers; tall thatched roofs, smoking chimneys; shops with their shutters and doors thrown wide open; people moving through the streets in bonnets and shawls, hats and caps. Out of one window, the tower of St Matthew's stood tall above the houses, its grey stone golden in the sun. Out of the other, Felicia could see the imposing facades of Ashpoint Hall and Ashpoint Brewery atop the hill to the north of the town.

A few men took off their hats and bowed as the carriage passed; the women curtseyed, and a handful of children pointed and cried out. The sight of the Eltons' carriage always caused a stir in Melford. Everybody knew who the Eltons were. Everybody knew of their importance. Everybody, rich or poor, man or woman, young or old, recognized the stately livery, knew the familiar family crest and the motto '*Superbia et honore*' painted in heavily ornamented letters on the carriage's side.

When they finally reached Maddox Square, the footman alighted to hand Mrs and Miss Elton down.

Felicia carefully avoided putting her satin shoes straight into a puddle. She really did not see why the streets could not be kept clean, why everywhere beyond Ludwell Manor was so very *dirty*.

She sighed and followed her mother down the street.

Melford was a thriving market town, one of the largest in Wickenshire, and Maddox Square was its heart. A market was raised twice weekly here, overlooked by the King's Arms Inn and the Lantern. Leading off the square to the

south was Grange Street, the principal shopping street, and
this Felicia and her mother now walked down. It was broad
and old-fashioned, lined by sandstone and wattle-and-daub
buildings, with thatched roofs and open shop fronts and a
regular throng of people. It had its polite side and its practical side. On the left stood Miss Nettlebed's dressmaker's,
the bookseller's, the stationer's, the milliner's, the tailor's and
Crayton's Bank. On the right stood the greengrocer's, the
butcher's, the baker's, the general shop and the butterman's.
Down one of the side streets was the pawnbroker's and a
less expensive dressmaker's – but no Elton had ever yet had
cause to visit either establishment.

As Felicia and her mother walked towards Miss Nettlebed's,
the shopkeepers raised their hats to them, as was only
proper, and the townspeople stared and curtseyed and
moved out of their way. It was a bright, warm summer's
day, and Felicia had to glance at her reflection in a shop
window or two to ensure that her cheeks were not reddened
by the heat.

As they passed the tailor's, the bell above the door tinkled,
and Major Alderton of Netherworth stepped out, almost
knocking into Felicia.

'I am terribly sorry – good morning, Miss Elton, Mrs
Elton.'

Felicia said, 'Good morning, Major Alderton,' before she
had the chance to consider whether or not she ought to
acknowledge a man of such low repute. Her mother said
nothing, but she visibly stiffened.

Major Alderton appeared determined to take no notice
of this – it must take a certain kind of pride, Felicia
thought, to withstand her mother's icy glare. But he smiled
at Felicia, all calm affability. 'I hope you enjoyed the ball on

Wednesday, Miss Elton,' he said. 'I was sorry not to have the pleasure of dancing with you, but perhaps next time.'

'Certainly,' said Felicia. He was dressed very well, in a crisp new tailcoat of the finest cut, his top hat evidently just purchased. He stood very upright, and it was hard not to be polite to somebody who so clearly had the bearing of a gentleman – who so clearly *knew* he had the bearing of a gentleman.

Major Alderton smiled, tipped his new hat to both Felicia and her mother and carried on down the street.

Mrs Elton took Felicia's arm in a tight grasp. 'My dear, you must not *speak* to such a man.'

'Oh, really, Mama – I could not very well ignore him when he spoke to me directly. And you cannot look at him and tell me that he is not a gentleman.'

'He is absolutely *not* a gentleman. Felicia, you know very well that he is' – and here Mrs Elton lowered her voice to a whisper, as though the word were not fit for the street – '*illegitimate.*'

'I saw Papa speak to him at the ball.'

Mrs Elton's lip curled. 'What your father sees fit to do I cannot help. I am glad that my uncle, the Marquis of Denby, is not alive to see my husband so demean himself. That *person* ought not to have been invited to a respectable occasion.' She shook her head in disgust. 'Come, Felicia, let us put the matter behind us,' she said firmly, before marching towards the dressmaker's.

The bell above Miss Nettlebed's shop rang lightly as they entered. Felicia walked in behind her mother, her head held high, her back straight. The familiar sight of silks and satins, ribbons and fashion plates, greeted her from each side. Miss Nettlebed stood behind the counter, discussing muslin with old Miss Waterson and Miss Maddon, while Mrs Palmer and a few of the Miss Palmers stood examining some new fabric by the window. They were talking quickly to one another in low voices, but Felicia caught the word 'Hurst' on Louisa Palmer's lips, followed by a giggle from her younger sister, Cassandra. The eldest sister, Anne, was apparently trying to steer the conversation back to haberdashery.

Miss Waterson, Miss Maddon and the Palmers were most definitely on the *town* side of the town and county divide, but they were at least respectable, and thus Mrs Elton bid them all 'Good morning' in a tone of such great stateliness that no one could doubt her superiority in rank. Felicia curtseyed and smiled her perfect smile. Neither of them acknowledged Miss Nettlebed.

'Have you heard the latest news, Mrs Elton?' asked Mrs Palmer, stepping towards her. 'It is all over the neighbourhood this morning that Mr Hurst's new bride – this *Mrs Roberts* – has children already.'

'Four of them, by all accounts,' declared Miss Waterson, turning around and launching herself into the conversation.

'Oh no,' said Miss Maddon. 'I have it on excellent authority that there are five.'

'I heard there's just a baby,' said Louisa Palmer with great relish, 'and so new a baby that the bride can scarcely be out of mourning.'

'I heard there are twins,' said Cassandra Palmer.

'Perhaps,' said Anne Palmer slowly, 'we oughtn't to speculate when—'

'Oh, do be quiet, Anne,' said Cassandra and Louisa together.

Felicia turned away from the conversation and flicked through the fashion plates on one of the tables, wondering if she would look better in crimson satin or dark-green silk. She did not much like the Palmer sisters, and she rather thought they did not like her. They were all silly girls, the kind who would end up marrying clerks and curates and the sorts of farmers who pretended they were gentlemen. Cassandra and Louisa were tolerably pretty, she supposed, but they laughed too much and were overly interested in gossip. Anne was meant to be the accomplished one, but Felicia thought her playing and singing both decidedly lacking. There was another sister or two at home, little girls not yet out in Society, but Felicia could never remember their names.

'Have you ever heard of this Matilda Roberts in London, Mrs Elton?' asked Mrs Palmer.

Mrs Elton shook her head. 'I have not.'

'I heard somebody say her first husband was in the army,' said Miss Waterson.

'Oh no,' said Miss Maddon. 'I am sure it was the navy.'

'But I asked my husband,' Mrs Palmer put in, 'and he could not think of a single admiral or commodore or captain or even a commander called Roberts.'

'I suppose Sir Frederick will know all about it,' said Cassandra Palmer. 'I hear he has gone to London, too, to be the best man at the wedding.'

That would, Felicia supposed, account for his not having called at Ludwell since the ball. At the start of the year, before the Eltons had gone to London for the Season, he had been at their house nearly every week. She had grown a little tired of his loud clothes and his quiet voice, of his stiff, formal manners and his complete lack of ease. But he was a baronet, and baronets must be borne. Her father might be doubtful of Sir Frederick's fortune, but her mother had quite made up her mind that Felicia was to marry him.

'Perhaps Sir Frederick will catch a taste for weddings,' said Louisa Palmer, with a sudden rush of giggles.

Felicia looked up to see Cassandra and Louisa staring at her, nudging one another, while Anne glanced towards them with an anxious frown.

Felicia forced herself to be composed. Let them laugh at her. They would not find it so very amusing when she wed a gentleman of title and they did not. They were only jealous. If she had been less beautiful, Felicia told herself, she might have had more friends – but she did not want to be less beautiful.

'I suppose nobody knows very much about this Mrs Roberts at all,' said Mrs Elton, with a fixed frown. 'It is most singular.'

And then, abruptly, Miss Nettlebed the dressmaker said, 'There are without a doubt three children.'

Everybody looked around at her in astonishment. She had had no part in the conversation thus far – she knew well enough not to intrude when her superiors were gossiping – and Felicia supposed her mother would never have thought of asking a mere *dressmaker* for her opinion. Even now, Mrs Elton held back, refusing to address Miss Nettlebed directly.

It was Miss Waterson who spoke instead. 'Goodness, whoever told you that, Miss Nettlebed?'

'Why, Mr Hurst's housekeeper was in here yesterday.' Miss Nettlebed looked down at her ledger book, cheeks reddening, as though she rather relished being the source of such news. 'She ordered three children's nightgowns,' she went on, with a triumphant smile. 'I should think, from the measurements, that the eldest must be about eight or nine and the youngest perhaps not more than two.'

There was a collective intake of breath. Miss Maddon and Miss Waterson exchanged curious glances, and Mrs Palmer nodded significantly at Mrs Elton. Louisa and Cassandra exploded in surprised giggles and even Anne appeared intrigued.

Felicia looked down at the fashion plates before her. It was certainly very remarkable. For Mr Hurst to marry a widow with a child of eight or nine – why, this Mrs Roberts must be a great deal older than they all had imagined. And *three* children, too. What on earth was Mr Hurst thinking? Felicia could simply not understand it. And if men made such wild, irrational decisions, who was to say what fate lay in store for the rest of the young ladies of Wickenshire?

CHAPTER VII

*In which cards are played and whisky
is consumed*

THE LANTERN WAS AN OLD ESTABLISHMENT. IT HAD BEGUN
as an inn in the sixteenth century, and over time the gentlemen of Wickenshire had claimed it as their own. It was a
tall, rickety building, with a wattle-and-daub frontage. The
top floor housed the staff, and the middle floor held rooms
for any gentlemen whose evening exploits with whisky prevented their riding home safely. Beneath that was the neat
room in which the elder gentlemen of the county convened,
and finally came the basement, which held the wine cellar
and the room where the younger gentlemen met.

In the upper room, the old gentlemen sipped port and
coffee; in the lower, the young gentlemen drank whisky. In
the upper room, they left the club before ten; in the lower,
they stayed into the small hours. In the upper room, the
largest debt from cards had been when Captain Palmer
once owed Mr Ashpoint three shillings ha'penny; in the
lower room, Lord Salbridge currently owed Mr Hurst ten
pounds, Mr Edmund Crayton twenty pounds, Mr Duckfield
fifty pounds, Major Alderton a hundred pounds and Mr
Diggory Ashpoint a whole two hundred.

The upper room of the Lantern was empty tonight, as
Lord Salbridge and Diggory Ashpoint came through the

doors and headed down the stairs. Diggory was excessively tired. It had been a dreadfully hot day, and he had spent most of it purposefully getting lost in order to miss the action of the hunt. What he longed for most was a large dinner and his own large bed – but what Lord Salbridge longed for was whisky and a card game. Salbridge's wishes had, as usual, prevailed.

'I say, old chap,' said Salbridge, as they reached the door to the lower room, 'could I borrow five pounds? I shall pay you back in a day or two, but I put money down for a new mare from that fellow at the hunt, and I haven't a penny to play with.'

'By all means,' said Diggory, as he reached into his pockets. He was fairly certain Salbridge owed him something already, but he was too tired to remember the sum. 'You can pay me back tonight, if you win. And listen, I cannot stay too long – I am meant to be at the brewery tomorrow.'

'Nonsense, dear chap.' Lord Salbridge slapped him on the back. 'Come, don't let your father ruin your fun.'

The lower room smelt of smoke, spirits and sweat, and was loud with a buzz of chatter. There were two card games ongoing: Major Alderton and Edmund Crayton were playing écarté at one table, while Monsieur Brisset, Lonsdale and Mr Duckfield played ombre at another.

Salbridge sat down near Crayton, and Diggory threw himself into the chair beside him.

'Playing for shillings, are you?' asked Salbridge with a laugh, as he looked across at the scattered coins. 'Can we not do a little better? Come, who wants to play high at speculation? Diggory and I are willing.'

Diggory, who had slumped back into his chair, did not feel very willing.

'I am, to be sure,' declared Edmund Crayton. He was two-and-twenty years old, worked very hard at his father's bank between the hours of ten and five, and spent all his free hours and money on cards.

'As am I,' said Major Alderton.

'Vicar?' asked Lord Salbridge, glancing towards the other table, where the game had just finished.

'Well, why not?' replied Mr Duckfield. He stood up, smiled half an apology at Lonsdale and Monsieur Brisset, then sat down at Salbridge's table. It never ceased to surprise Diggory how very fond their vicar was of gambling.

'Well, five of us will suffice,' said Salbridge, leaning forwards in his chair to shuffle the cards. 'I suppose we shall never have six around this table again, now that Hurst has decided to accept the chains of matrimony.'

'Unless Mr Lonsdale or Monsieur Brisset wish to join us?' said Major Alderton, turning with a smile towards the other table.

Diggory saw Salbridge scowl. He knew that his friend did not approve of Major Alderton, that he bore his presence in their card games only because he had enough money to always bet high and so much self-assurance that it was impossible to think of asking him to leave. Diggory often saw the major at the Lantern, but he had been rather surprised to see him at Lady Wickford's ball on Wednesday, dancing with people's daughters and sisters like everybody else. Still, he rather liked the man. The very fact that someone with such a fragile social position was always so thoroughly cheerful made Diggory think that perhaps his own situation was not so very bad after all.

But if Lord Salbridge tolerated Major Alderton's presence at the Lantern, he did not and never had tolerated

Lonsdale or Brisset. They were altogether a different class of men, as far as he was concerned. He never greeted them; he never acknowledged them. He certainly never invited them to play cards. Diggory had played with them once or twice, while Salbridge was in London, but then Diggory was not the son of an earl.

'Certainly they may join us,' said Salbridge calmly, 'if they can afford it.'

This was said with some pretence at a whisper, but the low conversation between Brisset and Lonsdale ceased at once. Brisset stood up, Lonsdale grabbed his arm, and Lord Salbridge laughed.

'Well, *gentlemen*,' he said, with a sneer upon the last word, 'are you to join us or not?'

It was the first time Diggory had ever heard Lord Salbridge address either of them directly. Lonsdale met his gaze as though ready for a challenge, and Diggory suddenly felt less tired.

Monsieur Brisset was shaking his head. 'I am going,' he said to the room in general. 'Goodnight.' He looked for a moment towards Lonsdale, who shook his head almost imperceptibly.

'I shall stay,' he said. His voice sounded unnervingly firm.

Diggory did not turn to see Brisset leave the room, but he heard the door open and close, heard Salbridge ring the bell for drinks. Around him, chairs were being moved and people were sitting down.

He glanced up as Lonsdale joined the table. He nodded once at Diggory, then looked away. Diggory knew him a little from the days when his father succeeded in dragging him into the brewery to help with paperwork and to 'contemplate his future'. This last year or so, Lonsdale had been a regular presence at the Lantern, too. At the brewery, Lonsdale was efficient, confident and easy in his manner. At the Lantern, he was almost silent.

Salbridge began to deal, and Diggory tried to sit up straight.

'Well,' said Mr Duckfield, as Salbridge placed a few crumpled banknotes in the centre of the table, 'what do you all think of this mysterious match of Hurst's?'

'I suppose she is terribly old,' said Edmund Crayton, 'if she has children.'

Major Alderton inclined his head. 'It is surprising that Mr Hurst has chosen a bride with a family already.'

'Perhaps the lady is very rich and not very beautiful,' said Salbridge, 'and Mr Hurst wishes to get her fortune and not be obliged to make heirs with her.'

Edmund Crayton nearly choked on his whisky.

'They say that Sir Frederick has gone up to London with him,' said Mr Duckfield, 'so I suppose he knows all about it.'

'What do we think he's wearing to the wedding?' asked Lord Salbridge, with a hearty laugh.

Sir Frederick Hammersmith was the only young gentleman in Wickenshire who never entered the Lantern, and thus he was considered a great joke here – at least on days when Mr Hurst was not present to be offended on his friend's behalf. Salbridge declared that Sir Frederick avoided the place because he was a strait-laced dull fellow who could not dress himself sensibly and was a snob about all life's pleasures. Diggory was inclined to think it was because Sir Frederick's father and grandfather had gambled away much of his estate, and he was determined not to do the same.

Salbridge turned over a nine of clubs, and Diggory

sighed. He hated speculation. He always lost. He was somewhat relieved when the waiter, Mr Graves, opened the door
with a tray of filled glasses.

'What's this, Graves?' said Salbridge, taking one glass and
gulping half of it down before it reached the table. 'Bring us
the bottle, man – I am quite parched. Hungry, too, in fact,
so if a chop—?'

'Very good, sir,' said Graves – with the same tone of disapproval as if he were saying 'very bad' – and bowed out
of the room.

'Anybody want to buy a nine of clubs?'

The game went on. Diggory lost track. He felt abominably drunk and sleepy, and he was sure everybody else must
be drunk, too. Certainly Edmund Crayton was drunk, and
Salbridge was drunk, and Duckfield was drunk. It was
harder to tell with Alderton and Lonsdale.

At last, the cards were turned over, one by one, but no
one had anything to beat Salbridge's king – until the final
card was turned, revealing that Lonsdale had the ace.

Salbridge swore, but Lonsdale only nodded and pulled
the pile of money towards him.

The cards were dealt again and Diggory, certain his hand
would once again be shockingly bad, wished he could be
somewhere else. It was pleasant enough to sit with a bunch
of other fellows in a half-drunken haze and slowly lose one's
money – but it would be pleasanter to be asleep in bed. Or
to be wandering the Wickford glasshouses with Lady Rose,
or dancing around a ballroom with Lady Rose, or dining
with Lady Rose, or, quite frankly, being *anywhere* with Lady
Rose. He thought of this morning, standing close to her in
the parlour at Wickford Towers, the flush on her face before
they were interrupted, the bright smile on her lips.

~

The card game was still going at half past one in the morning, by which time Major Alderton had won five pounds and Lonsdale fifteen. Lord Salbridge had lost ten pounds – the five Diggory had lent him earlier and another five in IOUs – and he was feeling rather sore about it. It did not do to associate with inferior men unless one was to win.

Salbridge often felt the lack of companions close to him in rank and status. At school, he had associated with the sons of dukes and marquises, but here, in this quarter of Wickenshire, there was nobody his equal. True, there was Augustus Elton, Felicia's brother – but since he had got into Parliament five years ago, he was almost always in London. Mr Hurst was a country squire, and that was something – but he had been off in Paris for much of the last decade, so Salbridge did not know him well. And as for Sir Frederick Hammersmith – he was infernally dull. The man did not drink, did not gamble, did not hunt, and so Salbridge scarcely saw the point of him. That the only other titled young man in the neighbourhood was such a bore was a great blow indeed.

It was one thing to sit down to cards with Mr Duckfield and Diggory Ashpoint. Mr Duckfield was a clergyman, and clergymen were always gentlemen. Diggory might be only a brewer's son, but he was a capital fellow, who always did what he was told. Edmund Crayton, too, was passable, for a banker's son was respectable enough.

But as for Alderton – well, good blood tarnished by bad. The name Alderton was, of course, a fabrication. He was a nobody, a legal nothing. So what if he was mightily rich? Alderton's father – some duke from the North of England, he had heard once – ought not to have given his bastard a fortune: he would have done better, Salbridge reflected, had he tucked Alderton away in a distant village, given him an apprenticeship to some trade and had done with him. Salbridge had been forced to put up with him at the card table for a year now, since Mr Hurst, not long after his return to the neighbourhood, had invited him to join them for a game.

But at least Major Alderton could pay his way and talk like a gentleman, which was more than could be said for this Lonsdale. Anybody could see that he was just a labourer dressed in finery, trying to pretend he belonged. It was beyond impertinent for Alderton to have asked him to play at all, when everyone knew this was *Salbridge's* game. Wickenshire was all his domain in its way, and there was certainly no doubt that he ruled the Lantern.

Still, it was useful to have enough fellows to make up a decent game. And if Lonsdale lost badly one night, he would probably not be able to afford his subscription to the Lantern, and then they might be rid of him for good.

'It is late,' said Major Alderton, rising to his feet at the end of a round. 'I had better go.'

'Come, come – one more game,' said Salbridge, with his most winning smile. 'And then I shall have to carry Diggory home, for he is already quite asleep.'

The major hesitated, smiled, then sat back down. He did it all very steadily, and Salbridge supposed he could not be as drunk as the rest of them. It was rather bad form not to be drunk.

Salbridge shook Diggory awake as Mr Duckfield dealt.

Cards were turned over, bought and sold. Salbridge purchased a queen from Lonsdale for another three pounds. The cards went around again – and Lonsdale, finally, turned over the ace of hearts.

Salbridge felt a stab of anger. Impossible – impossible, surely, for this fellow to beat his betters twice in one night with the same trick. He stood up sharply. 'I say,' he said, 'that's the second time that's happened.'

Lonsdale shrugged. 'Luck is on my side tonight.'

'Damn luck – I think you cheated.'

There was sudden silence around the table.

Lonsdale rose to his feet. 'I did not cheat,' he said firmly. 'Upon my honour.'

Salbridge laughed. 'And what is your honour? You're a foreman at a brewery.'

Major Alderton frowned. 'Really, my lord—'

'Oh, be quiet, Major,' retorted Salbridge. 'You are little better than him, and no one cares for your opinion.'

Alderton froze. All his cheery ease, his assured manner, was gone in a moment. Salbridge felt a faint glow of satisfaction.

Diggory was sitting up straighter. 'Salbridge, that isn't kind. And I hardly think Lonsdale would have—'

'Let it be, Mr Ashpoint,' said Lonsdale, bending down to sweep his winnings into his purse. 'I did not cheat, as I believe you know, as your friend will know when he is sober. A gentleman ought not to make such accusations.'

'And what would *you* know,' sneered Salbridge, 'about being a gentleman?'

'You ought not to have quarrelled with them,' said Diggory, as he and Salbridge stumbled upstairs after the others had left. 'I am sure Lonsdale did not cheat, and the major is a very good fellow. To touch him on what must be a sore point, really—'

'I dare say he has heard worse. And as for that Lonsdale – well, how the devil did he pull the same trick twice in one evening *without* cheating?'

'By sheer luck, I suppose,' said Diggory. He had some trouble saying the word 'sheer' distinctly.

'Wish I'd had some luck. Tonight, my dear fellow, I've lost all the damn money in my damn pockets, and I dare say my damn father won't give me any more.'

Diggory did not think it worth pointing out that the money in Salbridge's pockets tonight had been his. He had a headache, and he was wondering if it would be wise to leave his horse in the stables here and walk home by moonlight. He was thinking of Lady Rose and how she would probably not like to see him this drunk – except, of course, she probably did not care for him at all.

And then he thought of the card table again, Major Alderton's abrupt change of manner, the fury in Lonsdale's eyes. Lonsdale had won twenty-five pounds tonight and Diggory rather admired him for it. He knew what Lonsdale earned – he had seen his father's accounts books at the brewery – and the figure was about fifty pounds a year. To sit down to cards and win half your annual salary in one night seemed, to Diggory, a rather impressive thing to do. Lonsdale was very clever, to be sure, but Diggory could not imagine him cheating. The man had too much pride.

'Come, Diggory, do not look at me like that. Major Alderton is the bastard son of God knows who, and I dare say Lonsdale is a blackguard and a cheat, and if he is not – well, it does not make him any more a gentleman. Alderton ought never to have asked him to join us.'

Diggory frowned. He did not agree, but he could not

quite put his reasoning into words. 'But it is useful to have enough men to form a rubber,' he said at last.

'True – especially now that Hurst has been such a bore as to find himself a wife. I bet five pounds he will either give up the Lantern entirely or visit the upper room with all the old fellows instead.' Salbridge shrugged. 'Well, I shall make it up with Alderton and Lonsdale. If I am King of the Lantern, I am a very benevolent ruler.'

Diggory grinned. 'What you are is very drunk.'

They had reached the top of the stairs, and Salbridge squinted at the street door. 'Do you think, my dear fellow, that I would be able to mount a horse and ride five miles?'

'I rather think not.'

'Then I shall sleep here. Goodnight.'

Diggory was heading to the door when Salbridge said his name again. He turned to see his friend looking at him almost thoughtfully – and Diggory felt suddenly sober, because Salbridge rarely did anything thoughtfully.

'Diggory, old chap, there is something I was meaning to say to you.'

'Oh?'

'I was thinking, after Wednesday's ball ... well, you oughtn't to dance so often with my sister.'

Diggory felt a tightening in his stomach. He made himself say, 'Why ever not?'

'Come, Diggory, you must see my meaning. I know you intend nothing serious by it – you are a dear chap, and I should hate to think of you foolish enough to fall in *love* with anybody – but it wouldn't do to give Rose the wrong idea now, would it?'

'Salbridge, I would never trifle with—'

'My parents expect great things of Rose.'

Diggory felt rather sick. 'Oh.'

'You know I never mean to marry – what a bore that would be! – so any son of Rose's will be the Earl of Wickford after me. You see the significance.'

'I am not sure—'

'It's nothing personal, of course,' said Salbridge, with a drunk, lopsided smile. 'You know I'm terribly fond of you, but . . . well, I am sure you understand.'

Diggory blinked at him in the dim corridor. He did understand, and it was a true blow. He tried to concentrate, to think distinctly through the fuggy haze of alcohol. Yes, Diggory was the son of a brewer, and in time he would be a brewer himself – but the Ashpoints were rich, *very* rich, richer than the Earl and Countess of Wickford, richer than the Eltons. His father's income stood at a clear twelve thousand a year.

He thought of Rose's smile, how she had looked at him that morning. He wanted to shake Salbridge, to ask him if he really meant to say that his greatest friend was not good enough for his sister – but he was too mortified, too confused, too drunk. He said nothing. He only stared.

'You heard me, Diggory?'

'Of course.'

'You understand me?'

'Yes,' said Diggory slowly. 'Yes, I suppose I do.'

Salbridge turned to mount the stairs. 'Well, goodnight, old boy,' he said.

Diggory left the club and went out, dismally, into the night.

CHAPTER VIII

In which the Hursts return

THAT SUNDAY, ST MATTHEW'S HUMMED WITH TALK OF MR Hurst. Every resident of Melford hurried early to church, and a few gossips from Wickford, Ludwell and Radcliffe abandoned their own parishes to join the larger congregation in the town instead.

The pews were filled long before Mr Duckfield was to begin his service, and the worshippers whispered amongst themselves. As murmurs of gossip filled the church, Amelia nudged Diggory and rolled her eyes. Ada declared that it was all very exciting, and Laurie asked her *what* was exciting, and Mr Ashpoint told them all to be quiet – chiefly so that he could hear what Miss Waterson was saying about the new Mrs Hurst having *three* children.

And then, just as Mr Duckfield came up to the pulpit and opened his mouth to read the first prayer, the back door opened and Sir Frederick Hammersmith appeared. His attempt to walk to his box unobtrusively was undermined by his green pantaloons and tartan waistcoat.

St Matthew's gasped as one. As Mr Hurst's dearest friend, as his best man, Sir Frederick was currently the most sought-after man in Wickenshire, second only to Mr Hurst himself. Nobody had seen him arrive back in Melford, and for him to be home so soon could mean only that the wedding had already taken place. It took great strength of will within the congregation to resist interrupting Mr Duckfield to throw questions at the young baronet.

But Mr Duckfield must be listened to. The congregation stood and sang and prayed to know more of Mr Hurst's marriage and, after the service, clambered over each other to try to reach Sir Frederick.

He was not as obliging as they might have wished. Oh yes, he said to Miss Waterson, Mr Hurst was now married. Oh yes, it had gone off perfectly well, he assured Miss Maddon. Certainly, both Mr and Mrs Hurst were in excellent health, he told Louisa and Cassandra Palmer. It was a delight to see them all again, but he really must go – his mother was not well, as they all knew – and without so much as a 'Good day!' he was outside the door and up on his horse.

Some of the children ran after him, and little Laurie Ashpoint reached him first. He caught up with Sir Frederick just as he made it into Maddox Square and, summoning all his courage, called, 'When do Mr and Mrs Hurst return home, sir?'

Sir Frederick smiled at Laurie. He took a moment to consider the question, as though debating how much Society really ought to know. Then he said, at last, 'I believe it will be Wednesday. Good day, Master Ashpoint,' and rode off down the street.

❧

Monday and Tuesday passed slowly in Wickenshire. No one could wish them away fast enough. The shops sold, the brewery brewed, the farmers farmed and the servants served, and all the while there was only one topic of conversation on everybody's lips.

At last, Wednesday morning broke. In every breakfast table in Wickenshire, nobody spoke of anything but Mr Hurst and his widow-bride.

The breakfast room at Ashpoint Hall was large and grand, with an inlaid wooden floor and intricately patterned wallpaper. Mr Ashpoint sat at the far end of the table, a plate of cold meats and bread before him. He had managed to get mustard on his shirt cuff and wasn't quite sure how. (If he pulled his jacket down, would anybody notice? Lonsdale was just the sort of man who might see it and judge him.) To his left, Amelia was helping herself to cold mutton. To his right, Ada had spilt her tea everywhere and was attempting to mop it up with the tablecloth, while Laurie was arranging the fruit on top of his porridge into a smiling face. Diggory was still in bed.

'Laurence, my boy,' said Mr Ashpoint, with an attempt at nonchalance, 'I wonder if you might enjoy a ramble up Wayburn Hill this morning. There are some very fine raspberry bushes on the lanes.'

Laurie looked up in confusion. 'Wayburn Hill,' he repeated.

Amelia tutted. 'Oh, really, Papa,' she said. 'Do drop the pretence – we all know very well that Wayburn Hill has a view of Radcliffe Park. Was it not enough to send Laurie running off after Sir Frederick on Sunday for all the town to see? Now he is to turn spy as well?'

Mr Ashpoint took a bite of his bread and tried to look dignified. 'I simply suggested a ramble.'

'For the purpose of spying.'

'That is *not* what I said. Of course, if Laurie should *happen* to bring back any information, I am sure we should all be glad to hear it. Everybody is very eager to know more about Mrs Hurst, and we shall not be able to call for a few days, as we must wait for the wedding cards.'

'God forbid that we should break etiquette,' muttered Amelia, just as Diggory finally made his entrance into the breakfast room.

He was wearing silk pyjamas (really, how many times had Mr Ashpoint spoken to Diggory about *dressing* for breakfast?) and his hair was sticking up on end. He grunted a good morning to his family, then poured himself a large cup of coffee.

'Why on earth are you talking about etiquette?' he asked. 'It's all nonsense. *Everything* is nonsense – rules and rank and . . .' He trailed off, then drank his coffee with one large gulp.

'Goodness,' said Amelia. 'Had a little too much whisky last night, did we?'

Diggory pulled a face and threw a bread roll at her.

'You missed,' said Amelia, as the roll landed on Ada's plate. 'We were talking about etiquette because Papa is sending Laurie off spying again.'

'Oh,' said Diggory, and without further comment, he poured himself another cup of coffee.

Mr Ashpoint sighed very deeply. Diggory had been moping for several days now, and none of them could work out why. Mr Ashpoint's efforts to get his son into the brewery on Saturday had met with even more resistance than usual.

Laurie looked up from his breakfast. 'Will Mr and Mrs Hurst send wedding cake?'

'I am not sure widows get cake,' said Ada, pouring and spilling her tea once more.

Laurie appeared very put out by this and immediately began to change the strawberries in his porridge into a frowning face instead.

Amelia turned back to her father. 'What reason will you give Miss Thomas for taking her pupil out of lessons this morning?'

'I am not afraid of the governess, Amelia.' Mr Ashpoint glanced at his youngest daughter. 'Ada will find some excuse.'

'Papa, you know that Laurie will only eat a lot of raspberries and not bring back whatever scraps of information you are after.'

Mr Ashpoint frowned, then smiled. 'Very true, Amelia,' he said. 'You will have to go with him.'

This provoked a choked laugh from Diggory.

Amelia glared at them both. 'Absolutely not, Papa.'

'I suppose it would be rather upsetting for you to see Mr Hurst and his new bride,' Mr Ashpoint said solemnly, and Amelia's eyes flashed.

'Oh, fiddlesticks!' She slammed her butter knife down on the table. 'Very well, Papa – if that is what it takes to prove to you that I do not care a *fig* about Mr Hurst, then I shall go with Laurie. But as far as I am concerned, we had all better leave the Hursts alone.'

Half an hour later, Amelia had her little brother's hand in hers and was walking up the lanes towards Radcliffe Park. It was a two-mile walk, and she was not sure Laurie had the stamina. He kept lagging behind to pick flowers and eat raspberries. She ought to have told her father to leave Laurie in his lessons and have come on her own instead – or to have found some way to persuade him out of the idea entirely. She did not want to be traipsing up country paths today, not when she was two chapters into her new novel and had much to do.

Her boots were dirty and her hem thick with mud by the time they climbed Wayburn Hill. Laurie looked weary, but his eyes brightened as they neared the top and the house and park came into view.

Clara's father was right: Radcliffe Park truly was the finest house in the neighbourhood. Amelia had always admired it. It was not as large as Ashpoint Hall, but it was much, much older. Its roof was gabled, its central part set back a little from its two wings. It was one of those houses that changed colour in the sun, sometimes grey, sometimes gold, with trails of ivy embracing the stone. Around it, the lawns were neat and trim, stretching on one side to a lake, on the other to an orderly apple orchard.

Everything was calm, the gardens empty, the house still, and it dawned on Amelia that if they really were to catch a glimpse of the new Mrs Hurst, they might be here for hours.

And then, just as she was cursing her father in her mind, just as she had decided to turn homewards, just as she was wondering if they might make a detour into Melford for a visit to the bookseller's (for her) and the baker's (for Laurie) – there came the rumble of wheels and the neigh of horses.

Laurie leant forwards to peer down the hill. Amelia squinted in the sunlight.

A mile below, a figure emerged from the house, no doubt summoned by the noise. There was no parade of servants, no long line of respect as her father would have insisted upon were the Ashpoints returning from a journey. There was only a solitary housekeeper. She alone waited on the golden steps as the coachman pulled the horses to a stop.

Mr Hurst's carriage looked just as it always did: black and edged with faded silver, a few scratches glinting in the sun – no new livery or fresh paint in honour of the marriage. Amelia watched as the coachman leapt down, gave each horse a kindly pat, then called a faint salute to the housekeeper. She stepped up to open the carriage door, but before she had reached it, the door had opened from within and out climbed Mr Hurst.

He was *grinning*. He wore the broadest smile Amelia had ever seen on his face, and all of him, from the soles of his boots to the tip of his top hat, seemed to *shine*. He was laughing, turning back to speak animatedly to someone still in the carriage, and his happiness seemed so tangible, so bright, that Amelia herself almost laughed.

She had never seen him smile like that. Mr Hurst had always seemed to carry some shade of sadness around with him. When he first came back to Wickenshire, Amelia had presumed he was simply mourning his father or that perhaps he missed his life in Paris, but as the months passed by she decided that he had probably been disappointed in love, and she concocted several tragic histories for him. It was this, perhaps, that had made her feel at ease in his company, that had assured her that she might dance and talk with him as often as she liked, with none but her father likely to get hurt.

And now, he beamed and smiled like never before, and he was holding out his hand. Gloved fingers were pressed into it, and a female figure emerged from the carriage.

The new Mrs Hurst.

She looked, Amelia thought, delightfully ordinary. She

was a fairly small woman, wearing a pale-green dress – it looked to be muslin rather than silk or satin, so she was clearly not a lady of fashion. It was hard to tell from a distance, but Amelia rather thought she was not what Wickenshire would call a young lady. The woman had a way of holding herself that made her seem older, perhaps ten years or so Amelia's senior. She wore no hat, carried no parasol, and her gloves were plain and unassuming. She was laughing, too, beaming at Mr Hurst as she stepped down from the carriage.

Her laughter seemed to fade when she spotted the housekeeper waiting for them, and she put her hand up to hide her smile, like a child caught in play. She gave a quick curtsey and then turned to watch her husband as he helped the children out of the carriage.

Laurie tugged on Amelia's arm as Mr Hurst lifted out first one child, then another, then another.

The first was a boy of about eight years old, dressed in a little beige skeleton suit and with a mass of reddish hair. Next came a girl, five or six, with similar colouring to her brother, in a green dress with white pantaloons beneath. And finally came the smallest child, a little toddling boy in a white frock.

With one arm, Mr Hurst carried the youngest towards the house, and with his other hand, he reached out, ruffled the eldest boy's hair. Amelia smiled to see that Mr Hurst did all this himself, that the littlest was not passed to his mother or a nurserymaid or governess. Indeed, no servant followed from within the carriage, and it was the five of them alone who approached the house. They looked bright and cheerful, as though the gazes and whispers of Melford would slide from their smiles like rain from sloping roofs.

'What a lot of new children he has,' murmured Laurie. 'Do you think the oldest might like to play?'

Amelia smiled. 'Another day, we shall ask him.'

She put her arm around her brother's shoulders as the new family disappeared into Radcliffe Park.

CHAPTER IX

In which the Hursts do not call

AMELIA AND LAURIE ASHPOINT WERE NOT THE ONLY envoys sent to Radcliffe in the days following the arrival of the Hursts. Mrs Crayton strongly suggested that her husband take a ride in the direction of Radcliffe. Cassandra and Louisa Palmer walked up in the hope of catching some glimpse of the new arrivals. Miss Waterson and Miss Maddon borrowed a pony and trap from the inn and rode about the lanes, trying to gather gossip.

Word quickly rushed through Wickenshire that Mr Hurst and his bride and his three new stepchildren were safely ensconced at Radcliffe Park. Descriptions were soon in wide circulation of Mrs Hurst's age (old – no, young), of her beauty (exquisite – no, faded), of her features (fair – no, dark), but nobody could say anything for certain about the children except that there were indeed *three*.

Society waited with bated breath for the wedding cards that would tell them when the new Mrs Hurst was at home to receive visitors. Wednesday turned to Thursday, Thursday turned to Friday, and nothing came. Wickenshire began to whisper.

That Sunday, the pews were full at St Robert's church in Radcliffe. Parishioners of Melford, Wickford and Ludwell had all ventured afar for the sake of gossip. Even Mr Duckfield, the vicar of Melford, asked his curate to stand in for him at St Matthew's so that he might sit at the back of St Robert's instead and catch a glimpse of the new Mrs Hurst.

The congregation watched eagerly as five figures made their way up to the family box: Mr Hurst first, then a young boy and girl, hand in hand – and then there she was at last, the new Mrs Hurst, dressed in light blue, carrying her youngest child in her arms.

Everybody stared.

There was a tiny murmur of disappointment. She was a small, mousy-haired, pleasant-faced woman of a little over thirty, dressed with neither fashion nor vulgarity. There was nothing to especially admire and nothing yet to censure.

'She's not very handsome, is she?' Louisa Palmer whispered to her sisters.

Anne tried to say something about how beauty was not a person's most important quality – but nobody ever listened to Anne.

The children were plainly dressed and well-behaved. The eldest two sat quietly through the service, while the littlest boy entertained himself by playing with his mother's bonnet. To be sure, it was unusual that there was no sign of any nurserymaid or governess, but Mrs Hurst had only been in residence for a few days, and no doubt one would appear soon.

After the service, several people tried to catch Mr Hurst's attention to beg an introduction to his wife – but the toddling boy began to cry very heartily the moment they left the church, and the whole family was soon occupied in pacifying him. Mr Hurst gave a nod to an acquaintance or two,

but then, with an apologetic glance, followed his wife and
her children into the carriage.

The door was shut, the horses readied – and then they
were gone, leaving the congregation staring after them, with
no greater news to share with their neighbours than that
Mrs Hurst had two boys and a girl.

~

At half past six on Wednesday evening, Mr Ashpoint was
hurrying down the lane to Melford. It had been another
long day at the brewery, made longer still by his overpower-
ing need to wait until Lonsdale's departure before making
his own. He was going to the Lantern tonight, in the hope of
a game of whist and a gossip. Being market day, Wednesday
was the busiest day of the week in the upper room of the
Lantern. Mr Crayton and Captain Palmer were always present, along with some of the wealthier farmers. Mr Elton
often came in from Ludwell, and on some Wednesdays even
Lord Wickford patronized the Lantern.

If Mr Ashpoint arrived too late, all the best games would
have already started and he would be forced to sit alone.

But then a figure turned the corner, just as he was passing
by the corner of Maddox Court and turning onto London
Road, and Mr Ashpoint felt all the good luck of being late.
There, ahead of him on the path, was Mr Montgomery
Hurst.

Mr Ashpoint could scarcely believe it had been only a
fortnight since he had seen Mr Hurst at Lady Wickford's
ball, since he had watched him stride away as though every
eye were not turned upon him. And here he was, strolling
along, apparently lost in thought. Mr Ashpoint saw him

before he saw Mr Ashpoint. For a brief moment, he caught
the expression on Mr Hurst's face and fancied that his eyes
were brighter than before, his smile a trifle heartier.

Then the sound of his footsteps made Mr Hurst look up
and salute him with a nod. 'Mr Ashpoint, good evening.
How do you do?'

'Oh, capital, capital.' Mr Ashpoint tried to grasp hold of
the variety of questions hurrying through his mind. 'And
you, Mr Hurst – I hope you will allow me to offer my sincere congratulations.' He held out his gloved hand.

'Ah, yes – thank you.' A smile – a little bashful, a little
embarrassed – came over Mr Hurst's face, but he took Mr
Ashpoint's hand and allowed his own to be shaken. 'How
are your family?' Mr Hurst asked as he released his hand.

'Oh, they are all very well,' replied Mr Ashpoint. He said
it firmly, for he was aware that Mr Hurst knew that he had
wanted him to marry his daughter. It would be no good
trying to reassure Mr Hurst that Amelia did not care two
jots about him, just as it would be no good to pretend that
he himself was not very disappointed by the loss of such a
potential son-in-law. So all he said was, 'Mrs Hurst is well, I
trust?'

Mr Hurst blinked, as though to hear the words 'Mrs
Hurst' was still rather a surprise to him. 'Certainly, yes.'

'And Miss Roberts and the two Master Robertses?'

Mr Hurst hesitated, perhaps surprised to hear that the
particulars of his new stepchildren were known so fast. 'Yes,
they are quite well.'

'And happily settled at Radcliffe Park?'

'Oh yes.' Mr Hurst paused. Then he said, 'We are all
very happy,' so earnestly that Mr Ashpoint felt his questions
fall away.

Perhaps it was for the best that Mr Hurst had not made up his mind to marry Amelia, if he had found instead a wife who made his voice sound like that. And Mr Ashpoint thought for a moment of Charlotte, the early days of his own marriage, what sheer happiness it had been to bring her home, to map out their lives together. Fifteen years had not been enough. In five years' time, she would have been gone for longer than they had been married. It seemed almost impossible.

'That is a pleasure to hear,' said Mr Ashpoint. He was a little embarrassed by the faint quiver in his voice. 'Of course, all your friends and neighbours are glad to see you well settled.'

Mr Hurst's smile faltered. 'And not too . . . surprised, I hope?'

'Oh no,' replied Mr Ashpoint, ashamed by how easily the lie came. Seeing Mr Hurst before him now, he felt somewhat chastened about his own forays into gossip. 'It is quite natural, sometimes, to keep these matters private.'

This appeared to give Mr Hurst courage. 'Yes, that is my idea exactly,' he said quickly. He seemed about to say more, and then stopped, coloured, paused.

Mr Ashpoint felt that Montgomery Hurst was usually a rather better conversationalist; it must be some sense of guilt about Amelia. He tried to help him along by saying, 'I look forward to meeting her.'

'Ah – yes – thank you.'

'When Mrs Hurst has leisure to write her wedding cards, no doubt—'

'Oh, I am not sure we shall trouble ourselves with such things,' said Mr Hurst, with a hesitant smile. 'You know, of course, that this is not my wife's first marriage, and we are neither of us inclined to stand much upon ceremony.'

This took Mr Ashpoint rather aback. Perhaps one could simply dispense with such points of etiquette when one was from so old a family as Mr Hurst's, but Mr Ashpoint felt he would never have been brave enough to risk the disapproval of the Mrs Eltons and Lady Wickfords of the world.

'People will expect them,' he said gently. Mr Hurst might be his superior in rank, but Mr Ashpoint was the elder of the two, and Mr Hurst had always been the friendliest of the county gentlemen, the least proud. Mr Ashpoint did not think a little advice would be unwelcome.

Mr Hurst hesitated, frowned. 'Perhaps you are right,' he said, with an odd sort of laugh. 'But do not wait for them yourself – come and call, by all means, when your schedule allows. I have no doubt my wife would like to know you and your children. I think she will like Miss Ashpoint. And your youngest boy cannot be so much very older than John – the elder Master Roberts, that is.' Mr Hurst smiled. 'Well, I shan't keep you, Mr Ashpoint. It has been a pleasure to see you, as always.'

And Mr Hurst strode on down the road without another word, leaving Mr Ashpoint looking after him with a faint sense of puzzlement. He had never seen Mr Hurst so happy before – nor so ill at ease.

～

'Look, Clara,' said Lady Hammersmith, 'there is Mr Hurst, talking to Mr Ashpoint.'

Clara McNeil laid down her book, rose from her seat and

took a few steps towards the large bay window in which Lady Hammersmith sat. The elder lady was leaning up from her chaise longue, looking out over the little garden of Maddox Court and beyond into the road that ran along the edge of Melford.

'So it is.'

Lady Hammersmith watched for a moment longer. 'Ah, and off they go. I wonder of what they were speaking – this new marriage, no doubt.' She turned back from the window. 'I do hope Mr Hurst brings his bride to see me soon. I am always interested in new people, although I dare say I shall not like her as much as I like you.'

Clara reclaimed her seat. 'Are you so particular, my lady?'

'Oh yes, to be sure.' Lady Hammersmith leant back a little, winced as though at a sudden, sharp pain, then held up her hand when Clara moved towards her. 'I am all right. What was I saying? Ah yes, I *am* particular. For someone who has very little society, I have very decided views about our neighbours. I like Miss Waterson and Miss Maddon – they are very attentive, you know, and *very* entertaining. And I like you, Clara, for you have excellent taste in books – and I like Anne Palmer for the same reason. I like Mr Ashpoint, for he brings me gossip, and I am fond of Mr Hurst because he is fond of my boy – not that I ought to call Fred a boy, for he will be thirty this autumn, though I suppose he will always be a boy to me.

'But I do not like the Earl and Countess of Wickford, for they are too self-satisfied, and their *son* – well, I have seen him ride past a hundred times and he always kicks his horse dreadfully. And then,' she went on with a wry smile, 'I must admit that I quite detest Mrs Elton – one of the few benefits, you know, of a long illness and confinement to the house is *not* having to attend her dinners – and I cannot say that I like her daughter either. I feel as though Felicia Elton has tried to make herself into a jewel and has instead made herself into stone.'

Clara laughed. 'I must bring my friend Amelia to see you one of these days,' she said, 'for she is quite as wicked as you.'

'Is she? No wonder Fred is so afraid of her.' Lady Hammersmith leant back further into the chaise longue, shifted on her cushions.

Clara bit her lip. If Sir Frederick was afraid of Amelia, it was probably because he had overheard one of her passing insults regarding his taste in garments, about which Amelia loved to laugh – and she was starting to apologize on Amelia's behalf when Lady Hammersmith winced.

'Are you all right?' asked Clara. 'Do you need anything?'

'No, no – do go on reading. Miss Austen is all the balm I require for the present.'

So Clara lifted the book from beside her chair and began once more to read aloud.

She had been coming to Maddox Court to read to Lady Hammersmith for three or four months now. It had begun at her father's suggestion – through Sir Frederick, she understood, who was keen to secure more company for his mother. Twice a week she made the short walk to Maddox Court, passed through the well-trimmed garden, knocked on the big oak door and waited to be taken upstairs. It was a pleasant house – old-fashioned, built of rendered sarsen and limestone. It had once been the dower house of the old Maddox Court, the stately home of the Hammersmiths of Melford, but the old house had burnt down long ago and Mr Ashpoint's brewery now stood on the spot where it used to be. Most of the cottages that had once been on Hammersmith land were now under Mr Ashpoint's ownership. Maddox Court was not much of a court any longer, but it still retained its name.

Lady Hammersmith was a little over fifty years of age and had not been beyond her garden wall in five years. Clara knew that she was very ill, that she was in a great deal of pain. Her life was chiefly lived between her bedroom and her sitting room. Clara liked her a lot – she was straightforward, witty, good company, and the two of them had similar taste in novels. And she liked the rooms at Maddox Court, too, with their neat, old-fashioned furniture – the chintz curtains of Indian calico, the open armchairs, the stout bookcase filled with new and old novels. Between the jar of pot-pourri on the Pembroke table and the brightly coloured flowers Sir Frederick brought in every day from the garden to cheer his mother, the room always smelt pleasant, and the window was usually open to let in birdsong and summer air.

As Clara turned the page, the creak of a floorboard made her look up. The door was ajar, and through it she saw Sir Frederick approaching, dressed in a bottle-green frock coat. She paused at the end of the sentence as he eased open the door.

He gave a neat bow to Clara, then walked softly towards Lady Hammersmith's chaise longue. He knelt down at her side. 'How are you, Mother?' he asked in a quiet voice.

'Oh, I am all right. You know me.'

'I know that you never complain,' he said softly, 'even when you ought.'

'Nonsense.' She glanced over at Clara. 'I complain all the time, Clara, when you are not here.'

Sir Frederick chuckled. 'Can I bring you anything?' he asked.

'Oh, no, nothing,' she said, 'unless' – she was smiling slyly now – 'you have any gossip for me. Do you know, Clara,' she went on, turning back towards her, 'although Fred was at the wedding, he will tell me nothing of this new Mrs Hurst, aside from that he likes her.'

'I do like her,' said Sir Frederick, glancing towards Clara. 'She – well, she suits my friend entirely, Miss McNeil. What else am I to say?'

Lady Hammersmith laughed. 'That is just like you,' she said. 'I ask for information, and all I receive is your approval.' She turned to Clara. 'I suppose every neighbourhood always treats a newcomer with such interest. Miss Austen certainly seems to think so.'

'Wickenshire is not unusual,' replied Clara.

Sir Frederick smiled. 'I shall leave you to your reading,' he said. 'Good day, Mother. Good day, Miss McNeil.' And then, quickly pressing his mother's hand, he rose, bowed to Clara and quitted the room.

'I suppose *you* have not heard anything about the new Mrs Hurst, Clara?' asked Lady Hammersmith when Sir Frederick was gone.

'No,' she replied. 'Everybody who has seen her says she looks rather ordinary.'

'Oh? Now that *does* make me curious.' Lady Hammersmith smiled, her eyes bright. 'For you know, Clara, it is always the people who seem ordinary that are the most interesting in the end.'

CHAPTER X

In which Mrs Elton will not be deterred

FELICIA SAT POISED AT THE PIANOFORTE, FINGERS MOVING over the ivory keys. She was playing a sonatina in C major by Friedrich Kuhlau, and her music master, Monsieur Brisset, was sitting at her side, head bent, listening, every now and then interrupting.

'Quieter there, Miss Elton – keep those semiquavers steady. Do not count the beat; feel it.'

She liked this piece. She liked the steady rhythm of it, the swell of the quavers, the sharp introduction of accidentals, the way it veered between major and minor. It was still new to her, and she had not yet perfected it, but she was confident that she would soon. It would be a suitable piece to play the next time her mother threw a dinner, the next time she was called upon to impress. And in the meantime – well, the composition was excellent.

She finished the third movement just as the clock chimed two, and in the corner of the room, her maid sat up very suddenly, as though startled out of her reverie. It was an easy hour's work for Sarah, Felicia thought, her only responsibility being to chaperone. The girl stood up, crossed the room and opened the door, as she did at the end of every lesson, and Monsieur Brisset, too, rose to his feet.

'Do not forget, Miss Elton,' he said as he stepped back from the instrument, 'to let feeling into the music. It is never enough to play a piece correctly – you must *feel* it, too.'

Felicia did not quite understand his meaning, but nonetheless she nodded.

'I have sent off for some new music for you,' he went on. 'I thought you might like to try some Frédéric Chopin.' He smiled. It was a very faint smile, as all his were, and reached his eyes more than his mouth. 'I saw him play once. You will like his work, I think – it is very subtle but full of emotion.'

'Thank you,' said Felicia. 'I shall look forward to it.' She, too, had risen, and they stood side by side in front of the pianoforte. She hesitated, then asked, 'Have you never thought to compose yourself, monsieur?'

He looked at her, and there was that smile again in his eyes. 'I might ask you the same question,' he said quietly.

'Me?' Felicia shook her head. 'Oh, I do not think *ladies* compose.'

Monsieur Brisset blinked, then frowned. 'Perhaps I shall send off for some Clara Schumann as well,' he said, almost to himself. He tucked his bag under his arm, then lifted his hat from the chair upon which it lay. 'Good day, Miss Elton,' he said, with that quick smile of his, and then he was gone.

Felicia watched him leave, watched Sarah follow him into the corridor to show him out. She was still staring at the doorway, thinking about how one might manage to let *feeling* into music, when her mother appeared, stern and dignified as ever in dark-purple silk.

'You ought not to gossip with your music master, Felicia,' she said.

Felicia drew herself up. She did not like the idea of her

mother listening to their conversation from the corridor or the next room; she would no doubt disapprove both of lady composers and of *feeling*. Felicia began to tidy her sheet music, tucking the Kuhlau away behind a few Friedrich Kalkbrenner pieces and a J. N. Hummel. 'I was not *gossiping*, Mama,' she said, smoothing the edges of the paper. 'I was asking him about music. It is important for an accomplished young lady to know these things.'

Mrs Elton pressed her lips together, shook her head. 'Monsieur Brisset may be a talented musician, but I wish we had an Englishman nearby who might do as well,' she said. 'As my uncle, the Marquis of Denby, used to say, the French are far too prone to disorder.'

Felicia said nothing. Monsieur Brisset had been teaching her for more than two years, and her mother had yet to accustom herself to his nationality. She straightened her pieces on the pianoforte, closed the lid. 'Did you wish to speak to me about anything particular, Mama?'

Her mother blinked. 'Do not be impertinent, Felicia – it is most unbecoming.' She drew herself up. 'We are going to call upon on the Hursts,' she declared.

Felicia raised one perfect eyebrow. 'Have they finally sent their wedding cards?'

'That is immaterial.'

'Is it? You astonish me, Mama.'

'There are times when one must make the best of a situation,' said Mrs Elton firmly. 'Your father happened to see Mr Ashpoint at the Lantern last night, and he informs me that Mr Ashpoint, having met Mr Hurst by chance in the *street*, received a *verbal* invitation to call upon his new wife. It is all most irregular. I cannot possibly allow the Ashpoints to make her acquaintance before we do.' Mrs Elton turned towards the door. 'Come, don't dawdle – it is past two already, and it is a long drive to Radcliffe. I may be able to overlook the matter of the wedding cards, but no lady ever calls after four.'

~

An hour later, Felicia sat in the carriage, her mother across from her, while their footman knocked at the door of Radcliffe Park. After a short silence, Peter knocked again, and Mrs Elton peered out the window.

'Where on earth are their servants?' she asked Felicia.

Another minute passed – and then a very small maid opened the door, curtseyed, blushed and at last looked up at the footman. Peter handed her their card, and the girl closed the door.

The next pause was even longer.

Mrs Elton tutted. 'I am sure she is out. We have driven six miles for nothing. This is why wedding cards are essential. How else is one to know when Mrs Hurst is at home?'

But the door was opening again, the maid speaking to the footman, and now Peter was walking stiffly back to the carriage to inform them that Mrs Hurst *was* at home. He opened the door and helped the ladies out. Felicia adjusted her skirts, checked her reflection in the black shine of the carriage door – yes, she did still look perfect – and followed her mother up the path.

The tiny housemaid led them into the entrance hall, a stately room with a black-and-white tiled floor and a grand marble staircase. Looking up to the gallery of the floor above, Felicia saw the face of a little red-haired child staring down through the banisters.

'If you'll just wait in the parlour, please, ma'am,' said the housemaid, 'Mrs Hurst will be with you shortly.'

They were shown into an airy, sunlit room at the front of the house. The last time Felicia had been here, it was full of people, but now everything was calm. The old oak floor was covered by Indian carpets, the walls papered with a light floral pattern. Calico curtains were drawn back from the windows to let in the light. There was a satinwood Pembroke table and two small walnut settees, upholstered in needlework. Felicia made herself look away from the settees, for neither of them could sit until they were invited to do so.

Her eyes moved instead to the pianoforte. She had played a duet there with Mr Hurst, months ago, when her mother had thought it worth her time to play duets with him. He was not a bad musician, though inferior to herself, of course. She glanced at the large mahogany bookcase, at the stone surround of the fireplace. There were a few marbles and a spinning top tucked beneath the bellows.

'Where *is* she?' murmured Mrs Elton. 'Why did she say she was at home when she was not prepared to receive visitors? I simply cannot understand it.'

Five minutes passed before the door creaked again. Mrs Hurst opened it herself, but she turned back to the maid when it was half open and said, 'Jenny, dear, please would you ask for some tea and – well, ask Mrs Alley what she recommends. Meg can give you a hand bringing everything up. Thank you.'

The maid vanished, and Mrs Hurst walked forwards into the room.

She was a woman of no more than three- or four-and-thirty, but this, to Felicia, made her positively elderly. There was nothing unusual or striking in her countenance, and her dark hair, which held a few strands of grey, was done up high in a neat, if not fashionable, manner, tied with an orange ribbon. She wore a gown of pale blue – goodness, was it *cotton*? How very singular! – with no ornament but a silver chain around her neck. Her cheeks were country pink, her eyes dark. Her hands were small, and as she stood in the centre of the room, she seemed uncertain what to do with them. She curtseyed, smiled, blushed and said, 'Mrs Elton, Miss Elton – it is kind of you to call. Do sit down, please, and won't you take off your outside things?'

Mrs Elton kept her bonnet firmly on her head (as was only proper), but she did consent to sit down. Felicia sat at her side, and Mrs Hurst took the settee opposite. She sat on the very edge, as if not quite committing.

'I am sorry that my husband is out,' said Mrs Hurst. She spoke softly, almost musically. 'There is no one to introduce us.'

Mrs Elton smiled her most gracious smile, which was perhaps not as gracious as she wished it to appear. 'Then we shall have to make the introductions ourselves. Mr Hurst is a dear friend of the family, so I am sure we need not fear any impropriety. This is my daughter, Miss Felicia Elton. My son, Mr Augustus Elton, is MP for Melford and Wickford. He and his family are often kept in London because of his work, and we are in great hopes that he may be asked to join the next cabinet, so I expect we shall not see him this summer. I trust you will make his acquaintance in time. We hope to see much of you.'

Mrs Hurst gave a hesitant smile. 'That is kind.'

'You are, I hope, quite settled at Radcliffe?' asked Mrs Elton.

'Yes, thank you. Radcliffe is a very pleasant place, and Melford is a fine town. Montgomery's tenants are fond of him. I have already been visiting some of the cottages here.'

Mrs Elton pursed her lips, and Mrs Hurst, catching the expression, swallowed nervously. Felicia knew that her mother did not approve of cottagers – nor would she have ever referred to her husband by his Christian name.

'Your children are quite content?' asked Mrs Elton.

'Oh yes,' said Mrs Hurst with renewed enthusiasm. 'The countryside in these parts is very beautiful, and my eldest two are fond of sports.'

'I thought your second child was a girl, Mrs Hurst.'

Mrs Hurst blinked, as though surprised to hear knowledge of her family so firmly embedded in her neighbours' minds. 'Yes,' she replied, 'but Eleanor is quite as great a cricket player as her brother. Mont— Mr Hurst has been teaching them both bowls, too. We shall have a pleasant summer, I hope.'

'Indeed,' said Mrs Elton. Felicia could not remember ever having been allowed such improper liberties as bowls or cricket when she was a child. 'I am sure you have formulated some plan for the children's education. I suppose their governess was not willing to accompany you from – Richmond, I think it was?'

'Yes, Richmond,' said Mrs Hurst, and then paused.

Mrs Elton looked at her expectantly, and Felicia wondered when the tea would come. Usually when they made calls, tea was either on the table already or not served at all.

'We have not yet engaged a governess,' said Mrs Hurst. Her cheeks were a little red.

'If I might be of any service, you must simply say the word. Felicia had three different governesses in her younger years.'

'Well, I—'

'Miss Fuller, the last, was a very worthy woman, was she not, Felicia? French, Italian, painting, very skilled at the pianoforte. We only parted with her once Felicia was out.'

'I think,' said Mrs Hurst, with a glance at Felicia, 'that Mr Hurst mentioned a music master—'

'Oh yes.' Mrs Elton smiled graciously. 'My daughter's talents on the pianoforte are quite unrivalled – you must forgive a mother's partiality, of course. Does your daughter play?'

'A little, as does John. Mr Hurst thought that perhaps Miss Elton's music master . . .'

'Monsieur Brisset,' said Felicia.

'Yes, Monsieur Brisset. I know my husband thinks highly of him. We thought he might teach Eleanor and John music. I have been teaching the rest of their lessons, but—'

'But you will need a governess for your daughter, of course. School is far better for boys, to be sure. How old did you say your eldest was?'

'Oh, he is only eight.'

'Goodness, and not yet at school? Augustus went away at five. As my uncle, the Marquis of Denby, used to say, it is school that makes a boy a man.'

Mrs Hurst reddened. She opened her mouth to reply just as the door opened for tea. Two girls appeared – the small housemaid who had answered the door and a tall kitchen maid with an untidy apron and messy curls. Together they laid three cups and saucers on the low table, followed by a plate of dainties, before curtseying out of the room.

'What was I saying? Augustus was at Eton, of course, but I hear Winchester is—'

'I should not like the children to be parted from one another, nor from me,' said Mrs Hurst quietly.

Mrs Elton looked at her in astonishment. 'But, Mrs Hurst, when it comes to education, one must forget such fancies. And a mother whose children's education is settled has the proper time to attend to her husband.'

There was a long silence. Felicia glanced between her mother and their host. Mrs Hurst wore a cold expression on her face, and Mrs Elton seemed to hesitate, as though acknowledging that her current strategy was proving ineffective.

Then Mrs Hurst said quietly but determinedly, 'You forget, Mrs Elton, that I have been married before. I can manage my own affairs very well.'

'Oh, you quite misunderstand me. My dear—'

'Miss Elton,' said Mrs Hurst, turning to Felicia with calm resolve, 'my husband tells me you are a very fine dancer.'

'I am,' said Felicia. Her mother glared at her, and Felicia added, without a moment's blush, 'That is, I have been told so, and I enjoy dancing very much.'

'If you had only been here a few weeks sooner, you would have had the pleasure of seeing her,' said Mrs Elton, as Mrs Hurst passed her a cup of tea. 'Our neighbours, the earl and countess – Lord and Lady Wickford, you know; you will have heard your husband speak of them – they held a charming ball at Wickford Towers. You must throw a ball yourself, you know, for the ballroom at Radcliffe Park is delightful.'

'But I know no one,' Mrs Hurst said softly.

'And yet, my dear, everybody knows you.'

Just then the door eased open, and a small boy with a mass of uncombed reddish hair appeared in the entrance.

He looked between his mother and her two visitors before coming forwards into the room, letting the door slam behind him.

'Mama,' he said, 'Eleanor's in the pantry and won't come out.' He had an unusual voice – a trace of some unplaceable accent, an intonation a little like Monsieur Brisset's. They might have come from Richmond, thought Felicia, but they must have been abroad before that. That perhaps went some way to explaining Mrs Hurst's irregular manners.

To Felicia's amazement, Mrs Hurst, rather than scolding her son, began to laugh. 'Whatever is she doing in the pantry?'

'She pulled Mrs Alley's hair and ran to hide.'

Mrs Hurst laughed louder. 'Dear me.' She glanced back at Felicia and her mother before turning her attention again to the child. 'And is your new papa back from seeing the steward?'

'Not yet. And Meg can't stop Georgy crying, and Mrs Alley sent me for you because Eleanor says she won't come out unless we all promise she won't be scolded.'

'Does she deserve to be scolded?'

'Well,' said the boy slowly, 'Mrs Alley *did* touch Eleanor's hair, and Eleanor doesn't like anybody touching her hair, so then she pulled Mrs Alley's hair, and Mrs Alley told her she was a naughty girl, and then she ran into the pantry and says she won't come out, especially since she's ate up all the treacle tart in there and she doesn't think Mrs Alley will like that.'

Mrs Hurst laughed heartily. She turned towards her guests, attempting to hide her smile with an apologetic expression. 'I am ever so sorry,' she said, rising from the settee. 'I had better see to the children. Jenny will show you out. Do finish your tea before you go.'

~

'The incivility of it!' exclaimed Mrs Elton, as she and Felicia travelled homewards. 'It is for us to leave, not for her to dismiss us because her daughter decides to shut herself in the larder. And that nasty, foreign-sounding child – how shocking. I wonder if her first husband was a foreigner – Roberts is an English name, to be sure, but one never can tell. And imagine making time to visit mere cottagers but not to send one's wedding cards!'

Felicia sighed. 'I suppose she is reserved.'

'Either that or ill-bred – and yet she speaks like a lady.'

'What I wish to know,' said Felicia, 'is why a man such as Mr Hurst, with the pick of every young lady in the county—'

'I wish you would not say "the pick of", Felicia. It is terribly uncouth.'

'Well, I do not understand why Mr Hurst, with the *choice of* so many young ladies, would marry an awkward woman with three wild children. I never truly thought he would marry Miss Ashpoint, as some people did, but even *she* would have been a more understandable choice, for the Ashpoints are at least rich.'

'Why he should pay his attentions to either with a young lady such as you before him is hard to understand,' said Mrs Elton, 'but I have a little theory as to that. He is such a good friend of Sir Frederick's, and—'

'Oh, really, Mama.' Felicia scowled. She would have much rather discussed men whom she could never possibly marry than those for whom a real chance still existed.

'A true gentleman would never stand in the way of such a friend. Sir Frederick is of higher rank than Mr Hurst, and a few years his junior. Of course, if Lord Salbridge were a little less *wild*, we might have looked in his direction, but he does not seem likely to marry young – and so Sir Frederick is naturally the most suitable gentleman in the neighbourhood.'

Felicia glanced out of the carriage window. 'Papa does not think so.'

'Your father thinks of nothing but money. You and I, however, know that it is a far greater thing to marry a titled gentleman with one or two thousand a year than a commoner with five. What shall money matter when you are Lady Hammersmith? Who will mind what you owe and to whom? I said to your father this very morning, if you wish our daughter to think only in pounds, shillings and pence, she ought to have learnt arithmetic rather than the pianoforte.'

'What did he say?'

'Something preposterous, I am sure. I was not listening. He will forget these foolish things when you are Lady Felicia Hammersmith.' She shook her head. 'I must speak to him about this matter. Sir Frederick has only called once since we returned from London, and I am sure it is because your father has given him insufficient encouragement. He was here every week in the winter.'

Felicia said nothing to that. It was all very well to wish to be a baronet's wife, but she felt no need to sit opposite Sir Frederick while her mother spoke at him for half an hour each week. Far better to meet in a ballroom.

'I wonder what Sir Frederick makes of his friend's new bride,' said Mrs Elton. She frowned thoughtfully, but as the carriage passed through the gates of Ludwell Manor, her expression turned to one of resolve.

'Do you know,' she said, as the footman opened the carriage doors, 'I really think we must do something about Mrs Hurst.'

'Cut her?'

'Oh, dear me, no. We must bring her out. She is a little shy, a little unsophisticated – but then, she is new here. She must be helped along. I am thinking,' Mrs Elton continued, as they entered the house and walked towards the morning room, 'that we must throw a dinner. A select set of guests – not like Lady Wickford's ball. I know it is the duty of an earl and countess to show condescension to their neighbours but, really, they take the matter too far. It was very shocking to ask us to go amongst a crowd including that *person* Alderton. I have still not quite recovered from his *presuming* to address you in the street.' She shook her head solemnly. 'Why, Mrs Palmer told me that even the *foreman* of Ashpoint Brewery was at Lady Wickford's ball.'

Felicia removed her bonnet. 'I do not think Papa views Major Alderton as you do,' she said. 'He is very rich, you know, whatever may be said of his birth. And as for that foreman – well, I saw him dance with Miss Ashpoint. Perhaps she will end up marrying him, now that Mr Hurst has married somebody else.'

'*Felicia!*'

'Miss Ashpoint may have the largest dowry in the Wickenshire, but would it not be fitting, Mama, for the daughter of a jumped-up brewer to marry a brewer's foreman?'

Mrs Elton pursed her lips. 'Do not say "jumped-up", Felicia. Of course that wild, wilful girl will make a discreditable match one of these days – her mother married beneath her, after all – but let us speak no more of the matter. It is not seemly to discuss *foremen*.' She cleared her throat. 'As I said, we must have a dinner. The end of next week, perhaps. I have it in my mind to take Mrs Hurst under my wing, and I shall not be deterred. If she will not give me the time of day at her house – why, I must bring her to mine.'

CHAPTER XI

In which Miss McNeil receives a call and
Mrs Elton is outmanoeuvred

'LOOK AT THIS,' SAID AMELIA, HOLDING UP AN EMBOSSED
envelope, frowning as the silver border caught the light. 'A
dinner at the Eltons' house next week – however shall I
bear it?'

Clara laughed. 'Well, I am glad *I* am not fine enough to be
invited. That is one honour I am quite happy to forgo.' She
reclaimed the settee in the little parlour at 9 Garrett Lane,
and Amelia threw herself down beside her. They sat close together, not quite touching, as they always did when there
was any danger of being interrupted. Clara's father was out
on business, but the maid, Hannah, might come in without
warning.

'I shall have no fun without you.' Amelia sighed. 'And
why should you not be invited? The Eltons have the worst
kind of pride.'

'Oh,' said Clara, 'they are not really so different from everybody else. Father and I are not great county folk, and we
hardly expect to be noticed by people like *that*. We are always
invited to Wickford Towers, because the earl and countess
take a great pleasure in patronizing their *inferior* neighbours
and having enough persons to fill their *vast* rooms – but I have
never stepped inside Ludwell Manor and never intend to.'

Amelia leant back into the cushions. 'I shall hate every minute.'

'But surely the Hursts will be there,' Clara reminded her. 'Shouldn't you like to meet the woman all Wickenshire is speaking of?'

Amelia shrugged. 'I am bound to meet her soon enough, now that Papa has been invited to call. He will not stop speaking of it. He is ever so cross that this is a busy time at the brewery – he keeps consulting his pocketbook and sighing loudly.' Amelia laughed. 'Still, the chance to see Lady Rose may at least cheer Diggory up. He has been gloomy for a fortnight and won't tell me why. I keep finding him in the library, reading sad novels in *my* chair.'

'Speaking of *novels*,' said Clara, lowering her voice, 'is there any word from Lonsdale?'

Amelia shook her head. 'Oh, it is much too soon for that. It is not yet two weeks since he sent it to Browne. I think we must wait at least another fortnight before I have the right to collapse with anxious anticipation, and—'

She was interrupted by a tap on the door. Clara looked round as the family's maid-of-all-work appeared.

'Yes, Hannah?'

'Well, miss,' she said, handing Clara a card, 'Sir Frederick Hammersmith is here.'

'Sir Frederick?' Clara frowned in surprise. 'Did you tell him my father is out?'

'I did, miss,' said Hannah. And then, in a lower voice, 'But he asked if you were here. Will you see him?'

Clara looked between Hannah and Amelia. 'Very well, Hannah,' she said. 'Please show him in.'

Hannah departed, and Amelia looked curiously over at

Clara. 'Do you often have your Friday afternoons disturbed by baronets?'

'I am quite as surprised as you are. I hope his mother is all right. It will probably be business – you know Father has been his land manager when required, as well as your father's.'

'I didn't think Sir Frederick had enough land to be managed.'

Clara tried not to smile. 'Hush, Amelia. Still, I am not sure why he asked for me.'

'Perhaps the man has gone mad – his clothes have always been those of someone not in full possession of their senses.'

'*Amelia.*'

The door opened again, and Hannah announced, 'Sir Frederick Hammersmith,' then curtseyed away.

Sir Frederick walked straight towards Clara, then stopped abruptly at the sight of Amelia. He opened his mouth and shut it again. He was dressed in checked black-and-white trousers and a purple velvet waistcoat with silver buttons. His frock coat was black and undone, his cravat a lurid yellow. The hat he removed had a flower pinned to its side. Amelia suppressed a laugh.

She had concluded some years ago that Sir Frederick must be a very stupid fellow, for she was sure nobody wise would dress so ridiculously. He always looked like he had selected his clothes while drunk – and yet he never touched a drop of alcohol. Nor could she quite account for the clash of his bright clothes with his formal, awkward manners. It baffled her that a sensible man like Mr Hurst had chosen such a person as his dearest friend, but there was no accounting for taste – her brother's favourite companion was Lord Salbridge, after all. Clara inclined to a more charitable view of Sir Frederick – he was very kind to his mother, apparently – but Amelia was not sure that any degree of filial affection could make up for such preposterous outfits.

'Good afternoon, Sir Frederick,' said Clara, rising and giving a small curtsey.

He managed a 'Good afternoon,' with what was almost a smile.

Amelia inclined her head but did not rise.

'I think Hannah told you that my father is out,' said Clara, reclaiming her seat. 'He is in Melcastle on business until this evening.'

'Ah, yes,' said Sir Frederick. 'My apologies. I came to, um' – he hesitated, glanced at Amelia, seemed to lose his train of thought – 'yes, to see your father about some improvements up at Maddox. I thought – well, but he is out – I needn't bore you. Only—' He broke off, bit his lip.

'Would you like some tea, Sir Frederick?' asked Clara.

'Oh.' He looked pleasantly surprised at this offer. 'Thank you – yes.'

Clara smiled, nodded and stepped out into the corridor to speak to Hannah.

Sir Frederick shifted from one foot to the other – and then at last sat down in one of the armchairs and turned to Amelia. 'You are . . . quite well, Miss Ashpoint?' he asked.

He was looking at her oddly, almost anxiously, and for a moment Amelia thought he really had lost his senses – and then she realized that it was a look of something like pity, that he was asking how she was because he was afraid his friend Mr Hurst had slighted her.

She felt a wave of irritation and sat up sharply. 'I have never been better,' she declared. The sooner they were away from *that* subject, the happier she would be. 'What improvements are you planning for the Court, then?'

She hoped to provoke some kind of reaction by calling Maddox Court 'the Court' – Sir Frederick always called it simply 'Maddox', as though he knew it were preposterous to call a house with barely five bedrooms a court – but he merely blinked.

'Well, I am thinking of building a – a veranda,' he said at last. He glanced up as Clara came back into the room. 'My mother would like that, I think. Somewhere for her to sit in the summer. And – well, there is some need to improve the cottages, too. I do not have many tenants, but I aim for their lives to be as easy as possible. I hope – that is, what do you think of the scheme?' he asked, glancing at Clara, then warily back at Amelia.

'You should hardly ask me,' said Clara, with a laugh, 'for I am bound to approve of anything that brings my father employment. Although if it is to be a large project, you may be better sending to Melcastle for an architect.'

'Oh no,' said Sir Frederick. 'I am sure your father is quite capable. But, Miss McNeil, do you – do you think a veranda would – well, would it suit Maddox? I know, of course, from my mother, that you assist – that is, that you are a great help to your father in matters of – of business, and I thought – well, you must have knowledge of houses, and—'

'There is certainly space for one,' replied Clara. She paused, her brow furrowing as it always did when she thought things through. 'If you were to move the rose garden,' she said, 'and perhaps the pond, then there might be space to build out from the morning room – and then, as that is beneath your mother's sitting room, you might perhaps build a balcony on top of the veranda, so that, on days when she cannot come downstairs—'

'What a good thought,' Sir Frederick declared eagerly. 'Yes, that is just it. Quite perfect.'

Clara laughed. 'Well, you had better wait for my father's opinion,' she said.

'I am sure he could not improve upon the plan.'

The door opened again, and Hannah brought in a tray laden with a silver teapot, three blue-and-white china teacups and saucers, and a plate of sugared biscuits. She placed everything on the table, cast a faintly amused glance at Sir Frederick's outfit and was gone.

'How is your mother?' asked Clara.

'Oh, she is a little better today.'

Clara handed him a cup of tea. Amelia did not see what happened, but somehow Sir Frederick managed to slosh hot tea over his fingers. He swore loudly, then looked appalled with himself for having sworn in the company of ladies. 'Oh, God – sorry, I—'

He had always been a fool, Amelia thought, but she had never seen him quite so foolish as today.

'I'm dreadfully sorry,' he said.

Clara smiled. It was a kind smile, because Clara was always kind to everybody. 'You needn't worry,' she said. 'Amelia swears all the time.'

'I do not!' cried Amelia. She was a little surprised to hear Clara speak so frankly to a man she barely knew, but she supposed her friendship with his mother must excuse it.

Sir Frederick laughed. Clara's remark seemed to finally put him at his ease and he drank his tea a little more steadily.

Somehow, this ease vexed Amelia more than his confusion. It nettled her that this man was a baronet, that her own family was thought to be inferior to his, that the Eltons would forever invite him and snub the McNeils because of some

chance of birth. No foolish outfit, no stumbling conversation, would ever lose Sir Frederick his place in the world. He
was probably going to marry Felicia Elton one of these days,
and in the united powers of rank and gentility they would
possess everything the Ashpoints and the McNeils lacked.

'Have you been paying other calls this morning, Sir
Frederick?' asked Amelia.

'I – no, not this morning.'

'You have not been to Ludwell Manor to see the Eltons?'

Clara turned to Amelia with an unreadable expression
upon her face.

Sir Frederick looked rather red. His ease was gone as
quickly as it had come, and his face clashed with his waistcoat. 'No,' he said slowly. He glanced at Clara, then back at
Amelia. 'I do not often go to Ludwell. That is, of course I
call sometimes – the Eltons are my friends, I suppose, but—'
He hesitated, swallowed. 'I have been in Melcastle this
morning myself, in fact.'

'Waistcoat shopping?' asked Amelia, before she could
stop herself.

Clara shot her a pointed look of despair.

'No, I—' Sir Frederick broke off, swallowed, frowned. He
seemed to realize that he was being made fun of and had
not the faintest idea what to do about it. Amelia felt torn
between guilt and amusement.

There was a long pause before Sir Frederick rose from
his seat.

'I ought to go,' he said. 'Thank you for – for the tea. It
was very kind. I shall speak to your father, Miss McNeil,
about – about the plans for the house and the cottages.'

The young ladies rose. 'Good day, Sir Frederick,' said
Clara.

'Good day, Miss Ashpoint, Miss McNeil.' He raised his hat to his head, took it off again, bowed and, as Clara opened the door for him, said, 'I shall see you when you are next with my mother, I am sure, and perhaps at Mrs Elton's dinner next week?'

Clara hesitated, then said, in a low voice, 'You will not see me there, Sir Frederick.'

There was a dull, painful pause, and then understanding dawned in his face, and he looked very much as if he wished to swear again at his blunder. Instead, he said heavily, 'I see. Well, Miss McNeil, I must say, I think that a very great shame.'

～

Sir Frederick was gone, and Amelia was half sitting, half lying on the settee, helping herself to the biscuits, when Clara came back into the room.

'Amelia, you are dreadful!'

'Oh, it was not so very bad. Come, you cannot possibly feel sorry for such a fool.'

Clara sat down, her arms folded. 'He is not stupid, Amelia – he is *shy*. He knows you do not like him and it makes him anxious.'

Amelia took another biscuit. 'There was nothing shy about that waistcoat. Besides, any man in love with Miss Elton deserves to be teased.'

Clara shrugged her shoulders. She sipped her tea, looked thoughtfully down into it.

'What? All of Wickenshire knows the two of them will marry one of these days.'

'Very possibly,' said Clara. 'I do not think anyone can

resist the will of Mrs Elton for long. But I hardly think Sir Frederick is *in love* with Miss Elton.'

'What rot. Every man within ten miles of Melford is in love with her.'

'Mr Hurst is not in love with her. Diggory is not in love with her.'

'Diggory thought he was at one point,' said Amelia with a laugh, 'and Mr Hurst is the exception. You know well that nearly every gentleman thinks Felicia Elton the embodiment of perfection. I don't for the life of me know why.' Amelia reached out to touch Clara's arm, then caught herself, pulled back, for the door was still open. 'She is not half so beautiful as you,' she said softly.

Clara's frown softened. She sighed gently, looked round at Amelia. 'And I don't know why either,' she said, 'for she is not half so entertaining as you.'

'My dear Clara, is that a slight upon my beauty?'

'Oh, really, Amelia. Would I ever slight you?'

'Say that again, Mr Elton, I pray.'

It was Friday evening, and Felicia was dining with her parents. As always, they were in formal evening dress and the table was spread with an elegant feast – ten dishes or more, for the three figures who sat around it. At one end of the table, her father was eating his lamb with unconcern, while at the other end, her mother, dignified and stern, was sawing her beef with neat, studied movements. Felicia sat between them, eating very little. There was a dangerous air at the table tonight.

'No doubt you heard me, Mrs Elton,' said her father, in

that calm tone Felicia knew especially irritated her mother. 'I simply said that I happened to meet Major Alderton at the Lantern this afternoon and that I mentioned our dinner on the thirtieth. He said he would be delighted to come.'

'That *person*,' said Mrs Elton in an ominous tone, 'is not invited.'

Mr Elton met his wife's eyes. 'He *is* invited. I have invited him.'

Felicia looked down at her dinner.

Her mother dismissed the servants with a nod. 'Listen to me, Mr Elton,' she said, slowly and carefully. 'This is a respectable house. *I* am the niece of the Marquis of Denby, and *you* are a gentleman of land and property. Where is your sense of *dignity*? Our doors are not open to the *natural* sons of goodness knows who.'

Mr Elton waved a hand. 'It may all be rumour.'

'It is *not* all rumour, and you know that as well as I do. Rumours do not start themselves.'

'Well, if it is not all rumour, then he is the son of a duke.'

Her mother put her wine glass down on the table with force. 'A son born outside of the bonds of matrimony is no son at all. I should not care if his father were a prince when his mother was no doubt a – whore.'

Felicia flinched. 'Mother, really!' It was safer to remain silent in the midst of such battles, but the reproach was out before she could stop herself. Such language was not fit for the dining room. It was not fit for a single room in Ludwell Manor.

'That is quite enough,' said Mr Elton, more sharply than before. 'Whatever else Major Alderton may be, there is no doubt that he is an exceptionally wealthy man. And Felicia *must* marry money. We must look beyond the county families now. Mr Hurst is no longer an option; Lord Salbridge seems uninclined to wed. And you must give up this nonsense about Sir Frederick at once – he is little better than a pauper as far as we are concerned.'

'Really, Mr Elton—'

'Tell me, Sophronia, how else would you propose to pay our debts? And are we to deny Augustus funds the next time he is up for re-election and let the world say the Eltons cannot afford to keep their son in Parliament? Or would it flatter your sense of family importance if we were to sell off some of the Ludwell land?'

There was a stony silence in the dining room. Felicia looked down at her untouched dinner.

'Major Alderton will come here next week,' said Mr Elton, 'along with everybody else. You will be civil to him. Felicia will sit next to him at dinner. Do I make myself clear?'

Felicia glanced up, just once, at her mother. Mrs Elton's lips were pursed, her cheeks white. Her hands were clenched. If she could not master the situation, she clearly meant to master herself.

'Perfectly clear,' she said, and the words dripped with icy politeness.

Felicia sat quite still, gazing down at her plate. She tried to think of the J. N. Hummel piece she had been practising all afternoon, to sing it in her head. She thought about what Monsieur Brisset had said the other day, and she wondered if there were any pieces of music into which she could sink this feeling, this numbness, this fear – but she would not even know where to begin.

CHAPTER XII

In which Melford shops and Miss McNeil is slighted

It was market day in Melford, and the town thronged with people. There were queues outside the baker's and the butcher's, and determined servants weaved through the crowded streets on pressing missions. Lady Wickford and Lady Rose were trying on bonnets inside the milliner's, while Mrs Crayton and Mrs Palmer traded news outside.

Amelia Ashpoint and Clara McNeil stood at the corner of Grange Street, bonnets on, wicker baskets in hand. Amelia was attempting to steer them towards the bookseller's, and Clara towards the dressmaker's, when they were accosted by Miss Waterson and Miss Maddon.

'Miss Ashpoint, Miss McNeil, how *charming* to see you,' said Miss Waterson. 'You will *never* guess who we have just met.'

'The new Mrs Hurst,' declared Miss Maddon, before anybody could possibly have had time to guess. 'The new Mrs Hurst *herself*. At the bank. With Mr Hurst and her children. It was *most* exciting.'

'Mrs Hurst was *ever* so agreeable,' said Miss Waterson. 'A little older, though, than I expected. Four-and-thirty or thereabouts.'

'I should have said *three*-and-thirty,' said Miss Maddon. 'And she certainly *was* agreeable.'

Amelia wondered if Mrs Hurst had been given the opportunity to be agreeable; her words would have no doubt been lost in the constant stream of chatter that emulated from Miss Waterson and Miss Maddon.

'I wish we could have spent longer talking to her, but Mrs Palmer *would* come over and *would* start asking about her children.' Miss Waterson shook her head mournfully. 'One does not like to speak ill of one's neighbours, but Mrs Palmer is *such* a gossip.'

Amelia bit her lip to stop herself laughing. One of her great pleasures in life was to laugh at her neighbours, and Miss Waterson and Miss Maddon always gave her ample opportunity. Everybody thought them pleasant and harmless elderly ladies, and no doubt they were, but as long as they continued to relish gossip and take an undue interest in the doings of their neighbours, Amelia would continue to laugh at them.

'Oh – there is Mrs Crayton,' said Miss Waterson, peering over Amelia's shoulder. 'We must tell her the news, too. Good day, Miss Ashpoint. Miss McNeil, we shall see you on Friday.'

As they bustled off down the street, Amelia finally let herself laugh.

'Be kind, Amelia,' said Clara. She was pretending to frown, but they were standing close together on the street corner, and Amelia could see the smile in her eyes.

'What is happening on Friday?'

'My father is holding a rival dinner.' Clara raised an eyebrow. 'While the great and good of Wickenshire are at the Eltons, we shall be hosting Miss Waterson, Miss Maddon, Mr Lonsdale and the doctor.'

'The doctor?' asked Amelia, frowning. 'I did not know your father knew him well.'

'He doesn't,' said Clara, with a sigh of exasperation. 'But you know, Amelia, your papa is not the *only* father on the lookout for suitable matches for his daughter.'

Amelia laughed, though it did not sound quite as hearty as she might have wished. 'So the doctor is to be your Mr Hurst, is he? I wonder how long it will take *him* to find a widow with many children to marry. Your poor father *will* be disappointed, and unlike my father he does not even have a fondness for gossip to comfort him.'

Clara gave a faint smile. 'I dare say he will bear it. But now, Amelia, we had better go to the dressmaker's. You cannot possibly go to Ludwell Manor in two days' time wearing white gloves with soup stains on one palm and a hole in one finger.'

Amelia grinned at Clara. 'Even if you *do* force me to buy a new pair of gloves, perhaps I shan't wear them – you won't be there to know, because Mrs Elton is an uncivil fool.'

This was perhaps spoken louder than it ought to have been, and several passers-by looked round. Anne Palmer looked towards them, frowning, as she too made her way towards Miss Nettlebed's.

'*Amelia!*' hissed Clara, but she was laughing in spite of herself.

'What? Anne Palmer is only jealous that she does not have as much fun as we do,' said Amelia, grinning. 'Oh, hush, I know – I am very wicked, and you are shocked, and I am a disgrace, et cetera, et cetera. In apology, and only because of my great respect for you, *not* because of my respect for Mrs Elton – I have none – I suppose we *may* buy gloves.' She looped her arm through Clara's, pulled her as close as she dared. It was the fashion to walk arm in arm and no one would think anything of it. Together, they turned towards the dressmaker's. 'Do you need anything new for your rival dinner?' asked Amelia.

Clara hesitated. 'I haven't any money left this month,' she said quietly.

'Oh, well, that is no matter – you can charge anything to Ashpoint Hall. Papa will never know it is not mine, and he will be quite delighted if he thinks I have started to care more about my appearance.'

Clara turned to her with an expression of reproach, almost of irritation. Her grip on Amelia's arm loosened. '*Amelia,*' she said, 'I am not going to take your father's money. And what do you think *my* father would say if I came home with something he knew we could not afford? He has quite as much pride as your father, in his way.'

'Oh, I only meant—'

'I know what you meant. Forget it.' Clara shook her head, bit her lip, smiled. She held Amelia's arm tighter. 'Come on – today, our only mission is to make sure you are fit to be seen by the great, grand Eltons.'

Miss Nettlebed's dressmaker's and haberdashery was busy, as it always was on a Wednesday. The eldest three Palmer sisters were looking through a new selection of rather out-landish silks, while Felicia Elton stood at the counter, in a crimson satin dress with half boots and an overly trimmed bonnet, speaking to Miss Nettlebed about some new order. One of the Ludwell maids waited behind her, head bowed, hands folded together.

The Palmer sisters said good morning to Clara and Amelia, and they both returned the greeting.

Miss Elton said, 'Good morning, Miss Ashpoint,' rather coldly to Amelia. Her eyes passed over Clara, but she did not greet her. She simply looked away.

Amelia and Clara had released each other's arms as they came into the shop, but still Amelia was standing close enough to feel the shift in Clara's posture, to hear the catch in her breathing. It was one thing for the Eltons not to invite the McNeils to dinner, but for Felicia Elton to so blatantly cut Clara in public was another matter entirely.

Amelia did not reply to the greeting. She merely stared, frowning, while Miss Elton went on with her order for a new silk gown with large gigot sleeves.

'Look at this, Clara,' said Amelia loudly, waving her hand vaguely at the Parisian fashion plates upon the table. 'What an ugly gown this girl has on. I have always thought that gigot sleeves make one look rather like a soufflé.'

Clara bit back a smile. Cassandra and Louisa giggled. Anne laughed, then put a hand over her mouth as though she were ashamed of herself. The impassive maid tried hard not to smile. Miss Nettlebed looked unimpressed.

Miss Elton did not so much as flinch. She went on with her order, moving on to blue velvet and scarlet satin.

Amelia felt her anger rise. She would not let Miss Elton ignore Clara. She would not let Miss Elton ignore *her* either.

'If there is one colour I would never wear,' she said loudly to Clara, 'it is scarlet. It always makes me think of London streetwalkers.'

This time, the maid did smile. Clara shook her head at Amelia but said nothing. Cassandra and Louisa laughed a little harder, and Anne looked solemnly at Amelia, as though she thought she had let herself down.

Felicia Elton paused mid-sentence but did not turn. She breathed in and out, then went on with her order.

When Miss Elton was at last finished, she turned, the maid following quickly behind, and took a few neat steps towards the shop door. There, she paused and looked back at the crowd of customers. 'Good morning, Miss Palmer,' she said, 'Miss Louisa, Miss Cassandra.'

Anne murmured a 'Good morning' back, as though she could not help politeness, but the younger Palmer sisters only giggled. Cassandra hissed something about street-walkers to Louisa, and Louisa spluttered with laughter.

Felicia did not flush, but Amelia saw her swallow. She turned away and looked steadily at Amelia and Clara instead, but she said nothing to either of them. She simply left the shop without a word.

~

'Amelia, you should not have done that,' said Clara as they turned out of the dressmaker's and headed towards the bookseller's, new gloves finally acquired.

'Why not?' Amelia put her arm through Clara's. 'If Miss Elton wishes to slight you, she will find that I slight her in turn.'

'She has done that before, you know, when you weren't by,' said Clara, with a shrug. 'It is only how her parents have taught her to behave.'

'If I behaved as my father instructed *me*, I would be very dull indeed. Now,' she said, her hand on the door of the bookseller's, 'do you think Mr Mannering will have the latest instalment of *Master Humphrey's Clock* yet? Anne Palmer got there before me last time, and I had to wait while he ordered more.'

She pushed open the door, and the two young ladies stepped inside. Amelia felt her anger at Felicia Elton slip away as the smell of ink and leather and dust welcomed her. She loved the bookseller's, loved the long rows of beautiful bound volumes, the old and new friends beaming out from every shelf.

Amelia had been coming here with Clara for as long as she could remember. They had picked out childhood books together, measured their growth by the tallest shelves they could reach. They had kissed behind the bookshelves at the back of the shop, in the days when they were less careful. It was here that Amelia had first whispered to Clara that she would like to be a writer, and together they had traced their way along the spines, making up ever wilder *noms de plume* and pointing out where Amelia's book would sit amongst the other volumes.

The shop was usually quiet – the only customer who came more regularly than Amelia was Anne Palmer, and Anne always browsed books in grave silence, as though she were at worship. But today Amelia heard the chatter of children's voices, and she turned to see five figures assembled around a bookcase by the window: Mr Hurst, Mrs Hurst and the three Roberts children.

They did not look up at the sound of the bell. Mr Hurst was saying something that was lost in the sound of Mrs Hurst's laughter, and the two eldest children were talking loudly over each other. The little girl held up a copy of *Aesop's Fables*, and the boy held up Hans Christian Andersen's *Fairy Tales Told for Children*. Both books were being pushed up towards the littlest child, whom Mrs Hurst was holding on her hip. It appeared that he was to have the final say on which book was purchased.

Amelia glanced at Clara and smiled.

Finally, the child reached out a chubby hand towards *Aesop's Fables*. He took it from his sister and looked very much as though he might be about to chew the corners – upon which his mother pulled it out of his reach and carried it up to Mr Mannering at the counter.

It was at this point that Mr Hurst noticed the new customers. While his wife was paying, he turned, advanced a step towards the young ladies and wished them both good morning.

'I hope, Miss Ashpoint, Miss McNeil, you will allow me to introduce you to these young friends of mine.'

'We should be delighted,' said Clara, and Amelia nodded.

'This young lady is Miss Eleanor Roberts,' he declared.

The girl gave a shy curtsey and said, 'Good morning.'

'And this young gentleman is Master John Roberts.'

A very proper bow followed. 'Good morning.'

They both spoke with a faint accent that Amelia could not quite place.

The new Mrs Hurst turned from the counter with a question for her husband, and Mr Hurst left them for a moment. While the Hursts had a hushed conversation about whether or not to purchase the latest Edward Bulwer, Amelia asked the children how they liked Wickenshire.

The little boy and girl looked at each other.

'We aren't to speak to strangers when Mama or New-Papa are not here,' said Eleanor, 'in case we say the wrong thing.'

John shushed her loudly.

'John is always saying the wrong thing,' said Eleanor, 'but I am very wise and *I* know all about it.'

And then Mr and Mrs Hurst were back, two books neatly wrapped in paper clasped in Mr Hurst's arms.

'Miss Ashpoint, Miss McNeil, I should like you to meet my wife,' said Mr Hurst.

The words 'my wife' were spoken very softly, very tenderly, and Amelia felt a pang of something like longing. What would it feel like, she wondered, to declare in one word, before all the world, what Clara was to her?

'And this very young gentleman here is Master George Roberts,' Mr Hurst was saying. 'Do you remember how to say good morning, Georgy?'

The infant gave forth a random assortment of syllables, one of which almost resembled the word 'good'. Mr and Mrs Hurst appeared perfectly satisfied, and Amelia felt herself smile.

'I am pleased to meet you both,' said Mrs Hurst. 'I have heard your names often from Montgomery.'

'And we are pleased to meet you,' said Amelia, 'for we have heard your name from everybody for weeks. You, Mrs Hurst, are the most sought-after woman in Wickenshire.'

This was said lightly, but Mrs Hurst did not seem to take it as such. She clutched her little boy closer to her chest.

'My friend only means,' said Clara gently, 'that everybody is curious about you. Mr Hurst's neighbours are so fond of him that they all wish to meet his wife.'

My friend, thought Amelia. The word was never quite enough.

Mrs Hurst nodded slowly. She glanced sideways at her husband, who smiled at her with all appearance of brightness.

'There is nothing to fear from a little neighbourly curiosity.' He said this rather more earnestly than Amelia thought necessary, and she almost expected Mrs Hurst to laugh. But she only gave a faint smile and nodded.

John was tugging on his mother's coat. 'May we look at the toys in the market, please, Mama?'

She smiled down at him. 'Of course,' she said. 'Good morning, Miss Ashpoint, Miss McNeil.' She took a step towards the door, her husband close at her side. 'Will I see you both at this dinner of Mrs Elton's on Friday?'

'Not I,' said Clara quickly. 'I am not quite fine enough for Mrs Elton, I am afraid – but Amelia will be there, and I hope we shall often meet elsewhere.'

'Ah.' Mrs Hurst hesitated. 'For all that I have been invited,' she said, 'I am not sure that I am fine enough for Mrs Elton either.'

The family went out, and Amelia stepped to the window to look after them. 'I think I rather like her,' she said to Clara, as they watched them walk down Grange Street. 'She does not seem to have a high opinion of Mrs Elton, which gives me hope.'

She looked on, smiling, as the children stopped in front of the baker's and began to point, as Mr Hurst slipped inside and came out again a moment later, armed with a parcel of gingerbread.

Amelia glanced further down the street – and caught sight of Mr Lonsdale and Monsieur Brisset, walking together. Lonsdale noticed her in the window, touched his hat, and Amelia had just nodded her head to acknowledge him when she caught sight of Monsieur Brisset's face.

He had stopped in the street and was staring at Mrs Hurst, a clouded expression on his face.

CHAPTER XIII

In which we are told stories

'WHAT WAS ALL THAT ABOUT?' ASKED LONSDALE AS HE and Brisset settled in the tidy parlour of his house on Mill Lane. If Brisset had his suspicions that the rest of the house was not quite as respectable, he never mentioned them. Their friendship was based upon a shared knowledge that neither had as much money, nor as much respect, as they would have liked, but while Brisset was frank and open about the state of his affairs, Lonsdale rarely was. He was, in Brisset's words, too much the English gentleman.

'All what?' replied Brisset.

'You can't think I didn't notice you stare after Mrs Hurst in the street.'

Brisset shrugged, hesitated, wavered. Then he said, with a clear determination to change the subject, 'I am going to give up the Lantern.'

Lonsdale looked at his friend pointedly. 'You have been saying that every other week for a year. Now, moving back to—'

'The fact is, I cannot afford it.' Brisset began to move his fingers, playing the piano on his knees absent-mindedly. 'It was a foolish thought to begin with. They do not want me there. Why do you think they despise me – because I am French or because I am poor? It is so hard to tell.'

'Because they are fools,' replied Lonsdale. 'One day, I shall buy all their houses.'

Brisset laughed heartily – and then stopped. 'Do you know,' he said softly, 'I almost believe you will.'

Lonsdale smiled. 'Come,' he said, 'let me fetch you a drink, and then I shall force you to answer me. Tea, or something stronger?'

'Whichever you like. I suppose you have a cartload of beer somewhere you did not have to pay for?'

Lonsdale held up his hands. 'The benefits of the trade.'

'Then save your tea for when you need it – when Miss Ashpoint calls.'

'You know very well that she will never call here.'

Brisset raised his eyebrows.

'She has come to the door, once, to deliver her manuscript. Miss McNeil was with her, and neither of them crossed the threshold.'

Lonsdale stood up to fetch the drinks from the kitchen. When he returned, a bottle of Ashpoint beer in each hand, Brisset was looking at him thoughtfully.

'Lonsdale, I must confess I have wondered what your intentions are in that quarter. I do not think you would go to so much effort, these enquiries in London on Miss Ashpoint's behalf, these endeavours to further her ambition, were you not—'

'I ought never to have told you about that,' muttered Lonsdale.

'I am only suggesting,' said Brisset, 'that you are more interested in her than you care to admit.' He paused, his expression serious. 'You know, if you married her, it would be the making of you.'

Lonsdale shifted uneasily in his seat. 'Brisset—'

'Would it not?' asked his friend. 'You marry the daughter, you go into partnership with the father, and you are nearly as fine a gentleman as Mr Ashpoint in five years' time.'

'Stop it,' said Lonsdale, with sudden sharpness in his voice. 'I hope you know me too well to think that I would stoop so low as to marry simply for gain.'

Brisset looked across at him, eyebrows raised. 'It is not simply for gain if you also happen to love her,' he replied calmly.

Lonsdale flushed. 'We are not having this discussion. And really, Brisset, if we are to talk about ladies who are far above us, then—'

Brisset held up his hands. 'It was only a friendly remark. I apologize. Let it be.'

'Very well.' Lonsdale leant forwards in his chair. He was still smarting from Brisset's words. He tried to push them away, to stop the thought of Amelia Ashpoint blooming in his mind. 'Let us go back to Mrs Hurst. Come – out with it. You . . . recognized her from somewhere?'

Brisset frowned. 'I do not want to take part in all this petty gossip. Wickenshire is mad for it. Let the woman be.'

'But you might tell *me*,' said Lonsdale. 'I am not going to repeat it.'

Brisset inclined his head. He hesitated, opened his mouth, shut it again and then finally said, 'I think I recognized her. I am almost certain – by which I mean to say that I *am* certain. Only, it seems rather improbable.'

Lonsdale looked across at his friend. 'Am I to know any more than that?'

Brisset gave a pained smile. 'It was a very long time ago,' he said, taking a sip from his bottle of beer. 'It is the same face, to be sure, though she looks somewhat . . .'

'Older?'

'In truth, no. Happier, I suppose, freer from care. And the name *was* Roberts, to be sure . . .'

'Brisset, it's just as well you are not called upon to use more words in your profession. Tell me properly – where do you know Mrs Hurst from?'

'From Nice,' Brisset replied. He smiled at Lonsdale's vexed expression. 'All right. When I was a boy, I had a schoolfriend whose father took in lodgers. I was always in and out of this friend's house, and so of course I saw the lodgers from time to time, and I knew a little about them from my friend. For six months or so, a couple named Roberts took the upstairs floor.'

'And that Mrs Roberts is the same Mrs Roberts who is now Mrs Hurst?'

'I think so – well, yes, I am sure of it.'

'Any children at that point?'

'No – it must have been twelve years ago, I suppose.' Brisset paused, still frowning. He tapped out a rhythm on his knees.

'And?'

'Well, my friend and his father – and I also – had a very poor opinion of this Mr Roberts. He was a former military or naval man fallen on hard times – a difficult, cruel man. A gamester, you know. My friend's bedroom was beneath their sitting room, and we would sometimes hear Mr Roberts shouting – raging – at his wife. His wife, we rarely saw. She

XIII   MRS MONTGOMERY HURST   139

was a quiet young woman, and she always looked – well, exhausted, I suppose. Unhappy.'

Lonsdale felt a kind of tightness in his chest. 'I see.'

'They lived there for six months and only paid rent for three, and in the end my friend's father had to move them on. There was a big scene, my friend told me – Mr Roberts swore and shoved his father and when Mrs Roberts tried to stop him, he struck her, too.' Brisset sighed. 'They left, and neither I nor my friend ever saw them again. That is all I know.'

'And you are sure it is the same woman?'

'I did not think of it when I first heard her name, but when I saw her face . . . Well, I cannot doubt it.' Brisset looked across at his friend. 'I think Mrs Hurst's first marriage must have been a very unhappy one indeed.'

Lonsdale was silent. He thought of the family they had seen in the street that morning – Mrs Hurst's face bright at the sight of her new husband giving her children gingerbread. 'That is not the sort of history you imagine belonging to the wife of a man like Mr Hurst,' he said at last.

'No, it is not,' said Brisset solemnly. He sighed. 'I am going to Radcliffe tomorrow, to start teaching the children the pianoforte.'

Lonsdale frowned. 'I suppose she will not recognize you, if you were a child then. Will you say anything?'

'No,' came the slow reply. 'I think, for her sake, I had better not.'

～

Amelia and Clara lay side by side in Clara's bed in the little house on Garrett Lane. Amelia had dined with Clara and her father tonight and sent a message up with Hannah – whose sweetheart was one of the gardeners at Ashpoint Hall – to say that she would not be home until morning. After a day spent forever in the company of other people, it was a relief to be finally alone together, like removing a costume after a masquerade, like untying corset strings after a ball.

Clara's head was on Amelia's shoulder, her hand in hers. Amelia could feel her fingers brush her skin.

'Tell me a story,' said Clara.

Amelia turned her face on the pillow to look at her. 'What manner of story?'

'Any story. A happy story.'

'What shall it be about tonight?'

'Well,' said Clara, turning herself towards Amelia, pulling her closer, 'no marriage.'

'No marriage. Perfect.'

'And no balls. I am weary of them. No balls, no dancing, and no silk or muslin gowns. There must be no gentlemen—'

'No men at all?' asked Amelia, 'or just no gentlemen?'

'Author's discretion. But regardless of the men, we must have a young heroine named—'

'Clara?'

'I was going to say Amelia.'

'But I am the author. I do the naming.'

'Then you had better pick a name that is not mine.' They were lying close together, blankets pulled up over their bare skin. Amelia could feel Clara's breath on her cheek when she spoke.

'Very well,' said Amelia. 'So, we have a heroine called neither Clara nor Amelia, no marriage, no balls, no dancing, no muslin and no gentlemen. Anything else?'

'No historical settings,' said Clara, after a moment's thought. 'They have too great a scent of foolish romance.'

'Very good.'

They were silent for a few moments, looking at each other. Then Clara wrapped her arm around Amelia's waist, pulled her closer still, and Amelia felt her breath catch. They listened to the quiet, the safety, the peaceful hush of a house asleep.

'Can there be dragons?' asked Amelia after a while.

'Oh, to be sure. I like it best when your stories have dragons.'

'There will be a very fierce dragon,' said Amelia, 'the kind who will breathe fire at the Eltons and anyone else who dares insult you.'

Clara shook her head. 'Amelia,' she said softly, 'I can fight my own battles.'

'I know, I know, but – well, I wish you had no battles to fight.'

Clara laughed, but the laugh did not sound right. 'That's no good for storytelling,' she said. 'All good stories ought to have a battle or two.'

Amelia looked at her, and Clara looked back. She was smiling, but it was a slight smile, almost a little sad.

But then Clara leant in and kissed her, and Amelia forgot the sorrow at the edge of Clara's expression, forgot Miss Elton's slight in the dressmaker's, forgot Monsieur Brisset's odd look at Mrs Hurst in the street. She forgot Diggory's recent gloominess, her father's growing concerns about her matrimonial prospects, so much easier to laugh at than to feel.

She forgot it all. She let Clara's warmth warm her, let Clara's steadiness steady her. Let stories be. She blew out the candle, pulled Clara closer and kissed her in the dark.

CHAPTER XIV

In which Lord Salbridge collects rent and hearts

ON THE MORNING OF MRS ELTON'S DINNER PARTY, DIGGORY was woken by a loud noise. He pulled himself sleepily out from underneath the covers, wondering if he had overslept, if he had promised his father he would go into the brewery and forgotten about it again. But the mantel clock said only eight, and the noise appeared to be coming not from his door but from his window. He rubbed his eyes, wrenched open the bed curtains, then the main curtains, and opened the casement window. Leaning forwards, he saw Lord Salbridge outside, sat upon a fine chestnut mare. He held his hat in one hand and a pebble in the other.

'Diggory!' he called. 'You're up at last.'

'What are you doing here?'

'Summoning you. I want you to come on an adventure with me.'

'What sort of adventure?'

'A rather dull one – but with you at my side, infinitely less so.'

Diggory laughed. His annoyance at being woken was over-come by his relief at seeing his friend. He had barely him since that night at the Lantern, since Salbridge had warned him away from Rose. He knew that Salbridge only meant to be kind, to save him from the pain and embarrassment of a refusal – either from Rose or from their parents. And yet the thought of not seeing Rose again, not dancing with her, not talking to her – it was impossible, unendurable. He had spent the last couple of weeks sulking and reading novels with unhappy endings, and he felt thoroughly wretched.

So it was a true pleasure to see Salbridge grinning at him now, to know that their friendship at least remained intact.

'May I have five minutes?' he called down.

'But of course.'

He shut the window and rang for his valet, who seemed rather surprised to find his young master up so early. With some assistance, Diggory was soon dressed in cream trousers, dark boots and his favourite riding jacket. He took up one of his hats from the stand in the dressing room and examined himself in the mirror.

'You look splendid, sir,' said Ellington.

Diggory was never certain if Ellington really meant his compliments or was quietly laughing at him. Still, Diggory thanked him and headed downstairs, a full fifteen minutes after Salbridge had called him.

Outside, the air was cool, the sun dim behind misty clouds. One of the stable boys saddled Diggory's best horse, Ginger, and Diggory mounted, all the while watching Salbridge trot to and fro.

'What *are* we doing up at this hour?' asked Diggory as they rode out of the park.

'My father has decided that I ought to be a better heir,' said Salbridge, with a sneer. 'It is rent day and the steward is off visiting some sick relation, so I am now the rent collector – and you, dear fellow, are my assistant.'

Diggory frowned. This was not quite what he had expected

when his friend spoke of an adventure – but still, it was something to know that Salbridge felt his presence would be a help. 'Don't your people come to you?' he asked. Mr Ashpoint's tenants came up to the house once a month to pay their rents.

'Oh no. Some beastly old tradition that my father refuses to change. But I am bored to death of my father's commands and thought I might at least make it bearable with your good company. Besides, I have something to show you along the way.'

'Oh – what?'

'You'll see.'

It was nearly four miles' ride back to the village of Wickford. As they rode, they traded gossip and discussed the coming autumn months. They were planning to go into Norfolk in September to see an old Eton friend of Salbridge's, about whose wine cellar Diggory had heard great things. It was a relief to find this plan still intact.

Before they reached Wickford itself, they came upon several cottages scattered amongst the fields. Salbridge slowed his horse on approaching the first and sighed wearily as he dismounted. It was a very small cottage, scarcely bigger than the breakfast room at Ashpoint Hall. It was well constructed in sturdy grey brick, with a broad thatched roof, but one of the windows was broken and the front step was muddy. Diggory dismounted and tied up his horse.

The door stood half open to let in the summer air. Salbridge knocked, but he was already walking in before any answer came. Diggory followed him inside.

It was a dark, poky place, just one room with the range, table, bed and all. It was clean, however – cluttered but neat. Two little children sat upon the floor, squabbling over a rag doll. Their mother had put down her sewing at the sound of the knock and was rising to her feet.

Diggory tried not to think about how uncomfortable it must be to live in such a place. He thought of his own huge bedroom at home and felt the stirring of something like guilt. He wondered what his life might have been had his grand-father not made a success of the brewery. His mother had been from a very respectable family in Bath; she would never have met, never have married, his father, had he not been rich. He could almost imagine two different Diggorys: his mother's son by another husband, uncomplicated class and wealth, the kind of Diggory whom an earl and countess might have gladly let marry their daughter; and his father's son by another wife, a shopkeeper's boy or a farm labourer, living somewhere not so very different from here.

While Salbridge collected the money, Diggory knelt down and spoke to the children. He asked what their names were – Betsy and Jo – and asked the name of the doll – Jo called it Charlie, but Betsy said it was Maggie – and asked if they were well and if they were good children. Betsy said she was good but not very well and coughed to prove it. Jo, with admirable honesty, said he was well but not very good.

'You oughtn't to speak to them,' said Salbridge as they rode on to the next place.

'Why ever not? My father always enquires about his tenants.'

'Yes, I suppose he does,' said Salbridge, and the corner of his mouth twitched into a smile.

Another day, Diggory might have asked him what that smile meant, but the awkwardness of the other night was still fresh in his mind, so he endeavoured to ignore it.

The rest of the cottages were similar – small homes with

laundry strung up about the place and dust swept into the corners. Most of the men were already out in the fields, and some of the women were, too; in three cottages, they found only children, with instructions and money waiting. At several homes, they were told that not all the rent could be found. The first few times, Lord Salbridge reprimanded the women, but on the fourth occasion, the man of the house was at home and Salbridge seemed to lose his nerve. He simply nodded and said he'd tell his father.

'Oughtn't you to make a note of things like that?' asked Diggory as they left.

Salbridge frowned. 'Why should I? That will be the steward's problem when he returns.'

Later, they stopped at a cottage west of the village. Here again, the door was half open. Salbridge knocked and entered, and just before Diggory came through the door he heard a woman's voice say, 'Alexander!' in a tone of surprise, laced with something else he could not quite identify.

Nobody ever called Lord Salbridge 'Alexander'. The use of his Christian name was so irregular, so intimate, that Diggory felt his chest tighten. He knew at once, without wishing to know it, what Salbridge had meant when he said he had something to show him.

As they entered the cottage, the woman stood up, wiping her hands on her apron. She looked pale, startled – anxious, perhaps. She glanced hesitantly at Diggory, and then her eyes turned back to Lord Salbridge. She was about their own age, perhaps younger. She had light hair, delicate features and very blue eyes.

'Good morning, Grace,' said Salbridge.

'Good day, sir.' Her voice was low, and Diggory saw her swallow.

'This is my friend, Mr Diggory Ashpoint,' said Lord Salbridge. Unlike his tenant, he seemed entirely at his ease.

Grace bowed her head. Diggory was trying not to look at her, trying not to watch Salbridge's eyes on her figure. He looked around the room instead: neat, small, bare. A girl of five or six sat sewing in a shadowy corner.

'It's rent day,' said Salbridge.

With a nod and an exhalation, Grace stepped out from behind the table, turned to a chest behind her and began rummaging through. At last, she took out a handful of coins.

'I'm a few shillings short,' she said quietly as she put the coins into Lord Salbridge's hand.

Diggory saw him take her fingers for a moment in his, saw his other hand on her wrist. 'Oh,' he said, a half-smile on his lips, 'we needn't worry about that.'

∽

'Why did she call you Alexander?' Diggory asked as they made their way to the next cottage. He tried to speak lightly, but he found his voice laced with anxiety.

Salbridge shrugged. 'Well, I thought it best. There are hundreds of Alexanders in the world and only one Lord Salbridge – if she ever slips up and speaks of me, or if the child says something, nobody will be any the wiser.'

Diggory looked round at him. 'Is she . . . married?' he asked slowly.

'Widowed. Husband died not long after the brat was born. Isn't Grace a peach? She thinks herself rather in love with me.'

Diggory hesitated. 'And I suppose you have . . . encouraged her.'

Salbridge laughed heartily. 'Well, and wouldn't you – a woman who looks like that?'

They rode on in silence. The lane was quiet, the next cottage half a mile away, and Diggory was hot and weary with riding. He tried to work out what it was he meant to say. He knew that the situation was not right, but then Salbridge often did things that were not right, and it was hard to explain the grave difference here.

'Salbridge,' he said at last, 'it is not as though you can marry this woman.'

His friend gave a loud laugh. It was such a pleasant, cheerful laugh that Diggory almost smiled – and then stopped himself.

'My dear fellow,' said Salbridge, 'you are rather an innocent, aren't you? I said she was in love with me. I did not say *I* was in love with her. I have told you a thousand times that I am above love. I am the son of an earl, Diggory. I am not about to go and marry some cottager's widow – but that hardly means I am not allowed some *fun*.'

Diggory bit his lip. Once or twice, Salbridge had vaguely mentioned encounters with women in London or when he had been at Oxford, but Diggory had never really believed him. He considered his next words carefully. 'You know that is not the right way to treat someone, Salbridge.'

Another laugh. 'Really, Diggory. Tell me, in what manner I am treating her badly? Grace likes to see me. She likes to have me about the place. She likes—'

'What about her reputation?'

'Oh, come. It is not like that with these people. They are not like *us*. Besides, I am careful. Today is the first day I have come in my own clothes for two months – I usually steal something from one of the stablehands.'

'But—'

'My dear fellow, if you are going to read me a sermon on morals, I shall ride off and leave you. Come, don't you think her pretty?'

Diggory had stopped riding.

Salbridge pulled back on his reins and turned. 'Damn it, Ashpoint – I had rather thought to impress you.' He took a small flask from his waistcoat, took a gulp and leant over to pass it to Diggory. 'Drink up. You look as pale as a girl about to faint.'

Diggory took it, drank and winced. He felt sick. He did not want to think about Grace. He did not want to think about this morning at all. He did not want to think about the other Diggory, in the other life, the life where his grandfather had not grown rich. He did not want to think of another Amelia or Ada being treated like that.

'I have to go,' he said abruptly.

Lord Salbridge looked at him, frowned. 'All right,' he said, a little sulkily. 'You are ever so dull today, Diggory. Try to get some colour in your cheeks by this evening, won't you?'

∾

As Lord Salbridge rode on to the next cottage, he tried to put Diggory's expression out of his mind. He tried to think instead of Grace – of her eyes, her hands, her full figure. Perhaps, when he had finished this tiresome work for his father, he might find his way back to her cottage, see if she could get rid of that child for the afternoon, and—

It was no use. There was Diggory's face before him, talking about what was and wasn't the right way to treat someone, as though right and wrong had anything to do with it. This was his land; these were his tenants – he could do with them as he liked. It was simply the way of the world.

Diggory's reaction was not what Salbridge had antici-pated. He had been hoping to shake Diggory out of whatever nonsense he had got into his head about Rose, to show him the kind of woman a fellow *could* associate with if he were bored. He had been expecting a little surprise, to be sure, some expression of admiration for Grace's beauty, not to mention a healthy degree of envy – but he had certainly not expected *judgement*.

Salbridge did not relish the thought of being judged by anybody, let alone by Diggory Ashpoint, who was meant to look up to him in all things.

He frowned and kicked his horse to go faster.

CHAPTER XV

In which Mrs Elton presides over a dinner
of great splendour

AT TWENTY MINUTES TO SEVEN, FELICIA ELTON STOOD IN a green satin gown in the drawing room of Ludwell Manor, her parents at her side. As they waited for the guests to arrive, she examined herself in the looking glass above the fireplace. Her hair was adorned with artificial flowers, her dress trimmed with silver, and the pendant around her neck was very becoming. All in all, she thought she looked exquisitely handsome. Her parents appeared to think so, too, for her mother had told her that she was sure Sir Frederick would like her new gown, and her father had remarked (much to her mother's annoyance) that Major Alderton would certainly think her looking well.

The guests arrived so promptly at a quarter to seven that Peter had trouble announcing each party fast enough. In they all came, in their fine white muslin and coloured silks, in dark waistcoats, smart cravats and tails – the Wickfords, the Ashpoints, the Palmers. Mr Duckfield trailed in after them, looking very un-clergyman-like in a scarlet waistcoat and neat tails.

Sir Frederick Hammersmith came in next, in lilac trousers and a crimson-and-white striped jacket. He was greeted with ordinary civility by Felicia's father and with warm regard by her mother.

Behind him came Major Alderton, in a well-fitting navy-blue suit of clothes, a light smile on his face. Felicia's mother kept looking at him and looking away, as though she could not believe her drawing room was thus polluted – but if anybody else was taken aback to see Major Alderton at one of Mrs Elton's dinners, they were too polite to show it.

Mr and Mrs Hurst arrived as the clock was striking seven. If they had planned to slip in just before the dinner to avoid notice, they did not succeed. The moment the pair stepped through the door, all eyes turned to them.

Mrs Hurst looked less nervous than when Felicia and her mother had called, as though her husband's presence gave her strength. Felicia could not imagine that – having enough faith in a man not only to marry him but to trust in him afterwards.

When the dinner gong sounded, there was some diffi-culty between her parents about who was to take whom into the dining room. Mr Elton thought he ought to take in Mrs Hurst, for new brides were always given precedence, but Mrs Elton disliked such old-fashioned country customs even in the country and did not think it ought to apply to widows. Moreover, if Mr Elton took in Mrs Hurst, then Lady Wickford, as the highest-ranking lady in the room, would have to be taken in by Sir Frederick, as she could not very well be taken in by her own husband or son, which would mean Sir Frederick could not take in Felicia. In the end, Mr Elton triumphed, and Felicia was led into the dining room on the arm of Lord Salbridge.

'You look ravishing, Miss Elton.'

It was the sort of thing he always said, and she gave him

a mild smile in reply. She had no doubt that Lord Salbridge admired her beauty – of course he did – but her mother was probably right: he was not likely to marry young.

While Felicia's parents sat down at each end of the long mahogany table, the other guests were directed into their seats. Felicia took her place beside Sir Frederick (her mother's ruling), moved her bread to the left-hand side of her plate, took off her long white satin gloves, placed them in her lap, then spread her napkin elegantly over her knees. Major Alderton sat down on her other side (her father's ruling) and bid her a cheerful good evening.

The table was laid in silver splendour, with little flowers dotted between the settings. A fine spread already lay before them: bottles of sherry and champagne, oyster patties and sweetbreads, cod's head, curried mutton and pigeon pie, haricot beans and salad, with a large tureen of hare soup at one end and of white soup at the other.

Felicia glanced up and down at the guests as they took their places. At the far end of the table, Lady Rose sat beside Diggory Ashpoint in silence. She kept looking at him, and he kept looking away. Lord Salbridge was watching them from across the table, where he had been placed next to Amelia Ashpoint. Felicia's father was already engaging Mrs Hurst in conversation.

On Mrs Hurst's right, however, one seat remained empty, and as Peter closed the dining room doors, Felicia realized that everyone must already be inside. There was a gaping space between Mrs Hurst and Amelia Ashpoint. Felicia looked round at her mother, but Mrs Elton was already rising to her feet.

'But Mrs Palmer,' she said, 'where is your husband?'

Mrs Palmer frowned. 'I am afraid that the captain is

indisposed tonight. A headache. He deeply regrets his absence.' She glanced at her daughters. 'I thought one of the girls had told you.'

'Cassandra was meant to,' said Louisa.

Cassandra protested loudly, and Anne hurried to apologize on her family's behalf.

Felicia glanced at her mother. Mrs Elton had spent hours perfecting her table plan – Felicia had watched her do it – and she had thought it a masterstroke to place Mrs Hurst next to Captain Palmer, who was an excellent talker. And now it was all ruined. It was preposterous to have an empty space next to the lady in whose honour this whole dinner had been arranged. She saw her mother glance around the room, but there was nothing to be done. Felicia's father was already on Mrs Hurst's other side, and she could not ask any other gentleman to move without incivility.

Dignity must be maintained. Mrs Elton nodded at Peter to take the chair away, then gracefully raised her spoon and began her soup.

～

'How d'you do, Miss Ashpoint?' asked Lord Salbridge.

Amelia sighed. She wondered if Mrs Elton had put Lord Salbridge at her side purely to vex her.

'I am quite well, thank you,' she said stiffly. 'And you?'

'Oh, I'm all right.'

Amelia looked away, glancing up the table, to where Diggory sat with Lady Rose. Rather than being engaged in eager conversation as usual, both sat in silence. Diggory was looking beyond gloomy, his eyes fixed on his plate. Lady Rose glanced at him, bit her lip, then looked away.

Amelia wondered what *that* was all about, whether they had had some kind of quarrel, if that were the reason Diggory had been moping about so of late.

She turned back and found that Lord Salbridge was looking at her, apparently waiting for her to speak. When she did not, he began to pour himself a large glass of champagne. He clearly had no intention of waiting for his hostess to start her wine, nor of pouring any for Amelia. He glanced at her sideways. 'Sometimes, Miss Ashpoint, I rather think you don't like me.'

Amelia nearly laughed. 'I do not like gentlemen who drink too much,' she replied, lowering her voice, 'nor gentlemen who order my brother around.'

Lord Salbridge raised his eyebrows. He was looking at her hard, and his expression made her uneasy. 'Sometimes, Miss Ashpoint,' he said quietly, 'I do not think you like gentlemen at all.'

Amelia swallowed. There was a kind of cold dread blossoming in her chest, because if somebody *knew*, if somebody had worked out the truth about her and Clara – and worst of all, someone like *him*, with so little regard for her, so little regard for anybody – what would happen? She knew the world well enough to know that people who were not understood were ostracized or contained.

But surely it was impossible that he should really know. They were so careful. Perhaps she had misunderstood him – he might have meant, of course, that her taste was low, that she liked *men* more than gentlemen.

She forced herself to be calm, to push the unease away. 'I certainly do not like gentlemen who talk nonsense,' she said, as lightly as she could.

Lord Salbridge smirked, but Amelia did not give him the

chance to answer. She would not let him see that he had shaken her.

Instead, she turned firmly away, looking to the vacant space beside her, across which Mrs Hurst sat quietly, her cheeks pink, her eyes downcast. On her other side, Mr Elton was talking politics with her father across the table, apparently trying to secure Mr Ashpoint's interest in his son's career in London.

'Mrs Hurst,' said Amelia, forcing brightness into her voice, 'it is a pleasure to see you again.'

Mrs Hurst looked round in confusion, as though being addressed troubled her – and then recognition seemed to dawn. 'You are the young lady from the bookseller's,' she said, with a smile.

'I am indeed. I rather like the thought of being known as such. How are the children enjoying *Aesop's Fables*?'

'Oh, very much. At least, John and Eleanor are, but George seems to catch their excitement and starts to cry at the end of every fable.' She faltered, as though she were not much used to discussing her children with strangers. 'They all like stories,' she said at last.

Amelia smiled. 'As do you, perhaps? I think you purchased *Night and Morning*. It has been sat neglected on my shelf for a month already.'

Mrs Hurst nodded. 'Yes, I am fond of reading.' She paused, as if uncertain where to lead the conversation next.

Amelia tried to help her on. She was aware of the party's eyes on her, of Anne Palmer watching from across the table, of Mrs Elton peering down at them, of Lord Salbridge's presence at her side. 'And how do you find your new home?' she asked.

Mrs Hurst swallowed. 'It is very pleasant,' she said.

'Radcliffe is – it is just what I should have wished for, though I am not quite used to it yet.'

'And the children are happy?' asked Amelia, cutting into a slice of pigeon pie.

'Oh, thank you, yes.'

'They are fond of their new stepfather?'

Mrs Hurst blushed but nodded.

'That is as it should be. I have always had a lot for respect for Mr Hurst.' Amelia paused, let herself breathe. She pushed Lord Salbridge's words from her mind. 'You must forgive me for asking questions, Mrs Hurst, if you think them impertinent,' she said. She leant a little nearer to her and lowered her voice so that no one else could hear. 'We rarely have strangers here. You must know – you can hardly have failed to notice – that the neighbourhood is very much interested in you. I hate to see anybody suffering under the watchful eyes of Society. I wanted you to know that you should have a friend in me, if you would like one.'

Mrs Hurst was staring at her. She did not look annoyed; she looked almost touched. 'But, Miss Ashpoint,' she said slowly, 'why ever should they be interested in me?'

～

The first course was removed by the second. In came a large roasted fowl, a pig's head, mashed potatoes, stewed sea-kale, minced veal with béchamel sauce, snipes in jelly, broiled mushrooms, mashed swede – and Mrs Elton reigned over it all with a haughty smile. Felicia could see how pleased she was. The food was excellent. The guests looked content. Nobody other than Lord Salbridge was yet drunk, and Louisa and Cassandra Palmer were keeping their giggling to a minimum. Major Alderton was behaving as though he was quite as respectable as everybody else. And – as would please Mrs Elton more than anything – Mrs Hurst seemed to be enjoying herself, despite chiefly conversing with Miss Ashpoint.

All in all, Felicia thought, the evening must be considered a success.

She turned once more to Sir Frederick. 'How is Maddox Court?' she asked. 'The flowers must be out by now. You have the sweetest rose garden.'

'Yes, they are in bloom,' said Sir Frederick. 'Mother is delighted. The bright colours of the garden always cheer her. And I like the house best in the summer. I am thinking, in fact, of doing some renovation work – building a small extension – a veranda, and perhaps another room or two. If I . . . marry, I shall require a larger house.'

There was a moment's pause, and then Sir Frederick seemed to realize what he had said. He flushed, coughed and looked away.

Had Felicia not learnt long ago to control herself, she, too, might have blushed. His muddled hint ought to please her – but somehow it did not.

'I have been thinking of putting in a rose garden at Netherworth,' said Major Alderton, from her other side. 'You are fond of roses, Miss Elton?'

'Of course,' replied Felicia.

'I have made some changes to the house and the grounds since I bought the place,' he said, 'but I feel there is more to be done.'

'If you are doing anything extensive,' said Sir Frederick, finally looking up from his lemonade, 'then you must ask Mr McNeil – do you know him? He is really very good. He is as good as – as—' He looked around for a metaphor and finally managed, 'as good at managing land as Miss Elton is at playing the pianoforte.'

'I do hope you will play after dinner,' said Major Alderton. 'I do not think I have had the pleasure of hearing you before. I make no pretence of being musical myself, but I should very much like to hear you perform.'

'Of course,' said Felicia. She gave her best smile to Sir Frederick, because she still inclined to her mother's view of her matrimonial prospects, and her second best to Major Alderton, in case her father won. Of course she was used to admiration, but it all felt a little too real, sitting between these two men. Her parents' words at the dinner table last week kept coming back to her.

She let them talk over each other, let Major Alderton work up increasingly interesting things to say, let him drop in references to his expenditure and his large house, while Sir Frederick continued to talk about the planned extension to Maddox Court.

As Sir Frederick and Major Alderton talked at her, Felicia gazed out across the table. Mr Duckfield was boring Lady Rose with talk of some new card game. Mr Ashpoint was gossiping in whispers with Mrs Palmer. Diggory Ashpoint was looking thoroughly miserable. Miss Ashpoint was deep in conversation with Mrs Hurst, while Anne Palmer looked hard at them from across the table, as though she were trying to listen in. On Miss Ashpoint's other side, Lord Salbridge was gazing blankly about, looking vexed that no one was speaking to him.

Felicia turned back to Sir Frederick and, with a smile and an effort to engage him more once, asked him how his mother was.

CHAPTER XVI

In which Miss Ashpoint makes a new
friend and Lord Salbridge makes trouble

THE DINNER WAS OVER, AND THE LADIES HAD RETIRED TO
the drawing room. Amelia sat beside Mrs Hurst on a pair of
upright chairs beside the pianoforte, and the clusters of
women around the room occasionally shot bemused glances
in their direction. Louisa and Cassandra Palmer kept nudging one another, and Anne would not stop staring. Amelia
was aware that, unusually for her at a social occasion, she
was an object of envy. In the last few hours, she had discovered more about Mr Hurst's new wife than anyone else
had yet managed.

She had learnt that Mrs Hurst was an excellent walker,
who took great pleasure in the outdoors. She learnt, too,
that Mrs Hurst had spent a good deal of her life on the
Continent, on the Italian Rivera, in Verona, Venice, France,
Prussia, even Bohemia. This intrigued Amelia, who had
herself never been further than London. She had sometimes dreamt of adventures – of journeys she and Clara
might take halfway across the world in some other life. She
had written stories of places she knew nothing of, read
Shakespeare and Mary Shelley and Marco Polo with an
eager fascination for the foreign lands they described. Mrs
Hurst had actually been to most of Shakespeare's Italian

towns and spoke animatedly of the villages and landscapes she had visited – although on occasion she would falter.

'I lived abroad for convenience and economy, not fashion,' Mrs Hurst explained. 'I was a clergyman's daughter, although my parents died long ago, long before—' She stopped, pressed her hands together, went on. 'My mother died when I was quite a little girl, my father when I was some years below your age.'

'My mother, too, died when I was a child,' said Amelia, softly. 'Your father did not know your children, I suppose?'

Mrs Hurst shook her head, and a frown came over her face.

'And how old are the children, did you say?' Amelia felt almost ashamed of asking, of joining the rest of the neighbourhood in their insatiable curiosity – and yet she could not deny that she was interested in Mrs Hurst, both for her husband's sake, as she had always liked him, and for her own. Amelia had started up a conversation with Mrs Hurst chiefly to avoid Lord Salbridge and his insinuations, but she had found their discussion a more interesting diversion than she could have imagined. Mrs Hurst seemed a quiet, clever woman, clearly nervous of being in company – and yet she sat straight, held her head high, and had a smile younger than her face and frame.

'John is eight,' said Mrs Hurst. 'Eleanor is just six. Georgy is a little over two.'

Amelia smiled. 'And you are educating them at home?'

'Oh yes. I hardly know whether I ought to find a governess or not, but I can't abide the idea of John going away to school. Mrs Elton thinks—'

'Oh, bother Mrs Elton,' said Amelia. Anne Palmer looked round from her conversation with Lady Rose a few feet away, and Amelia lowered her voice. 'You must never listen to a word that woman says.'

Mrs Hurst gave a slight, nervous smile. 'I would rather educate them myself and bring in another master where one is needed. The children love to read, and they are all quick studies at language already, having lived so much abroad. Monsieur Brisset came yesterday to give Eleanor and John their first pianoforte lesson. Monty – Mr Hurst, I mean – is determined to make scholars and musicians of them all.'

'I am not surprised,' said Amelia. 'He is a kind man.'

Mrs Hurst nodded. 'He is the best man I have ever known.'

The door opened, and Mrs Hurst looked up as the gentlemen came in. Amelia saw Mr Hurst meet his wife's gaze. He came quickly over to join them, a bright, almost involuntary smile lighting up his face.

Diggory lingered in the dining room. Once the rest of the gentlemen had gone, he closed the door, sat back down at the table and poured himself another glass of port. He felt rotten. It had been unbearable, sitting next to Lady Rose and forcing himself into silence, feeling Salbridge's eyes on him every other moment.

After twenty minutes of brooding, Diggory found himself being glared at by two footmen, who evidently wished to clear the table. He rose slowly to his feet, apologized and walked miserably towards the drawing room.

He followed the corridor down to the entrance hall – and there, picking up her fan from the console table, was Lady Rose.

Turning, she saw him and said in surprise, 'Mr Diggory.'

They were entirely alone. He could hear the thrum of chatter from behind the closed drawing-room door further down the hall. She had fresh flowers in her hair, and her cheeks were pink.

He said, 'Good evening, Lady Rose,' as steadily as he could.

There was a moment's pause, and then Rose stepped towards him and said in a low voice, 'Have I offended you, Mr Diggory?'

'Offended me!' He stared at her, and all his misery seemed to double. 'Lady Rose, you are the last person in the world who could offend me.'

'Then why sit beside me in silence? I thought we were – friends.'

'We are, but—'

'What can I have done?'

'Nothing, of course. Only, your brother . . .'

She frowned. 'What?'

'He does not think I ought to – to talk to you. He thinks it – beneath you.'

'Beneath me?' she repeated. She sounded rather angry.

'Yes, he . . .' Diggory looked down at his feet. He was somewhere beyond tipsy, and he could not help the words that left his lips. 'The fact is, Lady Rose,' he said, in a low, cross whisper, 'that your brother knows I adore you and has warned me that, because my father owns a brewery and yours is an earl, your family would never allow us to marry.'

Lady Rose stared at him in astonishment. The colour rushed to her cheeks.

'I have been trying for weeks and months to ask you if you would – if you could – well, if you thought you could ever love me,' said Diggory miserably, 'but what is the use when your family would never allow it, even if you could?'

She was still staring. She said, 'Oh.'

'Don't tell me you wouldn't have me anyway, Lady Rose, for I am quite heartbroken enough as it is, and you may as well spare me. I am sorry I was uncivil all evening. Only, it is *very* hard. I have never met a girl quite like you, and now I shall have to keep away from you entirely. I'm very wretched, that's all, but what's a fellow to do?'

Rose blinked. She was silent for a moment, and then she began to speak in a hushed, exasperated voice. 'Well, I think a fellow's to ask me first, that's what *I* think a fellow's to do. Imagine taking orders from my brother! Papa lives still – and it is hardly as though you are a pauper. Really, I don't see why I shouldn't engage myself to anybody if I like to.'

Diggory stared at her. And then the meaning of Rose's last words sank in and his world flipped over.

'A-and,' he stammered, 'would you like to?'

Rose bit her lip as though to stop herself from smiling. She said, 'Maybe.'

Diggory was not sure he had ever smiled so wide, not in all his life. All thoughts of Salbridge vanished. All obstacles melted. All that was left was Rose, dear, lovely, brilliant Rose, beaming at him in the hall of Ludwell Manor. What if her parents did *not* object? If he could win them over, what could Salbridge do but make a fuss? He would come round in the end. Or perhaps not. At this precise moment, Diggory did not care. He was thinking of Rose and how they might buy a house on Lowick Terrace and how he could build glasshouses for her in the garden. He was think-ing of sitting beside her at dinner for evermore and talking to her night and day – and how much easier it would be to work for his father, to become a steady sensible brewery chap, if he were working for a future with such a partner.

He said, 'Rose,' and he had never heard his own voice sound like that before, tender and astonished and hopeful. She gave a kind of laugh, and he was just wondering how very bad it would be if he were to put his arms around her and kiss her in the middle of the hall, if he even dared to take her hand – when the door of the drawing room opened and Lord Salbridge walked out.

Diggory and Rose's smiles vanished. There was a moment's pause, and then Salbridge said cheerfully, without looking at his sister, 'Ah, Diggory, there you are. I have been looking for you. I need a partner at whist.'

Diggory said nothing. He tried not to look at Rose.

'I came out to get my fan,' said Rose quietly. She gave it a wave as proof, then walked down the hall, past her brother, towards the drawing room.

Salbridge's cheerful demeanour dropped the moment the door was closed. 'You know she will never have you,' he said coldly.

Diggory looked at him. He had seen Salbridge in many moods, seen him angry and bitter, irritated and disappointed, sarcastic and sour – but he had never seen Salbridge look at him like this, like he was nothing. It was the way he looked at Mr Lonsdale and Major Alderton at the Lantern.

'Listen, if you want a woman, you find someone like Grace – not my *sister*.'

Diggory felt his anger rise. 'Do you dare compare my behaviour with yours? I have every honourable intention towards Lady Rose. I know little of your relations with your tenant, but I think you know as well as I do that you are treating her abominably and—'

'I'm not going to discuss *that* with you! Grace is none of your concern. I thought you would understand. You do not – it is immaterial. But Diggory, you must give up these attentions to my sister. I *warned* you weeks ago. My parents won't stand for it. *I* won't stand for it. It is nothing personal, merely a matter of logic and blood. Our family has ten times the consequence of yours. Diggory, listen to me – you know you cannot possibly marry her.'

He looked up at Salbridge. This was his oldest friend in the world, the man around whom Diggory had built his life. He had loved him as a brother since he was ten years old, when Salbridge, a fine young man of twelve, had taught him one summer how to drink and smoke cigars and tie his own cravats. He had always gone where Salbridge told him, hunted when Salbridge wished to hunt, drank when Salbridge said so, lent him money when he asked, played cards at his request. He knew that Salbridge could be spiteful, cross, even cruel, that he talked of women in a way Diggory never would. But he had always thought it half an act, always believed in the kinder side of his friend, the side that smiled and made jokes, that could be charming to anybody.

But what if, after all, it was the charm that was the act, not the spite?

He thought of Grace's unease in the cottage, of Rose's smile, and he looked up to face Salbridge's cold expression.

He said, 'I am done listening to you.'

Salbridge's face hardened. 'This is ridiculous. Rose is the daughter of a peer, and you are merely the son of a tradesman.'

'And you are merely a scoundrel,' replied Diggory.

Upon which Lord Salbridge punched him in the face.

CHAPTER XVII

*In which Miss Elton overhears
what she should not*

FELICIA SAT IN THE DRAWING ROOM BESIDE MAJOR Alderton, who was regaling her with some story from his army days that she was not quite listening to. She wondered where Lord Salbridge and Diggory Ashpoint were, and as she turned to look for them, she caught her mother's eye. Mrs Elton angled her head discreetly towards Sir Frederick, who was speaking to Miss Ashpoint and the Hursts across the room. Felicia looked away.

Instead, she glanced around at the assembled ladies and gentlemen, the neat groups of conversation. Mr Duckfield and her father were engrossed in some political discussion. Mr Ashpoint was deep in gossip with Mrs Palmer. Anne was trying to tell her sisters about the novel she was reading, but Cassandra cut over her, saying that nobody wanted to talk about books at a dinner party.

In a moment's lull, Felicia caught Mrs Hurst saying, 'I have heard so much of Wickenshire's music.'

And then Mr Hurst turned and called, 'Miss Elton, won't you play for us? I have been telling my wife of your talents.'

'Oh yes,' said Sir Frederick, with a smile. 'Please do.'

This was seconded by Major Alderton, and Felicia, feeling

the eyes of the room gloriously upon her, left her seat and crossed to the pianoforte.

'I have heard so much of your talent,' said Mrs Hurst, 'both from my husband and from Monsieur Brisset.'

The room seemed to fall quiet. 'Monsieur Brisset?' Felicia repeated.

'Yes – he is teaching my children to play. He was telling me yesterday that you are by far the most skilled pupil he has ever had the fortune to teach.'

Felicia blushed. She was not sure she could remember the last time she had blushed without meaning to.

She sat down at the pianoforte and waited while Major Alderton and Sir Frederick debated who was to turn her pages. She thought of Monsieur Brisset, his rare sharp smile.

She lifted her hands and began to play.

❧

Diggory collapsed into a chair once Lord Salbridge had sauntered back to the drawing room. He held his hands over his face, mourning his bleeding lip and smarting nose. He was half in tears when he began to laugh.

Rose loved him. She would marry him if she could. He knew it as certainly as he knew his face would be bruised tomorrow. Salbridge would try to stop it, of course, and who could say what the earl and countess would think – but that was nothing to the knowledge that Rose *loved* him, that she at least thought him worthy.

So Diggory sat in the hall and laughed his heart out.

One of the maids crossed from the dining room to the drawing room at that moment and appeared to think him quite mad. She stared in astonishment at his uncontrolled laughter and then gave a start of surprise at the sight of blood on his hands and face.

'It's all right, it's all right,' cried Diggory, standing up. 'See, I'm not hurt. I just – fell.'

'Fell?' repeated the girl. She did not sound as though she believed him one bit.

'Yes. Would you—' He glanced around. 'Is there another room I might wait in? I can't possibly go into the drawing room like this, and I dare say your mistress would not like to find me in the hall.'

'I dare say not,' said the girl, with a weary sigh. She probably thought him very drunk.

It must be dreadful, thought Diggory, to work for the Eltons. He had seen this particular maid in Melford a few times, trailing after Miss Elton.

'You can sit in the morning room, sir,' she said, crossing the hall and opening another of the doors. 'I'll fetch some water for you to – wash yourself.'

'Thank you ever so much.'

Diggory crossed into the dark room and sat down heavily on one of the settees, while the maid lit a candle.

'Ought I to fetch somebody, the master or your father or—?'

'Dear God, not my father,' said Diggory. 'Not my upstanding, respectable father.' He grinned, but the maid remained unamused. 'I do not look very upstanding currently, I dare say.'

'No, sir. Surely someone ought to . . .' She trailed off.

'Perhaps,' said Diggory at last, 'you might go into the drawing room and ask for Miss Ashpoint?'

Ten minutes later – by which time Diggory was lolling on the sofa, trying very hard not to touch anything in case he stained it – Amelia appeared in the doorway. The servant was behind her, carrying a bowl of water and a strip of cloth, which she set down upon the table.

'I've told the master,' she said, in a low, hurried voice. 'I didn't tell the mistress, but it's more than my place's worth not to tell one of them.' She shrugged her shoulders in apology, then hurried out of the room, closing the door behind her.

'Oh my,' said Amelia, sitting down beside her brother with a smile, 'you have been in the wars.'

'Don't be disagreeable, Amy.'

'Whatever happened?'

He hesitated, and then he grinned. 'What would you say if I told you that I had just asked Lady Rose to marry me?'

Amelia let out one loud laugh. 'I should not have thought her aim so good!'

'What? No – no, Lady Rose did not *strike* me.'

'What a pity. I was set to be rather impressed.'

'No – she said yes. Well, she said maybe, but in a way that meant yes.' Diggory let out a laugh. 'I think I might be engaged.'

Amelia clapped her hands together and beamed at him. 'Well, that is excellent news. Congratulations!'

He looked round at his sister, then reached for the cloth and began to carefully clean his face, wincing all the while.

'I am so pleased. Lady Rose is a sensible and pleasant girl. She will suit you.' Amelia paused. 'Now, do tell me how on earth your proposing to Lady Rose brought you a broken face?'

'Because Lord Salbridge found me alone with her in the hall and did not like it.'

'Ah.'

'He doesn't know I asked her – he declares she'll never have me – and he thinks I'm a damned impudent fool to dare aspire so far above myself. This, from my oldest friend!' He scowled. 'Well, I am done with him.'

'Are you really? Then I am prouder still. The man's a – well, words for what he is aren't fit for Ludwell Manor.' Amelia looked very earnest – anxious, almost – as she said this.

Diggory thought of that morning, of Grace's expression when Salbridge walked in. 'I believe you're right.'

'What will the earl and countess think?'

'I hardly know.' Diggory's cheerfulness began to slip, and with the sensation of falling down to earth, he felt the misery of earlier this evening come crashing back. 'Salbridge is certain that they would never accept me as a son-in-law, but Rose did not seem to think it impossible. I hardly know what we shall do if they do not consent. We shall be forced to do something desperate like—'

'Like elope?' offered Amelia.

'I was going to say like Romeo and Juliet, but yes, I suppose there is that option, too.' He looked at his sister. 'You won't tell anyone, will you?' he asked earnestly. 'Rose and I had no time to settle anything, and I would rather not tell Papa until we have asked Lord Wickford, for Papa cannot keep a secret and the longer I can keep this from Lord Salbridge the better.'

'I won't breathe a word.'

'Do you think Papa will – will help me along? I cannot marry without being independent, of course, but . . . oh, I mean to show him I am old enough to marry and that I am worthy of marrying a girl like Lady Rose. Listen, Amy – I shall be a reformed character and I shan't get drunk – much – or play cards – high, I mean – and I shall be always at the brewery and—' Diggory broke off at the expression on his sister's face: eyebrows raised, lips curled in an incredulous smile. 'You doubt me,' he said eagerly, 'but you will see.'

'Well, you may yet surprise me,' said Amelia, laughing. 'But now, on to more pressing matters – what are we to do about your face? Should we try to get you home early or wait until the party disperses? Papa will be very cross. I expect a full hour's lecture on the importance of propriety and the appearance of gentility.'

Diggory groaned. 'I shall bear it the best I can. When I have an earl for a father-in-law, Papa will never dare lecture me on gentility again.'

~

The guests departed slowly. First the Palmers, then Mr Duckfield and Mr Ashpoint – the younger Ashpoints had disappeared earlier in the evening, no doubt because Mr Diggory had drunk too much wine. Sir Frederick bowed his goodbyes, and Major Alderton bid Felicia a warm farewell, praising her performance on the pianoforte in terms that made her suspect he knew nothing about music and only thought she looked beautiful when she played – which was, at least, true.

Finally, there was no one left save the Wickfords and the Hursts. Mr and Mrs Elton remained inside, giving instructions to the servants, while Felicia bid adieu to the Wickfords at the gate. The earl and countess were very gracious about the pleasantness of the evening. Lady Rose looked flushed and said little. Lord Salbridge kissed Felicia's hand and said, slurring, 'You look exceptionally handsome tonight, Miss Elton,' then gave a careless bow and climbed up into the carriage.

Walking back to the house, Felicia paused for a moment at the oak tree, letting the night air cool her. The Hursts were at the door, about to depart. As they walked down the hill towards their carriage, Felicia heard their voices.

'A good evening, Matilda?'

'Better than the calls. I like Miss Ashpoint.'

'I told you that you would. And these things will improve. You know that, don't you? You will grow more used to them, and I will, too. We have nothing to be afraid of.'

'Except—'

'Nothing, Matilda. Listen to me.' Here his voice grew gentle, solemn almost.

Felicia shrank further into the shadows. It was impossible to cross back to the house without drawing notice to herself, but she felt horribly embarrassed. It was all very well to know that people must and did marry, but to hear Mr Hurst address his wife in such a low, intimate voice was rather shocking. And it was highly improper to listen in on private conversations.

'Matilda,' Mr Hurst was saying, 'who can touch us now?'

'But if someone should find out—'

'I have no such fears. The world may turn their backs on us, and I would not care. We have each other. What does the rest matter?'

'But your position—'

'I am happy to occupy it as long as it suits us. No longer. We are safe, Matilda. We have nothing to fear.'

They had reached their carriage. Felicia heard the door shut, followed by the sound of wheels on gravel. She stepped out from the shadow of the oak tree and watched the horses pull off into the darkness.

VOLUME TWO

August 1841

CHAPTER I

In which Miss Ashpoint is out in the open and Lady Rose hides

'YOU HAVE BEEN SPEAKING OF MRS HURST ALL AFTERNOON,' said Clara, as she and Amelia walked the long path up to Tadrock Point. 'Ought I to be jealous?'

Amelia laughed. She caught up with Clara and looped her arm through hers, pulling her close. They were both in light summer dresses and boots, but they were warm from the walk, and she could feel Clara's arm pressed hot against her skin. 'That would be very unnecessary,' she said. 'I only meant that she is an agreeable and sensible woman. You liked her, too, you know, when we met at the bookseller's.'

'True. I am glad he married somebody sensible.'

'They are coming to tea at Ashpoint Hall on Saturday, with the children. I invited them, which I suppose was rather bold of me, but Papa is delighted to think of all the gossip he will gain.' She smiled. 'You can join us, if you like.'

'Not on Saturday,' said Clara. 'I have promised my father to help him sketch up a design for this new veranda of Sir Frederick's, and that is the first day he has time to attend to it.'

Amelia frowned. 'Your father works you too hard.'

'Nonsense,' came the reply, along with a faint smile. Clara's arm loosened from Amelia's, and she missed the pressure at once. 'Why should I not work hard for him? The business feeds us both. And I like it well enough, but – oh, I wish . . .'

'What?'

Clara paused, wind in her hair, her skirts blown against her. They were nearing the top of Tadrock Point, and the path had faded into mud and tangled grass. It was not a walk Felicia Elton would have felt herself able to make with dignity, especially not in the heat of the summer, but it was Amelia and Clara's favourite.

'Oh, I hardly know,' said Clara. She shrugged. 'What would you do,' she asked abruptly, 'if we were men?'

'If we were men?' repeated Amelia.

'Yes. I mean—' Clara swallowed. 'If I were a man, I think I would be an architect.' She said this very earnestly, and Amelia was surprised to hear a touch of something like dissatisfaction in Clara's voice. Clara seemed to hear it herself, for she went on in a lighter tone: 'Yes, I should be an architect. I should like to have a thriving business, a middling fortune, three children and a wife who looked like you.'

'Only looked like me?' Amelia laughed. 'Would she not talk like me, too?'

'Oh no,' said Clara with a calm smile. 'Much more docile.'

Amelia chuckled.

'And if you were a man?'

'Well,' said Amelia, 'I suppose I'd be a writer. I'd live in London, in a small but very fashionable town house, with, say, three servants.'

'No wife?'

'No indeed,' said Amelia.

'Too Greek in temperament, I suppose?'

They were laughing so hard by now that it was difficult to speak. Amelia found Clara's hand, warm and soft, bumps and calluses at the top of her fingers from too much time spent sketching. Her hands were as familiar to Amelia as her own, as every inch of Clara was.

'You and I,' said Clara, 'are atrociously unrespectable.'

'We knew that already.'

Amelia looked at her steadily. She laced her fingers through Clara's and tugged her nearer, so that they stood face to face.

They both stopped laughing. They stood for a moment, close together, hands and arms pressed tight, faces inches apart. Amelia could see Clara swallow. She could feel her breath on her skin. Such a small gap to close.

'Amelia.' Clara's voice was soft, warning.

'What? There is nobody here.'

'There is always somebody somewhere in Wickenshire. We made rules all those years ago for a reason.'

Amelia looked at her. She did not want reasons. She wanted to reach out, pull Clara towards her, press her lips to hers.

And then she thought of Lord Salbridge at Mrs Elton's dinner. *I do not think you like gentlemen at all.* She had not told Clara about that, because it was probably nothing, because she did not want to worry her. But after all, if somebody suspected when they were wise and careful, what was the point of being wise and careful? Better to be reckless and see what the world would throw at them. Better to take risks. Better to dare. Better to kiss on Tadrock Point beneath the vast skies of Wickenshire.

'Clara, aren't you ever tired of rules?'

'Always.' Clara's voice was low, pained, and she turned

her face away, then gently separated their hands and stepped back.

Of course Amelia knew she was right. Of course she did not really want to bear all the dangers the world could throw at them. Of course she did not want Clara to have to bear them. She knew the risks were too great.

And yet—

And yet the secrets, the caution, the constant hold over herself, the constant pulling back – it wearied her; it angered her. It made her want to shout and scream against the world.

'Come on,' said Clara, in a louder voice, a tone of forced cheerfulness, 'we are nearly at the top. Have you any news from London?'

Amelia shook her head, made herself speak. 'Not a word. Lonsdale has promised to send to me as soon as he has a reply. It may be weeks yet.'

There were just a few more yards to the peak of Tadrock Point. When they reached the summit, they stood together, a few feet apart, staring out at the view. The sunlit country-side stretched around them, miles of fields dotted with trees and hedgerows, the river and the odd hamlet breaking up the farmland. Melford looked small at this distance, a hand-ful of grey streets and houses in the endless green.

'Do you know,' said Amelia, 'Mrs Hurst has lived in Prussia and Bohemia.'

Clara laughed. 'I think I *shall* be jealous.'

'Don't be absurd. Only, promise that you will call on her with me some time.'

Clara looked round at her, and Amelia wondered how she must look, with her hair caught in the wind, her bonnet falling off, her petticoat thick with mud. Clara's boots were muddy, too, the ribbon in her hair catching in her bonnet strings, her face aglow in the afternoon sun.

'Very well,' said Clara, with a smile. 'You know I would go anywhere with you.'

～

'Rose? Rose, are you there?'

Lady Rose held her breath. She was tucked in the window seat of the library at Wickford Towers, hiding from her brother.

She had spent many hours of her life hiding from Lord Salbridge. He was eight years her senior, and they had never been on good terms. She held vague memories of younger days when he had enjoyed ordering her about, but he tired of her as soon as she was old enough to ask questions and wise enough to tell their parents when he misbehaved.

Before Rose came out into Society, he had contented himself with ignoring her, but this last year, as they were increasingly thrown together, he had made it abundantly clear that he resented her presence at the same social occasions as himself, that he thought her a bore at dinner parties and an embarrassment at balls. He started speaking to her once more: he would remind her how earls' daughters ought to behave, as though she had no mind of her own, and he would tell her, time and time again, that nobody cared about her stupid plants and that nobody would have borne her company for a moment if she were not the daughter of an earl.

To be actively sought by Salbridge could mean only trouble.

She kept motionless, tried to control her breathing, clutched her book.

The curtain to the window seat was wrenched back, and there was her brother, looking down at her, his lip curled in distaste. Rose started. Her book fell to the floor with a thud, and she forced herself to pick it up, to pretend it was nothing.

'Were you looking for me?' she asked, with an effort at ease she did not feel.

Salbridge glared. 'Impertinence does not suit you, Rose.'

She stood up, and though he was a great deal taller than her, it felt better than sitting down. She held her book to her chest as though it might help her and tried to fill her expression with greater courage that she felt.

'You needn't look so afraid,' said Salbridge with a cold laugh. 'I only wanted to speak to you.'

'What about?'

He paused, and then something like a smile – a sad, pitying smile – crept over his face. 'Listen here, Rose – you ought to stay away from Diggory Ashpoint.'

She felt the colour rush into her cheeks. She made herself speak, tried to keep her voice steady, to let her anger overrule her fear. 'If you are about to give me a lecture on titles and blood, I shall not listen. Do you think I am not capable of judging for myself?'

'I think,' said Salbridge, with complete composure, 'that you are young and naive. I know Diggory Ashpoint a great deal better than you do.'

Rose said nothing. She knew Diggory; she certainly knew that he was nothing like her brother. What a surprise it had been, the first time she was placed beside Diggory at a dinner party, to find him something entirely different from what she had always assumed. He was altogether gentler and less certain of himself than she had expected, and where Salbridge sneered at her and so many others dismissed her, Diggory listened to her, talked to her, looked at her as though she were really there.

Salbridge was smiling again, that insincere smile. 'I know you think him fond of you,' he said, 'but you cannot really believe he is in earnest. He is only having a little fun.' He paused, looking down at her. 'Seriously, now, Rose – why on earth would anybody want to marry you?'

Rose flinched.

She told herself that she would not rise to it. She would not listen to her brother's words. She would think of Diggory in the hall at Ludwell Manor, the way he had smiled when he said her name.

'Stay away from him,' Salbridge repeated. 'Do not listen to a word he says. For your own good. Do you understand?'

Rose swallowed hard, pushed down her anger. 'Yes,' she said. 'I do.'

CHAPTER II

In which Miss Elton plays a sonata

DIGGORY HAD BEEN WALKING THE STREETS ALL MORNING. It was market day, and he had been in great hopes that Lady Rose and her mother might come into Melford, as they often did, and that he might get to speak to her. But a heavy shower of summer rain seemed to be keeping everyone away. Apart from a brief glimpse of Anne Palmer hurrying into the bookseller's and Miss Waterson and Miss Maddon sheltering in the greengrocer's, Diggory had seen no one he knew for hours. Despite his umbrella, he was soaked through, but he was determined to walk until he saw Rose – or until the shops shut.

Since Friday, he had been in a state of considerable excitement, wavering between outlandish joy and anxious despair. Lady Rose and he were engaged. (Although, *were* they engaged? He kept replaying her *maybe* in his mind to be sure her tone meant exactly what he had thought.) Lord Salbridge and he were no longer friends – all that was at an end forever. His life had been turned upside down, and all he could think of was Rose, Rose, Rose.

He was strolling along Grange Street for the fifteenth time when he spotted the Wickford carriage rolling through the mud. He stood back, sheltering in a shop doorway, feeling very warm and very nervous, as Lady Wickford and Lady Rose stepped out of the carriage.

The countess walked briskly up to the dressmaker's, umbrella held over her head. Rose followed, but as she did so, she looked over her shoulder. She saw Diggory, and he felt himself smile as Rose beamed at him.

Diggory stood beneath his umbrella and watched through the window as Lady Rose joined her mother at the counter. It was enough, he thought, for her to look at him like that. If he did not manage to speak to her today, so be it; he would wait until she came out regardless. He would wait a long time, in any weather, for the chance of such another smile.

And then, when five minutes had passed, the bell above the shop door rung abruptly, and Lady Rose stepped out.

She came quickly towards Diggory, glancing once over her shoulder to check if anybody was looking. But in the torrent of rain, very few people passed by.

'We haven't long,' Rose said quickly, as she came up by his side and began to walk, leading them further from the shop. 'I told Mama I was going to the milliner's for some ribbon, but she will come after me if I am not back soon.' She glanced round at Diggory, a shy smile spreading over her face. 'This is a lucky chance,' she said, 'for I have been longing to see you.'

Diggory beamed at her. 'It is not really luck,' he said, 'for I have been walking up and down all day, hoping you might come into town.'

Rose laughed. Her cheeks were reddening, and she bit her lip. 'It is not so great a chance on my side either, for I asked Mama if she would take me into Melford today – just so that I might look for you.'

They stopped walking. Diggory turned to face her, holding his umbrella so that it sheltered her more than him.

'I have so much to say to you,' he said, 'that I do not know where to begin.'

'Nor I.'

Diggory looked at her, and she looked back. What a thing it was, to stand in the middle of the street in the summer rain with Rose looking at him. He felt shaky with happiness.

'On Friday,' he began, 'you did – when you said *maybe*, you did mean – that is—'

'Yes,' said Rose quickly. 'Of course I meant yes.'

'Right.' Diggory swallowed. If he went on feeling this happy, he thought he might start to cry. 'Do you think your family will . . . ?'

'I don't know.' Rose's voice was quiet, almost a whisper. 'You will have to go to Papa, but – oh, not yet. I must think over what is best. My brother is—' She stopped, as if a new thought struck her, and looked closely at Diggory's face. He was suddenly much more aware of the faint bruise still present around his nose. 'Are you all right?' she asked. 'On Friday, my brother didn't – hit you?'

'It was not so very bad,' said Diggory. And then, because he could say such things now, he said, 'It was worth it.'

Rose laughed, almost tearfully.

'Are *you* all right?' he asked.

'He has been trying to – to turn me against you.' Her voice shook. 'He has been trying to tell me that you are not serious about me.'

Diggory stood aghast. 'Rose,' he said urgently, 'you must know – surely, you must know that—'

'I know,' she said. 'I trust you. My brother has never been – kind to me.'

There was something in her tone, her voice, in the look on her face, that made Diggory know she meant more than that. He felt a wave of rage, of despair.

'I am done with him,' he said. The rain was falling harder now, but he did not seem to feel it. He was thinking of Salbridge, of how long he had listened to him, looked up to him. They had known each other for so many years, and he supposed he had been flattered, as a boy, to be the chosen companion of the son of an earl – but nothing, he thought, could excuse his blindness.

'You were always too good for him.' Rose glanced back over her shoulder, towards the dressmaker's. 'I had better go,' she said. 'Listen – when can we meet? If I say I am simply riding, I can get away from home for a time. There is a clearing in the woods, between Wickford and Ashpoint Hall – up near Cobnar's Farm. Do you know where I mean?'

'I do. Tomorrow?'

'Noon?'

Diggory nodded quickly. 'I shall be there.'

'Good.' Rose looked up at him, her smile radiant. 'I have to go,' she said.

She looked over her shoulder, then, finding the street empty, reached out and pressed his hand quickly in hers before turning and hurrying away.

Meanwhile, as rain fell beyond the windows of Ludwell Manor, Felicia Elton was attempting to play the first movement of Schubert's Piano Sonata No.16 in A minor. Her fingers skimmed the notes, back and forth between pianissimo and forte, quick quavers and chords that took up every finger – and all the while Monsieur Brisset sat quietly at her side, staring at the keys as though he could not hear the voices coming from next door.

On the other side of the wall, Felicia's parents were arguing over her prospects. Today's grievance was that Sir Frederick had not called lately; Mrs Elton blamed her husband for not inviting him to do so at the dinner on Friday. As her mother's voice rose again, Felicia played her staccato chords very hard and took full advantage of the marked fortissimo.

She could hear her father saying something in that low, calm way that infuriated her mother. She caught the word 'lessons' and heard her mother's sharp's reply: 'What is music for, save to gain the girl a husband? And now, when a promising suitor—'

'*Promising?*' Felicia heard her father snap.

Felicia played a loud chord with her left hand, then ploughed on, despite Monsieur Brisset's whispered, 'Mezzo piano, Miss Elton.'

'He is a baronet!' her mother cried in the next room.

The piece returned to its first motif for the climax, and Felicia played it softly, gracefully, beautifully. And all this, this practice and strain and care, all this glorious sound – was it really for nothing but to gain her a husband?

'Do not forget to keep those grace notes steady,' said Monsieur Brisset. He tapped it out for her, left hand and right, fingers on his knees. Something about it saddened Felicia. This great man, for whom music was like breathing, who played with such skill and earnestness – it pained her to see him turn a blind eye to her parents' behaviour as though he were nothing more than a good servant. Even her maid, Sarah, was looking rather uncomfortable, though she had often heard this kind of row before.

As Felicia played on, her mother continued her tirade about title and respectability, declaring that the relations of the Marquis of Denby were not to be sullied, and the only words she caught of her father's reply were 'money', 'land' and 'debt'.

Felicia wished Monsieur Brisset would comment, look at her, anything. But he only told her to play a different piece – a louder one.

She played slowly, loud and mournful, flats and sharps and clashing notes. She missed a bar, and Monsieur Brisset did not correct her. She did not look at him.

'And who would *you* have Felicia marry?' she heard her mother cry. 'Tell me, Mr Elton, *who*?'

'She is nineteen,' her father replied. 'There will be suitors enough.'

Felicia played her semiquavers as rapidly she could. The music grew louder.

A sudden pianissimo. Her mother's sharp voice could be heard clearly, rising with every sentence in her own crescendo. 'And how are we to get to London to find these suitors when you say we can no longer afford it? And nineteen, you say, as though nineteen were nothing. People must know we are not as rich as we once were. Felicia's greatest attractions are her youth and beauty. If we leave it too long, both will fade and no one will have her.'

Felicia flinched and missed her note. A moment of discordance, and then her hands left the keys. She sat in silence for a moment, and Monsieur Brisset turned towards her for the first time. He said nothing, but he looked at her, and she was sure that if she glanced up she would see some kind of comfort, a solemn expression on his face, a glimpse of anger on her behalf. But she did not look up, and at last he looked away.

He said, 'Continue from the bottom of the page,' and she did so, lifting her hands to the keys as her father spoke on calmly next door.

This was usually her favourite part of the piece, moments of brightness, the hint of a major chord. During a quiet passage, she caught her mother say, in a tone of disgust, 'Major Alderton!' And then, between steady quavers, after further muffled conversation, her mother cried, 'That *person* will never wed a daughter of mine.'

The next thing Felicia heard was her father shouting, 'You mustn't stand in my way, Sophronia!'

Felicia played on, moving through the key change with scarcely a breath. The major chords grew bitter. The room next door grew quiet. Felicia played on, growing louder even when she was not meant to, playing faster and faster, her hands across the keys like wind across grass.

She reached the final cadence. She played the notes heavily, majestically, and left her fingers on the keys for a long time after the notes faded.

They sat there for some moments in silence.

'I think today's lesson is at an end,' said Monsieur Brisset at last.

Sarah rose from her seat in the corner to open the music-room door.

Felicia looked up at Monsieur Brisset as he closed the lid of the pianoforte and rose to his feet. He was a tall man, imposing when he wished to be, handsome in his way. He said, 'You played very well today, Miss Elton.'

Then he quitted the room, and Felicia stared at the space he left behind.

CHAPTER III

In which the Hursts come to tea

ON SATURDAY AFTERNOON, THE DOORS BETWEEN THE morning room and the best parlour at Ashpoint Hall were thrown open to form one long room. The tables were set with fine china teacups, and the settees had been thoroughly dusted. Laurie had brought up armfuls of his favourite toys: a smart new doll, a few spinning tops and marbles, an army of little soldiers and a grand toy theatre were all tidily arranged in one corner.

Amelia was lounging on a settee, waiting for her father to tell her to sit in a more ladylike position – it was bound to happen at any moment. Beside her, Diggory was cheerfully asking Laurie about the various toys. Ada was standing hesitantly by the piano, wondering aloud what she could play to entertain the Hursts. Their father was gazing out of the window, watching for the arrival of their guests.

'Ah,' came the sudden exclamation, a ripple of excitement in his voice, 'the carriage has come through the gates.' He turned back towards his family. 'Amelia, sit up properly. Ada, leave the music. Everybody, maintain composure and do not forget civility. Remember the Hursts and the Robertses are our guests today and . . .'

Amelia stopped listening. She rolled her eyes at Diggory, and he grinned back.

'. . . and above all, do not forget that four out of our five guests are still new to the neighbourhood. It behoves us to welcome them kindly, and—'

He was cut off, mid-flow, by the opening of the parlour door, the appearance of one of the footmen and the announcement of 'Mr Hurst, Mrs Hurst, Master Roberts, Miss Roberts and Master George Roberts.'

And then there they were: Mr Hurst in his usual blue frock coat, smiling broadly; Mrs Hurst, in a pale print gown, holding Master George on her hip; the elder children following behind. Eleanor and George were dressed smartly in white frocks, while John wore a neat blue skeleton suit. In the hurry and flurry of good afternoons, Amelia saw Eleanor nudge John and point towards Laurie's toys; the two of them stared, wide-eyed, at the paper theatre.

Seats were taken as tea was brought; plates of dainties appeared while chatter filled the room. Within less than ten minutes, Laurie and Ada were settled amongst the toys, showing each in turn to the Roberts children. Mr Hurst was sitting beside Diggory, and Mrs Hurst was between Amelia and her father. Amelia watched as he plied Mrs Hurst with tea and questions.

'And you have lived abroad, I think Amelia said?'

'Yes.'

'It must feel strange, being settled once more in England.'

Mrs Hurst hesitated. 'Yes. And I have chiefly lived in cities and towns on the Continent, so the countryside is . . . different.' She hesitated, and Amelia thought again that Mrs Hurst did not seem to like speaking about herself.

'How are you finding the new Edward Bulwer novel?'
Amelia asked brightly.

Despite her father's slight frown, this was more success-
ful, and Mrs Hurst seemed to relax as she answered.

After half an hour of talk and tea – by which time Laurie's
toys were entirely in disarray – Eleanor and John came shuf-
fling up to their mother and asked quietly if she thought
they would be allowed a tour of the house.

Mrs Hurst glanced at her husband, then towards Amelia
and Mr Ashpoint. Amelia smiled.

'I think,' said Mrs Hurst to the children, 'that perhaps if
you ask Miss Ashpoint here *very* nicely, she might show you
around.'

'Oh, would you, please?' asked Eleanor.

'Please,' echoed John.

Amelia laughed. 'Of course.'

There was a moment's debate about whether Mrs Hurst
would go with them – but then Georgy managed to fall over
in his excitement to reach a new toy, and it took the combined efforts of Mr and Mrs Hurst and Laurie's doll to
comfort him. In the end, Amelia and the two elder Roberts
children set off alone.

She led them through the gallery, the green sitting room,
the blue sitting room, the drawing room and the music
room. Eleanor and John looked and stared and appeared to
be trying very hard not to touch anything. They did not
seem much inclined to talk, so Amelia told them stories
about the rooms and furnishings, where various items had
been acquired, how she and Diggory had used them for
mischief as children, which nooks were Ada and Laurie's
favourites.

'And beneath this table,' said Amelia as they passed into

the library, 'I once hid for a whole day and night. Nobody could find me. I took supplies with me – a cake I found in the kitchen and seven books.'

'What happened then?' asked Eleanor.

'I was discovered at last by Laurie, who was quite a baby – even younger than your brother George is now. He crawled in to join me, then began to cry and spoilt all my plans.'

The children laughed, and Amelia smiled.

'What a lot of books you have,' said John.

'My mother loved books very much, and my siblings and I are all fond of reading. You like to read, too, I know, for I saw you in the bookseller's.'

The children nodded but said nothing.

Amelia crossed the room, pulled open the door to the study and led the children inside. They walked forwards eagerly, then came to a stop in front of the globe, peering down at the countries of the world. Eleanor turned it with a hesitant finger.

'You are both great adventurers, I know,' said Amelia. 'Can you show me where you have lived?'

The children hesitated, then began to puzzle over the continent of Europe. They spoke softly to each other, fingers darting from one place to the next: first Prussia, then France, the Italian Lakes.

'That's not right,' she heard Eleanor mutter.

'It is, it is,' said John. 'Papa showed us on the map, remember?'

Eleanor flinched and froze. She looked at John – Amelia could not make out the girl's expression from where she stood, but she saw John swallow. Both of their hands fell to their sides.

Amelia watched them carefully. She thought of her

mother's death, ten years ago: how her father had sunk beneath his grief, not eating, not sleeping, wandering the rooms in an endless, aimless march; how Diggory had wept for what felt like weeks; how Amelia had bolted herself in the library and refused to see anyone but Clara. Ada had been five, the same age Eleanor must have been when the Roberts children lost their father, if Melford's gossip was to be believed. Ada did not really understand what had happened at first; she was unable to make sense of the fact that their mother had been replaced with a small, squalling new brother who was not yet old enough to play with. Every time she asked Amelia and Diggory when Mama was coming home, it made everything so much worse.

For a few years, there had been speculation amongst the gossips of Melford that Mr Ashpoint might remarry – but he had never shown the slightest inclination to look for a new wife, and Amelia was rather glad of it. She could not imagine what it must be like for these children, to lose their father, to see him now replaced with Mr Hurst, to find their lives entirely uprooted.

'You must miss your father very much,' Amelia said gently.

The children turned and stared at her. Eleanor seemed pale. She looked at John, and John looked at her.

'Papa was very kind,' said Eleanor. She said it strangely, almost stiffly – not with the sorrow Amelia had expected from her reaction to John's very mention of their father. Amelia peered at her, trying to make out her expression, but Eleanor only looked away.

John asked abruptly, 'May we go back to Mama now, please?'

So Amelia walked back to the parlour, the children

following a step or two behind. They murmured to each other as they went, not in English this time but in a language Amelia did not know – Italian, perhaps, or Spanish. When she turned to look at them, they ceased speaking at once, and both looked very grave.

She thought of Mrs Hurst's hesitance to talk about her past, her pauses mid-speech, the children's odd manner when they spoke of their father. She wondered what Mrs Hurst's first marriage had been like, what sort of man Mr Roberts might have been.

~

Diggory was sitting on the floor with Georgy and Laurie and the toy theatre when Amelia and the other children came back into the room. The paper dolls were getting married – which had been Diggory's idea, for he had thought of nothing but Rose and weddings for a week. Rose loved him, and that was everything. He hardly knew what the future held; of course, Salbridge was against him, but ultimately it would all depend on the earl and countess, and on how generous an allowance his own father was prepared to make him. Rose and Diggory had discussed the problem at length in the clearing near Cobnar's Farm on Thursday, and in an attempt to show that he could be responsible, Diggory had spent all of yesterday at the brewery, doing accounts and writing out orders for his father.

Laurie and Georgy were making the paper dolls dance when Eleanor and John joined them. Diggory turned to see Amelia reclaim her seat beside Mr and Mrs Hurst, and within a few moments they were all talking about books. Ada was at the pianoforte, playing the piece she had been practising for days with an air of great concentration and trying to appear every inch the young lady.

'Had you ever been to Wickenshire before, Mrs Hurst?' Mr Ashpoint was saying, trying to steer the conversation away from literature and back to the Hursts themselves.

'No, never. It is a pleasure to see it at last.'

'The two of you met in Paris, I suppose?'

Diggory looked around to see Mr and Mrs Hurst exchange glances. 'No,' said Mrs Hurst. 'In Richmond.'

Mr Ashpoint smiled. 'I only thought, as you are so well travelled and Mr Hurst used to live there—'

'I have not been back to Paris since my father died,' said Mr Hurst. 'We met in Richmond.' He looked once more towards his wife. 'We spoke of our travels on the Continent, of course,' he said slowly. 'We became acquainted by comparing notes.'

Diggory turned back to the children. Georgy was mumbling a series of indistinct syllables that may have been the marriage ceremony, and Eleanor had picked up Laurie's tin soldiers and was making them invade the theatre. Laurie and John were throwing spinning tops at it in the place of cannonballs. Diggory feared the game had got away from him.

Then came the noise of voices outside and the door opened abruptly. The company all looked up, and Diggory turned to see William, the footman, with Lonsdale at his side.

William bowed and looked anxiously at Mr Ashpoint. 'If you please, sir—'

'I am sorry to disturb you,' said Lonsdale, cutting over him in a quick, urgent tone, 'for I know you have company, but there has been an accident, and I thought—'

Mr Ashpoint was on his feet immediately, all thoughts of gossip clearly forgotten. 'What sort of accident? Is anybody hurt?'

Lonsdale gave one glance towards the children, as though to check they were not listening. 'John Parcels is in a bad way,' he said, 'and Sam Fedmouth and Oliver Magner have burns to their hands. The doctor is already with us and is hopeful, but . . .'

Diggory winced.

'What happened?' asked his father.

'Some pipework cracked overhead in the mash room – not badly enough to collapse, but enough to leak. It was the same pipe we repaired last month, but further down. Parcels was beneath, and Fedmouth and Magner tried to stop it before they fetched me.'

'Dear God.' Mr Ashpoint raised a hand to his forehead, and Diggory knew this was serious by the faint tremor in his father's fingers. 'I had better come at once. Mrs Hurst, Mr Hurst, you will excuse me, I know.'

'Of course,' said Mr Hurst, and his wife nodded her sympathy.

Lonsdale gave them each a quick bow and then glanced around the room. His eyes lingered for a second on Amelia. Diggory saw it. Mrs Hurst saw it, too – Diggory saw her catch Lonsdale's hesitant expression, his sudden swallow. His father did not seem to notice it; even Amelia hardly seemed to do so.

'We had better make haste,' said Mr Ashpoint.

Diggory stood up before he quite knew what he was doing. 'Can I help?'

His father looked at him. There was a flicker of surprise

in his expression – and then something like gratitude. 'Come if you will,' he replied.

And then Lonsdale and Mr Ashpoint were filing out of the door, and Diggory was following close behind.

~

Mr Ashpoint, Lonsdale and Diggory hurried down the long path that stretched through the gardens of Ashpoint Hall to the brewery. Mr Ashpoint questioned Lonsdale as they went – quick, direct enquiries given quick, direct answers. There was no time for panic, for blame. By the time they reached the towering buildings of the brewery, Mr Ashpoint was master of the situation, if not quite master of himself.

The brewery felt oddly quiet. The usual whirr of the steam engine was absent, and the endless clicks and clanks of machinery no longer emanated from the central tower. In the courtyard, some were carrying on with their usual tasks – one lad was stacking up a dray with bottles, while a man filled buckets of water from the handpump. Others were gathered around the door to the tower, peering in and up with hesitant curiosity, and several workers stood around the entrance to the supper-house, where Lonsdale and the doctor had moved the three injured men. They stepped aside to let Mr Ashpoint, Lonsdale and Diggory through.

Magner was sitting up now, his wounds dressed, and Fedmouth sat cross-legged on one of the tables, bandaged hands held palm up, tears in his eyes. Parcels lay on his side on another table, wincing as the doctor tended to his burns. Mr Ashpoint could see the raw red of his skin at the side of his head, could see where some of his hair had come away.

It might have been much worse, Mr Ashpoint told himself, but it did not stop the pang of guilt, the anger at himself that such a thing had happened here.

After ascertaining the situation from the doctor, he went to each man in turn, asking after their injuries. Magner was bearing up well, but Fedmouth could not stop crying. He was muttering about his hands, about missing pay, and he barely seemed to hear Mr Ashpoint's reassurances. Parcels was clearly suffering too greatly to take in much of what was said to him, and in the end, Mr Ashpoint could do nothing but leave him in the doctor's hands.

When he turned from his workers, he saw Diggory and Lonsdale standing at the edge of the room, talking together in low, quick voices. Lonsdale was explaining what had happened once more, in slower, clearer terms, while Diggory listened, stopping him if he did not understand a term or know exactly what a piece of machinery was for. He looked pale and grave, his eyes moving every now and then towards the injured men with a kind of awed horror. Mr Ashpoint saw him swallow and try to steel himself.

'Diggory,' Mr Ashpoint said in an undertone as he approached his son, 'will you stay here? Lonsdale and I had better look at the tower, but why don't you remain? Talk to the men – Fedmouth most. He needs it. Give what little comfort you can. He has two girls – five and seven years old. Ask him about them. Distract him. Understood?'

Diggory nodded once. 'Of course,' he said, and Mr Ashpoint watched as he crossed the room, as he heaved himself up onto the table beside Fedmouth and began to speak.

'Lonsdale,' said Mr Ashpoint, as the two of them headed back into the courtyard, 'when the doctor is content that the men are well enough to leave, will you ask Harris to fetch one of the drays to help them home? Five pounds each, and orders not to return to the brewery for a fortnight at least – and even then, only if the doctor sanctions it. Tell him to see all three again tomorrow – at the brewery's cost, of course.'

'Certainly.'

Inside the tower, where the accident had occurred, the heat was worse than normal. Together, Mr Ashpoint and Lonsdale climbed the wooden stairs up to the mash room. He could see it at once – the long crack in one of the pipes overhead, leading up to the largest mash tun, the thin trail of hot liquor oozing down from it, sometimes in drips, sometimes in a steady train. Several barrels had been placed below to catch the leak, but the crack was long and the floor-boards were still soaked.

'We ought to have replaced the whole pipe, not simply repaired what we could see,' said Lonsdale, and his tone was suddenly anxious, vexed. 'I ought to have suggested it.'

'You weren't to know,' said Mr Ashpoint, and he heard his voice shake. 'It is my responsibility – you know that.'

There was a moment's pause. Lonsdale glanced round at him, and his expression seemed to steady. 'Accidents happen,' he said quietly. 'We could not have foreseen it.'

'We shall replace the whole pipe now, at any rate.' Mr Ashpoint sighed. He was thinking of the first time his father had taken him into the brewery, when he was six or seven years old, how he had stared at the towering chaos of wood and metal, the strange mess of pipes, gazing up and up into the heights of the brewery. All that industry and power. All that danger. 'How soon could we do it, do you think?'

'A few days at least – perhaps a week.'

'And how safe is the tower in the meantime?'

Lonsdale hesitated. 'If we block up this pipe, redirect the liquor down the other, into the second mash tun, perhaps—'

Mr Ashpoint was shaking his head. 'Too dangerous – it's all the same age. We had better replace every pipe in the room.' He raised a hand to his forehead. 'Parcels, poor man, looked wretched, and Fedmouth . . . It might have been so much worse.' Mr Ashpoint glanced up at the pipework, dared to take a step closer. Then he looked down at the wet floorboards, the liquid dripping and oozing from the long crack into the barrels. 'How much more will flow through?'

He watched Lonsdale squint, calculate. 'We emptied the cold liquor tank by hand, but I would not let the men bail out the hot tank in case of further accident.'

'Quite right.'

'It was full, though. It will flow down for another few hours at least.'

Mr Ashpoint nodded, glanced upwards. 'And you stopped the engine, of course – will the tank have cooled?'

Lonsdale's expression shifted again. 'Not enough,' he said slowly.

But Mr Ashpoint was shaking his head. 'A few hours is too long – that much liquid will damage the floor beyond repair.' He hesitated, swallowed. He thought of Diggory down in the supper-house, out of his element, trying his best. 'I shan't have any more of my men injured today,' he said, 'but if you fetch me a bucket or two, Lonsdale, I shall deal with the hot tank myself.'

Lonsdale's mouth twitched into a smile – but not, Mr Ashpoint thought, an amused one. If he was not mistaken, he had managed to impress his foreman a little.

'Yes, sir. I will help you, if I may?'

'If you are happy to take the risk, please do.'

Lonsdale nodded. Mr Ashpoint watched as he took off his jacket and rolled up his sleeves, and headed down the wooden stairs to fetch what was required.

Despite everything, Mr Ashpoint thought, despite the smart waistcoat and the silver watch chain and the at times infuriating manners, Lonsdale was really not so bad a fellow at all.

CHAPTER IV

In which Miss Ashpoint offers some advice

'SO YOU SEE,' AMELIA WAS SAYING, 'I HAVE COME TO THE conclusion that her first marriage must have been an unhappy one. Her hesitancy to speak of it, the children's strange reaction – it is all quite clear.'

'Do you not think,' replied Clara, 'that you are turning Mrs Hurst into one of your adventure stories?'

'Certainly not. I am judging by the evidence of my own eyes. If you had seen the children's reactions when they realized they had mentioned their father . . . Eleanor looked almost terrified.'

They were on one of their regular rambles, heading back to Melford from Tadrock Point. The air was warm and humid, the sky a wispy grey.

'Well,' said Clara, 'and if she *has* had a hard life, what business is it of ours? Amelia, you are nearly as bad as your father.'

Amelia pretended to be very deeply wounded. 'I am *not*!'

Clara laughed. 'Admit it – you are a gossip.'

'I am not a gossip! I would never speak to anyone but you about such things. I am only trying to puzzle her out. Besides, I like her. And if she *has* had a hard life, if she is in need of a friend, then – well, perhaps I could help her.'

Amelia looped her arm through Clara's, felt Clara's warmth pressed to her side. 'When you call at Radcliffe with me next week, you will judge for yourself.'

They walked on for a little longer in silence, their boots bringing up dust, their arms pressed together. They crossed the stile from a field onto a bridleway, and Amelia held out her hand to help Clara over, let their fingers press together firmly for a moment. Then onwards, down the path.

'Look,' said Clara suddenly, squinting into the distance. 'Is that your brother?'

Amelia followed Clara's gaze. There, across a stretch of crops and hedgerows, was Diggory. He stood at the edge of a wheat field, leaning back against an oak tree, and beside him was Lady Rose. Diggory had his arm around her waist.

Clara raised her eyebrows. 'They look rather . . . intimate.'

Amelia spluttered. 'He finally managed to propose to her,' she whispered, 'but it is all a great secret for now.'

'It does not *look* much like a secret.'

Diggory and Rose were now kissing very enthusiastically.

Amelia put her head in her hands. 'I know my brother is a complete fool, but I really thought Lady Rose had more sense.'

Clara stifled a laugh. 'What they need,' she said softly, 'are *rules*.'

'How can they be so careless? Anybody might see.'

'Anybody might indeed,' said a voice from behind them.

Amelia and Clara both turned at once. Mr Lonsdale was standing between them, looking in the same direction, an expression of faint amusement on his face. He must have come down one of the other lanes, and Amelia was vexed that she had not heard his approach. She glanced sideways at Clara; she had said nothing, really, only a

mention of rules that Lonsdale could not possibly understand, and Amelia's answer had only spoken of Diggory
and Rose – but still, it startled her. She might so easily have
said something else.

'My, my . . .'

'They are engaged,' said Amelia quickly, for any other
assumption was worse, 'but – well, it is a secret.'

'Well, you may rely on me.' Still, Lonsdale looked rather
too amused for Amelia's liking.

She turned and began to walk down the lane, attempting
to move them all to somewhere they could not see Diggory
and Rose. Clara followed, and Lonsdale fell into step with
them.

'Where have you been walking to, Mr Lonsdale?' asked
Clara.

'Radcliffe.' He glanced back over his shoulder. 'I have an
aunt in the village there. She is – unwell. Your father gave
me leave for the morning. I am on my way back to the brewery now. Are you going to the house?'

'Amelia is,' replied Clara, 'but I heading back to Melford –
I have promised to help my father at his work this afternoon.'
A few yards later, she peeled off onto the path into the town.
'I shall see you at dinner tomorrow, Mr Lonsdale?'

'Oh yes. And my best wishes to your father.'

Clara smiled and looked towards Amelia. She held her
gaze for a moment, nodded, said, 'Goodbye,' in the lightest
tone imaginable and walked off down the lane. Amelia
watched her go.

As Amelia and Lonsdale turned their steps towards
Ashpoint land, he began talking about the accident at the
brewery, about how the men were doing, how long they had
to wait for new equipment. Amelia tried to listen, but her

thoughts were still on Diggory and Rose in the field, their careless stupidity.

'Look, Mr Lonsdale,' she said when he finished, 'this matter of Diggory and Lady Rose . . . They have not spoken to my father yet, nor to Lord Wickford. You must promise not to say anything – you must swear.'

'Certainly,' said Lonsdale. The smile returned to his face. 'I suppose this is why we have had the pleasure of seeing much more of Mr Diggory at the brewery lately – a sudden need to prove to your father that he is mature enough to be married.'

Amelia grimaced. That was undoubtedly true. 'You will not say anything to my father, will you?' she asked, more urgently this time. 'I know Diggory's position at the brewery must be . . . vexing for you, when you are so much better qualified to assist my father, but please do not—' She broke off, struggling for the words.

'Do not what?' asked Lonsdale sharply. He was looking at her now with dawning understanding and rising anger. 'What do you mean by that, Miss Ashpoint? Do you imagine I would repeat your brother's secret to your father in the hope of gaining his good opinion and shaking his faith in his son?'

Amelia flushed. That was more or less what she *had* meant, but it had not seemed quite so accusatory in her mind. She liked Lonsdale well enough – he was interesting and witty, and he was helping her with her novel, for which she was truly grateful – but she knew he was ambitious, and she could not tell what form that ambition might take.

'Is that what you think of me?' said Lonsdale. He sounded – horrified almost.

Amelia winced. 'I am sorry. I only meant—'

'I know what you meant,' said Lonsdale, 'and you have misjudged me most unfairly.' He was staring at her. 'Miss Ashpoint,' he said, in a low whisper, 'do you really think I am that base, that I have so little regard for common decency, even passing over my regard for your family? Have I not shown myself to be trusted? I have kept *your* secret. I am doing all in my power to further your literary ambition, as is my friend Browne. It is a great favour I have asked him on your behalf, and—'

'You need not list me your merits, Mr Lonsdale. I am sorry to have offended you. I only wanted to be sure you would not say anything.'

There was a short silence. 'Of course I won't.' His voice was cold. He looked sideways at her, then looked down. 'I have heard nothing from London, by the way,' he said, in an altered voice. 'I shall inform you as soon as I do. Browne will let me know when he has a reply.'

'Thank you.' It was a very low thank you, and she scowled to think that he had managed to make her feel abashed.

They parted at the end of the next field, Amelia going up to the house, Lonsdale down to the brewery. Their good-byes were quiet, hers as cold as his. She watched him go, still frowning, feeling that perhaps she really was, this once, in the wrong.

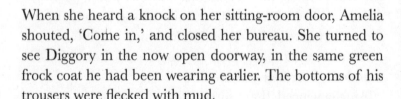

When she heard a knock on her sitting-room door, Amelia shouted, 'Come in,' and closed her bureau. She turned to see Diggory in the now open doorway, in the same green frock coat he had been wearing earlier. The bottoms of his trousers were flecked with mud.

'I say,' he said, closing the door behind him, 'every time I come in here you shut up that bureau as though you had a thousand secrets to hide. Really, Amy, I have no intention of reading your love letters.' He gave a weary shrug. 'Ada said you were looking for me.'

Amelia crossed the room and took a seat in a ladder-back armchair. 'Sit down.'

Diggory snorted. 'You sound like Papa.' Still, with a flourish of his frock coat, he threw himself heavily down on the settee. 'What was it you wanted to talk to me about?'

'Diggory,' she said, 'you must be more careful.'

Her brother looked sharply down at his clothes, as though he expected to see his shirt untucked or some other grave misdemeanour. When nothing struck him, he glanced back at Amelia. 'About what?'

'How many people know about you and Lady Rose?'

'No one but you.'

Amelia folded her hands in her lap. 'After today,' she said slowly, 'two more people know.'

'What? Who?'

'The first is Clara.'

Diggory sniffed. 'Well, I suppose you do tell her everything—'

'I didn't—'

'And she is the sort to keep one's confidences, so I have no real objection. Who is the other person?'

Amelia sighed. 'Mr Lonsdale.'

Diggory raised one eyebrow. 'Goodness.'

'I didn't *tell* him – and nor did I tell Clara. We saw you, this morning, from the lane just outside Melford.'

Diggory's smile was gone. 'They – they saw—'

'What were you thinking? You simply cannot go about

kissing people beneath trees as though it were a perfectly respectable pastime. Why, even if you were openly engaged – even if you were *married* – it would still be thought unseemly behaviour. As it is – well, it is beyond foolish of you both. Even walking together alone would be suspect. For goodness' sake, you must be more *careful*.'

Diggory sat straight upright. 'Oh dear.'

'Lonsdale has given his word not to tell Papa – can you imagine what he would say if he learnt you had kept such a secret from him? Clara, of course, is to be trusted a thousand times over, but who can say that no one else saw you? Diggory, if you are going to carry on a secret love affair, you must have your wits about you. You must meet as indifferent acquaintances or harmless friends in public. Otherwise, you must meet in places where you *know* you will not be disturbed. You must remain calm and unromantic in the presence of others and not allow yourselves to even *feel* that you are lovers until you are entirely and unquestionably alone.'

'I say, Amy, you certainly seem to know a lot about secret love affairs.'

Amelia felt a little queasy and tried to ignore him. 'If you and Lady Rose are to go on in secret, you must be more discreet. You know what little regard I have for propriety, and I haven't the least idea of it being *morally* wrong – but if you continue as you are, you will ruin her reputation and your own. If her father discovers you have been going on all this time without his consent, he will be less likely to give it, and this kind of indiscretion is hardly going to make *our* father give you a larger allowance either.'

'I am sure I have been very unwise,' muttered Diggory, 'but you needn't lecture me. It is very hard, when we so long to see other.'

Amelia flinched. She felt a wave of sudden anger. If he only knew. 'Have a little self-control, Diggory,' she snapped. 'Besides, why *is* your engagement secret?'

Her brother looked rather crestfallen at this. He leant further back into the settee, as if its plump cushions might hide him.

'Why have you not spoken to Lord Wickford yet? It has been a fortnight, and these things are best settled quickly. It is beneath you to trifle with Lady Rose's reputation.'

'I am not trifling!' cried Diggory, shrinking even further into the cushions.

'Then what? Lord Wickford may be an earl, but we are far richer than they are. I know you are worried that Lord Salbridge disapproves, but what can he really do, if his parents consent?'

Diggory emerged a little from the cushions. 'He could make Rose's life a misery,' he said in a low voice. 'He *will* make her life a misery. If I knew I could speak to the earl tomorrow morning and marry Rose tomorrow afternoon and take her out of that house, I might feel easier – but for all I know, we may not be able to marry for months, perhaps years. I shall have to ask Papa to increase my allowance so that I can afford to marry – I am entirely at his disposal. You know he thinks I am reckless and careless and all that. What if he decides I am too young and irresponsible? What then?'

'Why not ask him and find out?'

Diggory shot her a weary look. 'If *you* are concerned about the impropriety of our keeping the engagement from Lord Wickford, imagine what palpitations Papa would suffer with such a secret. I cannot go to Papa until I am ready to go to Lord Wickford, and I cannot go to Lord

Wickford without being certain that I can get Rose away from Salbridge.'

'If Lord Wickford gives his consent, I am sure he can protect you both from his son. Salbridge will be a greater danger to you if he finds out by accident.' Amelia put her hand to her forehead; she felt suddenly very tired. 'Do not live in hiding when you have no need to,' she said softly. 'It is a hard life.'

'I do not mean to hide forever. We have a plan. Listen,' he said, leaning forwards, his elbows on his knees. 'In a few weeks' time, Salbridge is going to stay with a friend of his from Eton. I was supposed to go with him, but – well, that is hardly going to happen now. He will be away for a full month, and while he is gone, we shall ask her father and mine, and pray they are disposed to be generous about money and let us marry quickly. I am trying very hard already to show Papa that I am a reformed sort of fellow – I have been at the brewery every day but today this week – but that is all by-the-by. We must wait until Salbridge is away.'

'A few weeks, then,' said Amelia, with a warmer smile. 'Well, I am glad you have a plan, at least. I shall hold you to it.'

Diggory smiled at her. And then something else flashed across his face. 'Hang on a moment though, Amy – you said that Lonsdale saw me with Rose when you were on the lane to Melford together? And *you* have been taking the high ground with *me*!'

'Oh, really, Diggory. Clara was—'

'Look, I know what you have been saying is very sensible, and I *shall* talk to Lord Wickford as soon as Salbridge leaves, but what I wish to know is: why is it perfectly acceptable for you to walk about with Lonsdale, but if I am seen with Rose, it is the end of everything?'

Amelia folded her arms. 'That is not the same thing at all,' she said. 'We were not alone – Clara was there, as I told you – at first, at least. We met Lonsdale by accident, not by arrangement, and I walked back towards the house with him. That is all. And we were certainly not *kissing*.' She wrinkled up her nose. 'If anyone were to spread rumours about Lonsdale and me, we could simply deny them. You and Lady Rose, as you actually intend to marry, could not. Besides, I have no demonic brother to fear – only an indolent one. And,' said Amelia, with a look of weary triumph, 'when most of Society look at Lonsdale, they see a servant, not a threat. My father's foreman is hardly a scandalous chaperone.'

Diggory looked at his sister for a long time. At last he said, in a solemn voice, 'You know Papa will never stand for it.'

Amelia sat up straight. 'Oh, no, it's not—'

'I can see why you like him,' Diggory went on. 'I see a lot of him at the brewery, and he is a very fine fellow – intelligent and witty and all that. And, Amy, I am so desperately in love with Lady Rose that I'd give my blessing if you were in love with a footman. But when it comes to Papa—'

'Diggory—'

'Where Lonsdale is concerned, his pride is at its height.'

'Diggory, you have completely misunderstood the situation. There is nothing—'

'You don't have to lie to me! I know you are writing love letters every time I come into your sitting room. And I saw the way he looked at you, when he came up to the house to tell us about the accident. And I know you go to Clara's so often because you think you may see him there. You need not lie to me, Amy. I am in love, too – I understand!'

Amelia stared at him, uncertain whether to laugh or to cry. She wished so very, very much that she could tell him everything, that she could sit with her brother and calmly explain that she *was* in love. She wished she could tell him how difficult it was sometimes, the uncertainty, the strangeness, the solitude of secrets. She wished she could tell him that Clara was the greatest person in all the world. And for just a moment, she thought about it, weighed up the chance that Diggory – kind, romantic Diggory, her favourite sibling, Diggory who loved her unconditionally – might understand. It was almost possible.

And then the fear came – the knot of panic in her stomach, the stilling of her heart. A blurry terror of asylums and banishments and enforced separation from Clara. And the more tangible fear of being sunk in his opinion, of losing him.

But if she could not tell him about Clara, she could tell him something else.

'Diggory,' she said, 'you are so entirely *wrong*.' She stood up and hurried towards her bureau. Her hands were trembling as she unlocked it, let the writing surface clatter down, then pulled out a large stack of paper and turned towards Diggory triumphantly. She walked across the room and thrust it at him. 'Read it.'

Diggory was on his feet, trying to push the papers back. 'I don't want to read your love letters! And I must say, quite why Lonsdale is writing you such huge stacks of paper is beyond me. Ought I to be writing this sort of thing to Rose?'

'It is not a *love letter*. Read it.'

With an expression of the utmost distaste, Diggory lifted the papers towards him and read aloud, ' "In the year of eighteen-hundred-and-thirty, a lady by the name of Eliza Wallace turned five-and-twenty." ' He stopped, frowned, looked at his sister. 'What is this?'

'It is my novel,' said Amelia. She wrenched the papers back from him and clutched them tightly to her chest. 'I have not been writing *love letters*; I have been writing stories. Lonsdale has a friend in London who is an author – Mr Browne, the old curate of Radcliffe. Mr Browne has been giving my manuscript to publishers. Lonsdale is not my lover, Diggory – he is my middleman.'

Diggory stared at her for a few moments. Then he sat down heavily on Amelia's settee. 'So you are not in love with Lonsdale?'

'Not remotely.'

'And you really wrote all that?'

Amelia nodded.

'Gosh,' said Diggory, and in his shock, he seemed to forget his usual flippant tone. 'It looks terribly long.'

'It is.'

'What's it about?'

Amelia hesitated. Then, with a burst of relief, she sat down beside her brother, dropped the manuscript between them and turned eagerly towards him. It was something, to speak of this to him – one secret fewer to weigh her down. 'I have called it *The Life and Times of Eliza Wallace*. It is an adventure story, following the life of a poor girl who stows away on a ship to explore the world, and then, when she finally returns to England, she is mistaken for the missing Lady Winifred Allington, who was kidnapped seven years earlier. Seeing an opportunity to make her fortune, she pretends to be Lady Allington, which lands her in all sorts of difficulties.'

'Until,' said Diggory, who was partial to serial novels himself, 'she dances with a very charming man at a ball.'

Amelia pulled a face. 'I should think not! All the men in my novel are scoundrels. As, for that matter, are the women. There will be no happy endings and wedding bells in anything *I* put my pen to.'

Diggory looked down at the manuscript with a combination of fear and curiosity. 'What will Papa think of this?' he asked.

'I do not suppose he would much like a lady novelist in the family. It is perhaps not quite so bad as a brewery, but I hardly think Mrs Elton will forgive *both*. Papa is far too concerned with propriety – which is why I have no intention of telling him about the book. It is being read by publishers under the name of A. A. Oaksharp. That was Clara's idea; I think it mightily impressive. You won't tell Papa, I know.'

'Well, you have kept my secret.'

'Yours will be a shorter secret, I hope, than mine.'

Diggory leant back into the settee. 'You might have told me,' he said at last, in an almost wounded voice.

'I have told as few people as possible. Only Clara and Lonsdale know – and now, you.'

'Well, you may rely on me completely.' He paused. 'Could I – read it?'

Amelia hesitated. 'I suppose so. But it does not leave this room. The only other copy is with Mr Browne in London, and I cannot afford to lose either. I have started another novel, but not even Clara has read the first chapters of that yet.'

'Then I shall read it here,' Diggory declared, reaching for the manuscript.

'I did not mean now!' said Amelia – but her brother had already settled further into the settee, the stack of paper on his lap, a smile spreading across his face.

CHAPTER V

In which Mr Lonsdale revises his opinion

THE FOLLOWING WEDNESDAY, AS THE CLOCKS CHIMED eight, Lonsdale headed towards the brewery gates, Mr Diggory Ashpoint at his side.

It had been a long day. The new pipework had arrived that morning, and after hours of strain and effort, everything was finally in place. Mr Ashpoint had departed earlier in the afternoon to meet a customer near Melcastle, but Lonsdale had remained, along with Mr Diggory and a few others, to carry out checks on the new equipment. At last, Lonsdale was satisfied.

'We shall have no more accidents in the mash room, at any rate,' he said as they neared the gates.

Diggory nodded. 'How are Fedmouth, Magner and Parcels?'

'All right, I think. Magner is determined to be back at work next week. Parcels will need longer, and Fedmouth . . . well, I don't know. I am not sure he will feel at ease in the tower again. I shall suggest to your father that we reassign him.'

'We are in need of another hand in the stables,' said Diggory. 'Roke will be too old to drive the drays soon and had better train somebody else.'

Lonsdale looked around at him, a little impressed.

'What?' asked Diggory.

'Well, sir, you would not have known that a week ago.'

Diggory inclined his head. 'No, I do not suppose I would have done. But, Lonsdale, you really cannot call me "sir" – you are older than me and have a much clearer sense of what you are doing. I shall only ever think you are laughing at me.'

Lonsdale chuckled. 'All right, Ashpoint,' he said. 'Will that do?'

'Perfectly.'

They were out of the gates now, into the lane, and Diggory turned towards Lonsdale, his face all earnestness. 'Listen, Lonsdale, do you think – well, do you think I shall ever be any good at all this?'

'What, brewing?'

'Yes. I am *trying*, but my father said something about how all the best brewers are chemists, and I do not think I am any good at science, and . . .'

Lonsdale laughed. 'You will do fine,' he said.

He had discovered, in this last week or two, that he rather liked Mr Diggory Ashpoint. Having for so long associated him with Lord Salbridge, Lonsdale had at first been wary and made an effort with Diggory only because he was his employer's son. But he was beginning to discover that Diggory Ashpoint without Lord Salbridge was a very different young man to Diggory Ashpoint with Lord Salbridge. He seemed a well-meaning, good-hearted fellow beneath his languor and shiny shoes. And he was not unintelligent – true, Diggory might not make as great a scientist as Mr Ashpoint or himself, but he would make a decent business-man. He was quick enough to pick up the ins and outs of the brewery, thoughtful enough to get to know the workers – and he seemed, finally, to be trying. In the last few weeks,

Diggory had gone from being a rare sight at the brewery to being present every day – not arriving until ten, it was true, but usually staying until Lonsdale left.

'Lonsdale,' said Diggory suddenly, lowering his voice, 'I know that you know about—' He turned somewhat red and glanced around to ensure the lane was empty. 'Well, I know from my sister that you know about my engagement.'

Lonsdale blinked, nodded. He was surprised that Amelia had told Diggory what he had seen last week, and the idea of Amelia and Diggory discussing it made him feel some-how uneasy. He thought of her on the lane to Melford, all but telling him she considered him an opportunist without principles. Was that why she believed he was helping her, in the hope of some advancement of his own?

It stung him more than he cared to acknowledge, even to himself. He had let his guard down, let the careful walls he built around his feelings slip. He had let Brisset's words get into his head.

A year ago, he had barely known Amelia; she had simply been his employer's handsome, witty daughter. Then, he had met and befriended Mr McNeil, who had been over-seeing some building work at the brewery, and he had begun to see Amelia at the McNeils' house, laughing, smiling, shooting witty remarks across the dinner table. And he had begun, vaguely, slowly, to hope. When Amelia had agreed to dance with him at Lady Wickford's ball, he had thought she might merely wish to irritate her father – but when she had asked him to write to Browne in London for her, that was another matter entirely. What he could not work out was: had Amelia asked this of him because she wished for an excuse to bring them into closer contact, or had she asked because she saw him as a friend – or, worse, as a servant?

She had not asked him like she would have asked something of a servant. But nor was her behaviour last week
consistent with her having any respect for him at all.

Better to crush the hope now. Lonsdale believed himself
to be a prudent man – and falling in love with Miss Ashpoint
would definitely not be prudent.

'Nothing is quite settled yet, as you know,' Diggory was
saying, 'and I have not spoken to my father, but I am trying
to prove to him in the meantime that I can be – that I *am* –
responsible and hardworking and – well, that I am no longer
a boy but a man.' He winced. 'But I am so dreadfully afraid
of doing everything *wrong*.'

Lonsdale smiled. He felt a spark of fondness for Diggory.
Perhaps it was not so very strange that his sister was protect-
ive of him. 'You are not doing anything wrong,' he said
gently. 'As far as I can see, you are doing well. Come to the
brewery every day, listen and watch, and do as your father
and I say, and you will learn. You have the brains for it,
Ashpoint, as long as you have the will.'

'I do have the will,' said Diggory. 'Rose has given me
the will, but – well, I am not sure I *do* have the brains. I do
not understand half of what you do about brewing. My
father would have been a great deal better off with you as
a son.'

Lonsdale did not know how to say that he would not be
what he was had he been a son of Mr Ashpoint's. If Diggory
had possessed the will to work for a fortnight or two – well,
Lonsdale had had it since he was ten years old. 'You are sure
to understand it all in time,' he said instead.

'Perhaps,' said Diggory, 'if you teach me.'

Lonsdale laughed. 'I will do my best.'

They had reached the turning now, where one path led

back up to Ashpoint Hall and the other down into Melford, and here they paused.

Lonsdale turned to Diggory. 'I am going to the Lantern to meet my friend Monsieur Brisset, if you are minded to play a hand of cards – that is,' he added, with a faint smile, 'if you do not object to playing with two half-gentlemen like us.'

Diggory laughed. 'I think you are rather more than half a gentleman, Lonsdale,' he said. 'And I should be very glad to come.'

~

Lord Salbridge sat in the corner of the Lantern, playing écarté with Edmund Crayton. It was by no means his favourite game, and Crayton was by no means his favourite companion, but both would have to suffice. At least Crayton put his money down freely, and at least he liked to drink. It was only eight o'clock, but they had both been here for two hours and had already consumed three glasses of port wine and many more of whisky.

Salbridge was wondering, with vague, tipsy intent, if he ought to make Crayton his new Diggory. To be sure, the Craytons were not nearly so wealthy as the Ashpoints, but a banker's son was much the same as a brewer's son, and Edmund Crayton had not, thus far, shown any disinclination to lend him money when asked. And there was no doubt that young Crayton respected him. *He* would not have acted like a girl when shown the stunning features of Grace Abbott. He certainly would never dare to set his cap at an earl's daughter. Nor would Crayton have called Salbridge a scoundrel and failed to apologize even after he had been punched in the face.

Salbridge was finished with Diggory forever. He might as well have somebody else to play cards with.

'. . . and I was telling you, you know, about this girl I met at a ball in London, when I was there with Father on business last month. A jolly pretty girl, she was, too – *excellent* figure.' Crayton made a hand gesture to indicate exactly how the young lady was well-favoured, and Salbridge snorted. 'And I march up to this beauty and say, "Won't you dance?" and she says—'

The door of the lower room opened and in came two young men. The first was Diggory Ashpoint, in a scarlet waistcoat, an auburn frockcoat and cream trousers dotted with stains. The second was Lonsdale, dressed neatly in grey, his top hat in his hand. God save us, Salbridge thought, from upstarts. They were discussing something about the brewery as though it were terribly important. He rolled his eyes.

Salbridge had been hidden from view in his easy chair, but when he leant forwards to attend to the cards, the chatter abruptly ceased. His eyes met Diggory's, and there was a moment's silence. Lonsdale was looking between them with hesitant interest, and Crayton was gazing on in eager anticipation.

Lord Salbridge threw down his cards and claimed the pile of notes on the table – he would have won sooner or later anyway – then stood up very deliberately. 'Crayton, don't you wish they'd reserve the Lantern for *gentlemen*?' he said loudly. 'I am going to the King's Arms – care to join me? At least there we shall *know* to expect low company.'

Crayton sniggered and hastened to stand up. To be sure, he was a puppy, but at least he was an obedient one.

As Salbridge turned towards the door, he glanced at the new arrivals. Lonsdale looked entirely unmoved, but he saw

Diggory's scowl, caught the flush on his cheeks. Good – he had seen that the words were for himself as well as for Lonsdale.

They were taking seats opposite each other now, and as Salbridge stepped out the door and began to climb the stairs, he heard Lonsdale say, 'Ignore him – he never says anything worth listening to.'

In the upper room, Salbridge saw his father at one of the round tables, playing cards with Mr Elton. Salbridge studiously ignored him. As he and Crayton crossed the room, the door opened and in came Major Alderton. He nodded to them. Salbridge did not deign to acknowledge him, but Crayton nodded back – Salbridge would have to teach him better.

He expected Major Alderton to head down to the lower room to join Diggory and Lonsdale, where he would, Salbridge thought, fit in perfectly – dear God, what degrading company he was expected to keep here! – but instead, he was surprised to see Alderton walk up to the table where the two elder men sat and address himself to Mr Elton.

'I beg your pardon, sir, but I wonder if I might have a moment's private conversation with you?'

Salbridge raised his eyebrows. He wondered what the devil a person like *that* could want with Mr Elton – but he was at the door now, and Crayton was stumbling along behind him, and the thought of another drink was more interesting than the dull affairs of other men.

Damn the Lantern. If he could not reign here, he would find somewhere else.

He wrenched the door back and stepped out into the street.

CHAPTER VI

In which cricket is played and tea is drunk

AS AMELIA AND CLARA NEARED RADCLIFFE, THE LANES grew narrower. It was a hot summer's morning, and they were warm with walking. They walked arm in arm, as they always did – the safest way to be close, when they might pretend to cling to one another only for support, not affection. It was as necessary as that, sometimes, Amelia thought: whenever she was weary or restless, she needed Clara's touch to lift her spirits.

They passed the cottages and farms of Mr Hurst's tenants, then the apple orchards and rose gardens of the park itself – and finally, just as the house was nearly in view, they heard voices – cheerful shouts, a muddle of hoorays and cries. They looked at each other and smiled.

As they came to the edge of the orchard, they saw the family playing cricket in the sunshine. Master John was standing, bat in hand, while Mr Hurst bowled. Miss Eleanor had her hands up to catch the ball, while Mrs Hurst, bonnetless, her dress muddy, was waiting to bat on one of the stone benches, an even muddier Master George sitting on her knee. Beside her, to Amelia's surprise, sat Sir Frederick.

Of course she knew Sir Frederick and Mr Hurst were good friends, but she felt faintly vexed to find him here. He looked more at ease than usual: his jacket off, legs stretched out, his fuchsia waistcoat lurid in the sun. Master George was playing with Sir Frederick's hat, trying it on his head and sticking his feet into it, and the young baronet did not appear to mind at all; he was pulling faces at George in response. George giggled back.

Amelia and Clara watched from the trees for a moment as Mr Hurst bowled, as John hit out and began to run, as Eleanor scrambled for the ball. She threw it to her step-father, who missed it, and the ball rolled through the grass to Sir Frederick's feet.

He reached down, picked it up and handed it to little George, who promptly tottered forwards to tap his brother out.

'Out!' cried Mr Hurst. 'Five runs.'

'That's not fair!' cried John. 'I made six. And, Sir Frederick, you are meant to be on *my* team.'

'I don't know what you mean.' Sir Frederick was smiling, feigning an air of nonchalance. 'It was all George – nothing to do with me whatsoever.'

'Oh, you are too slow for Georgy,' said Mrs Hurst. She lifted up her youngest child, kissed his forehead and smiled at John. 'My turn to bat. You will get your six runs next time, John.'

Amelia was just wondering whether they ought to return another day when George, looking up, cried indistinctly, 'Mama – ladies in the trees!' and the cricket players all looked round.

Mr and Mrs Hurst smiled, and Sir Frederick stood up so quickly he almost lost his balance.

Amelia and Clara came forwards together, letting their arms slip apart.

While Mr Hurst nodded and Sir Frederick bowed, Mrs Hurst approached them with a bright smile and reached out to take Amelia's hands in hers. 'I am glad you have come, Miss Ashpoint,' she said gently. 'And Miss McNeil – it is a pleasure to see you again.' She turned back to the children. 'John, Eleanor, George,' she said, 'you remember Miss Ashpoint and Miss McNeil? Say good morning.'

'Good morning,' echoed John and Eleanor together. George hid behind his mother's skirts.

'We are delighted to see you both,' said Mr Hurst.

'And I,' began Sir Frederick, stumbling over his words. 'That is, I did not expect the pleasure today, and it is . . .'

He appeared to have lost his train of thought, and Clara helped him out by saying, 'How are you, Sir Frederick? I hope you received my father's plan for the veranda?'

'Oh, yes, I did – thank you – capital – it is quite perfect. Although I think, Miss McNeil, you are being modest, calling it your father's plan, for my mother recognized your handwriting on parts of it.'

Clara gave a faint smile. 'Oh, I did not do much,' she said.

Sir Frederick hesitated, as though he would like to protest and did not know how. Amelia wondered if he had noticed that Master George was currently dragging his discarded yellow jacket through the grass.

'You have both had a long walk here, in the heat,' said Mrs Hurst. 'Would you like to come inside for a cup of tea?'

Amelia glanced at Clara, then back at their hosts. 'But we can't disturb your game.'

'Yes, you can,' said John, 'for if we finish now, Mama, Sir Frederick and I have won.'

'But that's not fair!' cried Eleanor.

Mrs Hurst shook her head at her children with a smile. 'Then perhaps the two of you had better join forces. What do you think – can you two and Georgy beat your new papa and Sir Frederick?'

John scowled and said, 'I can beat *anyone*.'

'So can I,' declared Eleanor.

Mr Hurst glanced at Sir Frederick and smiled. 'What do you think, Fred? Have we a hope of victory?'

'It will be quite a challenge,' replied Sir Frederick, 'but I am ready for anything.'

Mrs Hurst laughed. 'Enjoy your game,' she said. 'Miss Ashpoint, Miss McNeil and I shall have tea.' She smiled at her children, put her hand on her husband's arm for a moment, then led her guests up to the house.

The last time Amelia had been inside Radcliffe Park was only a few months ago, when she had come for dinner with her father and Diggory, but something in the house had definitely shifted. It felt brighter, airier, happier. New pictures hung on the walls, and the softening signs of children were scattered through the house – a wooden duck hidden behind the grandfather clock in the hall, a bat and ball nestled under a table.

They followed Mrs Hurst from the entrance hall into the parlour, where she rang for tea.

'Do you see much of Sir Frederick?' asked Clara as they sat down.

Mrs Hurst nodded. 'He is often here,' she said, smiling. 'He and Monty have been friends for so many years, and I like him. He is such easy company, and he is ever so good with the children.'

Amelia wondered that her new friend saw anything to like in Sir Frederick, but she supposed his long friendship with Mr Hurst would make it difficult for her to criticize him.

'I hope you will forgive the disorder,' said Mrs Hurst, glancing towards a discarded abacus on the floor by the hearth. 'The children use every room as their nursery. We are not used to having so much' – she blushed – 'so much space. Radcliffe is already quite a home to us. I hope we never have to leave.'

Amelia gave an incredulous smile. 'That is hardly likely.'

'Oh, no, of course not. It is only that I am not used to staying in one place for so long.' She hesitated, then turned to Clara. 'I have heard so much about you, Miss McNeil. Your father is a surveyor and land agent, I think?'

'That is right.'

'I believe he oversaw some repairs here last year? My husband thinks very highly of his work,' said Mrs Hurst. 'And he is carrying out some work for Sir Frederick, I know. Did I understand that you sometimes help your father with the architectural drawing?'

'Sometimes, yes, although I fear Sir Frederick overestimates my abilities,' said Clara, with a laugh.

As the maid brought in the tea, Amelia watched Mr Hurst, Sir Frederick and the three children through the window. The cricket bats were laid in a pile on the grass now, and they were playing skittles, John bowling along the open grass, his siblings cheering.

'Mr Hurst seems very fond of the children,' said Amelia softly, once the maid had gone.

'He is.'

'They must miss their father a great deal.'

Amelia was vexed at herself the moment she had said

it – she knew that she meant to pry, and she knew that it was wrong of her, but somehow she could not hold her tongue. Clara's foot nudged hers in reproach.

Mrs Hurst looked confused, then uncomfortable. She opened her mouth, closed it again, and then began to pour the tea without a word.

'I am sure they never feel the want of a father with Mr Hurst present,' said Clara softly.

'That is just it,' said Mrs Hurst, as she handed Amelia and Clara a cup each. The china was delicate, blue and white, old but meticulously clean. She raised her own cup shakily to her lips.

Amelia conquered herself, changed the subject and said, 'You told my father that you and Mr Hurst met in Richmond, I think?'

'We – yes. I was back in England for a time and . . .' Mrs Hurst trailed off, and Amelia began to feel that she had not chosen her new topic wisely after all. 'But I have been talking about myself, and I am far more interested in you. Have you both always lived in Wickenshire?'

'More or less,' said Clara. 'I was not born here, but it is all I remember.'

'And I *was* born here.' Amelia sipped her tea. 'My mother's family were from near Bath, but my father is all Wickenshire. I have never been beyond London, and even London I have only visited twice. My father hates it, and I am not fond of it either. In London, a girl cannot so much as step outside her front door without a chaperone.'

Clara set her teacup down. 'So you see, Mrs Hurst, we are both delighted to find you such a seasoned traveller.'

Mrs Hurst blushed. 'Oh, but I fear you are setting me up as a woman of high fashion. It was not like that at all. It was—' She broke off and looked down at her tea as though she did not know what to say. 'Travelling is all very well,' she said at last, 'but it is a fine thing to have a home.'

At that moment there came the sound of closing doors and footsteps, then a burst of chatter from the hall.

'But *I* won,' John was saying, and Amelia heard a soft laugh from Mr Hurst before Eleanor said, 'No, you didn't, *I* did.'

Clara and Amelia smiled as Mr Hurst came into the parlour, holding George on his hip, Sir Frederick and the two elder children following behind. Sir Frederick was still in his shirtsleeves; George had his hat upon his head, and John was now wearing the yellow jacket, which entirely swamped him.

George was put down on the settee next to his mother but promptly scrambled off, Sir Frederick's hat still firmly on his head. He picked up the abacus and began to shake it, while Eleanor and John claimed another of the settees. Mr Hurst sat down beside his wife, and Sir Frederick stood hesitating by the door, until his friend inclined his head to the seat beside him.

'Can I keep this, Sir Frederick?' asked John, his hand upon the lapel of Sir Frederick's jacket. 'It is so very smart.'

'*John!*' said Mrs Hurst. 'You cannot ask to have other people's clothes.'

But Sir Frederick was laughing. 'You can have it if you like,' he said, 'or better still, your new papa and I can take you to my tailor, and you can have one all of your own. What do you think?'

'Can I?' asked John eagerly. 'Oh, thank you, sir!'

Amelia watched all this with some amusement and some surprise. Of course *John* liked Sir Frederick's clothes, she thought – he was eight years old – and yet she could not deny that Sir Frederick was at his best with the Hursts in a way he was not in other circles. She was not sure what to make of this, and so she pushed the thought aside: she was too fond of laughing at Sir Frederick to lose him as an object of ridicule entirely.

'I was about to ask your mama about her travels,' said Clara, leaning forwards to address Eleanor and John, 'but perhaps the two of you can tell me your favourite places that you have visited?'

The children looked at each other – and then they both looked towards Mr and Mrs Hurst. Amelia saw Mr Hurst smile encouragingly, saw Mrs Hurst give a slow, measured nod.

'Venice,' said John, at just the same time as Eleanor said, 'Florence.'

'You are both fond of Italy?'

'I was born there,' said Eleanor, with a quick glance at her mother.

'And I was born in France,' said John, 'and Georgy in Prussia.'

'You are quite the world travellers.' Amelia felt a strange, solemn pang of envy. Then she thought of the globes at Ashpoint Hall, of the conversation the children had carried out behind her in some other tongue. 'I suppose you speak all manner of languages.'

'Oh, they are better scholars than I am,' said Mrs Hurst. 'Italian and French and German and a smattering of Spanish—'

'*You* don't speak Italian, do you?' John asked Amelia abruptly – adding, with a glance at Clara, 'Do you?'

When they both shook their heads, he looked a little

relieved, then turned to his mother and began a stream of fluent Italian.

Mrs Hurst spoke over him at once. 'English, please, John. You know that you are to be an Englishman now, and we have guests today.'

'I like England,' said Eleanor abruptly. 'It's big and green, and all the rooms are large, and there are toys all about.'

'That's not England, silly,' said her brother, 'that's just here.'

Mrs Hurst smiled gently, though her face looked pale. She glanced down at where Georgy was tottering towards the settee and lifted him up onto her lap. 'Now,' she said, turning to Amelia, Clara and Sir Frederick, 'how should you all like to stay for lunch?'

~

'Well,' said Amelia, as they walked homewards two hours later, 'what do you think now of my theory that Mrs Hurst's first marriage was an unhappy one?'

'I think you had better leave well alone.'

'But you saw for yourself how very pale and strange she went when I mentioned the children's father—'

'Which you ought not to have done.'

'And at lunch, John and Eleanor asked their mother something in Italian before they answered some of our questions – I am sure they wished to know what they might and might not say about their former lives.'

Clara looked at her, eyebrows raised. She pressed Amelia's arm.

'I know, know, I am very wicked and quite as bad as my father – but, Clara, it is not gossip; I am simply *interested* in Mrs Hurst. What did you make of her?'

'I like her.' Clara shrugged. 'She seems a pleasant, sens-ible sort of woman – a little nervous, to be sure, but she is in a new place with new people. From all she and the children said, it seems that she was not in Richmond for long before she met Mr Hurst. And if she were abroad for so many years before that, she must feel almost like a foreigner here. No wonder she is anxious.'

'You do not agree with me, then, that there is some great tragedy in her past?'

'I think, Amelia, that you would like everybody to have some great tragedy in their past – so that you might write a novel about them.'

Amelia pulled a face at her.

'I hope Mrs Hurst does not let John get a jacket like Sir Frederick's,' said Amelia lightly as they walked on. 'The boy will look like someone has poured custard over him.'

Clara stopped walking, and Amelia felt herself pulled back, felt their arms slip from one another.

'*Amelia!*'

'What? You cannot deny me a laugh simply because Sir Frederick was kind to John. It is still a ridiculous jacket, and he is still a ridiculous man.'

Clara sighed. 'Oh, Amelia, let him be.'

'You are simply flattered,' said Amelia, laughing, 'because he likes that veranda, which was chiefly your design.'

'Well, and if I am? Nobody else thinks my work of much value.'

Amelia stopped laughing. She felt a sudden spark of – what, anger, injustice? '*I* do,' she said. 'Your father does.'

'I know, but—'

'But what?' said Amelia, eyebrows raised. 'But we are not baronets?'

Clara looked at her. For a moment, Amelia thought she was actually affronted, and she felt a knot of panic somewhere deep in her chest – but then Clara laughed.

'Oh, this is absurd,' she said. 'Amelia, you are being as absurd as – as—'

'As one of Sir Frederick's waistcoats?'

'*Amelia!*' said Clara, but she was still laughing. Clara looked at her, and there was love in her eyes, fondness and forgiveness and indulgence and acceptance and a thousand other things she could not put into words. Amelia took a step towards her and put her arm gently through hers.

'Thank you for coming with me,' she said, when they reached the place where the lane split. 'I am glad you liked Mrs Hurst.'

Clara smiled. 'I did. And, in return, you must make a call with me next week – I owe one to Miss Waterson and Miss Maddon.'

Amelia groaned. 'Must I?'

'You must – and you must be kind.'

'I am *always* kind,' protested Amelia.

As they parted, Amelia pressed Clara's arm, and Clara returned the pressure with a smile

As Amelia walked home alone, she thought again of Mrs Hurst, her awkward smile, her unusual life. She was half annoyed with herself for being so interested in her. When the news first broke that Mr Hurst was to be married, she had held every intention of remaining aloof from the fascination and gossip of Society. But she could not deny that she liked Mrs Hurst, that the pair seemed suited to each other. Barely six weeks married, and already they were so familiar with the other's wishes and plans. No stepfather could have treated Mrs Hurst's children with more respect and affection than Mr Hurst did. No wife could have been better pleased with Mr Hurst's home.

And Mrs Hurst seemed so different from their other neighbours. She had been nervous and awkward in the large group at Mrs Elton's dinner, and even with Amelia and Clara today she had blushed, hesitated, left her sentences to die in the air. But for all her small embarrassments, she seemed genuinely glad to see them. Amelia thought she might really be able to make a friend of her.

It would be good to have a friend. Of course, she had Clara – but that was something altogether different. She had wondered, from time to time, with a sudden anxiousness, what life would be like if anything were ever to change between her and Clara. Not, of course, that she could foresee such an eventuality – they had agreed long ago that they were to pass all their lives thus, never marrying, never changing, in and out of each other's houses, perhaps even living together one day if the opportunity arose. But still, it unsettled her somehow, the knowledge that, without Clara, she would be so very alone.

Amelia shook the thought from her head. She climbed the steps of Ashpoint Hall, let herself in the front door and walked upstairs to her sitting room. She opened her desk, took out her ink and began to write.

CHAPTER VII

In which Miss Elton's fate is discussed

IT WAS A BRIGHT, WARM MORNING AT LUDWELL MANOR, and Felicia Elton was in her dressing room, standing in front of the cheval mirror, examining herself. She tilted the mirror upwards and considered her reflection.

She had been trying on dresses for an hour. The difficulty was that she looked well in everything. Her blue silk was very fetching, and no one wore frills better than Felicia Elton. Her green satin showed her figure to the best advantage. There was the cream gown, too, which had the largest gigot sleeves and would go with whatever jewellery she wore. She pushed the thought of Miss Ashpoint's joke about soufflés out of her mind. Perhaps not that one, after all.

Felicia's current gown was of pale-pink satin, with a pleated neckline and a very tight waist. Her hair was done up at the back, with three columns of ringlets to each side of her face; she wore a band of flowers in her hair, a thin gold chain and ruby cross around her neck, and elegant satin shoes.

'You look beautiful, miss,' said her maid.

Felicia did not respond, because of course it was true.

There was a knock on the bedroom door, and Felicia turned. 'Is that you, Mama? Do come in.'

Her mother stepped inside and came through the bedroom. She stopped in the dressing-room doorway, looking at the maid. 'What is Sarah doing here?' she said sharply to Felicia. 'She ought to be attending to the parlour by now.'

Sarah scowled. 'But, ma'am—'

'I needed her,' said Felicia calmly. 'I am trying to decide whether I require a new gown for the Harvest Ball.'

'I did wonder why you were in evening dress at such an hour. Did you mention the matter to Mrs Jennings?'

'I should hope, Mama, that I do not need to ask the housekeeper for use of my own maid. Sarah is my own maid, is she not? Mrs Jennings will have to make do without her.' Felicia glanced back at her reflection in the mirror. 'Well, Mama, what do you think?'

'The gown becomes you very well.'

'I wore it twice in London.'

Mrs Elton considered this. 'A new gown would be more fitting. It is only the Harvest Ball, a foolish affair, in my opinion – as if any of us wished to sit down to supper with farmhands and workpeople! Yet it is important, at such' – she glanced sideways at Sarah – 'indiscriminatory events to clearly preserve the difference of rank and station. Perhaps something splendid in silk might—'

Another knock – and her father's voice came through the bedroom door. 'Felicia, a word, if you please?'

Mrs Elton looked pointedly at Sarah, and Sarah went to open the door. She stood back as Mr Elton came into the bedroom.

'Ah, you are both here. Good. Sarah, you may go.'

Sarah glanced at Felicia, raised her eyebrows slightly, then departed.

'But, Papa, she was helping me – I am contemplating a new dress for the Harvest Ball.'

'Have you not enough dresses already?' Mr Elton held up a hand to stave off any replies. 'Let it be. I have a word to say to you about your marital prospects, Felicia, and your mother may as well hear.'

'Her marital prospects?' Mrs Elton was immediately on her guard. 'Mr Elton, if you intend to once more disparage Sir Frederick's fortune—'

'What fortune?' Mr Elton's calmness dropped, and Felicia felt a wave of uneasiness wash through her. 'The man has no money, and we *must* have money. What shall we do the next time Augustus is up for election? Campaigns cost, and his wife's parents clearly don't mean to give a penny more than they have already. Let us turn, for a moment, from Sir Frederick to Major Alderton. He has money *and* high connections.'

'High connections!' cried Mrs Elton. 'And pray, *how* is he connected to them? With infamy and sin. My uncle, the Marquis of Denby, would never have stood for—'

'Pooh pooh, what does it all matter? You may ask a favour of a duke whether the law recognizes you as his son or not. Let a man like Major Alderton marry into a respectable family and most people will simply forget the past.' He turned from his wife to his daughter. 'What do you think, Felicia?'

She hesitated. Her father did not often seek her opinion; he was a man who liked to have his own way.

'Well? Who would you rather marry – Major Alderton or Sir Frederick?'

Felicia stared at him.

They were both fairly young, both tolerably good-looking. Major Alderton always seemed surer of himself – but she was not certain whether that was to be valued. She could not imagine Sir Frederick ever arguing with her, but Major Alderton, she thought, would hold his own. And she would like to be Lady Hammersmith – well, to be Lady Anybody. But then, she would also like to be very rich. She liked fine clothes, fine company. She would like a large country estate and a house in town for the Season.

It would lower her in the eyes of the world to be united to such a man as Major Alderton – but, then again, it would lower her in her own eyes if she could not have a new dress for each public occasion.

'I shall marry whomever you and Mama think best,' she said at last.

'You hear her?' said her father, turning towards her mother.

'Felicia distinctly said that she would marry whom you *and I* think best, not whom *you* think best.'

'And I suppose, Mrs Elton, that Sir Frederick has actually said something to you of his intentions towards Felicia?'

Felicia saw her mother hesitate. 'Not in so many words, but—'

'And has he spoken to you, Felicia?'

'No, Papa.'

'When was the last time he even called at the house? You both know we have seen less of him since we returned from London than we did over the winter.'

'Because you do not invite him,' retorted Mrs Elton, 'because you—'

'Enough.' Mr Elton held up one hand. 'Yesterday evening, at the Lantern, Major Alderton asked my permission to pay his addresses to Felicia.'

Felicia stared. She looked at her mother, who was pale with anger. She looked at her father, who stood near the door, an expression of calm triumph upon his face.

Felicia felt rather sick. Of course, she must marry some-time. The whole purpose and business of her life was to marry, to secure an establishment – and yet she was hardly eager to come to the point. Once she married, everything would change. Her beauty would be no longer be a possibility for each man she met. It would be something out of reach, and people forgot what was out of reach. She liked her life. To be sure, her mother infuriated her, and her father bored her, and she longed sometimes for a friend, a girl of her own age with whom she might talk – but nonetheless, she was happy in her way. She had her beauty, her dresses, her music. If she mar-ried, it would all change. No more basking in the glory of her many admirers. No more days to herself. No more Mama to organize the household for her. No more freedom.

No more music lessons.

'What did you say to him?' her mother asked in a hoarse voice.

'I told him fairly that I believed my daughter had other admirers but that I was quite happy for him to pay his addresses. I did tell him that the decision must ultimately be my daughter's – but of course, Felicia, I hope you will be guided by those with more experience of the world than yourself – and moreover, I told him that I thought it proper for him to call here a few times and dine with us once or twice more before making any formal proposal – in order that you may both come to judge him at his own worth and not by hearsay with regards to his origins.' He turned towards his wife. 'Yes, Sophronia? You look as though you would rather like to speak.'

'Of course I should like to speak!' cried Mrs Elton. 'How could you, Mr Elton, how could you – the man is a—'

'What the man is, Sophronia, is exceptionally wealthy. That is, quite frankly, the most important consideration.' He nodded at Felicia. 'I have nothing more to say on the matter. He will call in a few days' time, and he will dine with us next week. I do not need to say that I expect him to be treated with the utmost respect by both of you – do you understand, Sophronia?'

Mrs Elton said nothing. Her lips were pressed together hard, and Felicia felt all the force of her cold rage.

'Very good,' said her father. 'Good morning to you both.' And then he opened the door and stepped out of the room.

Mrs Elton sat down heavily upon the bed, and Felicia stared at the closing door, feeling the world spin around her.

CHAPTER VIII

In which calls and plans are made

IT WAS MARKET DAY IN MELFORD, AND THE STREETS WERE full of people. The queue outside the baker's was exceeded only by the queue outside the butcher's, and both Market Square and Grange Street were thronged with shoppers.

As always on market day, the population of Wickenshire had three purposes: the first was to shop; the second was to gossip; and the third was to watch their neighbours.

Mrs and Miss Elton watched Lady Rose walk into Miss Nettlebed's and wondered what she was buying. Captain Palmer watched Major Alderton go into the tailor's and wondered if he ought to take his own business elsewhere. Mrs Crayton watched Mr McNeil walk towards her and crossed the road to avoid greeting him. Lady Wickford watched, frowning, as her son stepped into the King's Arms, though it was scarcely noon.

Everybody watched as Mrs Hurst walked alone down Grange Street and made her way to the stationer's.

~

'Miss Ashpoint, Miss McNeil, can I not help you to more tea? Are you *quite* sure?'

Not far from Grange Street, Amelia and Clara were sitting in the little house shared by Miss Maddon and Miss Waterson. They had been there for thirty minutes, and Amelia had been trying to leave for twenty-seven. She shook her head as politely as she could manage and did not point out that she had already drunk three cups of tea at Miss Maddon's insistence.

'I am afraid we had better go,' said Amelia, 'for we have business at the dressmaker's.'

'Ah,' said Miss Waterson, 'are you both to have new dresses for the Harvest Ball? I have purchased one myself – silk, you know! I have never worn silk in my life, but Gertrude said—'

'I said, Arabella, that you would look splendid in silk, for so you will – quite regal, you know.'

Amelia coughed to cover a laugh. Clara refused to meet her eye, refused to be drawn into her amusement.

'I shall probably wear muslin,' said Clara, 'but I am trying to persuade Amelia to satin.'

'Charming,' said Miss Maddon, 'quite charming.'

Amelia rose as though to depart, but Miss Waterson stopped her.

'My dears,' she said, 'I have not yet asked you about Mrs Hurst. I hear that you have been to tea with her.'

Amelia suppressed her irritation. 'We have.'

'And what did you make of her? Was she charming? Interesting? Intelligent?' asked Miss Maddon.

'Do tell us,' added Miss Waterson.

Amelia snapped. Thirty minutes of Miss Maddon and Miss Waterson was simply too much to bear. 'I like her a great deal,' she said. 'She is far more interesting than anybody else in Wickenshire.'

Miss Waterson stared at her. There was a flicker of reaction of Miss Maddon's face, but whether it was offence or confusion or amusement, Amelia hardly knew. She did not let herself dwell on it.

'I am so sorry,' she said, 'but we really must get to the dressmaker's – good day to you both.'

~

As they walked towards Grange Street, Clara turned to Amelia with a frown.

'You needn't scold me,' said Amelia, still smiling. 'I know I am an unrepentant reprobate.'

'Why make such a comment? You might as well have told them outright that you thought them dull and foolish. They are not *dull*, Amelia – they are *happy*.'

'They are gossips.'

'For that matter, so are you.' Clara stopped walking and looked round at her. 'They are interested in everything that goes on in Wickenshire – what is so wrong with that? I like Miss Maddon and Miss Waterson. I think they are interesting. I think they are—' She stopped abruptly.

'What?'

'What I mean is, you should not *dismiss* them.' Clara spoke emphatically. 'You think Mrs Hurst supremely interesting because she is a stranger, but you can never be persuaded to find interest in the sights, scenes and people you have grown up amongst. You are always contemptuous of Melford. You take great delight in finding all our neighbours ridiculous and dull.'

Amelia stared at her. Her first instinct was to defend herself or simply to laugh, but there was something in Clara's manner that stopped her. She sounded – vexed. She sounded – exasperated, almost. But Clara *liked* her humour, her wit; she liked it when Amelia made her laugh in spite of herself, when Amelia said things she never would. She had always liked that about Amelia. Amelia knew this; she knew it like she knew every line and freckle of Clara's skin. If that fact could change, then—

No, she would not think of that. And it wasn't true, was it, that she delighted in showing contempt for those around them? Of course she found people ridiculous and dull when they *were* ridiculous and dull, but surely all sensible people did?

But then she thought of Mrs Hurst speaking warmly of Sir Frederick, of Clara's kindness to Miss Waterson and Miss Maddon, and she felt, for a moment, a prickle of shame.

'I am sorry,' said Clara abruptly. She stepped towards Amelia, put her arm through hers. She sounded anxious, as though she were aware her words had cut harder than she meant. 'I don't know what is the matter with me today – I am out of sorts, I dare say.'

Clara's voice was low and warm and familiar, and Amelia felt the knot in her stomach untangle, felt her spirits calm. She pushed the fear from her mind.

'As long as you do not detest *me*,' Clara said gently, almost lightly, 'then you may laugh at whomever you like. Now come – let us see what we can do about your satin at Miss Nettlebed's before I am due up at Lady Hammersmith's.'

In the dressmaker's, they found Lady Rose near the fashion plates and the three Miss Palmers contemplating new gloves.

The young ladies all bid each other good morning, and

while Clara examined some fine silks by the doorway, Amelia took Lady Rose to one side, on the pretence of showing her some shawls. She had not spoken to her since Mrs Elton's dinner, since her brother's proposal, and she had long wished to say something to her on the matter. Besides, she would show Clara that she did not think *all* their neighbours ridiculous.

'I have been wanting to see you, Lady Rose,' she said, in a low voice.

Rose beamed at her. Her cheeks were red, her eyes bright. She *shone* – and Amelia felt a sudden ache, a sombre and hopeless stirring of envy that Rose and Diggory were permitted to be this happy.

'And I you,' Lady Rose replied. 'And you must call me only Rose now, for I hope we are to be good friends.' She said this very softly, and the ache seemed to fade – not entirely, but enough to be ignored.

Amelia smiled. 'Of course.'

Across the room, the Palmer sisters were watching them. Louisa nudged Cassandra and whispered something, while Anne looked on with an expression of deep curiosity.

'And now,' said Amelia, taking up the shawl and running it through her fingers, 'we must look very hard at this ugly thing before the gossip begins.'

Amelia's order for a new gown was placed quickly, for she left the bulk of decisions to Miss Nettlebed herself – a suggestion about colour and a categorical refusal of gigot sleeves and Amelia was done. Clara went up to the counter next, and took out the dress she wanted altered, discussing the changes with Miss Nettlebed with careful consideration. Lady Rose left to meet her mother; Anne Palmer headed to the bookseller's and her sisters to the milliner's – and after another five minutes, with Miss Nettlebed and Clara still deep in discussion, Amelia grew bored. She gazed out of the window, looking up and down Grange Street at the hustle and bustle of market day, the carts dragged to and fro, the traders hurrying towards the square – and then she spotted Lonsdale walking along the other side of the road.

She turned back to Clara, waved her hand in the direction of the street – she would understand – then hurried out of the shop.

'Good day, Mr Lonsdale,' she said, when she caught up with him.

He turned, his cheeks a little flushed, his expression one of surprise. 'Good day, Miss Ashpoint.'

'I did not mean to startle you,' she said. 'I only wanted to ask if – well, you have not heard anything from London, I take it?'

A smile crossed his lips, but it was very faint. 'I have not, no. I would find a way to tell you, if I had.'

She nodded. They stood for a moment in silence, and Amelia found herself thinking of the last time they had met, when they had seen Diggory and Rose together almost a fortnight before. She thought of Clara's rebuke, and if she had not thought Lonsdale ridiculous or dull – well, she had thought him worse. Her conscience smote her. 'I meant to say, I – well, I wanted to apologize for the way I spoke to you the other day. I have no right to question your integrity. I know you are to be trusted.'

An odd smile spread across Lonsdale's face. 'Thank you,' he said, so earnestly that Amelia felt guiltier than ever. Was Clara right, then? Was she more partial, more prejudiced than she allowed herself to believe, too quick in her judgements of others?

'As it happens,' Lonsdale went on, lowering his voice, 'your brother has spoken to me of his secret himself.'

Amelia laughed. 'Has he indeed?'

'Well, he had it from you that I already knew, and he wanted to discuss it with me. We have been thrown much together at the brewery these last few weeks, and I think – well, I think Mr Diggory is in need of a friend.' He smiled. 'I had better go – I am on my way to see one of the men from the brewery who was injured in the accident.'

'Fedmouth? How is he?'

'He will be all right with time. Good day, Miss Ashpoint.'

'Goodbye, Mr Lonsdale.'

As she turned back towards the dressmaker's, she saw Anne Palmer looking at her from the doorway of the bookseller's, an odd expression on her face. She thought of Diggory, his assumptions about her and Lonsdale, and she felt suddenly that it had been a stupid thing to do, to run after Lonsdale in the street like that. Anne was by no means as much of a gossip as her younger sisters, but nonetheless: people would talk.

She wanted so much to hear about her book. She was tired of waiting and wondering and doubting whether she were good enough. She was weary of not knowing what the future held.

But still, she ought not to be foolish. She made herself smile at Anne Palmer, as though to show she had done nothing amiss. Anne Palmer looked surprised – pleasantly surprised, perhaps. She inclined her head and smiled back.

～

Felicia had just left the milliner's with her mother when she spotted Miss Ashpoint across the street. She saw her not only run after her father's foreman but also stop and speak to him in the street, quite alone – not a friend or a maid to be seen. She saw them talk in whispers, saw Miss Ashpoint laugh. Felicia was appalled.

And yet she wondered, with a sort of pang: had she been a different kind of young woman, in a different kind of life, would she ever have stopped to speak to someone in the street like that? Would she ever have wished for someone's company enough to ignore what others might think?

Her mother had not noticed. She was looking further down the street, to where Mrs Hurst was stepping out of the stationer's.

'Ah,' she said, in a tone of firm determination. 'Come, Felicia.'

She marched towards Mrs Hurst, Felicia walking quickly behind; her maid, Sarah, followed with a weary sigh that did not escape Felicia's ears.

Felicia did not really wish to speak to Mrs Hurst. She could not forget that strange conversation she had overheard between the Hursts after her mother's dinner, those low intimate tones, that mention of fear. There was something . . . if not exactly improper about it, at least something unex-plained. It made her feel perturbed.

'Mrs Hurst,' Mrs Elton was saying, having successfully ambushed her on the street. 'How do you do? And your dear husband and the children – all well, I trust?' She did not stop for an answer. 'It is a pleasure to see you. I was saying to Felicia only a moment since that I cannot quite believe it is more than three weeks since my dinner – and to think we have scarcely met since! But pray, Mrs Hurst, how do you come to be quite alone today?'

Felicia watched Mrs Hurst's face. She had looked unnerved

at Mrs Elton's first salutation; now she looked alarmed. She glanced at Felicia, then at Sarah trailing behind them.

'Mr Hurst and the children are at home,' she said slowly. 'The children were in need of more paper, so I walked into Melford.' She raised her basket, as though to signify her purchases.

Felicia looked at her mother, to see how she bore this.

'Walked?' repeated Mrs Elton, in a tone of grave surprise. 'From Radcliffe, in this hot weather? But, my dear, it is nigh on four miles. Surely a servant might—'

'It is not much more than two,' said Mrs Hurst. 'I am fond of walking, and it is such a pleasant day that I thought I might as well go myself.' She glanced at Sarah and, to Felicia's amazement, smiled at her.

Mrs Elton pressed her lips together. She did not look at Sarah – as usual, she ignored her presence entirely – but Sarah nonetheless seemed to feel the force of her expression. She shifted backwards a little, bowed her head lower.

Felicia thought for a moment about what it might be like to be Sarah. They were nearly of an age, after all. She wondered whether Sarah were permitted to choose her own sweethearts, whether her future ever stretched out before her in a grand expanse of uncertain unease – and then chided herself for such foolish thoughts.

'It is lucky to meet you here,' said Mrs Elton, 'for I have been meaning to call. It is always such a pleasure to spend time in a neighbour's company. And I had a word to say to you, too.' Mrs Elton lowered her voice to that warm, confidential tone that so unnerved Felicia. 'I wanted to say that if you need any advice, Mrs Hurst, about anything – any little matter at all – you really must ask me. I should be most glad to help.'

Mrs Hurst blinked. 'I hardly know—'

'My dear,' said Mrs Elton, laying a hand gently on Mrs Hurst's arm and smiling with an effort at sweetness, 'you will forgive me, I am sure, for speaking plainly. I heard that you had Miss Ashpoint and that friend of hers for luncheon, and to have paid *those* young ladies such an honour *before* inviting the earl and countess . . .' She inclined her head. 'Well, it might be seen as a slight, the Wickfords being the most *significant* family in the neighbourhood.'

A faint red crept up Mrs Hurst's cheeks. Felicia was not sure whether it was due to anger or embarrassment. And then she wondered abruptly if this would be her position in a few months' time: a new bride, planning the first dinners in her own house, thinking over invitations and courses and dresses and discussing these plans with – the face in her mind was Major Alderton's one moment, Sir Frederick's the next – with her *husband*. The thought made her feel a little giddy, a little sick.

'Mr Hurst will not have considered the matter,' Mrs Elton went on, 'for gentlemen so rarely put their minds to such things, but we ladies must ensure we maintain good relations with our neighbours. I thought I would mention it, for I know you are but recently returned from the Continent and . . .'

Felicia stopped listening. She was thinking of her father's words in her room last week. She was thinking of Major Alderton, of what it would be like to marry a man with a stain upon his birth so great that no fortune could truly wash it out. She was thinking that surely her mother was right, that she – *she*, Felicia Elton, the great beauty of Wickenshire – could do better. She was thinking of what it would mean to be married, to no longer be Felicia Elton but

Felicia So-and-so, a different person altogether. Here was Mrs Hurst, once Mrs Roberts – but before that, who had she been? Her original name was wiped from memory, her first self lost to the wind.

Her mother had finally stopped talking, and Felicia heard Mrs Hurst sigh deeply, as though steeling herself for some great trial. 'I shall ask the Wickfords to come to us on Monday evening,' she said shortly. 'Would you like to come, too?'

Mrs Elton hesitated. This was, Felicia was certain, exactly what her mother had planned, and yet something in Mrs Hurst's manner gave her pause. Although Mrs Hurst had asked them, it was evident that the invitation gave her no pleasure. But Mrs Elton drew herself up, no doubt determined to take it as a triumph. 'How very kind. Mr Elton, Miss Elton and I would be delighted to come. That is, of course, if we do not throw off your table, for *nine* is an awkward number. Of course, if you were to ask somebody else . . .'

'I am sure Sir Frederick will come,' said Mrs Hurst, 'and that makes it even.'

Mrs Elton smiled. Felicia did not doubt that this had been her mother's intention, too.

Mrs Hurst looked almost as if she knew that. Her cheeks were pink, and she wore a strange expression, half anxiety, half amusement. 'Monday, then – shall we say half past six?'

'How delightful,' said Mrs Elton. 'I shall look forward to it with infinite pleasure.' With her mission fulfilled, her warmth seemed to seep away. 'Goodness, do I hear the church bells ring for one o'clock? Felicia, we had better get home, or you will miss your music lesson. Good day, Mrs Hurst.'

Felicia curtseyed to Mrs Hurst and followed her mother

towards their carriage, stationed around the corner in Garrett Lane. She glanced once over her shoulder to see Sarah trailing behind, and beyond her, Mrs Hurst, standing motionless in the street, as though she had been turned to ice by the sheer force that was Mrs Elton.

CHAPTER IX

In which new friendships are established

MEANWHILE, MR ASHPOINT WAS IN THE OFFICE OF THE King's Arms, having an in-depth conversation with the proprietor about the price of beer. The King's Arms had sold Ashpoint beer for thirty years and was not likely to stop – but nonetheless, there were deals to be struck and haggling to be done and contracts to be renewed.

He had walked down into Melford half an hour since with Lonsdale, who was to visit Fedmouth at his home on Rattern Street and speak to him about coming back to the brewery. Mr Ashpoint had left the works under the temporary supervision of Diggory.

This last month or so, his elder son had been behaving very strangely. There had been the incident at Mrs Elton's dinner party, when Diggory had apparently fallen over, drunk, and cut his face – and since then, Diggory was waking up earlier, drinking less and apparently seeing nothing of Lord Salbridge. He had developed a new passion for long rides and, stranger still, a sudden interest in the brewery. Since the accident, he had been there nearly every day, helping with the clean-up and repairs, making himself useful in the counting house and studying brewing techniques. He kept asking Lonsdale questions as though he desperately wanted to know the answers.

Mr Ashpoint did not quite understand it. Every morning, he woke prepared for Diggory to revert to his old ways, and every morning, Diggory appeared at the brewery looking eager and determined.

Today was a kind of test. He had suggested that Lonsdale see Fedmouth at the same time as he was due at the King's Arms in order that Diggory might feel the weight of responsibility. Of course, Diggory was not *actually* in charge – Mr Ashpoint had instructed Magner and several of the more senior men to keep an eye on things – but it might do Diggory some good to feel that he was.

Mr Ashpoint felt almost sure that Diggory had turned a corner. Now all he needed to worry about was his other three children.

He sighed and went on talking about beer.

At six o'clock that evening, Diggory followed Lonsdale out of the brewery gates and down the lane towards the Lantern. They had formed a habit, this last week or so, of meeting Monsieur Brisset there for a hand or two of cards after their day's work was done. Sometimes another fellow might join them – Major Alderton or Mr Duckfield, sometimes Edmund Crayton, but never Lord Salbridge. If Salbridge found Diggory present, he would leave at once.

Diggory liked going to the Lantern with Lonsdale and Brisset. They chiefly played low, did not drink too much and usually left at a reasonable hour. Diggory was surprised to find just how much easier it was to wake up in the morning if one went to bed early and relatively sober. Besides, he liked Lonsdale and Brisset, and it seemed so much more natural to work each day if one's companions did the same. Salbridge had always laughed at him and called him dull for going into the brewery. Now, he had been at the brewery every day for more than a fortnight – with a few breaks to meet Lady Rose – and was feeling immensely proud of himself. Today, his father had left him in charge for a full two hours, and nothing at all had gone wrong.

'I have been reading that book you lent me,' said Diggory as they strolled onwards. 'I am not sure I understand half of it, but I am learning ever so much. Do you think we ought to buy one of Levesque's mash-tun thermometers?'

Lonsdale smiled. 'We already have two.'

'Ah,' said Diggory, wincing. 'I ought to have known that. It is only that whenever someone writes about *new* equipment, it seems as though we ought to have it. Come, I see you smile, Lonsdale – you think I am getting ahead of myself.'

'I think,' said Lonsdale, 'that your father would be very pleased to see you excited about mash-tun thermometers.'

They were approaching the side entrance to Maddox Court now, and Diggory saw two figures standing at the gate: Sir Frederick, in a mauve tailcoat and umber waistcoat, and Clara McNeil, a blue ribbon in her hair and a basket under her arm.

They passed close by, so Diggory waved to Clara and nodded to Sir Frederick, and Lonsdale bowed to both. Sir Frederick had presumably come out to bid Clara goodbye – Diggory knew from his sister that she came up to Maddox Court to read to Lady Hammersmith – and Diggory hesitated, half wondering if they ought to wait and offer to walk

Clara back down into Melford; but Clara and Sir Frederick appeared deep in conversation about verandas, and so Diggory and Lonsdale walked on.

At the Lantern, they found Brisset sitting alone in an armchair in the corner of the lower room. He had a glass of whisky before him, barely touched.

'I really am going to give up the Lantern,' he declared, as Lonsdale and Diggory rang for drinks.

Lonsdale laughed very heartily, and Diggory assumed this must be a long-standing joke between them. For a moment, he missed Salbridge, their easy familiarity – but thoughts of Rose and of Grace pushed that out of his mind.

'Our friend thinks I am not serious,' said Brisset, address-ing Diggory, 'but I mean it this time.' He turned to Lonsdale. 'It is too expensive and, besides, it is a bore. And there is always the danger of meeting Lord Salbridge, whom I would rather keep at the other end of the earth from myself.' He glanced at Diggory. 'Not that I intend any offence, Mr Ashpoint, but—'

'What offence could there be?' said Diggory. 'He is no friend of mine any more.'

'Well said,' replied Lonsdale.

'Certainly,' said Brisset. 'But I would be quite as happy to drink beer at the King's Arms. We needn't pay so much for the pleasure of paying more for our drinks.'

Lonsdale laughed. 'I suppose that is true. And yet, I rather like it here.'

The door opened, and Lonsdale turned to see Major Alderton stepping in. He greeted them with a hearty, 'Good evening, gentlemen,' and began to take off his hat and jacket.

'Lord Salbridge has fewer friends here than he thinks,'

said Lonsdale quietly, 'and we have more. At this rate, we shall run the place soon enough.'

Diggory smiled faintly. 'Salbridge told me once that he was the King of the Lantern.'

'Then I suggest you usurp him,' said Lonsdale.

Diggory could not help but laugh.

Brisset held up his hands. 'I have nothing to do with this,' he said, but he was laughing, too.

'Join us for cards, Major?' asked Diggory, turning as Alderton approached.

'By all means.' He pulled up a chair to join the table, glancing between the three of them. 'What's the joke?'

'Lord Salbridge,' said Brisset shortly, and Major Alderton laughed.

'Excellent,' he replied. 'I'll drink to that.'

Diggory smiled. He looked around at his three companions, and he did not think he would miss Salbridge for long.

CHAPTER X

In which Radcliffe Park is invaded

FELICIA ELTON SAT IN THE FAMILY CARRIAGE AS IT JOLTED along the roads to Radcliffe Park. Her father sat opposite, a newspaper open before him, and beside him was her mother, with a tight smile of determination upon her lips. It was a fine evening, just gone six o'clock, the sun low but still bright in the sky. Felicia gazed out of the window as they passed labourers and sheep in the fields, clusters of farmhouses and clumps of woodland. Then the trees cleared, and Felicia looked up as Netherworth, Major Alderton's house, came into view.

It really was very grand – a large, square house built in red brick, with white about the windows and a grey-tiled roof. The grounds were extensive, the gates made from stately iron. When Felicia was a little girl, it had belonged to the Devenports, one of the old county families, but they had melted away a decade ago. An unwise speculation, the death of a son and the marriage of a daughter to somebody from the North – and the great Devenports of Wickenshire were suddenly no more.

She saw her father's gaze turn towards the gates as they passed, saw him glance meaningfully at her. Netherworth was, Felicia supposed, a very respectable house. No doubt this was why Major Alderton had purchased it.

There were not so many great families in the area these days. The Eltons, the Hammersmiths, the Hursts, and the Earl and Countess of Wickford were rather above their neighbours – but no one could dine with only three other families, and so Society spread further and thinner. To be sure, Felicia did not consider Major Alderton her equal. But then, she did not consider *anyone* her equal.

The question was whether there would be any better prospect. Here in Wickenshire, Sir Frederick, Major Alderton, Lord Salbridge and Diggory Ashpoint all had either rank or fortune enough to impress one of her parents – but Lord Salbridge did not seem likely to marry any time soon, and Diggory Ashpoint paid her little attention these days. She had barely noticed when he stopped asking her to dance last summer; at the time, it had not seemed to matter.

There was the London Season, too, of course. For all she knew, next spring might bring a devoted peer to her feet. But London was unpredictable – and there was a chance, she feared, that her father might say they simply could not afford to go next year.

'I trust, Sophronia,' said her father, 'that you will find this evening to your liking. As we have invited ourselves to Radcliffe Park, let us hope it will prove worth your efforts.'

Mrs Elton drew herself up. 'Mr Elton, you know perfectly well that you are speaking nonsense. Mrs Hurst invited us.'

'At your insistence.'

'No, indeed. I do not know what Felicia has told you, but I merely hinted – the barest suggestion—'

Mr Elton straightened himself, returned his gaze to the newspaper. 'It is not civil, Sophronia, to make up parties at other people's houses.'

'Nor is it civil,' said Mrs Elton, 'to live two months in a

neighbourhood without asking the county's best families to dinner. To invite Miss Ashpoint and that Irish girl before the Wickfords, before *us* – it would be insulting if I did not believe it had been done in error. Mrs Hurst does not understand Society, and I am determined to make her understand.'

Mr Elton said nothing. He only raised his newspaper and read on.

Netherworth had slipped from view. The carriage trundled up and down the roads, past farmers packing up for the day and children skipping down the lanes. At last, they rolled through the gates of Radcliffe Park, slowing as they reached the house. Peter jumped down and rang the bell.

In the long pause before the door was answered, Felicia saw the Wickford carriage pulling up alongside them, their footman likewise moving towards the door. She could not see all the occupants from where she sat, but she caught a glimpse of Lord Salbridge leaning forwards, his eyes finding her.

At last, the small maid answered the door, dressed a little more smartly than last time, though her mobcap was askew. She curtseyed, said a few words, then looked anxiously back into the house as Peter and the other footman hurried towards the carriages. Felicia adjusted her skirts, checked that her hair was still perfect (it was), then walked gracefully up the steps to the door.

The party assembled in the drawing room. Sir Frederick was already present, standing beside his hosts at the pianoforte. Mr Hurst looked as agreeable as ever, while Mrs Hurst looked somewhat anxious. The little Robertses were also here, no doubt to the indignation of Felicia's mother. Surely they were not expected to *dine* with the children? It seemed impossible.

Felicia found herself addressed, her hand taken, found herself saying 'Good evening' to everyone in her most charming tones. Sir Frederick did not seem to take her hand for as long as usual, but perhaps that was her imagination. The Earl and Countess of Wickford had filed into the room close behind her, and of course he had to greet them, too.

A few minutes later, while Lady Rose entertained the children, while her parents spoke to the Hursts, while Sir Frederick and the earl and countess talked amongst themselves, Felicia found Lord Salbridge standing close behind her.

'Isn't this a bore?' he muttered. 'I do hope you will entertain me, Miss Elton, or God knows what mischief I shall get up to.'

She suppressed a smile but said nothing.

'We appear to have been invited to a children's tea party,' he said. 'At least my sister will feel at home.'

Felicia could not help a laugh at that. Perhaps this evening would not be so very dull after all.

❧

Lady Rose was sitting on the sofa, Miss Eleanor Roberts on one side of her, Master John Roberts on the other. She liked children in general, but these Robertses seemed nervous of her. She wished she might have been with the littlest one, for infants were not so very hard to please – but Master George Roberts was currently playing peek-a-boo with Sir Frederick's hat and appeared entirely satisfied.

'How do you like Wickenshire?' she finally managed to ask.

'It is very pretty here,' said Eleanor.

'And not so hot as Italy,' said John. 'Do you ever get real summer here?'

'Why, it is summer now.'

'Not real summer, though,' said John. 'Not like in Italy.'

Rose smiled. 'Do you enjoy travelling?'

'Sometimes,' said Eleanor.

'I do,' said John. 'I mean to always travel when I am grown. I shall be an explorer or a soldier or a sailor and see *everywhere*.'

'Of course,' said Rose gently. 'It is in your blood. Your father was a sailor, I know.'

John froze. There was a pause, and Rose felt that she had said something foolish. She ought not to have mentioned their father, whose loss they must feel so keenly. Eleanor looked at John, then glanced over towards her mother, perhaps to see if she had heard.

And then Eleanor turned to her brother and said, in a low voice, '*Questo è ciò che la mamma ha detto a tutti.*'

'*So che,*' John hissed back.

Rose frowned. It clearly did not occur to either of them that she might know any Italian. But what did Eleanor mean by saying that that was what their mother had told everybody? Had Mr Roberts not been a sailor after all?

Rose was trying to think what to say next when the doors to the drawing room opened, and in stepped two servants. The little housemaid who had answered the door came to take the children to their supper in the nursery. Another servant followed behind her, to lead the rest of the party into dinner.

Rose started when she recognized the second girl. She looked around at her parents, saw her mother glance at her father. She watched as Salbridge's eyes fell on Meg, as he raised his eyebrows in recognition, a smile of something like amusement forming on his lips.

Meg had once worked at Wickford Towers – until, a little over a year ago, she had left very quickly and without explanation. Rose disliked being kept in the dark and was not averse to listening at keyholes when necessary, and it soon became clear that Meg had been involved in some indiscretion with Salbridge. As far as she understood, her father had recommended Meg to Mr Hurst – but evidently, Rose thought now, he had not given a full explanation of why it had been expedient for Meg to leave Wickford Towers.

That they might see Meg this evening had never occurred to her. At Wickford Towers, she had been a kitchen maid, rarely seen upstairs. It was usually footmen who served at table – and yet, as the party were led into the dining room and settled into their seats, it appeared that the Hursts had no footmen at all. So here was Meg, the housemaid or kitchen maid or whatever she was, helping serve the dinner.

If Meg felt any discomfort at being in the same room as Lord Salbridge, she did not show it. She studiously avoided looking at him as she brought around the bread, but that was all. Salbridge kept his eyes on her, following her figure from place to place. Rose watched him and felt unease bloom in her stomach.

Mr Hurst sat at one end of the table, Mrs Hurst at the other. Mrs Elton was at Mr Hurst's side, as though Mrs Hurst had deliberately put her as far away from herself as possible. Rose was between her father and Sir Frederick. She heartily wished that Diggory was here, that she could spend the evening talking to him instead.

Soon, she told herself. Her brother was heading to Norfolk tomorrow, and while he was gone, Diggory would speak to her father. Soon, she would be able to eat dinner with Diggory forever, to talk to him forever, to know that some-body was forever listening to her, loving her, caring what she said and thought.

CHAPTER XI

*In which Miss Elton is slighted and Lord
Salbridge is enlightened*

THE DINNER HAD BEEN BEARABLE, FOR LORD SALBRIDGE
was beside her, but Felicia found the drawing room inter-
minably dreary. Her mother and Lady Wickford had
cornered Mrs Hurst and were talking to her loudly about
the best methods of education for children and the best
changes to make to one's home. Felicia was with Lady Rose
on a settee at the other side of the room.

'I wonder how long the gentlemen will be,' Felicia said,
for she must say something.

Lady Rose looked at her but did not reply.

Felicia tried again. 'Have you a dress ready for the Harvest
Ball?'

'Oh, yes. I think I shall wear what I wore to your mother's
dinner.' Rose smiled. 'I am looking forward to it.'

'Yes, the Harvest Ball is all very well in its way. Of course
it is a shame to be amongst so many low people, but it is
rather an interesting occasion.'

Lady Rose looked at her, her mouth curving downwards.
'I don't know what you mean by *low* people,' she said in a
quiet voice. 'I like the Harvest Ball, for everyone behaves as
they wish and not as they think they ought, and it is . . .
much more honest, I think. I danced with the greengrocer

and several of the farmhands last year, and they were all very pleasant.' Rose was smiling now, absorbed in memory. 'And Anne Palmer danced with the bookseller's daughter because neither of them could get partners, and Amelia Ashpoint swore not to dance all evening – and went through with it, too.'

Rose was intolerably dull, and Felicia had lost all patience. She spoke her next words without thinking. 'How ridiculous. But I suppose I should expect no less from a girl who spends so much time with her father's foreman.'

Rose stopped smiling. 'What on earth do you mean?'

Across the drawing room, Felicia saw Mrs Hurst's eyes flick towards them. Lady Wickford and Mrs Elton carried on talking, oblivious.

Felicia hesitated. She ought not to have said that, but she was feeling reckless this evening. 'I saw them speaking to each other in the street the other day,' she said, a little more softly, 'quite alone. Of course it is not her first Season out, but even Miss Ashpoint might do better than *that*.'

Rose looked quickly at her mother and then back at Felicia. Her eyes were dark, her expression defiant. 'You are talking nonsense on purpose to injure her,' she said sharply. 'Amelia has no thought of marriage at all. Diggory thinks she will never marry anybody.'

'You seem rather intimate with the thoughts of Mr Diggory Ashpoint,' Felicia remarked.

Lady Rose turned red in an instant. Very red. Red enough that Felicia felt she had hit closer to the mark than she had expected.

Rose glanced very quickly over at her mother, then back at Felicia. 'And why shouldn't I be?' she hissed. 'Not everyone has to be in love with *you*, Miss Elton.'

It was as if someone had struck her.

Of course she wanted everyone to be in love with her – surely everybody wanted that! – and yet it sounded rather vulgar when spoken aloud.

Felicia was trying to think of how to respond when the doors opened. The gentlemen came in, Mr Hurst and Sir Frederick deep in conversation, the other three trailing behind.

'I am really very sorry,' Lady Rose was saying hurriedly, 'I didn't mean—'

But Felicia was already on her feet.

Before she could speak to any of the gentlemen, the little figure of Master John Roberts darted forwards through the open door, followed quickly by the small maid, who was holding Master George in her arms and looking very apologetic.

'Mama,' said John, tugging on his mother's sleeve, glancing around at Mr Hurst as though to include him in the question, 'mayn't we come down and be adults for the evening? We have been good all day and Mrs Alley said there would be sweets with the coffee, and Eleanor said—'

'I said you are very naughty,' Eleanor called from the doorway.

To Felicia's surprise, Mrs Hurst began to laugh and her husband joined in heartily. Even Sir Frederick smiled.

'What do you think, Monty?' said Mrs Hurst, addressing her husband as though nobody else were present.

'Oh, why not? Very well, John, you *may* stay – but if you are not very good, you will go to bed at once.'

'Thank you, thank you!' John pulled Eleanor forwards by the hand, and Mrs Hurst helped the youngest boy down to the floor to let him toddle about.

Felicia thought that this was quite the oddest dinner she had ever been to.

When the maid had departed and the children were scattered about the room, she found herself beside Lord Salbridge.

'What a dreary hour I have passed, Miss Elton,' he said, in a low, confidential voice. 'You would not believe, would you, that Hurst is only five years my senior? He seems to have grown years older since his marriage. All those blasted stepchildren, I suppose.' He turned towards her, looked her up and down. 'How do you do, Miss Elton? I suppose my sister has been boring you to death.'

Felicia supressed a smile. She glanced sideways at Lord Salbridge. His lips were very red, and his jacket hugged his figure. She was standing near enough to see him breathe. Perhaps, she thought, she would not have to marry either Major Alderton or Sir Frederick. There was always Lord Salbridge. Yes, she supposed he drank too much and was not what one would call a *good* man, but he was at least handsome, and it would be something to be a countess one day. Her mother had dismissed him in favour of Sir Frederick because she did not think him likely to marry, but surely if anybody could capture an uncapturable man, it was Felicia Elton. Perhaps things were not so very desperate as her father thought. There were still choices, and while there were still choices, there was still time.

She was contemplating this when the doors opened again and the coffee was brought in.

The maid carrying the tray was the one with the curly hair who had served them at dinner. She leant over the table to arrange the cups and coffee pot, to position the milk and the plate of bonbons – and all the while, Lord Salbridge was *staring*.

The girl kept her gaze upon her work, but Felicia watched

Salbridge's eyes track her every move, follow the curves of her figure as she stooped and straightened, watched him stare as she unlatched the glass doors to the terrace.

The rest of the party were heading outside to watch the sunset. Sir Frederick went out with Mr Hurst, without a glance back at Felicia. When she, too, stepped forwards, she found that Lord Salbridge was no longer beside her.

She looked around, but he had moved back towards the door.

He smiled at her. 'If anybody asks where I am, Miss Elton, tell them I have gone to explore the grounds or something like that, won't you?'

And then he slipped out of the drawing-room door, leaving Felicia to stare after him.

She thought of how very red Lady Rose had turned at the mention of Diggory Ashpoint's name, of how keenly Lord Salbridge's eyes had trailed that maid, of how little Sir Frederick had spoken to her this evening. She felt as though she were sinking.

She made herself move, forced herself to follow the others out onto the terrace, did her best to gaze up at the sky. She joined the group just as Lady Rose was saying how very beautiful the sunset was – and just in time for Master George to totter forwards, look up at Felicia and promptly vomit up his bonbons over her satin shoes.

~

Lord Salbridge found the servants' stairs easily enough. He made his way down slowly, careful not to be seen by the rest of the staff, and paused at the kitchen door. There was Meg, quite alone, her back turned, washing dishes at the sink.

He'd not thought of her for more than a year, but seeing her tonight was rekindling memories. He had come home from the London Season a few years ago to find Meg eighteen years old and suddenly good-looking, and he had paid her the kind of attentions he paid to women of her class as a matter of course. When he tried his usual sort of thing, pledges of love and vague murmurings about marriage and the difficulties of his position, she had laughed in his face, but she still let him touch her. This had confounded but amused him: he liked women with a little fire. They had carried on intermittently for a few months – encounters in the pantry, in the gardens, in the back of the glasshouses – until his father had caught them and promptly arranged for Meg to work elsewhere.

And here she was. He had not cared much when she left; he was distracted by a barmaid at the King's Arms at the time, and not long afterwards he began to pursue Grace Abbott. But he was growing tired of Grace these days. He hadn't seen her for over a week, not since he'd asked her to come to London with him – for he had, unbeknownst to his parents, given up his plan of going to Norfolk now that Diggory was not to accompany him, and he intended to head to London for a few weeks of entertainment instead. Grace had said no, not without this and that, and then she'd started going on about that brat of hers, how she could not go away without somewhere to place her, how he had promised to do something about the girl's education, which he supposed he probably had said something about once. It was all such a bore. Meanwhile, Meg appeared to have grown only better-looking in the past year.

'Evening, Meg.'

She flinched and turned around sharply. 'What the hell

are you doing down here?' she demanded. She looked even prettier when she scowled.

Lord Salbridge smiled and took a step closer to her. 'I've missed you,' he said, in his most charming voice.

Meg took a step back. 'No, you haven't – I am no fool. Go upstairs now. Imagine if someone caught you! It's quite enough that you lost me one place – you needn't lose me another.'

Salbridge frowned. He was debating his next move when there came a noise outside in the corridor, the sound of voices, and Meg froze.

She swore under her breath. Then, 'In here,' she whispered urgently and shoved him towards the pantry. She shut the door quickly behind them, bolted it, then pressed her back against it, frowning hard.

They were close together in the pantry, and Salbridge reached his arm around her waist.

Meg shoved him back. 'I've a carving knife in my apron,' she hissed, 'so you'd better not try anything.'

Salbridge could hear voices in the kitchen now – the housekeeper's first and then, to his surprise, Mrs Hurst's. He wasn't really listening to what they were saying – something about a child's frock, about that little boy being sick. He was busy looking at Meg and wondering which tactic to try next.

'Mrs Alley, we must try to get the stain out,' Mrs Hurst was saying. 'Poor Georgy, being so ill.'

'It is terribly unlucky,' the housekeeper replied, 'and at your first party here, too.'

'I know,' said Mrs Hurst. 'And Miss Elton's shoes! Whatever will they think of me?' She gave a slight laugh. 'Perhaps I should not have dressed him in this tonight – but it is his best. Oh, Mrs Alley, I do hope you can save it. You know how precious this frock is. Monty wore it himself as a boy and brought it over from England when John was born.'

Salbridge frowned, a new curiosity sparking in his mind. *When John was born.* But—

'I think I have something in my own room, ma'am – if we try . . .'

His mind was racing as the voices faded, as the sound of footsteps echoed away up the corridor.

Meg turned and made to open the pantry door – but Salbridge put a hand out to stop her.

'What was all that about?'

'What?'

'What they were saying – how could John Roberts have worn Mr Hurst's childhood things when he was younger, when Mr and Mrs Hurst met only a few months ago?'

Meg went red and bit her lip. She looked so very self-conscious, so very anxious, that he knew he had hit upon something significant. She reached for the door again, but he kept his hand firmly in place. A thought was already taking seed in his mind.

'That does not make sense,' he said, 'unless—'

'You mustn't say anything,' Meg hissed. 'It's not so very bad. I am not supposed to know, but one of the children let it slip and—'

Salbridge stared at her. She flushed again, as though she feared she might have made things worse.

Monty brought it over from England when John was born.

'Forget it,' Meg said, wrenching his hand off the door with sudden force. 'Go upstairs and forget it.'

But Salbridge did not think he would.

If Montgomery Hurst had been in that family's life since before John's birth, surely that meant only thing.

How had he not seen it before? It was so very odd to begin with that a man like Mr Hurst should marry a widow with three children from her first marriage. And then Mr and Mrs Hurst did not seem like a couple wed but a few months. Nobody in Wickenshire knew much about Mr Hurst's life in Paris before his father's death, and since his return to the neighbourhood, there had been all those trips to London – perhaps to further afield.

And now that he thought about it, the elder boy did have a look of Mr Hurst about him.

If it were true, it meant that Mr Hurst was not so respectable after all. He wondered if Diggory would dare look down upon him if he knew that Mr Hurst – upstanding, irreproachable Mr Hurst – had done something like *this*.

If he hadn't been leaving tomorrow, Salbridge would have had half a mind to spread it about a bit, see what people made of the rumour. What a scandal it could be.

He smiled to himself as he walked back up the stairs.

He did not know whether Mrs Hurst had been married to begin with, whether she had left her husband for Mr Hurst and the man had lately died, or whether she had simply been content to be Mr Hurst's mistress until now.

But if there *had* ever been a Mr Roberts, Lord Salbridge would bet he was not the father of those three children.

VOLUME THREE
September 1841

CHAPTER I

In which Diggory Ashpoint rides and Mrs Hurst calls

DIGGORY WAS STANDING IN FRONT OF THE MIRROR IN THE entrance hall, contemplating his reflection. He looked smart. He did – didn't he? His shoes were shiny and his cravat was neat. He looked gentlemanly and respectable and presentable and all that. Perhaps if he were to comb his hair one more time, then—

'Diggory,' said Amelia from the doorway of the library, 'what on earth are you still doing here?'

Diggory jumped. 'Amy! You needn't sneak up on a fellow.'

'Apparently I do need to,' declared his sister, 'if you have not left yet.' She came towards him, arms folded. 'If you delay your visit to Lord Wickford one day longer, I am going to have to tell Papa about your engagement.'

Diggory gaped at her. 'You wouldn't.'

'Wouldn't I? How much do you bet?'

He scowled at his sister. 'Stop . . . tormenting me,' he said. 'Look, I have told Papa I shall not be at the brewery today. I am dressed to go. You needn't scold me for not doing what I am just about to do.'

Amelia raised her eyebrows. 'And yet you have been standing in front of that mirror for an hour. Do I need to drag you to the stables?'

'*No!*' said Diggory. 'You would only spoil my jacket if you tried. I *am* going.' He swallowed and looked back at himself in the mirror. 'That is – do I look all right?'

'I am warning you, Diggory. If you continue to dither—'

'I have not been *dithering*,' Diggory protested. 'I have been busy at the brewery, and Rose and I had to work out the best plan, and I had to – to get my hair cut.'

'You are afraid,' said Amelia gently.

'Well, and why shouldn't I be?' Diggory felt hot and awkward and strangely tearful. 'It is all very well for you to tell me I ought to go and be brave, Amy, but you are not the one who must go and lay your heart out before an earl and get rebuffed and all that. What if he says – well, what if he will not give his permission? What if he treats me as Lord Salbridge has? What will I do?'

'You will bear it,' Amelia replied, 'and Rose will do her best to change his mind. But' – and here a smile crept over her face – 'he has not refused his permission yet. You and Rose do not wish to go on like this forever. You will never know until you try.'

~

Half an hour later – after combing his hair again and changing his cravat twice more – Diggory was finally on his way to Wickford Towers. He rode slowly up country lanes and roads, through woods and copses and past little farms, sweating and panicking and going over his rehearsed speeches in his head. Amelia was right: he was afraid. He was terrified.

He and Rose loved each other. They were both determined to marry. Diggory was his father's heir, and his father was one of the richest men in Wickenshire. This, surely, was all in his favour.

Yet Diggory could not shake off his melancholy. He kept thinking of Lord Salbridge's warning at the Lantern and again at Ludwell, and he could not shift the unease that came from weeks of being slighted by his former friend. If anything could smooth over shopkeeper ancestors and a fortune made in trade, it was the fact that the said fortune was worth twelve thousand a year – but everybody knew that earls were proud.

He had dramatic visions of Lord Wickford's fury. They would take Rose away from him, out of Wickenshire, out of the country, hide her somewhere where he could not reach her – or perhaps they'd take her at once to London to marry some duke's son or marquis, the kind of fellow whose hair always looked dashing and who had even shinier shoes than Diggory. He could imagine the disappointment turning to fever like it did in novels, the fever leading to madness and death, and Rose, broken-hearted and despising her new husband, taking a post-chaise from London to Melford to weep on Diggory's grave – and all in all, by the time he had finished his ruminations, he rather thought that if he did manage to marry Rose after all, he'd have to lend his ideas to Amelia for one of her books.

He was a mile away from Wickford Towers – still riding very slowly to put off the inevitable for as long as possible – when he realized that he was being followed. At first, he thought his nervousness was placing shadows in the trees and on the hedgerows – and then, as he made to turn one corner, a figure stepped out in front of him and he nearly fell off his horse.

'I didn't mean to startle you, sir.'

Diggory clung tightly to the reins as he adjusted his position. The figure on the road was a woman, one of the cottager's wives by appearance, a blue shawl wrapped around her head and shoulders, so that he could not fully see her face.

'What the devil did you mean, then?' said Diggory, rather more gruffly than he intended, because a moment before he had been practising loud retorts to Lord Wickford in his head. The woman seemed to shrink at his words, and he said more softly, 'Forgive me. Did you wish to speak to me?'

She moved a step closer and said, 'Do you recognize me, sir?', taking down her shawl – and it was then that Diggory saw the blue eyes and delicate face of Grace, the woman from the cottage, the woman who had called Salbridge 'Alexander'. He felt unease blossom in his chest.

'I do.'

'I saw you riding, and I . . . I wondered, sir, if you would help me.'

Diggory frowned. 'Certainly, if I can, Mrs . . . ?'

'Abbott,' said the woman quietly. She looked very pale. Her eyes seemed less blue, her cheeks less pink than when he'd last seen her. 'Do you know where Alexander is?' Her voice was thick with feeling. She sounded anxious, frightened, angry, perhaps – Diggory hardly knew what.

'It's only,' she went on, 'that I haven't seen him for nigh on a fortnight, and one of the village lads said he'd gone away somewhere. I need to . . . Do you know where he's gone?'

Diggory swallowed. 'He is staying with a friend in Norfolk for a month – the friend's name is Balfour, but I do not know the address.' And then, because Grace Abbott flinched, he added, 'I believe he is well.'

'He may be, but I'm not,' she said. And then, hurriedly, 'Look, sir, I'm in trouble, and I need to speak to him. I thought you might—'

'What kind of trouble?'

Grace Abbott looked at him as though she thought him rather a fool.

Diggory said, 'Oh,' and felt his stomach flip. 'Look, Mrs Abbott—'

'He asked me a fortnight back if I'd go away with him somewhere, and I said I wouldn't, not unless he married me like he always said or unless he put Janey in a school somewhere, which he has said he would. He didn't come after that, and – look, do you know how long he is away?'

'A few weeks at least, I believe.' Diggory felt suddenly sick. His words poured out in a rush that he could not help. 'Listen, Mrs Abbott, Lord Salbridge is a not a good man. He is a bad kind of fellow to place your trust in. He cares for no one but himself.'

Mrs Abbott stared at him. 'And this from his friend!'

'I am not his friend. Not any more.' He looked at her. Her eyes were wide, her arms wrapped tightly over her stomach. She looked steady – Diggory's hands were shaking more than hers – but she was certainly very pale. If Diggory were to turn the next corner and ride into Lord Salbridge, he thought he would knock him down. He said, in a gentler voice, 'He ought by rights to marry you.'

She shook her head. 'If he's as bad as you say he is, I wouldn't have him. No good could come of being tied to a man like that.' She hesitated. Then, 'Sir, I wouldn't have you think' – her face flushed crimson – 'well, that I am either a whore or a fool. When he first said that he meant to marry me, of course I reckoned he was lying. But he said it so many times and came so very often, and you can't say no to your landlord's son forever, not when there's rent owing and repairs that need doing, and to have someone on your side to ask favours – well, it's something. My daughter's five years old. And I thought, if he really did mean to marry me, if there were any chance – well, what a thing for her. And even if he didn't, he said he could put her in a school, and I—' Her voice caught, but she steadied it. 'No doubt I've been foolish, but he's been worse.'

Diggory was too embarrassed, too distressed himself to know what say, what words of comfort he was able to offer. 'Listen, my name is Diggory Ashpoint. I live at Ashpoint Hall. You know it?'

She nodded. 'You're the brewer's son?'

'Yes. If I can do anything for you – if you need money or – well, you could come and find me.'

She gave a harsh laugh. 'Are you mad, sir? I couldn't go to a grand house like that and ask for a gentleman. It would do me no good, and it might do you some harm.'

Diggory frowned. He had not thought of that, of what it would mean for his own reputation, his own good name. If Salbridge heard any scrap of scandal to use against him with the earl, it would be a calamity indeed.

'Perhaps you are right,' he said, 'but if you asked for my sister—'

'If it came to that, I'd sooner go to the countess.'

'The countess! Do you mean it?'

'Do you think she'd have pity on me? Do you think she'd help me if I kept quiet?' Grace shifted her weight from foot to foot. 'If Alexander means to throw me over, I'll bargain for a better life for his child – we've all heard about that Alderton fellow at Netherworth, the natural son of some gentlemen or other with all that money at his disposal – I don't suppose his mother was so very different from me. And if the countess won't help me . . . well, I can try to make some noise hereabouts.'

'You'd ruin Salbridge.'

She almost laughed. 'I think not. A man like that may do as he pleases, as far as the world's concerned. And if I *could* ruin him, why shouldn't I? He has ruined me.'

Any last remnants of Diggory's affection for his old friend seemed to crumble. 'You are quite right,' he said solemnly. 'Listen, he has been gone only a week. I do not know if he means to throw you over, but I do know he has no intention of marrying you. I am sorry for it.'

'Your pity does me no good, sir.' She glanced behind her. 'I must go,' she said. 'Janey's with a neighbour, and I said I wouldn't be long.'

She turned her back on him, leaving Diggory staring after her as she walked away into the trees.

∾

Meanwhile, at Ashpoint Hall, Amelia was hurrying to the morning room, where Mrs Hurst was waiting for her. It was not often that Amelia received calls. Her father was at the brewery, her younger siblings up in the schoolroom, and Diggory had *finally* gone to Wickford Towers, so Amelia opened the door alone and stepped forwards to meet her new friend.

'I have come to repay your visit,' said Mrs Hurst hesitantly, 'that is – I thought—'

'Of course, you are very welcome. I am always glad to see you.' Amelia waved a hand towards the settee. 'Do sit down. I'm afraid you will have to content yourself with only me today.'

Mrs Hurst smiled. 'I don't mind that,' she said. She sat down, and Amelia was just wondering if she ought to ring for tea when Mrs Hurst said, 'I wanted to mention – that is, we had the Eltons and the earl and countess to dinner last week and I shouldn't like you to think – I mean, I should infinitely have preferred to have your family, but Mrs Elton—'

'Bullied you into it, I suppose?' said Amelia, half laughing. 'I am not surprised. Was it very dreadful?'

Mrs Hurst hesitated. Then she said, 'Yes,' and bit her lip. 'We had the children down before and after dinner – they always dine with us, and really, I could not keep them away for the whole evening – and Mrs Elton clearly thought this the height of vulgarity. And then – oh, poor Georgy ate too many sweets and was sick – all over himself and all over Miss Elton!'

Amelia could not help herself. She burst out laughing.

Mrs Hurst was laughing, too, now. 'It was very dreadful, but I suppose it *is* rather funny.' She shook her head. 'I fear I shall never get on in Society here.'

'Well, you needn't if you don't wish to. Mr Hurst does not mind much, I take it?'

'Oh no. He does not care much for Society himself. We have—' She broke off, hesitated. 'Sir Frederick, of course, has been my husband's friend since they were boys, and Monty is fond of your family, I know, but he does not care much about Society for its own sake. He is happy with a quiet country life.'

Amelia smiled. 'You are clearly very attached to one another.'

'Yes.' Mrs Hurst hesitated, looked down at her hands in her lap. 'I am very lucky to have found such a man.'

This was said so earnestly, so solemnly, that Amelia felt suddenly sombre. She thought of how lightly she had spoken to Clara of theories and assumptions, and she felt a sudden surge of warmth and fondness for Mrs Hurst. She leant forwards in her seat.

'Mrs Hurst,' she said quickly, 'I am going to ask you something very impertinent, and I hope you will forgive me, because I hope that we are friends. You don't have to answer if you choose not to, but . . .'

Mrs Hurst had gone very pale. 'What is it?'

'Well, I have sometimes thought, from your own words and from one or two things the children have said, that perhaps your first marriage was not – not a happy one? And I only wanted to say that – well, that I am sorry for it, and that, if it would ever be a relief to you to talk to a friend, I should like to be that friend.'

Amelia looked across at her. Mrs Hurst's face was unreadable – pale still, her lips set – and for a moment Amelia felt she had made a grave error, crossed an unforgivable boundary. She ought to have followed Clara's advice and left well alone – but she wanted to help, if she could. She wanted to clear the shadows that hung over Mrs Hurst's life. She kept thinking of Clara's words in the street a fortnight ago, and if it were true that she only laughed at her neighbours, that she made sport of them when she might have been kind – well, here was one person to whom she might be of some use, some comfort.

And then Mrs Hurst gave a sigh of what might have been relief. She leant back on the settee as if letting go of something and looked up at Amelia with a changed expression.

'Well-meant impertinence is better than ill-intended civility,' she said at last, with something like a smile. Then she shook her head, and the smile faded. 'Miss Ashpoint,' she said slowly, 'circumstanced as you are' – a glance at the room around them – 'I do not think it likely that you have ever felt the . . . pressure, the urgency to marry.'

'Well, I—' Amelia stopped herself. She had been thinking of her father, that sorrowful look in his eyes when she would not dance, how unhappy he had been to learn that Mr Hurst was to marry another woman. But she knew what Mrs Hurst's look had meant, and it was true: money, at least, had never been lacking. A roof over her head had always been a given. Food, dresses, books – there had never been a shortage. She had no greater danger to fear from spinsterhood than her father's disappointment – and that, she had decided long ago, she must simply bear. 'No,' she said, 'I have not.'

'The press of poverty, of . . . uncertainty, can drive one to . . . to make foolish decisions.' Mrs Hurst shook her head. 'I do not regret – I *cannot* regret anything that has brought me to where I am now, but . . . Well, to answer your question, Miss Ashpoint: no.' Her voice was thick. 'My first marriage was not a happy one.'

'I ought not to have asked,' said Amelia quietly.

'I am glad you did,' returned Mrs Hurst. 'It has been a long time since I have had a friend.'

Amelia allowed herself a smile at this. 'When did he die?' she asked gently.

Mrs Hurst gave a shaky sigh. 'A little under a year ago.'

'And it was a – a relief?'

Mrs Hurst bit her lip. She looked down at her hands, folded in her lap. 'Yes,' she said slowly, 'in ways that I cannot explain. I wish I could tell you, Miss Ashpoint—' She broke off, shook her head. 'No,' she said under her breath. Then she roused herself, sat up straighter, folded her hands in her lap. Whatever she had momentarily let go of seemed securely in place once more. 'Miss Ashpoint,' she said, with a faint smile, 'you will forgive me, I am sure, if I let the subject drop. Let us talk, instead, of books.'

CHAPTER II

In which Miss Elton's confidence is shaken

'REALLY, MAMA,' SAID FELICIA ELTON, AS THEY WATCHED their footman walk up the short path from the carriage to the doors of Maddox Court, 'I hardly see the need for this. It will be such a bore. And if she is too ill to see us, as she was last time, it will have been a wasted journey.'

'It will not be wasted if Lady Hammersmith knows we have called,' replied her mother. 'It is an important sign of respect. Everybody knows one must woo the mother as well as the man. Besides, as she cannot return a call to us, Sir Frederick will have to come in her stead. He has not called for some days, for which I can only blame your father.'

Felicia sighed and adjusted her hair. It was not *some days* since Sir Frederick had last called at Ludwell; by Felicia's reckoning, it was more like three weeks.

Peter came back from the door to inform them that Lady Hammersmith was 'at home'. No one commented on the fact that she was always at home. They alighted from the carriage, and Felicia was rather disconcerted to find the path so dirty. It took considerable care to keep her satin shoes clean. She had still not recovered from the mortification of having her other pair ruined at Radcliffe Park.

'If you please, ma'am,' said the maid, as they followed

her through the doors, 'Lady Hammersmith sends her apologies but says she must see you in her chamber. She cannot come down today.'

'Very well,' said Mrs Elton, rather tartly, as though *she* would never have had the bad manners to be too ill to come down the stairs. When the maid did not move, Mrs Elton grew vexed. 'Have you anything else to say, girl?'

'If you please, ma'am, my lady has asked me to inform you that she has one other visitor present – Miss McNeil.'

'What, Clara McNeil?' asked Felicia.

Her mother glared at her for failing to hide her surprise.

'Oh yes. Miss McNeil comes often to read to my lady.'

Felicia pursed her lips, then immediately rearranged her face; she hated her habit of adopting her mother's expressions. Instead, she examined herself in the mirror on the stairs to ensure her hair looked at its best (it did) and wondered what on earth made Lady Hammersmith take a fancy to a girl like Clara McNeil, the daughter of an Irish land agent with not a bit of beauty about her.

The maid showed Felicia and her mother through Lady Hammersmith's sitting room into the bedchamber. Felicia had never been in anybody else's bedchamber before, aside from her mother's, and it was a degree of intimacy she was by no means prepared for – but here they were, in a light, pretty room, with lace curtains across the open window and sketches on the walls. There was a large four-poster bed with the drapes pulled back, in which lay Lady Hammersmith, propped up on her pillows. On the far side of her bed, in two upright chairs, sat Miss McNeil and Sir Frederick.

Felicia blinked. She had not expected Sir Frederick to be present; the servant had only said Clara McNeil was there. She noticed that Miss McNeil was not wearing her bonnet, and she wondered how long she had been here, how late into the day she planned to stay.

She caught a murmur of cheerful conversation between the three of them, but it ceased as she and her mother entered the room. Sir Frederick gave a slight bow. Miss McNeil stood and curtseyed. Lady Hammersmith turned her head to look at them.

'It is kind of you to come and visit me,' she said, although Felicia did not think she looked very pleased. 'I am sorry I am not well enough to receive you properly. You both know Miss McNeil, I am sure?'

Mrs Elton nodded very briskly, and Felicia gave a kind of curtsey. She thought of that day, some weeks ago, in the dressmaker's: how she had passed over Miss McNeil as a matter of course, and endured Miss Ashpoint's sharp remarks. She made herself look away.

'And pray, how is your health, my dear?' Mrs Elton asked Lady Hammersmith.

'I am afraid to say it is rather indifferent. Today is neither the worst of days nor the best.' She smiled, then turned to the servant and asked if she might bring two chairs in from the sitting room. 'Fred will help if they are too heavy, Beth.'

Sir Frederick and the maid left the room, returning shortly with a Windsor chair each. Mrs Elton looked on in disapproval, and even Felicia was somewhat disconcerted to see a baronet carrying chairs. Somehow, it did not seem proper.

'How are you both?' asked Lady Hammersmith, as Felicia and her mother sat down.

'Oh, very well,' said Mrs Elton. 'And Felicia, too. Don't you think she looks well?'

'Remarkably. I am sure she always does.'

They fell into silence. The servant left the room, and

Felicia glanced at Sir Frederick, at his bright cheeks, his salmon-pink waistcoat. He was handsome, she supposed, in his way. Perhaps if she really were to marry him, she might persuade him to adjust his wardrobe.

Across the room, Clara McNeil began to rise. 'I had better go home,' she said. 'My father will be wanting me, and—'

Sir Frederick was on his feet in a moment. 'Oh, but you must stay. I am sure—'

He was silenced by a look from his mother. Lady Hammersmith then turned to Miss McNeil. 'Of course we shall not keep you from your father, Clara,' she said gently. 'I shall see you on Wednesday, I hope?'

'Certainly,' said Miss McNeil, with a smile of – what, relief?

Felicia shifted uneasily in her seat. That Clara McNeil did not want to remain in her presence was clear – and it was clear, too, that Lady Hammersmith understood this and was unsurprised. And she had called her *Clara*, as though they were intimate friends. Ought Felicia to have paid more attention to Miss McNeil? How was she to have known the girl was on good terms with somebody like Lady Hammersmith? She wondered, with a sudden sense of something like shame, if Clara McNeil had told Lady Hammersmith about that day in the dressmaker's, if Lady Hammersmith judged her for it, if she had told Sir Frederick in turn. She thought of Amelia Ashpoint's words that day, the sting of them, and she wished, with a sudden, deep longing, that she had anybody in the world who loved her enough to say spiteful things in her defence.

'Good day, Lady Hammersmith,' said Clara. 'Good day, Sir Frederick, Mrs Elton, Miss Elton.'

She curtseyed, took her bonnet from the chest-of-drawers in the corner and left the room. Sir Frederick remained on his feet for a moment, watching Clara until the door swung shut behind her. Then he slowly sat down.

Something seemed to shift in Felicia. Oh, she thought. *Oh.*

No wonder they had seen less of Sir Frederick since their return from the London Season than they had earlier in the year. No wonder he had barely spoken to her at Mrs Hurst's dinner.

She felt a sinking in her stomach. She was suddenly cold.

'Is she a regular visitor of yours?' asked Mrs Elton, turning to Lady Hammersmith and adopting one of her kinder smiles.

'Oh yes. She has been coming to read to me since the spring.'

Since the spring. Felicia swallowed. She had gone to London in the spring, taking Sir Frederick's admiration for granted. She had returned, months later, days before Lady Wickford's ball, danced with him as usual and assumed that nothing had changed. And yet – if she really thought about it, had his attentions been so marked these last two months as they had before? And that muddled hint about marriages at her mother's dinner, all his talk of verandas and extensions – had he not, a moment later, recommended to Major Alderton the services of Mr McNeil?

When he had spoken of marrying, he had not meant *her* at all.

'A sweet girl, I am sure,' Mrs Elton was saying. 'Her family are not gentlefolk, of course, and it is a pity she is Irish, but there is no denying that she is a sweet girl.'

'Her father is a very respectable man,' said Sir Frederick

coolly, and Felicia's skin seemed to grow colder. 'There is no one more intelligent in Wickenshire.'

'I have been quite flush with visitors of late,' said Lady Hammersmith, with a visible effort to change the subject. 'I had Mr and Mrs Hurst here on Thursday. I must say, I like her very much.'

'She suits my friend so well,' said Sir Frederick, with a slight smile.

Mrs Elton nodded. 'Certainly, she is a very agreeable lady – a little reserved, to be sure, but we shall break the ice yet. Society is what every lady needs. I have often thought it a great shame, Lady Hammersmith, that we are prevented by your ill health from having the pleasure of your company in Society. It is a great loss to the neighbourhood.'

Sir Frederick looked almost amused by this statement, and even Lady Hammersmith could not suppress a smile. 'I dare say *Society* copes,' she said softly. She adjusted the pillows and shut her eyes for a moment. 'I wonder,' she said, in a lower voice, 'whether you might leave me now. I am sorry to be so uncivil, but I am overtired this afternoon.'

Mrs Elton pressed her lips together. 'It is kind of you to see us at all, Lady Hammersmith,' she said. 'You must rest, of course. Pray do remember that if you ever need company, you may send a note to me.'

<hr>

'Well,' said Mrs Elton, as the carriage trundled home, 'it is a shame she was so very ill as to cut the visit short, but at least Sir Frederick was there. He looked delighted to see you.'

Felicia glanced over at her mother – so self-assured, so

firm in her convictions. 'Do you really think so?' she said quietly.

'And no wonder Lady Hammersmith is tired. It must be exhausting to be confined to a few rooms and to the society of such a person as Clara McNeil! I must call more often. Now, child, when you are the young Lady Hammersmith—'

'I do not think it likely, Mama.'

'Really, Felicia! I hope you have not been listening to your father's *absurd* suggestions about Major Alderton.'

'It is not that, Mama. Only—' She paused as the carriage went over a patch of rough ground just outside of Melford. 'Mama,' she said quietly, forcing the words out, 'I am not so very sure that Sir Frederick likes me after all.'

Her mother stared at her in astonishment. 'Come, Felicia. Modesty is always admirable, but you and I must be frank with each other. Why ever should Sir Frederick not like you?'

Felicia swallowed. It was so hard to explain, so hard to make her mother understand. 'Mama, I have been out for two years now. He has paid me intermittent attentions for most of that time without any serious outcome, and you must admit that since we arrived back from London he has come to the house less often.'

'That is only because your father has not asked him. Besides, he is reserved.'

'Or indifferent. I do not wish to wait for a gentleman who may never pay his addresses to me. I do not want to be left without a husband because I have been complacent.'

Her mother's eyes were dark, dangerous. 'You are not considering Major Alderton, Felicia? Tell me, child – assure me that you will refuse him. The thought is abhorrent. For *you*, Felicia Elton, *my daughter*, the great-niece of the Marquis of Denby, to marry the natural son of goodness knows who!'

'Beggars cannot be choosers.'

'Don't be vulgar, Felicia. You know I detest idioms. Besides, you are not a *beggar*. You are Miss Elton of Ludwell Manor. You are the most beautiful and accomplished girl in the county.'

'It is not enough, Mama!' Felicia shook her head. She felt suddenly very angry and very tired. 'Do you know, sometimes I wish you had taught me to be kind rather than to be perfect.'

Her mother stared at her. 'Whatever do you mean?'

Felicia turned away. She watched the countryside stream past their window, caught glimpses of cattle and sheep, flowers and hedgerows, puddles of muck in the path. 'I only mean to say, Mama,' she said, more softly than before, 'that I shall not dismiss Major Alderton without consideration. General admiration is all very well, but he is the only man who has declared himself.'

Her mother grabbed her wrist. 'There will be others. I shall take you to London again next year.'

'Can you afford to, Mama? Papa does not think so.' Felicia shook her head. 'If Major Alderton asks me to be his wife, how can I say no? If I have too many scruples, I shall end up an old maid – oh, don't frown so, Mama. I know it sounds preposterous. I know I am accomplished and beautiful, but accomplishments and beauty are not everything. It would be unwise to refuse a man simply because his birth is rather ... discreditable. At least he has money.' She wrenched her wrist away. 'There is no future for me if I do not marry. You know that as well as I.'

CHAPTER III

In which a storm breaks at Wickford Towers

WHEN DIGGORY REACHED WICKFORD TOWERS, HE WAS aware that his hands were shaking and his head was spinning. He had been quite terrified enough when he left home, and his encounter with Grace on the road had entirely thrown him. He had just about enough self-possession to dismount his horse and ask at the door to see Lord Wickford, but by the time he had been shown up to the earl's study and was walking through the door, he could remember barely a word of his prepared speeches.

Lord Wickford stood up, held out his hand to shake and said, 'Ashpoint, how are you?' quite as though he did not realize that this was one of the most important moments of Diggory's life – which, Diggory supposed, he did not.

He hoped his hand was not too sweaty.

He said, 'Good morning, my lord,' and his voice sounded odd – scratchy and shaky and strangely high. Oh God. This was not a good beginning.

But Lord Wickford did not appear to notice. He was sitting back in his chair, waving a hand for Diggory to do the same. 'What can I do for you? It is about Salbridge, I suppose. Do *you* know where he is?'

Diggory stared at him, entirely taken aback. 'Where he . . .

is?' he repeated, thinking back to Grace's words on the way here. 'Why, with the Balfours, I thought. Is he . . . not?'

'Apparently not.' Lord Wickford leant forwards, lit his pipe. He was frowning. 'My wife wrote to thank Lady Balfour for having Salbridge with them, and she received a rather confused note in reply. It appears my son has changed his plans.' The frown was deeper now, his brow furrowed. 'You know nothing of this, Ashpoint?'

'Nothing at all,' said Diggory. 'I think you must know that Lord Salbridge and I have . . . quarrelled.'

'I did gather something of that sort.' Lord Wickford puffed on his pipe and sighed. For a moment, he seemed lost in thought, and then he sat forwards again, looking Diggory full in the face for the first time. 'Well,' he said, 'if you did not wish to speak to me about Salbridge, why are you here?'

Diggory breathed in. He was trying to remember some of the clever phrases he had concocted last night and this morning, to recall what words Rose had advised him to use when they last discussed this. And at the thought of Rose, he felt his hands still. He swallowed and looked up.

'My lord,' he said simply, 'I should very much like to marry your daughter.'

Lord Wickford blinked. He put down his pipe and looked at Diggory but said nothing. His face was unreadable.

'And I would like,' Diggory went on, 'that is, *we* would like – your permission.'

Another blink. He saw Lord Wickford take in his words, the '*we*'. 'I see,' he said slowly. He opened his mouth once more as if to speak, then shut it. His brow furrowed, and he looked at Diggory carefully, as if weighing him up. 'This is a matter requiring a great deal of thought,' he said.

The tone in which he spoke these words did not, to Diggory, sound especially promising.

Then a new jolt of understanding seemed to pass over Lord Wickford's face. 'This is what you and Salbridge have quarrelled about?' he said abruptly.

Diggory flushed. 'Well – yes. That and – other things. He did not think – that is—' He broke off, tried again. 'My lord, I—'

There was a sudden knock on the door – a harsh, urgent noise that made Diggory start.

Lord Wickford dropped his pipe, and before he had the chance to answer, the door was opening and the butler, red-faced from running, was coming through the door, an envelope held in one hand.

'I am ever so sorry, my lord, but an express – just come – I thought—'

'Quite right.' Lord Wickford snatched up the envelope, then dismissed the man with a quick nod of thanks. He tore it open, his eyes darting over the closely written words within.

Diggory swallowed hard. Lord Wickford seemed almost to have forgotten his presence, and he sat motionless, awkward, as the earl read on.

First, his face reddened. Then it went deathly pale. The pipe rolled from the desk and landed on the rug without his noticing. Lord Wickford put the letter down, and then he swore so loudly that Diggory almost fell out of his chair.

'My lord?'

The earl looked up, as though startled by Diggory's presence. 'Oh, Ashpoint, I – listen, I must—' He was standing up, shoving the letter into his jacket pocket. His voice was

laced with something Diggory could not identify – fear, perhaps, panic. 'I have to go – I am sorry we cannot continue
this – another day, to be sure, but – I—'

And then, without finishing his sentence, Lord Wickford
hurried out the door, leaving Diggory behind to marvel at
how very badly this had all gone.

≈

Lady Rose had been watching from the library window as
Diggory rode up to the house, and she was watching still
as he left. She could not see his face from the window, but
the way he sat on his horse looked somehow *sad* – and it
was surely not a good sign that he was leaving, that her
father had not called her to his study while Diggory was
still there.

She willed him to look round, to look for her, but he
was riding on, onto the drawbridge, across the moat and
out onto the road.

Rose told herself she would not cry. She was going to
marry Diggory Ashpoint, and nobody – no father or mother
or brother – could stop her.

She walked quickly down the stairs towards her father's
study. It would be best, surely, to have it out with him at
once, to tell him that she was quite determined, to beg or
plead or ask for her mother's interference – whatever
would help. If there were to be a scene, she had better get
it over with.

She was halfway down the staircase when she heard
raised voices. Her father's first, and then her mother's,
carrying through the closed door of the study. She could not
hear the words, but her father sounded – anxious, panicked?

And her mother was – crying. Surely not. She could not remember having ever heard her mother cry before.

Rose felt faintly sick. They surely could not be so against the match as that. She knew that Diggory was worried and that Salbridge would be against them – she had half-expected some degree of strife and persuasion – but she had not expected this. Why, her mother was sobbing heartily now, and she caught the word 'ruin' suddenly audible in her father's grave, desperate tone. As if it would ruin her to marry Diggory! She would be able to hold her head up far higher as Diggory Ashpoint's wife than as Lord Salbridge's sister.

Rose moved quickly down the rest of the staircase, walking heavily so that they might hear her approach. She knocked hard upon her father's door.

The raised voices ceased at once, followed by a stream of murmurs and whispers, and then Lady Wickford called out, 'Rose, dear, is that you?' in a trembling voice.

'Yes, Mama.'

'You had better come in,' said her father.

Rose pushed open the door and stepped inside. Both her parents stood by the desk, her father paler than she had ever seen him, her mother with tears in her eyes.

'What has happened, Papa?' she asked.

'Well, Rose,' said her father, sitting down heavily in his chair, 'two things have happened this morning. I have received an express from my brother in London, and Mr Diggory Ashpoint has called to see me – you know on what errand, I presume.'

Rose swallowed and stood her ground. 'Yes,' she said firmly. She barely heard the words about the express; they were lost behind the thought of Diggory, the image of Diggory riding away.

'You have given him your own answer, I suppose,' said her father, 'as young ladies like to these days.'

'I have,' said Rose. She looked between her parents – her father's odd expression; her mother's faint attempt to stem her tears. 'What did you say to him?' she asked her father.

'I told him I must think about it,' he replied, 'and then this damned letter came, and I sent the fellow away.' He waved a sheet of paper in his hand. It was crumpled, as though he had crushed it in his fist.

Rose frowned. 'What letter?'

But her mother spoke over her. 'Do you wish very much to marry him?' she asked, and she sounded somewhere between relieved and upset.

'Yes,' replied Rose. She looked at her parents, their stricken faces. She could make no sense of any of this. 'Mama, Papa, must you really leave me in such suspense? Am I to have your consent or not?'

There was a moment's pause.

'I shall tell you plainly that I intend to marry Diggory with or without it,' said Rose. This felt like a very brave and daring thing to say, and she was aware that her hands were shaking. 'If we must wait until I am one-and-twenty and may do as I please, or if we must go to Scotland, so be it, but I am going to marry Diggory.'

Still there was silence. Her father frowned, and her mother looked pained.

'And why should I not?' cried Rose. 'He is kind and clever, and he works hard, and I love him, and he loves me, and I really do not know what more I could want. I know my brother would not think him worthy, but what is blood compared to goodness? What is birth weighed against affection?'

Her father winced at the mention of her brother, but that was all.

'Well,' Lord Wickford said at last, 'it is not what I would have once hoped for you, Rose, but I hardly see how I can prevent it now.'

'And the Ashpoints have money, to be sure,' said her mother, in a trembling voice. 'We will not need to worry about *you*, at least.'

There was an odd emphasis here that Rose did not quite understand. She frowned. She felt that she had triumphed, that this was, perhaps, the best she could have hoped for – and yet there was still something in her parents' manner that unsettled her. 'You are . . . giving me your consent?' she asked.

'I suppose we are,' said her father gravely. 'Only, listen here, Rose – this express contains some very grave news about your brother.' He held up once more that crumpled sheet of paper. 'It appears he has not been with the Balfours this last week but in London, and his activities there . . . well, there are certain – financial implications, shall we say, even leaving aside the . . . scandal. I shall spare you the details, but . . . it will all be known soon enough.'

Rose frowned. 'I don't understand. What has Salbridge done?'

Her father shook his head very solemnly. 'What has he not done?' he muttered.

Her mother gave a sob. She said something else, mumbled words that came tumbling out between tears: something about Wickford Towers, something about ruin, something about wedding clothes.

'What your mother means,' said Lord Wickford, 'is that we shall not be able to afford your trousseau, and we shall not be able to pay for the wedding, and we shall not be able to give you a dowry.' He gave a very weak smile. 'But you may marry Mr Diggory Ashpoint if you wish, Rose – that is, if he still wants to marry you.'

CHAPTER IV

In which a new tide of gossip spreads through the county

THE RUMOURS BEGAN SLOWLY. THE BUTCHER WHISPERED to the baker that the Wickfords had not paid their bills. Mr Graves at the Lantern was informed that Lord Wickford and Lord Salbridge would not be renewing their subscription and that neither were to be let in. The servants from Wickford Towers gathered around the newspapers in the King's Arms to read advertisements for new positions.

Mr Elton received a letter from his son in London, telling him that Lord Salbridge had been arrested for debt, that he had been released into his uncle's custody after his uncle had paid some of his bills, the total sum of which was beyond anything even Augustus Elton MP thought proper. *Enough for an election campaign*, he declared, which Mr Elton supposed was a hint.

One of Mr Crayton's banker friends in the city wrote to tell him that it was all up at Wickford Towers, that the place had been mortgaged for years and that the mortgage was, at last, forfeited, that the house and land were to be sold.

In short, the Wickfords were ruined, and everybody would know soon enough.

'Tell me again,' said Diggory softly to Rose, 'what exactly did Salbridge do?'

They were sitting together on one of the settees in the parlour at Ashpoint Hall, while their fathers sat in Mr Ashpoint's study down the hall, talking about money. Diggory was feeling so anxious he had already drunk three cups of tea, and Rose looked pale and shaky. This last week, he knew, had been a shock for her. She had known her family were not as wealthy as they had once been, that Salbridge's expenditure worried her father – but she had not known that the situation was so very hopeless.

And now it had come to this – some final escapade of Salbridge's, and the family's fortunes were all dried up. Wickford Towers was to be sold, and Lord Wickford, Lady Wickford and Lord Salbridge were to go abroad, where they might weather the storm and live off the very little they had left. Rose was – Diggory hoped, *prayed* – to stay with him, but it would all depend on the conversation currently happening three rooms away.

'I hardly know,' said Rose. 'Papa will tell me so little. I do not think he has told Mama everything either.' She shook her head. 'I *hate* that,' she muttered. 'He might have told us how bad things were years ago, and we would have been prepared. Instead, we have gone on acting as though we had all the money in the world – and why? Because Papa was too proud for economy, too ashamed to admit that we had less than he thought we ought? I am so *angry*.' She sighed, gulped her tea. 'The fact is that Papa made some speculations when he was younger that were not – well, not wise – and Salbridge has been in and out of debt since he left school.'

'And recently?'

'Recently,' said Rose, wincing, 'Salbridge went to London instead of to Norfolk and – oh, God knows what he did. I know that he was arrested when he struck a bailiff who was after him on account of some unpaid bills. I know that he bet some ridiculous sum of money on a horse. I know that he has been using bills apparently undersigned by my father and my uncle, all of which were – forged.' Rose bit her lip, glanced sideways at Diggory. 'I think he would be going to prison, were my uncle not a judge. And I overheard some – some things about women,' she added, in a quiet voice, as though she were not quite sure that she ought to say more. 'I don't know exactly what.'

Had Grace Abbott gone to the countess, then, as she had said she might? Diggory looked over at Rose, uncertain whether he ought to tell her about that, too, but she looked so tired and tearful that he was not sure he should add to her worries. He reached out and put his hand over hers. 'It will be all right,' he murmured.

'Will it?' asked Rose, in a low voice. 'And what if your father says no – what if he says he does not want you to marry into a family tainted by all of *this*?'

Diggory swallowed. It had been his great fear, too, since the rumours began to circulate. Everything had shifted now, and whether Mr Ashpoint thought the family more likely to be raised up by Diggory marrying an earl's daughter or dragged down by the fate of that earl, it was difficult to say.

'We shall find a way,' he whispered, pulling Rose towards him, arms around her shoulders. 'I promise we shall find a way.'

~

Meanwhile, Mr Ashpoint sat in his study, looking across at Lord Wickford. He had never seen the earl like this – cowed and anxious and eager to please, all that Wickford self-importance vanished with the wind.

Lord Wickford had spent the last half an hour laying out the facts. Diggory and Rose were in love – which Mr Ashpoint had gathered for himself by Diggory's manner of greeting Rose when she and her father arrived at Ashpoint Hall – and Lord Wickford was very willing that they should marry and as soon as possible. He had then gone on to confirm that, yes, the rumours circulating this last week were quite true: the family was all but bankrupt, and Wickford Towers was to be sold at once. Lord Wickford had not dwelt long on his son's misadventures, but he had gone into enough detail to leave Mr Ashpoint in no doubt of both Lord Salbridge's infamy and his excess.

'And so you see, Mr Ashpoint,' Lord Wickford finished, with what seemed a brave attempt at cheerfulness, 'this romance of our children is rather timely. My wife and I shall have to leave Wickenshire, of course. We are to go to the Continent. We shall take Salbridge with us and try to correct him as best we can. But Lady Rose will be spared the disgrace. She will be able to stay. That is' – he hesitated, and the feigned cheerfulness slipped into agitation – 'that is, if you are quite content to . . . ?'

The question hung in the air.

Mr Ashpoint sat forwards and sipped his coffee. His head ached. He could not quite grasp the magnitude of everything he had heard this last hour. Diggory wanted to marry an earl's daughter, and this earl's daughter wanted to marry him. Wonderful, glorious news – a fortnight ago, Mr Ashpoint would have been beyond delighted to see Diggory

united to such a family. But the tidings of the Wickfords'
ruin startled him. Of course, it made the match less straight-
forwardly grand than it might have been – but that was
nothing to the shock he felt at its happening at all. Here was
Lord Wickford, with all his eminent ancestry, with his title
and his grandeur and his old, old house. Lord Wickford, the
leading man in the neighbourhood – ruined.

Mr Ashpoint felt, suddenly, for the first time in his life,
that it was a better thing to be a brewer than it was to be
an earl.

Lord Wickford cleared his throat, and Mr Ashpoint realized he was waiting for an answer.

He thought of Diggory: Diggory lounging in the parlour,
coming down late for breakfast, pulling faces at Amelia;
Diggory at the brewery, working harder this last month than
Mr Ashpoint had thought him capable of; Diggory throwing his arms around Rose in the entrance hall as though
nothing else mattered.

And he thought of his own youth, so many years gone, of
the great trepidation with which he had asked Charlotte, so
far above him, to be his wife, of that burst of joy in his heart
when she had said yes.

'Of course I shall not stand in their way,' he said.

Lord Wickford's shoulders dropped, and he sat up a little
straighter. 'You understand that – that I can give Lady Rose
no dowry?'

'Yes,' said Mr Ashpoint. He paused, his mind working
quickly. 'Of course, Diggory is my heir, but it will be some
years before Ashpoint Hall and the business go to him. I
am prepared to settle three thousand a year on him for his
own use in the meantime, and I would encourage him to

purchase a house of his own in Melford upon his marriage. Their circumstances will be quite easy.'

Lord Wickford nodded and swallowed hard. Mr Ashpoint wondered what it must cost him, to have this conversation.

'Lady Wickford is concerned about Lady Rose's wedding clothes.' Lord Wickford almost winced as he spoke. 'And there is the wedding itself, of course – we are not . . .'

'I can pay for it all,' said Mr Ashpoint. He looked across at the earl, who was shifting uncomfortably in his seat, and he asked gently, 'When are you to leave?'

Lord Wickford gave a long sigh. 'As soon as we can, I suppose – a month, perhaps two. We shall have to – to auction the contents of the house. For the sake of the past, I should dearly love to preside over one last Harvest Ball, and of course we must stay for the wedding, but after that . . .' Lord Wickford trailed off and gazed down at the desk, as though unable to meet Mr Ashpoint's eye.

Mr Ashpoint felt a great wave of pity for this man. What a long way it was to fall.

'If I can be of any assistance,' he said, 'if there is anything at all I can do to help – if your present expenses . . . ?'

Lord Wickford said nothing, but Mr Ashpoint saw from the look on his face that such an offer was not unwelcome.

'Let me write you a cheque for five hundred pounds,' said Mr Ashpoint, and Lord Wickford looked as though he might cry – whether in relief or at the indignity of taking such a sum from a man like him, Mr Ashpoint hardly knew.

He told himself that it did not matter. If he could help, he would. This man was to be Diggory's father-in-law, after all.

'Must you really leave Wickenshire?' he asked gently. 'I am sure we might be able to arrange—'

'We must,' said Lord Wickford, and Mr Ashpoint knew that his pride was not yet all burnt away.

'Of course.' Mr Ashpoint rose to his feet. 'Well,' he said, with an attempt at a smile, 'we had better go and tell Diggory and Lady Rose to be happy.'

~

The tide of rumour changed direction.

When Miss Waterson exchanged thoughts about the Wickfords' ruin with Mrs Crayton at the dressmaker's, she was told that Lady Rose, at least, was to be saved – that she was to marry Mr Diggory Ashpoint. Mrs Crayton had heard it from Lady Hammersmith, who had heard it from Lady Wickford herself.

On Miss Waterson's return home, she relayed the news to Miss Maddon. They drew out their large blackboard to firm up the dotted line already in place between Diggory Ashpoint and Lady Rose.

Miss Nettlebed, who traded in gossip quite as much as in gowns, told Mrs Palmer what she had overheard – but Mrs Palmer declared she knew already, for she and her daughters had spotted Lady Wickford taking Diggory Ashpoint and Lady Rose to view a house on Lowick Terrace, only a few doors down from them.

The word spread fast down Grange Street. The tradespeople of Melford waited for orders to come in – and sighed to each other when they saw the Ashpoint carriage departing on shopping trips to Melcastle.

It was soon common knowledge at the brewery, and Diggory announced it himself at the Lantern. Lonsdale smiled knowingly, and Brisset shook his hand, and Mr

Duckfield asked if they intended to marry from the church at Wickford or from St Matthew's. Edmund Crayton wondered if per-haps he'd better shift his allegiance from Lord Salbridge to Diggory Ashpoint – it was rather less fun being friends with an earl's son now that he was disgraced. Major Alderton congratulated Diggory heartily and wondered if the old tale of one marriage following another would do him any good.

The neighbourhood was divided on the coming marriage. The first faction (consisting of, amongst others, Mrs Elton and all the servants at Wickford Towers) believed that Diggory Ashpoint was not good enough for Lady Rose. The second (consisting of the Craytons and all the men at the brewery) believed that Lady Rose was not rich enough for Diggory Ashpoint.

News of the Wickfords' ruin and news of the wedding now came hand in hand. Everybody knew without a shadow of a doubt that it was all over at Wickford Towers, that Lord and Lady Wickford and Lord Salbridge were to leave the county, the very country, mere days after the wedding. In two weeks' time, the Harvest Ball would take place. A fortnight after that, Diggory and Lady Rose would be united, and three days later, the family would be gone. Wickford Towers was to be boarded up and sold.

The news of the bankruptcy at Wickford Towers and the family's coming flight caused almost as much pleasure as the news of the coming marriage. To be sure, Society was aghast. To lose the highest family in the neighbourhood seemed almost unbelievable. And yet more than a few residents of Wickenshire allowed themselves a smile. Mrs Crayton told her husband that she had always thought young Lord Salbridge a reprobate, and Captain Palmer remarked to his wife that it was about time someone pulled those swells down to earth.

The earl and countess had always been too proud: proud of their rank, of their house, of their moat, of their children. The Eltons might frown to see a great family fall, but for the residents of Melford, the professionals and the shop-keepers and the farmers in the surrounding fields, it was a different matter entirely. With the fall of the earl and count-ess, the rest of Wickenshire felt themselves a little higher up the ladder than before.

CHAPTER V

In which two young ladies are made uneasy

ALL THIS TALK OF MARRIAGE AND RUIN MADE FELICIA feel despondent. She tried not to think of it. She tried to concentrate on Kuhlau's sonatina opus 20, to keep her notes steady. She tried not to feel Monsieur Brisset's eyes on her hands, tried not to think of how soon her lesson would be over.

There was a knock on the door. She did not stop playing. Her maid, Sarah, crossed the room to answer it, and Felicia forced herself to look up as the parlourmaid peered in.

'If you please, miss,' she said, 'Major Alderton enquires whether you are at home.'

Felicia tried not to wince. She said, her fingers still moving, her eyes once more on the keys, 'Please tell him to wait. I shall be with him in a quarter of an hour.'

The girl nodded, the door was closed, and Sarah sat back down. Felicia kept on playing, feeling Monsieur Brisset's eyes not on her fingers now but on her face.

It was the fourth time this had happened within a fortnight.

Major Alderton was now a regular caller at Ludwell. Mr Elton was always pleased to see him, shaking his hand with great enthusiasm, inviting him to stay for lunch, telling the parlourmaid to interrupt Felicia's lessons. Mrs Elton was coolly polite and in vain glanced out of the window each day to see if perhaps Sir Frederick was coming instead.

He was not.

Felicia did not really know what to do. She had thought of writing to her brother or sister-in-law in London, of asking their advice. But Augustus was nearly ten years her senior – she did not know him well – and she had only met his wife a handful of times. She had no close friend to talk to, no girl of her own age with whom she might discuss her prospects. There were only her mother and father, and she knew their opinions well enough. She must decide her future alone.

The news of the earl and countess's ruin had shaken Felicia. All her father's talk of debts and financial difficulties felt a great deal more real now. Even her mother seemed disheartened by it. Mrs Elton had refused to believe the reports at first and, when they were proved true, had sat at the dinner table and spoken at length about blood and rights and asked what the world was coming to until Felicia was sick of it all.

The sonatina finished and the lesson complete, Sarah opened the door for Monsieur Brisset and stood in the corridor, awaiting his exit.

Felicia closed the piano, and as Monsieur Brisset packed up his sheet music, he turned towards her and said, in a low, calm voice, 'Miss Elton, we might move your lesson a quarter of an hour earlier if it is more convenient.'

She felt her cheeks flush. 'Oh no, it—' She stopped, swallowed, made herself speak. 'No, nothing need change.'

There was a moment's silence. Monsieur Brisset glanced

towards the door, towards Sarah. He said, in a voice so quiet that Felicia had to strain to hear it, 'I do not think you love him, Miss Elton.'

'No,' she said softly, 'but what has that to do with anything?'

She knew Monsieur Brisset was looking at her, but she turned away, refused to see his expression. He left quietly, and she walked down the hall to the parlour in solemn silence.

Major Alderton stood up when Felicia came in, reclaiming his seat only when she took hers.

They talked vaguely about the weather and the news from London – their usual topics of conversation. She had tried, once or twice, to engage him on the subject of music, but he could name few composers, and her praises of Chopin, Kuhlau and Clara Schumann fell on deaf ears.

Felicia glanced at the door and wondered whether her mother would join them, as she usually did.

She did not. Her father's doing, no doubt.

And then Major Alderton said, in that cheerful, assured way of his, 'It is but a fortnight until the Harvest Ball, I think. I wonder if I might have your hand for the first two dances?'

She inclined her head. 'Yes, if you wish it.'

There was a pause. And then Major Alderton said, 'I have something else to ask you, too.'

Felicia swallowed. She wanted to close her eyes, to dream herself back at the piano, fingers on the keys, the sound of Monsieur Brisset's breathing. She said nothing.

'I wonder, Miss Elton,' said Major Alderton, sitting forwards in his seat, 'if you would do me the great honour of becoming my wife?'

For a moment, with a dull sense of horror, Felicia thought she might cry.

'I am aware that my position in the world is a little – well, unusual, shall we say? But I have been brought up as a gentleman, and my circumstances, as regards to fortune, are very secure. I was on active service in the army for ten years and, I believe, distinguished myself in that time. I am currently only on half-pay, but I have . . . other sources of income. Indeed, I have seven thousand a year from capital settled upon me, and Netherworth brings in another two thousand. You would always be quite comfortable with me. I am a steady, practical man – I hope – and I have admired you for a long time. I think you and I would suit each other perfectly.'

It was an odd sort of love speech, Felicia thought. What was she to say? Here was a man willing and ready to marry her. She knew – she *knew* – she must marry someone, and someone wealthy, too. She had been brought up for it. It was all she was good for.

'I do not expect an answer at once,' Major Alderton said calmly. 'I have spoken to your father, of course – he is all in my favour – and I am sure you cannot have been in any doubt as to my intentions. Yet I think it right to give you time to fully consider my offer. I believe you may have' – he coughed – 'other suitors. Your mother has gone to some lengths to inform me of this. In the meantime, here I am. I appreciate that you will need time to think, so I suggest that I return for your answer after the Harvest Ball. Does that sound reasonable?'

It sounded so entirely reasonable that it made Felicia uneasy. This was not like her idea of a proposal at all. She did not expect to be calmly informed that she had won an admirer; she expected outpourings of devotion. She did not expect to be told that she might have time; she expected to demand it. She did not expect to be reminded that she had other suitors; she expected to toss her hair and tell him so herself.

Everything she would have said to delay the necessity of giving an answer had been said by him already. Felicia Elton sat, powerless, and could think of nothing to say.

'A fortnight, then, Miss Elton? Please – if I have no hope, you would do better to tell me now.'

Felicia swallowed hard. 'You have my permission to hope,' she said, in a quiet voice that did not sound like her own. 'I shall think it over. You will have an answer soon enough.'

~

'Are you happy?' Amelia asked her brother the following night. It was nearing midnight, and they were sitting up by candlelight in the best drawing room, a decanter of wine and two glasses on the table before them. Lady Rose had spent the day at Ashpoint Hall and had departed but an hour since. Clara had been there earlier, but she, too, had gone home. Their father was sleeping, as was little Laurie. Ada was no doubt reading in bed, pretending to be asleep, as was her custom. Diggory lounged back on the settee, his legs resting on another chair, and Amelia sat on the ottoman, her skirts billowed around her and her arms wrapped around her legs. He did not look very much like a gentleman, and she did not look very much like a lady.

'Certainly,' said Diggory. 'Rose and I are getting married, and Salbridge will be out of the country soon enough. We are to have that pretty house on Lowick Terrace with the high windows, and the glasshouse in the garden is nearly finished. Why shouldn't I be happy?'

Amelia surveyed him for a moment. 'You often used to be gloomy enough when you might have been happy.'

'Well, I mean to be always happy now.' He made a great effort to lean forwards, raised his wine glass from the table and drank it back.

'Do you . . . miss Lord Salbridge?'

Diggory looked across at her. 'In a way. We were friends such a long time . . . But the sort of fellow who thinks one not good enough for his sister clearly does not hold one in high esteem. I have been a pet to him – someone to drink with when there was no better company. And then' – Diggory's face turned scarlet – 'I think he is a scoundrel. A proper cad, I mean. There is . . . a woman, one of his father's tenants, and . . . well, the story is not fit for the drawing room but I dare say you have heard some of the rumours. Lord Salbridge is not a good man. The person I thought was my friend was . . . not him, not really.'

Amelia stretched out on the ottoman. She lay back, her head on the cushions, her eyes on the ceiling. 'I am proud of you.'

Diggory snorted. 'You needn't say it like that. I am a whole year older than you.'

'But I *am* proud. You are a far better man than you were a few months ago – and you are a far better man than Lord Salbridge.'

Diggory leant back into the cushions. 'I wish I could see you as happy, Amelia.'

'Oh, I am happy enough. And perhaps Lonsdale's friend

will get my novel published one of these days. That would make me very happy.'

'Well, it is an excellent novel,' said Diggory. 'I think you are quite as good as Mary Shelley and Edward Bulwer.' He glanced round at her. 'And you really aren't in love with Lonsdale?'

Amelia laughed. 'Not one bit.'

There was a pause, and when Amelia looked up, Diggory was frowning. 'I rather think he might be in love with you,' he said slowly.

Amelia shook her head. 'Don't talk nonsense. I think Lonsdale is too shrewd for love.'

'Maybe. I almost wish you *were* in love with him, for I do like the fellow. We are good friends these days, you know.'

Amelia smiled. 'I am sorry to disappoint you.'

'I shall bear it.' Diggory yawned. 'I suppose you are not in love with anybody.'

'No man shall ever win my heart.' Amelia sat up lazily and reached for her wine glass. 'No, Diggory, I shall never marry. Papa will sulk and look solemn, but Ada will marry, I suppose. As long as she does not marry one of the Lord Salbridges of this world, I do not care whom she chooses. Laurie will probably marry, too, and I shall be the greatest maiden aunt all your children could wish for. I shall spoil them a dozen times over and turn them all against you.'

'I think you would be a very good maiden aunt,' said Diggory. 'Only, are you sure? It seems a dreary sort of life to me.'

'I am quite sure.' Amelia looked at him. She wondered what he would think, if he knew everything, but the mere thought of telling anybody produced an uneasy lurch in her stomach. She wondered if she could write it into a story, hint at it somehow, gauge his reaction through fiction. She had grown used to secrecy, to the deep, distant pain it brought, to smothering a sense of unfairness with wit, to papering over sorrow with joy.

'How does it feel to be the talk of Wickenshire?' she asked, to change the subject.

'A little odd. People do seem to be dreadfully excited about matters that really are nothing to do with them.' Diggory poured himself another glass of wine. 'I suppose Mr and Mrs Hurst must be rather pleased that we have stolen the county's gossip. Goodness knows what everyone will talk about after we are married.'

'Oh, you and the Wickfords will be the town's talk for months – until Sir Frederick marries Felicia Elton.'

Diggory looked across at her. 'Do you really think that will happen?'

'Have you ever known Mrs Elton's will not to prevail?'

He rested his head on the cushions. 'Well, no,' he said, his voice casual, his eyes closed, 'but Lonsdale thinks Sir Frederick admires Clara.'

Amelia sat up so fast her wine glass smashed to the floor. There was a moment's pause, in which Diggory opened one eye and looked over at his sister in confusion. She glanced down and grimaced at the stain spreading over the rug. Then she sat up, frowning, her face flushed. All her tipsiness was gone. She felt as though she had been struck, burnt.

'That is impossible,' she said.

'I don't know,' replied Diggory. 'We saw her leaving Maddox Court the other week, just when we were heading down to the Lantern, and Sir Frederick was seeing her off at the gate. They were ever so deep in conversation. I didn't think much of it, but Lonsdale has been speculating. And I have to say, now that he has said it, Sir Frederick does rather stare at Clara in church . . . Whatever is the matter, Amy? You look rather serious.' In a burst of energy, Diggory sat up almost as quickly as she had. 'I say, you're not in love with Sir Frederick yourself?'

'Of course not!'

'Oh, Amy, you always said you thought him rather silly.'

'I *do* think him rather silly,' cried Amelia, 'which is why I think he does not like Clara. He is far too ridiculous to see her worth.'

And yet she could not stop the memory of Sir Frederick at Radcliffe Park, praising Clara's work with her father; of Sir Frederick at Garrett Lane, months ago, stumbling over his words, spilling his tea when Clara passed him a cup.

'You are talking nonsense,' she said, as though to say it could make it true.

Diggory frowned, and she winced to think that he must have heard the pain in her voice. He would know. Surely he would know. If he asked, she would tell him – of course she would – and what then?

He said earnestly, 'You would not lose Clara if she married. You are too good friends for that, surely.'

She looked at him, his oblivious expression, his anxious entreaty, his firm belief that *that* was her only concern. She was half relieved, half disappointed. And then the words *if she married* seemed to ricochet through the drawing room. She felt as though she might be sick.

'This is ridiculous,' she said. 'It is impossible that he likes her, and more than impossible that she would—' Amelia rose to her feet. Her head spun. 'This is all foolishness. I am going to bed.'

'But whatever is the matter?' Diggory's face had changed, and he was looking at her very steadily. 'Amy—'

Amelia barely heard him. She was walking quickly up the stairs, cheeks blazing, her stomach churning. She thought of all Clara's visits to Lady Hammersmith, how often she must see Sir Frederick there.

And then she thought of Clara, Clara dancing, her grace and charm, Clara's bright laugh and eternal powers of conversation, her quick understanding, her mind so far above the other minds of Wickenshire. She thought of Clara's beautiful smile and soft voice, the way she held her cup of tea, walks with her on summer mornings, stories told, memories shared, the warmth of her lips against hers.

She ought not to be surprised that someone else had fallen in love with Clara. Was it not only natural that someone else would, in time, notice her brilliance, her loveliness?

And yet it had never occurred to her that this might happen. They existed in their own unit, quite apart from the world of Society, the world of men. The idea that either one of them would ever be the object of some man's desire, some man's affection, was unthinkable. She had always thought they were safe from such things. To be sure, she had not liked to hear Sir Frederick compliment Clara, because Sir Frederick was a fool whose good opinion was not worth having, but she had never seriously thought that—

She shook her head. She shoved open the door to her sitting room and crossed through to her bedchamber. Her mind was spinning, and she must control it. They *were* safe. Of course they were. Clara loved her. Clara was her world. Some foolish baronet with a passing fancy for her could never alter that.

Still, she could not shake the feeling of nausea. And she was furious that her brother had noticed how Sir Frederick looked at Clara and never noticed how Amelia looked at her, too.

She threw herself down on the bed, feeling hot tears build in her eyes.

CHAPTER VI

In which Lord Salbridge returns home

LORD SALBRIDGE WATCHED THE FIELDS OF WICKENSHIRE roll by through the carriage window and let his anger mount.

He had been locked up in his uncle's odious house in London for nearly a fortnight, confined to a single bedroom and sitting room, harassed with constant reprimands about the irregular signatures on those bills, about the fight with the bailiff, about the trip to a police station. The first three days had been bad enough, but when he had not returned to the actress he had been in London to see, she had found him out at his uncle's, and suddenly there was talk of suing for breach of promise or some such nonsense – as if she had ever really thought he would marry her! – and his father was writing from the country to say that Grace Abbott had been to see them, that she was asking for support for her unborn *child*.

And, really, Salbridge was tired of being told how very wicked he was. His uncle kept trying to have dull, earnest conversations with him, and his aunt kept reading sermons. It had been the dreariest fortnight of his life.

At last, they had grown so frustrated with him that he was packed off back to Wickenshire with two servants to guard him. By all accounts, he would be there for little more than a month, enough time to see his sister marry Diggory Ashpoint – dear God, what was the world coming to? – before his parents took him to the Continent.

Salbridge was livid with his uncle, his aunt, his father, his mother, for denying him the life he ought to live. He was furious with Rose for degrading herself with this appalling engagement. He was angry with that damned actress for daring to take her ridiculous story to his uncle, incensed with Grace for concocting some foolish lie to gain his parents' money and sympathy.

He let his eyes wander to the window again, as the carriage moved down old familiar tracks. It seemed unreal that they were to leave this place. This was his home, his birthright. He would be the Earl of Wickford in time, and for the Earl of Wickford not to be in Wickford, in Wickenshire, was impossible. It was not the natural order of things. These trees were his trees; this land was his land. These roads and these cottages and this sky and these people – they all belonged to him.

As the carriage turned a corner, Salbridge caught sight of a group of figures coming down one of the lanes, heard a child's laugh. He sat up a little straighter as he recognized the three Roberts children and Mr and Mrs Hurst, and his mind went back to Meg in the pantry. He squinted at them. Yes, that boy did have a look of Mr Hurst about him – and the girl, too. And Mr Hurst was carrying the smallest child in his arms with such natural fondness that Salbridge almost laughed.

How had nobody seen it before?

He had thought it over, once or twice, in the dreary drag of the last few days. It seemed unlikely that Mrs Hurst might have lived for the best part of a decade as Mr Hurst's mistress and then suddenly persuaded him to marry her. It was more likely that there had once been a Mr Roberts, that some separation or desertion had occurred, that Mr Hurst and Mrs Roberts had lived in unholy union until her husband's death allowed them to stamp the seal of respectability over their sin.

And really, what a feat of brave, idiotic daring, to bring one's bastard children into one's house under the respectable guise of one's stepchildren, to install one's mistress as one's wife and let the world flock to see her. That Mrs Elton had been so eager to make the acquaintance of Mr Hurst's whore would have amused Salbridge at any other time – but it rankled him now, the thought that the world would glower at *him* but continue to lavish its praises on Mr Hurst, the thought that *his* sins would be counted so heavily while Mr Hurst remained respectable.

No, he would not let Mr Hurst's name go unstained. The world might punish Salbridge all it liked, but he was damned if he would fall alone.

Lady Rose retreated from the window when the carriage made its way through the gates of Wickford Towers. She did not want to see him: this brother whom she had never liked; this person who had ruined their family, who had taken their home and smashed it to pieces; this man who took up and dropped women as though they were worth nothing; this fool who had not thought Diggory worthy of her, who had tried to keep them apart, who had endeavoured to mislead them both. She wanted to strike him. She wanted to pick something deadly from her glasshouse and put it in his wine.

And yet she was afraid of him. The idea of being in the same house as him once more made her heart tight with unease.

Rose did not like being at Wickford Towers any more, even without Salbridge's presence. It seemed a very different place now from what it had been just a few weeks ago. More than half the servants had already been dismissed, and the house was partly shut up. In a few months, perhaps a year, some new owner would change everything, rip out the glasshouses, let the plants die. The thought stung. In the past fortnight, she had spent as much of each day as possible at Ashpoint Hall or at the new house at Lowick Terrace, where she and Diggory were to live after their marriage. Mr Ashpoint had managed to find somebody in Melcastle who could build a small glasshouse in the garden at speed, and Lady Rose had already begun transferring her favourite plants. She was concentrating on Diggory, on their plans for the future, endeavouring to forget the sorrows awaiting her at home.

'Rose?'

She turned to see her mother standing in the doorway of her sitting room.

'We had better go down and see him, don't you think?' Lady Wickford hesitated. She looked pale.

Rose stepped forwards, laid a hand on her mother's arm. 'If you wish it, Mama.'

Her mother made a valiant attempt at a smile and put her arm through Rose's as they descended.

They were halfway down the grand staircase when Salbridge was pushed through the front doors by two burly servants. Lord Wickford stood at the foot of the stairs, looking at his son with an expression of such stark disappointment that Rose thought it must touch even her brother's cold heart.

But Salbridge only shook the servants off and glared around the hall. He looked first at his father, then up at his mother and finally at Rose. His lip curled into a sneer.

'Well? You needn't all stare at me.'

Lord Wickford stepped forwards. He stood before his son, his face grave, his back straight. 'And you needn't expect a welcome here, Alexander,' he said. 'I call you Alexander because you do not deserve the title Salbridge. You do not deserve to be my heir.'

Salbridge said nothing; he glared at his father.

'Now, listen to me. We shall be in England for only a month more. Within that time, you are not to leave this house without permission. You are allowed outside only within the courtyard – you are not to venture into the park. You are not to have any money, any tobacco, any drink. You are not to stir one step out of line. And I hope to God you repent of the disgrace you have brought us.'

Rose felt that she would have wilted under such a speech, but Salbridge looked his father full in the face, then glanced up to where Rose stood. She flinched.

'You speak of the disgrace I have brought you,' said Salbridge slowly. 'And what of the disgrace Rose has brought? Are you quite serious, *sir*' – this said with mocking derision – 'in allowing *my* sister, *your* daughter, to marry a man with the merest pretentions towards gentility, whose grandfather was a shopkeeper, whose great-grandfather was God knows what?'

Rose took two steps forwards, but her father spoke before she got closer.

'I am quite serious,' he said, 'in blessing your sister to

marry a man whose position in life is secure and whose character is honourable. If the Ashpoints can pull her from the wreckage you have made, I am grateful and I am glad.' He shook his head. 'I wash my hands of you, Alexander. You will stay at my side because somebody, it seems, must control your self-indulgence, must place you on a leash. But I renounce you as my kin.'

Salbridge looked up at him and – Rose could hardly credit it – smiled. 'And is that supposed to frighten me?'

Lord Wickford stared at him. 'Go to your room,' he said, with cold ferocity. 'Get out of my sight.'

Salbridge shrugged and obeyed. He moved slowly, languidly up the stairs. As he passed Rose and his mother, he paused. 'Well, Rose,' he said, 'I hope you are satisfied.'

'And I hope you are damned,' she replied.

Her mother was saying something about unfit language for young ladies when Salbridge started to laugh.

'Good riddance,' he muttered, as he climbed the stairs. 'Good riddance and damn it all.'

CHAPTER VII

In which we witness an act of sabotage

BEING SHUT UP AT WICKFORD TOWERS WAS QUITE AS BAD as being shut up in London. Lord Salbridge lounged about the house, cursing his family, cursing the world. There was nothing to entertain him. All his usual pleasures were forbidden. He thought about reading – but his father had confiscated, and apparently burnt, all his favourite books, declaring them filth. He was not to go out, and even his own family would not speak to him. Every door in his path was locked, and the servants were under strict instructions to prevent him leaving the house. Even if he could have found his way past them, his father had promised that, on the first sign of misbehaviour, his uncle would withdraw his influence with the law, and he would find himself in prison.

None of the servants remaining at Wickford Towers were very good-looking, but still, he amused himself by flirting hard with one of the housemaids – Susan or Betsy or whatever she was called – asking her what she meant to do next and if she would be very sad to leave Wickford Towers.

'Yes, it has been a good place here,' she said, with a glance back at the door. She had brought him his morning coffee and was evidently under orders not to speak to him for long. 'But I am hopeful of finding another. They do say the Hursts are not flush with servants, and I've a friend on the staff there, so I thought I might ask her to put in a good word for me.'

Salbridge looked at her. 'I shouldn't do that if I were you,' he said, in his gravest voice. 'A good, respectable girl like you in a house like that? No, I should hold out for something better.'

She looked at him, faltering. 'Whatever do you mean?'

'Oh, but surely you must know.' Salbridge attempted to look very shocked. 'They do say that Mrs Hurst was Mr Hurst's mistress before this patched-up marriage of theirs, that the children are really his.'

The housemaid stared at him. 'I – I am not sure I believe you.'

'It is quite true,' said Salbridge. 'Ask your friend at Radcliffe Park. Or you've only to look at the children to know.' He sighed, as though the world's sins appalled him. 'Perhaps you had better tell the others – I shouldn't like any of you to end up in so very wicked a place.'

And so, in the week before the Harvest Ball, a new rumour began. It started as a trickle. The upper housemaid at Wickford Towers – whose name was neither Susan nor Betsy but was in fact Bertha – mentioned the matter to her fellow servants, adding that she was not quite certain of the veracity of the report but that it was well to be aware of what was being said. Lady Rose's maid told her friend Sarah at Ludwell Manor. One of the footmen told his brother, who worked at Maddox Court. The Wickford butler told the valets at Ashpoint Hall.

The servants listened and the servants talked. They knew how important it was in Wickenshire to be always one step ahead of one's masters, to know the news before they did. Maids and footmen murmured as they went about their work. Stable boys and kitchen girls passed whispers to each other. What if Mr and Mrs Hurst had known each other longer than they claimed? What if the tide of public opinion was about to turn against them?

~

Lady Rose had kept out of her brother's way since his return, seeing him only at mealtimes, hastening to leave any room he entered. But on Thursday morning, three days into his imprisonment at Wickford Towers, he sauntered into the library and threw himself into one of the armchairs.

Rose went on writing her wedding invitations, refusing to look at him, ignoring the prickle of unease blooming in her chest.

'I do hope you're not inviting the Hursts to your wedding,' he said suddenly.

'And why should I not?' she replied coldly. 'You know we are to have a large breakfast and a dance afterwards, for it will be Mama and Papa's last day in Wickenshire.'

'Do you suppose *I'll* be permitted to come?'

Rose said nothing. This had already been the subject of much debate between her and her parents. She did not want Lord Salbridge there, but her mother thought it wrong to demonstrate the division within the family so publicly. It was one thing to ban him from the Harvest Ball – her father thought it far too dangerous to risk Salbridge's presence in a large crowd where there would be drink and temptation – but his absence at his sister's wedding would be far more conspicuous.

He said again, 'You shouldn't invite such people.'

Rose moved to the far side of the table and wrote on.

'They are not respectable.'

Rose's anger flared. That her brother should dare talk of anybody else's respectability! Still, she did not speak. She kept her eyes on the papers before her.

'Seriously, though, Rose,' he went on, 'have you never noticed how fond Mr Hurst is of those children? If you came upon them without knowing their names, you would think him their father rather than their stepfather, would you not? And the eldest boy looks—'

Rose could bear it no longer. 'What on earth are you talking about?'

'I am telling you not to invite the Hursts to your wedding. It is bad enough that you are to marry the son of a brewer, but you might leave off inviting Mr Hurst's mistress and his bastards.'

Rose dropped her pen. 'What rot!' she cried. 'Why must you paint others with the same brush as yourself? Who are *you* to talk to me of such things? I know very well about the actress and the cottager's widow – did you think such secrets could be kept in this house? Don't warn me off the Hursts as you once tried to warn me off Diggory – they are all so much better than you!'

She stood up angrily, her hands shaking. She grabbed her pile of paper, her blotting pad and her pens, and stormed out of the room.

❧

And yet, as the day wore on, as Lady Rose wrote out invitation after invitation, she began to think over what her brother had said.

She knew well enough that Salbridge was not to be trusted,

that he took great pleasure in lies, in slander. He had tried to poison her against Diggory, and he had failed, and now he was trying to shake her faith in others, simply because he could, because he found satisfaction in her discomfort. It was nothing, of course – a foolish story she ought not to credit.

True, the children did look a little like their stepfather, now that she thought about it – but that was easy to account for. Perhaps Mrs Hurst had married two men with some superficial resemblance to one another; she might easily have a preference for auburn-haired gentlemen or those with dark-blue eyes.

But then Rose kept thinking of the pair of them at Mrs Elton's dinner and at Radcliffe Park a few weeks ago, the smiles and looks that passed between them – and was it not true that they seemed more familiar, more comfortable with one another than most couples married but a few short weeks? And when Rose mentioned Mr Roberts to the children, they were so strange about it – and John had said that odd thing to Eleanor in Italian about what their mother had told the world about their father, as though it were all lies.

She told herself that her brother's words could not be true – and yet, such things did happen. Not everybody followed the rules laid out by Society. Her brother was evidence of the fact, and no girl as keen a reader of Gothic novels as Rose could be ignorant of the scandalous ways of the world.

She went over it again and again in her mind until, that evening, riding in the carriage from Wickford Towers to Ashpoint Hall for dinner, she found herself almost believing it. She thought she might put the question to Diggory, but at the same time she felt it was a very unladylike thing to do. It would be different when they were married – in a month's time she was quite prepared to say all manner of forward things to him – but at present it seemed rather indelicate.

Nonetheless, when they sat playing cards alone together in the drawing room later that evening, she said slowly, 'Did you ever wonder – well, no, it cannot be.'

'What is it, Rose?'

She paused, sighed and faltered. 'Diggory, I have been thinking about Mr Hurst.'

He laughed. 'Have you? I hope I've no need to be jealous.'

'It is – something Salbridge said.'

'Then it is probably nonsense.'

Lady Rose hesitated. 'Yes, it must be.' She bit her lip. 'But – well, have you ever noticed that Master John Roberts has quite the same nose as Mr Hurst, or that Eleanor has eyes rather like his and – and Salbridge said – and it can't – surely you don't think it can be – could it?'

'Whatever are you talking about?'

'And they act as though they have been married for a longer time, and the children are wary of talking about their father, and—'

'Rose, what *are* you saying?'

'Well,' she said slowly, lowering her voice, 'you don't think that the Robertses could be Mr Hurst's natural children?'

Diggory said, 'Oh,' and went rather pale.

~

Mr Ashpoint, passing by the open door, nearly dropped his newspaper.

For once in his life, he did not feel the need to spread the latest gossip. He had his hands and mind full. The Harvest

Ball was just one week away, his son's wedding only a few weeks after that, and the brewery was building up to its busiest time of the year. He simply did not have leisure to dwell on other people's secrets.

Besides, what Lady Rose had said was a very serious suggestion indeed. It could not be true, of course – surely it could not be true. Mr Hurst was a squire, a respectable man, a member of the gentry. Mr Ashpoint had known him intermittently since he was a boy. Say, perhaps, it *were* true – say the Roberts children were not Robertses at all – what did that mean? That Mr Hurst had kept a mistress for nine years and married her at the end of it? That when he told his father he was living alone in Paris, he had in fact been living with his mistress and their children? That on all his trips to London since his father's death, he was visiting Mrs Hurst? No, it was impossible. The Hursts were respectable people.

And yet Mr Ashpoint knew that such talk was very dangerous. People might tolerate Major Alderton in the corners of their ballrooms. They might murmur about and forget the indiscretions of someone like Lord Salbridge. But Society was not so kind to women. The suggestion that Mrs Hurst was not respectable, that she had been involved with Mr Hurst before their marriage – well, it could ruin her forever. The children's prospects would be destroyed. The family would be cast out from Society.

It was all nonsense, Mr Ashpoint told himself. It would surely blow over soon.

∽

Yet the words had been said and could not be unsaid.

Mrs Palmer was appalled when her housemaid suggested

that Mrs Hurst was not a respectable woman. She told Maggie that she was a bad girl, that she was sure such things did not happen in Wickenshire.

Mrs Elton's 'own woman', Hubbard, heard it from Sarah, and calmly mentioned the matter to her mistress. Mrs Elton nodded sharply and dismissed Mrs Hubbard with a solemn word of thanks. Then she pressed her lips together and glided from the room.

Mr Crayton was informed of the situation by his gardener, who had been told by the coachman of Wickford Towers. Lonsdale heard the news from the men at the brewery, who had heard it from the clerks at the bank. Major Alderton learnt it from his steward, who had learnt it from Mr Graves at the Lantern, who had learnt it from someone who worked at Wickford Towers.

The tide became a flood.

At St Matthew's in Melford that Sunday, the whispers spread. The Hursts themselves were safely at St Robert's in Radcliffe, but this did not prevent the townsfolk discussing them. Miss Waterson and Miss Maddon whispered urgently together. Mr Crayton muttered something to Captain Palmer. Cassandra and Louisa told everybody who would listen about what they had heard, and ignored Anne when she tried to quieten them.

At the front of the church, Amelia Ashpoint sat motionless, listening. She thought of her new friend, the way she had spoken of her first husband, the love in her face when she looked at her second. She thought of Mr Hurst and the children, in the bookshop in Melford, playing cricket at Radcliffe Park – of the five of them so quickly a family.

What would happen to them now, if this rumour did not fade?

CHAPTER VIII

In which Melford consumes a feast

ON THE DAY OF MELFORD'S HARVEST BALL, EVERYONE IN Wickenshire was dressing with care.

Mr and Mrs Crayton put on their most expensive clothes, and Edmund Crayton wore two waistcoats because he'd read it was the fashion in London. Miss Waterson donned her new silk, and Miss Maddon wore a fine satin gown. Mr Duckfield dressed in his best tails. Major Alderton put on his newest cravat. Mr McNeil brushed off his old dress coat, and Clara put on her retrimmed muslin.

At the Palmers' house, everything was in disarray. Even the littlest sisters – fifteen-year-old Julia and eleven-year-old Elizabeth – were to be allowed to come tonight, and so the flurry of preparations and excitement was noisier than usual. While Captain and Mrs Palmer admired their youngest girls' new dresses, Cassandra and Louisa fought over the mirrors and loudly discussed who looked best. Anne attempted to calm them down, but nobody was listening to her.

At Ludwell Manor, Felicia Elton examined her cream silk gown in the mirror – low at the bust, long at the ankles, inordinately wide at the sleeves. She looked perfect, of course, but then she always looked perfect. She did not *feel* perfect. She had been trying all day to play a Mozart sonata in her mind, to let the melody of it drown out her worries. She would have to dance with Major Alderton tonight.

In the little damp bedroom of his home on Mill Lane, Lonsdale smoothed out his waistcoat with his fingers. He did not have a proper looking glass, but he had tried to angle his shaving mirror so as to give some impression of his appearance. He had bought a new suit of clothes with what was left from the twenty-five pounds he won at the Lantern months ago – half of the money had gone to his aunt in Radcliffe village, the woman who had raised him after his parents' deaths, and much of the rest on repairs to the house. He looked very respectable tonight – respectable enough to seem more than half a gentleman, respectable enough to ask Amelia Ashpoint to dance. He pulled on his jacket and gloves, then lifted a crisp envelope from his straw mattress and folded it into his breast pocket with a smile.

At Wickford Towers, one of the few remaining maids helped Lady Rose on with her lilac satin gown. It would be her and Diggory's first public appearance as a betrothed couple, and she was determined to look her best. She was scrutinizing herself in the mirror when she heard a shout from down the hall and sighed. No doubt Salbridge was complaining about not being allowed to come.

At Ashpoint Hall, Amelia's maid insisted on tying her corset tighter than she would like. She had been fending off advice from her father all morning, suggestions about her dress, warnings about her behaviour. At the last Harvest Ball, Amelia had refused to dance with anybody. This year, she intended to annoy her father by dancing with all the men who worked at his brewery and next to nobody else.

Ada and Laurie were getting ready in the nursery. Children

were always welcome at the Harvest Ball, but Ada had put on her best muslin and done up her hair like the Queen did (according to Ada's shiniest shilling), and she thought she looked very grown-up. Laurie, meanwhile, was having great difficulty tying his cravat.

Down the corridor, Diggory gazed at himself in the looking glass, at his shined shoes and carefully shaped hair. Rose had assured him that Salbridge would not be allowed to come, but he still felt a little anxious. He sighed, and Ellington, thinking him worried about his looks, said brightly, 'You look splendid tonight, sir,' which did, admittedly, rather cheer Diggory up.

At Maddox Court, Sir Frederick dressed carefully. He had never had a valet, though his father had kept two; the staff of five who managed the house and garden had enough to do without helping the master dress. On went his best pinstripe trousers, his favourite cravat of dark maroon, his purple waistcoat, his black tails with gold trimmings. He looked at himself in the mirror, shrugged, then walked swiftly into his mother's room. She was lying in bed, a cold towel thrown over her forehead, pillows propped up behind her. She looked up at him with a weary smile.

'How are you?' he said gravely. 'I'll not go if you are not well enough to be alone.'

'Beth will keep me company,' she replied. 'Of course you must go. You look very handsome. Your bright colours always cheer me.'

Sir Frederick smiled. 'I know.'

'You light up this old house.' She smiled, studying his face. 'You seem anxious, Fred.'

He sighed. 'These rumours about Montgomery . . . they are very bad. I am afraid for him.'

'But they cannot be true,' said his mother. 'Surely it will blow over.'

Sir Frederick said nothing. He shook his head.

'You have not . . . changed your plans? About tonight?'

He sat down in a chair beside her bed. 'I don't think so. I decided that today would be the day, and . . . so it will be. I thought – well, it would be an occasion.'

She reached out a hand towards him. 'There is no time like the present.'

Sir Frederick nodded. Then, with a kind of pained smile, he said, 'Do you think she'll have me, Mother?'

'I honestly do not know,' said Lady Hammersmith with a solemn smile. 'She is hard to read. But I hope she will. I hope it with all my heart.' She pressed her son's hand. 'You can do no more than ask, Fred. You have my blessing. I wish you the very best of luck.'

~

By six o'clock that evening, the crowds had gathered. A wide assortment of people lined the long tables that ran up and down the town hall. Held every year on the day of the harvest moon, the Melford Harvest Ball welcomed everybody – and everybody came: baronets and country squires, shopkeepers and farmers, tradesmen and cottagers, workers from the brewery, maids and footmen, little children and aged parents, everybody from miles around.

The town hall was decorated with bright fruits and vegetables and flowers, corn dollies in pride of place, ribbons strung from the ceiling. Each table was already bursting with food, with empty plates set at each seat. A little quartet – pianoforte, violin, violoncello and cornet – was playing in one corner as the guests began to take their seats. After the feast – the gentlefolk present called it dinner; the rest called it supper – there would be hours of dancing, on the town green itself if the weather remained dry.

One table at the top of the hall was reserved for Sir Frederick, Lord and Lady Wickford, and the members of Melford town council: Mr Ashpoint, Captain Palmer, Mr Crayton, a local corn merchant, a miller, and a handful of wealthy farmers from just beyond the town's main streets. In the rest of the hall, people mingled. Mr Duckfield had a farmhand to his left and Sir Frederick's gardener to his right. The younger Ashpoints, joined by Clara and Lady Rose, shared a table with Miss Nettlebed and her apprentice.

Not everybody approved of the Harvest Ball. Mr Duckfield had dedicated his sermon last Sunday to the dangers of overindulging in alcohol – but he was here all the same, eagerly drinking his wine and talking cheerfully to one of the clerks from the bank about which were the best card games. Mrs Elton, too, appeared displeased. She was with her husband and daughter, trying not to look at the group of brewery men beside them, who were poorly dressed, loud and merry – and altogether looked as though they were having rather a better time than she was.

～

Amelia did not mind the Harvest Ball. There was none of the grandeur of the dances restricted to county families and professional men, and in the chaos of music and wine people were less likely to notice if one did not dance, or if one happened to stand up with a lady because gentlemen were scarce.

She glanced around the room, picking out familiar faces from the crowd. Anne Palmer was reading a book under the table. The McNeils' maid, Hannah, was sitting very close to one of the gardeners from Ashpoint Hall. Miss Maddon and Miss Waterson were talking to some of the elderly cottager's wives, and Lonsdale was conversing with the baker.

To one side of Amelia, Diggory and Rose were telling Ada and Laurie about their new house; Ada was listening with rapt attention, declaring that she could not wait until the day when *she* might have a house of her own, while Laurie was untying and retying his cravat.

To Amelia's other side, she caught snatches of conversation: local disputes and predicted marriages, worries over work and trade – and in the midst of it all she heard one of the brewery men say something about Mr and Mrs Hurst. Then she began to catch their names again and again, a low background whisper rumbling through the hall.

These rumours might be nonsense, of course – some concoction of Lord Salbridge's to deflect talk from his own messy affairs, the sort of thing that a place like Wickenshire put about because a woman was not given much to Society – and yet she kept thinking of Mrs Hurst's expression in the morning room, the little she had said about her former life. *I wish I could tell you, Miss Ashpoint.*

She was glancing around to see where the Hursts were sitting when the doors of the town hall opened and in they walked: Mr and Mrs Hurst, arm in arm, followed by the three Roberts children.

The room as one turned and stared. Amelia saw a frown form on Mr Hurst's face, saw the colour deepen in his wife's cheeks – and then the people looked away and a low buzz of murmurs began. Everyone turned to speak to their neighbours in hesitant voices as the newcomers found a few seats at the back of the hall. The farmhands they sat down beside tipped their hats hesitantly, and one of them nudged his neighbour and laughed. Amelia saw Mrs Hurst whisper something to her husband. He shook his head, but the panic in his wife's eyes did not fade.

'Clara,' murmured Amelia, 'have you heard what they're saying in town?'

'Of course.' She paused. 'Do you think it is true?'

Amelia stared at her. 'I hardly know. She has said one or two things to me before that make me wonder, but . . . what do you think?'

'Well, Amelia,' said Clara, very quietly, careful that no one else at the table might hear, 'we of all people know that not everybody follows the rules.'

Amelia glanced across the room at the Hursts. How much worse, she thought, with a sudden wrench in her throat – how much worse for them if all this talk were true.

The music stopped, and the corn merchant from the town council stood up to say grace. There was a moment's pause, a second's silence – and then the assembly began to serve themselves from the rows of food that lined the tables: piles of thick warm bread, geese baked with apples, plates of potatoes and carrots and turnips and onions, watercress and cabbage and radishes and beans, chestnuts and hazelnuts, bowls of grapes and gooseberries and the last of the season's plums.

As Amelia served herself, she gazed across the room and caught the eyes of Mrs Hurst turned in her direction. When Amelia smiled at her, Mrs Hurst looked surprised, then gave a solemn smile back.

CHAPTER IX

In which Melford dances

AFTER THE MEAL, THE PIANOFORTE WAS WHEELED OUTSIDE, and the dancing began in the fading light. Great torches were lit around the edges of the green, and chairs and benches were moved outside for the elder members of the party.

Amelia watched from the side as the dancers gathered. Sir Frederick was to open the ball with the daughter of the farmer who had been proclaimed by his fellows to be this year's Lord of the Harvest. The second couple were Diggory and Lady Rose. Then came Felicia Elton, led up by Major Alderton – that *was* a surprise; Amelia heard a few hushed whispers from the crowd, a few mutters and exclamations of wonder. She saw Mrs Elton press her lips together.

Next came Edmund Crayton and Louisa Palmer, then Mr Duckfield and the miller's daughter. Clara stood up with the doctor, as Mr McNeil watched from the edge of the dance. Beyond them were pairs and pairs of people Amelia knew by sight, servants from Ashpoint Hall and the other great houses, shopkeepers, farmhands and labourers and workers from the brewery, people she had walked past a hundred times.

At the end of the line were a few pairs of children. Ada

was standing across from a farmer's son, grinning very broadly at being allowed to dance. Amelia saw Mr and Mrs Hurst urge John Roberts on, and he moved forwards with all the awkwardness of a boy of eight to ask the baker's daughter to dance. Amelia watched as the little girl smiled and put her hand in his. The girl's mother looked on from the side, a scowl forming on her face; she leant over to her husband and said something in an urgent whisper. Amelia felt unease blossom in her chest.

'Would you care to dance?' asked a familiar voice. Lonsdale had appeared beside her, dressed even more smartly than usual.

Amelia roused herself. 'Well, why not? I suppose I had better dance one or two dances to please my father.'

'I should hardly think your dancing with *me* will please him.'

Amelia gave him a weary smile.

'Are you quite well, Miss Ashpoint?'

'Oh yes,' she said softly. She was watching the scene before her unfold. The dance was over, and while the baker's daughter was still chatting away to John Roberts, her father approached from behind and led her quickly away with a hushed reproach. Mr and Mrs Hurst were standing alone, given as wide a berth as the busy green would allow. Sir Frederick was looking at them from the top of the dance, his face pained – and then Amelia saw him turn, saw him look directly at Clara. He smiled at her, and Amelia saw Clara smile back.

'I am only tired,' Amelia told Lonsdale.

'I have something that may cheer you.'

She looked up sharply. 'What?'

'A letter,' he said, 'from London.'

The music was starting up again, and Lonsdale held out

his hand to her. She took it without knowing what she did
and let herself be led up to the dance.

~

Felicia danced four times in a row with Major Alderton, and
when he asked her again, she merely shook her head. It was
improper, impossible, to dance so much with one man. She
knew that it was already the cause of much speculation –
not only their sharing so many dances but their dancing
together at all. That Major Alderton, about whom all of
Wickenshire had gossiped for so long, should be the marked
favourite of so proud a young lady must be, to everybody,
scarcely believable.

He led her to the edge of the green, saying something
about last year's Harvest Ball, but she was not quite listening.
She was looking across the grass, where she caught a glimpse
of Monsieur Brisset in the torchlight amidst a cluster of
people. Major Alderton talked on. Was this what marriage
was like? A thousand hours of the same person saying the
same things? It was not that there was anything *wrong* with
him – leaving aside for a moment the question of his birth.
He spoke well, danced better, smiled with a cheerful, bright
air – but he did not appreciate music, and it irked her that
he seemed to know, categorically, that she would eventually
accept him.

'If you will not dance with me,' he said with a smile, 'I
shan't dance at all.'

'I wish you would not say such things,' replied Felicia.
'You ought to dance. Otherwise, people will talk.'

He frowned. He seemed to be looking about for somewhere for the two of them to sit together when Felicia,

spotting Louisa Palmer a few feet away, said softly, 'Look, there is one of the Miss Palmers. Ask her.'

He hesitated. 'You are quite sure?'

'Of course.'

Major Alderton vanished into the darkness, and Felicia was left alone. She stood listening to the song for a moment, the steady one-two-three-four, and she wondered what it would be like to be a common musician, playing for money at parties and balls, knowing that the very meat and core of your life was decided by music. She thought of Monsieur Brisset, and her eyes sought him out again. He was walking up to dance with Anne Palmer.

She watched the couples assemble, watched Major Alderton take Louisa by the hand, watched Lady Rose and Diggory Ashpoint dance, watched Amelia Ashpoint stand up with one of the hands from her father's brewery – oh, how dreadful! She had danced with that Lonsdale fellow already, but this was far worse. Felicia frowned as Sir Frederick walked to the top of the line with Clara McNeil beside him.

It was only when the music grew louder and the couples began to move that Felicia realized she was herself without a partner.

She could not remember ever before having wanted for a partner at a dance. Last year at the Harvest Ball, everybody had beseeched her to dance with them. Even at Lady Wickford's ball, not three months ago, men had argued for the honour of her hand. And now she stood alone, cut off, cut out, watching the dance go on without her.

She had not lost her beauty. She knew that. Only, some-how, inexplicably, abominably, all her admirers had fallen away from her. They had talked to her, danced with her – and found her, for all her perfections, less attractive, less admirable than the other women around her. Diggory Ashpoint, whose admiration she'd felt certain of eighteen months ago, was now engaged to somebody else. Mr Hurst, with whom she had often danced, was married. Lord Salbridge was in disgrace – and it was clear he had never cared much for her. And Sir Frederick, who had always seemed her destiny, who last year had opened every ball with her and called regularly at Ludwell Manor – if he had ever really liked her, he had since found out the better qualities of somebody else.

She watched them dance, watched Sir Frederick's eyes on Clara McNeil, her hand in his, his bright eager smile – and she knew it was over. She had lost him. She had lost them all.

Diggory and Rose agreed to take one dance off in ten for the sake of their feet. During one of these short breaks, Rose half-collapsed into a bench on the lawn and began talking to the Palmer sisters, while Diggory crossed the green to fetch them both glasses of wine. On his way back, he fell into step with Lonsdale.

'I hope you have had a lot of partners tonight, Lonsdale,' said Diggory.

'A few.'

'I believe I have seen you dance with half the town.'

'Well,' replied Lonsdale, with a slight smile, 'as you have been dancing only with Lady Rose, someone must dance with everybody else.'

Diggory grinned. 'I have danced so much I hardly know how I shall get out of bed and to the works tomorrow.'

Lonsdale shrugged. 'You might sleep in.'

'I doubt *you* will sleep in.'

Another smile. 'Perhaps not.'

'Well, I mean to be your equal, Lonsdale. I shall be a very good, productive sort of fellow now I am to be a married man. I shall be up at eight every morning and in bed by ten every night. I shall give up drink – after tonight, of course – and give up playing cards except with Rose. I shall devote myself to the brewery entirely and surprise everybody. What do you think?'

'I wish you every success,' said Lonsdale, 'although I myself am always up at six.'

Diggory laughed. 'Listen, there was something I wanted to ask you.' He hesitated. 'Well, I – I wondered if you should like to be the best man at my wedding. Once upon a time, it might have been Salbridge, but he and I have quarrelled dreadfully, as you know, and you – well, Lonsdale, you are just the sort of fellow one should like to have for a true, steady friend.'

Lonsdale stared at him. He looked so thoroughly shocked that Diggory wondered if it were possible that he could be offended, and for a strange moment he thought Lonsdale might be about to cry. And then Lonsdale took one of the wine glasses Diggory was holding in order to shake his hand heartily and said, 'Of course, Ashpoint, of course. I would be very, very glad.'

~

Mr Ashpoint watched the scene before him from the edge of the green. Ada and Laurie were dancing with Julia and Elizabeth Palmer, and Diggory was up again with Rose, spinning her around. Lord and Lady Wickford were dancing solemnly together. Amelia was talking to Clara at the edge of the dance, and Mr McNeil was chatting to Lonsdale some feet away.

Beyond them stood Mr and Mrs Hurst and the three children, lingering in the shadows of the town hall. Eleanor and John Roberts had tried once or twice to dance, but their efforts to befriend the other children present had been met with hesitation, and at last they had retreated to their mother's side.

The Hursts' names were on everybody's lips tonight. Eyes were constantly turned upon them and hushed whispers flowed beneath the music. Nobody outright snubbed them – passers-by nodded and turned quickly away – but nor did anyone approach them. Across the green, Mr Ashpoint saw Captain Palmer say something to his wife and incline his head in their direction.

'Have you heard what is being said about that woman?' It was Mrs Elton, addressing her husband, some feet behind Mr Ashpoint. Her sharp voice carried.

'It is probably all nonsense,' said Mr Elton, 'although I suppose there is some resemblance between Mr Hurst and the eldest boy.'

Coincidence, thought Mr Ashpoint. It was madness to think it anything else. He glanced over to where the Eltons stood. Mr Elton met his eye, frowned a little and lowered his voice.

'I am not surprised in the slightest,' Mr Ashpoint heard Mrs Crayton whisper to her husband as they passed on their way to the drinks table. 'Did not I say so when we heard the news about Lord Salbridge? These grand county families are awash with sin – while truly respectable people like us are never given their due.'

This was not going to blow over. It had gone too far for that. And besides, Mr Ashpoint thought, with a sudden sense of shame, when had anything in Wickenshire really blown over? Wickenshire loved to talk. Of course it did. He was no exception – he, too, liked to feel he understood his neighbours, that he was not behindhand in learning what others knew. A few weeks' discussion of the Wickfords' ruin had left a thirst for some new tale, some new scandal.

He looked at Mr Hurst, his pale cheeks, his hand placed gently on his wife's arm. Of course he must already have some inkling of what was being said, but he deserved to know it like a gentleman: somebody was going to have to speak to him about it. And as Mr Ashpoint glanced around at the assembled crowds, at Mr Elton's frown and Captain Palmer's stare, at Mr Crayton's narrowed eyes, he knew that somebody would have to be himself.

CHAPTER X

In which Sir Frederick overcomes his shyness

THE HARVEST BALL SPIRALLED ON. PARTNERS WERE exchanged, songs requested, quadrilles danced, punch consumed. Gossip was traded in low whispers. Hushed remarks were passed between partners.

Amelia and Clara were standing with Cassandra and Anne Palmer at the edge of the dance. Cassandra was telling Clara how many partners she'd had, and Anne was trying to tell Amelia something about the Harriet Martineau novel she was reading, and although Amelia was trying to listen – she had liked *Deerbrook* herself – she was distracted by what was happening a few feet away from them. She was watching Eleanor Roberts talk to the tailor's daughter, watching as the father summoned her away.

Amelia glanced at Mrs Hurst and saw the grave look on her face.

'If you'll excuse me,' she said, stopping Anne mid-sentence and stepping away.

Anne's cheeks flamed, and Amelia felt that perhaps she had been rude. She smiled to soften it, but as she walked away, she heard Cassandra mutter, 'I *told* you, Anne. Nobody ever wants to discuss books at a ball,' and she felt a pang of guilt.

She crossed the green in the dimming light, and as she grew nearer, she heard Mrs Hurst say softly to her husband, 'You know what they are saying now. We shall have to leave.'

'Surely not,' murmured Mr Hurst. 'It is not as bad as that yet.'

Amelia paused, swallowed and marched up to them. 'Good evening, Mrs Hurst.'

'Miss Ashpoint.' Mrs Hurst's whole face had changed. Her pale cheeks glowed. She smiled widely, as though anyone who approached her amidst all these glares was a saint to her. 'How are you? Have you enjoyed the ball?'

Mr Hurst gave her a grateful smile, then moved a few paces off to speak to Sir Frederick, leaving the ladies alone to talk. Amelia answered her steadily, telling her about her brother's preparations for his wedding.

'I think they will be very happy,' said Mrs Hurst.

Amelia looked out to the centre of the green. Rose and Diggory were now the top couple of the Scotch Reel. 'I agree,' she said. 'Any couple who can dance for that long without tiring must be either very much in love or very much mad. I can vouch for Lady Rose's sanity, even if not for my brother's. But how are you? I have not seen you for a few weeks. We have been so busy with the wedding and setting up Diggory's new house.'

'We have been well enough,' she replied, a little hesitantly. 'The children's lessons keep us both busy.' She glanced over to where Eleanor was now leading Georgy by the hand around the edge of the dance. Beyond them, Master John Roberts was dancing with young Elizabeth Palmer. Amelia noticed Captain Palmer and his wife frown as they watched. They turned to each other, spoke in rapid whispers.

Mrs Hurst saw it, too, and flinched.

'Are you unwell, Mrs Hurst?' asked Amelia gently.

'No, no – it is nothing.' She gave a weak smile. 'I am very fond of Wickenshire, in its way,' she said suddenly. 'It is strange, Miss Ashpoint, when you have lived in as many places as I have, when you are three-and-thirty and have had no settled home since you were nineteen – the thought of a home is . . . well, it is almost a danger. It is so tempting, is it not, to believe nothing can trouble you if you are happy?' She paused, as though she had half forgotten what she was saying. 'Forgive me, Miss Ashpoint. I am speaking nonsense. Perhaps I have had too much punch.'

The dance was finished, and Captain Palmer was stepping forwards, taking his youngest daughter by the hand. He pulled her from the dance and knelt down before her, his hands on her shoulders, speaking quickly with a grave expression on his face. The girl glanced back over her shoulder at John.

'Do you know,' said Mrs Hurst, her cheeks pale, her voice barely more than a whisper, 'I really do think it is time we left. It has been a long day for the children. Goodnight, Miss Ashpoint.' She turned away, then looked back. She pressed Amelia's hand with her own. 'Thank you for coming to speak to me, Miss Ashpoint. I fear it will not be long now before everyone in Wickenshire will refuse to.'

Amelia watched as Mrs Hurst was swallowed up by the crowd. She caught no more than a glimpse of her, a blue dress, a figure bending to lift a child. In the dim distance, she saw Mr Hurst leave Sir Frederick and step forwards to meet his wife.

～

'What do you make of all this talk, then?' Lonsdale asked Brisset in a low voice as they watched the Hurst family leave the ball from a bench at the side of the green.

Monsieur Brisset hesitated, gave a solemn shrug. 'I think it is bad news for Mr and Mrs Hurst. I think is hard luck for the children.'

'And do you think it is true?'

He paused, sipped his wine. He looked pained. 'I am certain she was once married to another man. But it was so long ago that I saw her in Nice. Who can say what has happened in the meantime?' He swallowed. 'Mr Roberts seemed the sort of man who might drive his wife to something desperate,' he said at last. 'And Mr Hurst is certainly very fond of those children.'

Lonsdale nodded. He looked over at Amelia Ashpoint, still standing where Mrs Hurst had left her, an anxious frown on her face. 'You have told nobody but me what you remember?'

'Nobody,' repeated Brisset, 'and I shall say nothing now. A testimony that she was living with her first husband twelve years ago can hardly help, and any knowledge of the state of her marriage at the time would almost certainly harm her. I hope the rumours wear out. That is all.' He turned away with a sigh and sipped his wine. 'Have you ever thought of leaving Wickenshire?' he asked abruptly.

Lonsdale blinked. 'Never. I could not hope to get on so well anywhere but Ashpoint Brewery.' He felt a sudden tightness in his chest, a burst of fondness for his friend. 'You are not saying you are thinking of leaving? Brisset, I cannot do without you.'

Brisset laughed. 'What, even though you are such fast

friends with young Ashpoint now? You will survive –
especially if you go on dancing with his sister.'

Lonsdale shook his head gravely. 'Enough of that, Brisset.'

'You see – you will not miss me really.' Brisset smiled
faintly. 'Still, it is only an idle thought. I am sick of gossip
and Society – that is all.'

Lonsdale followed his gaze out towards the middle of the
green, to where Felicia Elton and Major Alderton were
leading the dance.

'At the very least,' said Brisset, in a lighter tone, 'I shall
certainly give up the Lantern.'

∾

The Harvest Ball ran on. As the night grew cooler, the
number of couples lining up to dance began to diminish.
Volunteers gathered by the town council brought supper
out onto the green: trays of cold meats and pastries, bread,
fruit and cheese. Mrs Elton was dismayed to find herself
eating grapes from the same plate as her own gardener.

Amelia was halfway through a bite of cheese when
Lonsdale appeared at her side. 'Have you opened your
letter, Miss Ashpoint?' His voice was soft, almost inaudible.

She shook her head, swallowed. 'Not yet.' She had been
putting it off, preparing herself for rejection.

'Read it.' Lonsdale paused. For a moment he did not
move. Then he said, in a changed voice, 'Miss Ashpoint?'

'Yes?'

Another pause. Lonsdale smiled and shook his head. 'No,
it is nothing. Do not think of it. I had better go home.
Goodnight.'

She watched him for a moment as he walked off the

green, and then she turned back and felt for the place where her letter was tucked away. The party was quieter now, the dancers slowing. Who would miss her, for just a few moments, if she slipped into the town hall to read it?

~

Ten minutes later, Clara was walking through the empty hall. The central room was a chaotic tumble of dirty plates, drained wine glasses, napkins tossed to the floor, fruit left in great bowls. She wondered where Amelia had gone. Anne Palmer said she had seen her speaking to Lonsdale a few minutes ago, and now she was nowhere to be found. Clara had come into the hall hoping to find Amelia and Lonsdale a civilized distance apart, discussing her novel, but there was only the silence of the empty plates.

She opened the door of the first side room she came to. It was deserted. She was just about to move on to the next room when the main doors of the hall opened and in stepped Sir Frederick. He gave a slight bow but said nothing, and there was an odd silence before Clara made herself speak.

'I was looking for Amelia.'

'Ah. She is not here?'

'I think she must have gone into one of the side rooms.'

A pause. Clara began to move, and Sir Frederick stayed rooted to the spot. She saw him swallow. His clothes were very bright, but his face was exceptionally pale.

'Sir Frederick, are you unwell?'

He gave a strange, anxious laugh. 'Quite well,' he said, and there was something in his tone that filled Clara with a sudden sense of apprehension, with a desire to run from the hall and outside into the cool night air, to throw herself beneath one of the dining tables and not listen to a word he had to say.

He said, 'As it happens, I came to find you, Miss McNeil.'

She let the words rest for a moment in the air. She said, 'I see.'

'I wanted to – to speak to you, Miss McNeil. In fact, I have something rather important to say.'

CHAPTER XI

In which an answer is not given

AMELIA WAS SITTING IN ONE OF THE ROOMS AT THE BACK of the town hall, at a long wooden table surrounded by a dozen chairs. This was the room in which the town council met, and here she was, in what was usually her father's seat, a lit candle before her. Beside it was her letter, still sealed.

Lonsdale had implied good news – but he might not know the contents of the letter, or he might think her lucky to receive an offer to read her next book or an invitation to print at her own expense. She hesitated, flexed her fingers, reached for the letter, then dropped her hand back to her side. She had been here a quarter of an hour and had still not managed to break the seal. While she did not know, hope remained. She could not quite bear to risk knowing.

When the door creaked, she sat up sharply, grabbed the letter from the table and slipped it back inside her dress. But it was only Clara. She had found her, as she always did. Amelia breathed out.

Only, no, something was not right, and—

'Clara, are you crying?' Amelia was on her feet at once, but Clara had already thrown herself down into one of the chairs. Her eyes were red and wet, her face pale. Her lips trembled. Her hands shook. 'Whatever is the matter?'

'My God,' muttered Clara. She wiped her eyes on the back of her bare arm.

'What's happened? Are you unwell?'

Clara gently shook her head. She covered her hands with her eyes and spoke without looking at Amelia. 'Sir Frederick has just asked me to marry him.'

'Oh.' Amelia stared at Clara. She did not move. Her first instinct was to laugh. Sir Frederick was silly. They had always thought him silly – or at least, *she* had always thought him silly; Clara's appraisal of everybody was reliably more charitable. Her next instinct was to cry, because Clara was crying, because Diggory had been right, because the world was falling apart. Instead, she said, in a very low voice, 'Why are you crying?'

Clara shook her head.

'Clara, you did not say yes?'

Her hands fell from her eyes. 'Of course not! How can you ask that?'

Amelia breathed out. 'You said no?'

'Well, I – it happened so fast that I hardly know what I said. I ran away as soon as I could. But I shall say no, of course.' There was something in Clara's tone that stung Amelia, a hint of false cheerfulness, almost resignation. 'I shall write to him. I shall say no properly.'

There was a long pause.

At any other time, Amelia would have held Clara as she cried. Now, she sat down heavily two chairs away from her and stared. She saw more tears build in Clara's eyes.

'Surely this is a mere inconvenience. I am sure it is unpleasant to reject someone but – Clara, why are you so upset?'

Clara gave a weak smile through her tears. 'I suppose I never thought I would have to – to make that choice.'

'What *choice*?'

'For Heaven's sake, Amelia, you know what I mean. It is one thing not to marry when you do not have the option. Oh, don't look at me like that, as if to say it is a betrayal – have we not always been honest with each other? Amelia, tell me, don't you ever tire of our lives?'

'What do you mean?' Amelia could not keep the fear out of her voice.

'I am not saying I shall marry Sir Frederick. I am not saying I want to marry him – you know I don't *want* to – but look at our lives. What is there for us, Amelia – another forty years the same as today? We have no opportunities. We have little hope of ever leaving Melford. We are entirely dependent on our families. But say we were to marry men. It would not change our . . . our connection – how could it? We hide so much from our families now – what would be the difference?'

'Every difference! How can you say such a thing?'

'Because it is true. We could do it. It is not ideal, but life will never be ideal for us. Think about it for a moment. We could have full lives, and it would not part us – we would find a way to be together, as we always have. I could marry Sir Frederick. I think Lonsdale would ask you if you gave him any encouragement.'

Amelia was on her feet. 'I don't want to marry *Lonsdale*,' she cried. 'I want to marry *you*.'

There was a long, long silence. Clara stood, too. She stepped away, and for a dreadful moment Amelia thought she was going to leave the room – but she only turned the key in the lock.

'There is no point talking of impossible things,' Clara said very softly, but she pulled Amelia back from view of the window and pressed her forehead to her forehead, her lips to her lips. Amelia could feel Clara's tears on her cheeks, could feel her breath warm against her skin.

'Amelia,' she said gently, 'you cannot doubt me. You have had my heart for years and years. You had it when we first met. You had it when we were ten years old and you began to tell stories. You had it when we were thirteen and realized that we were not like other people. You have it now.' She pressed Amelia's fingers to her lips. 'I shall write to Sir Frederick tomorrow and reject him.'

Amelia wrenched her hand away. 'Because that is what you choose or because you think that is what I want?'

'Both. Either. What is the difference?'

Amelia shook her head and stepped back. She felt dizzy, as though the world were tilting on its axis. 'How can you want it?' She spoke quickly, barely looking at Clara. 'How can you even consider it? What would it give you?'

Clara gave a weak smile. 'Independence,' she said. 'Children. Status.'

'*Status?* Oh, Clara!'

'It is not the same for me as it is for you!' Clara's voice was sharp. 'You have grown up rich. Your father may be a brewer, but he is still one of the leading men in Wickenshire. You cannot know how it has been for my father, for me, every time the Eltons hold a dinner and snub us, every time we are sneered at and left out of social occasions. My father is only a land agent. We are Irish. We are second-rate here, Amelia, and that is hard. Don't – I know what you will say, that it is shallow to care, but that is all very well when you do not *have* to care.'

Amelia felt sick. She thought of Mrs Hurst sitting in the parlour at Ashpoint Hall. *I do not think it likely that you have ever felt the pressure to marry.*

'And if you married Sir Frederick,' she said, her voice shaking, 'you would be Lady Hammersmith.'

'Yes,' said Clara softly. 'That is something.'

'*Is it?*'

'Oh, Amelia, aren't you *bored*? Tell me, what do our futures hold? In forty years, we will be like Miss Maddon and Miss Waterson – is that the life you want?'

Amelia stared at her. 'Miss Maddon and Miss Waterson . . . You don't think they are – like us?'

'Sometimes, Amelia, you are so blind! Do you never see the way they look at each other? And tell me, really, is that what you want, to think of nothing but gossip and the marriages of young people because you cannot marry whom you wish to yourself?'

Amelia stared at her. 'But – I know I laugh at them sometimes, but – well, they do not seem unhappy to me. You have said so yourself before. And there is more to life than marriage, Clara.'

'Is there?' said Clara. She was shaking her head. 'It is one thing for you, Amelia. You have siblings. You will have nieces and nephews to watch grow up, to take care of. You have wealth to comfort you. You have Ashpoint Hall and all that brings. You have your stories and whatever career you make with them. And what about me, Amelia? What do I have?'

'You have me,' said Amelia.

'I know. I know.' Clara raised her hands to her forehead. 'But it scares me, Amelia, to think of the future. If I had been a man, I would have taken over my father's business, but that is impossible, however much I might like the work. For women in my position, the only step in life is marriage. Otherwise, I shall live off my father forever – no independ-ence, no income of my own, no hope of anything beyond this, living forever with the fear of what would happen if you and I were discovered, knowing that nobody would ever understand.'

Amelia stared at her. She felt as though someone had knocked her down, as though the world were spinning. 'I didn't know you were unhappy,' she murmured. 'You never said – you never—'

'What would have been the point?' Clara's voice was low. She felt for Amelia's hand, held it gently in her own. 'There has never been another path.'

There was a long, stretching silence. Clara leant against Amelia. Amelia steadied her, her arms around her. For a long time, they stood, words unspoken, answers not given.

Then Amelia said, 'You are crying again.'

Clara stood up straighter, smiled. Her eyes were wet.

'What are we going to do?' asked Amelia, her voice trembling.

'I don't know.' Another pause. Clara said, 'I must think.'

'Yes.'

'I should go. My father will be looking for me.'

'Yes.'

They pulled apart, slowly, almost awkwardly, and for a moment they looked at one another. Amelia thought of the letter folded in her dress. She thought of Clara, the ribbons in her hair, the stories they had shared. In all their years together, this was the first time she had really feared the future.

'Will I see you tomorrow?' asked Amelia, as Clara moved towards the door.

'Of course,' said Clara softly. 'Of course.'

When Clara was gone, Amelia sat down heavily on one of the chairs. She felt winded, faint, and she could not quite process what had happened, what had changed, what had shattered. It all seemed impossible, and she felt the weight of their conversation heavy on her heart.

She would have to go home soon. Her father would be looking for her. Her siblings would wonder where she had gone.

Blinking back tears, hands trembling, she reached for the letter in her dress. She had given up on suspense, on hope. What did it matter now? She tore the seal, unfolded the sheet of paper and read.

To Mr A. A. Oaksharp,

It is with great pleasure that I write to you. I have completed the manuscript so kindly bestowed upon me by our mutual friend Charles Browne and am more than interested. I should be glad to purchase the novel for the sum of one hundred and fifty pounds and shall return your manuscript care of Mr Browne, with some suggested amendments.

Amelia read on in a flurry of words. A book published. A hundred and fifty pounds.

It was not what her father would call of a lot of money, but nor was it a small sum, and it would be the first that was truly her own. She could use it for – well, what? To build a better, different life?

Her mind was racing. Clara had said there was no other path. But what if there was?

From the main hall she could hear someone calling her name – Diggory, sent to find her before the family departed. She folded the letter and tucked it back into her dress, wiped her eyes and stood up, hoping she would look presentable, hoping he wouldn't know.

'Are you all right, Amy?' were his first words when she walked out of the side room.

'Yes,' she said slowly, and then, in a stammering voice, 'I have received a letter. Somebody in London has purchased my book.'

It was a relief to have a credible reason for her tears. It was a relief when Diggory caught her in his arms and embraced her tightly, grinning and laughing, saying all the joyous things that she wished herself to feel.

VOLUME FOUR

October 1841

CHAPTER I

In which Mrs Hurst gives some advice

AMELIA PASSED A SLEEPLESS NIGHT AT ASHPOINT HALL. She lay in bed, her mind on fire, alternating between fear and hope. Sir Frederick's proposal, Clara's tears and the letter about her book filled every thought.

The idea that had taken seed after she read the publisher's words had grown and grown. It was impossible – *impossible* – for her to lose Clara. If Clara was unhappy, if Clara wanted change – well, she could give her that. She would have one hundred and fifty pounds of her own that no one could take from her. They could live on that for two or three years, surely, if they were careful – and when she finished the next novel, there might be more. She and Clara could leave Wickenshire behind, move to London or beyond – Italy, France, Switzerland, where nobody knew them. They could see the world.

She knew it would not be easy, that they would have to leave their families behind, that they would have to leave no trace. She knew it would mean running away from the world they had known.

But it would be worth it, for Clara. It would be worth it, to be with her.

They could build a life of their own – no pretence, no hiding, no family, no lies.

Or fewer lies, perhaps. There would always be lies.

By seven in the morning Amelia had given up on sleep entirely. She got out of bed, dressed hurriedly without waking her maid, then crept slowly downstairs and out into the half-light. She began to walk without even knowing where she was going.

As the rising sun warmed her shoulders, Amelia realized she was heading in the direction of Radcliffe Park. Who else could she talk to but Mrs Hurst? Clara was her usual friend and support. Diggory she loved with all her heart, but this was a problem with which he could not help. But then she thought of the rumours that had spread these last ten days, Mrs Hurst's quiet manner last night. *She* might be able to help.

It was a little after eight o'clock by the time Amelia reached the woods around Radcliffe. She had been walking through the fields of Wickenshire for an hour and her boots were caked with mud, the hem of her dress dirty, her hair loose and wild. She had been crying as she walked, and she knew her face must be wet with tears.

She hardly knew how to present herself to Mrs Hurst in this state, at this hour. It was madness to have come here at all.

She was just thinking of heading homewards when she heard a voice say, 'Miss Ashpoint?'

Mrs Hurst was sitting on a bench in a clearing, a book in her hand, an expression of surprise on her face.

Amelia stared at her. 'Mrs Hurst, I was coming to see you. I was—' Her voice cracked.

Mrs Hurst stood up. She looked confused, concerned, anxious.

Amelia straightened her bonnet, brushed down her dress, blinked back her tears. She swallowed hard.

'Are you quite well, Miss Ashpoint? It is always a pleasure to see you, but it is early for a call. I am only out myself because I could not sleep.'

'I am perfectly well, thank you. I—' Amelia breathed in and out, closed her eyes so she did not have to look at Mrs Hurst. It all seemed so senseless now. What a thing to do, to walk across the fields at this time of the morning with a question too offensive to be asked. She felt tears at the corners of her eyes and blinked them away.

'I came to ask you something,' she said at last, and the words trembled in the air. 'And now I am not sure I can – but I *must* know, and, if it is true, I should like to – well, I have a decision to make and I – oh, I cannot explain it. It is too much to say. Mrs Hurst,' she went on, beginning again in a lower voice, 'you implied the other day that – that there was something else, something about your life you would have liked to tell me, and – and you must have heard – yesterday, at the Harvest Ball, I mean. You must know what people are saying – about you and Mr Hurst.'

A pause. The colour rose in Mrs Hurst's cheeks. She opened her mouth, then paused. She sat down heavily on the bench. 'Yes,' she said, after what felt like a long time. 'Yes, I heard.'

'I wanted to ask whether – whether it is all true. Not simply because I wish to know,' Amelia went on hurriedly, 'but because if it is true, I wanted to ask your – your advice, I suppose. I wanted to ask you, if it was worth it, if, say, I loved someone, someone whom I could not—' She stopped, caught her breath, shook her head. This all felt too dangerous. She could not think. She felt hot tears on her cheeks.

It was all too much. Amelia turned hopelessly to go.

'Stay, Miss Ashpoint – Amelia. Sit down. Tell me what it is you think you know, then tell me how I can help you.'

Amelia looked back at Mrs Hurst. She was flushed, yes, but her voice was steady. Amelia sat down at her side and looked off into the trees.

'They are saying in town that – that John, Eleanor and Georgy are Mr Hurst's natural children. Which would mean – were it true – that you and Mr Hurst had – had lived together, as man and wife, long before your marriage. It does not seem beyond the realms of possibility. We saw little of Mr Hurst here until his father's death – he had always said that he was living in Paris, but I suppose he might have been elsewhere – and even since he settled in the neighbourhood, he has been often away. You have said yourself that your first marriage was unhappy, and I can see that if – if you were married to a man you did not love, a man with whom you could not live, then you might live with another and, if one day your husband were to die, you might marry the man you had always been as much as married to, begin life again and pretend – pretend that you had not known each other as long as you had, that your children were the legitimate children of someone else. You must stop me, Mrs Hurst, if I am talking nonsense.'

Mrs Hurst's voice was quiet. 'You are not talking nonsense.'

Amelia swallowed. 'You – left your husband? For Mr Hurst?'

'I did. He did not follow me. He was – glad to be rid of me, I suppose.'

Amelia looked round at her. She felt that she ought to be shocked, or at least surprised, but somehow, she felt only very sad. 'You said – the other day – that when Mr Roberts died, it was a relief – more than you could say.'

'Yes.' Mrs Hurst sighed, leant back on the bench. 'We read of his death in the newspaper. I had not seen him for more than a decade, and – there it was. Mr Henry Roberts, deceased. The knowledge that Monty and I might finally be married . . .' Her voice caught, and she trailed off. 'And now, this.' Mrs Hurst sighed. 'We shall have to leave Radcliffe. It is a shame. I like it here, and the children are happy. Monty is fond of the place – it is his home. But we shall have to leave. We will move somewhere far away and start a newer, easier life. We will pretend we have been married for ten years, call John and Eleanor and Georgy Hurst, not Roberts – or take a new name altogether. It will be an easier lie.'

'I am loath to lose you,' said Amelia, and she heard her voice crack. 'I feel as though we might have been such friends.'

Mrs Hurst gave a solemn smile. 'So do I. But I am afraid we have no choice. While people know about us, we will never be welcome here. We will never be welcome anywhere.'

There was a long silence.

'What did you wish to ask me?'

Amelia blinked back tears. She steadied her voice. 'I wanted to ask you if – if it was worth it?'

Mrs Hurst turned to look at Amelia. Her face bore a small smile. 'I should not have done it,' she said, 'if I had not known it was worth it. But you said you had a decision to make. What did you mean?'

Amelia swallowed. 'Say I loved someone,' she said, in a low, shaking voice, 'say I loved someone whom I could not marry. Say I could leave behind my entire life, live in secret with them. Say I would never be able to see my family again. If that were possible, what ought I to do?'

'Miss Ashpoint,' said Mrs Hurst gently, 'if you mean Mr Lonsdale—'

Amelia started.

'You must forgive me, but I saw how he looked at you that day at Ashpoint Hall. And I really don't think it is so very desperate as you believe. I admit that he occupies a different station to you, that his being in your father's employ is an obstacle, but if you love him, if he loves you, your family could be persuaded to accept the match. He might be made a junior partner in time.'

Amelia was shaking her head. She almost laughed, but it came out more like a sob. 'Oh, that it were only that! My God, it is not *Lonsdale*.'

'No?'

'No. I wish it were something so simple.'

'Then I am afraid you have me at a disadvantage, Miss Ashpoint. It is a – a more difficult match than that?'

Amelia nodded. She did not look at Mrs Hurst.

'You are not in love with – with a married man?'

Amelia shut her eyes. She felt the truth form on her lips and pushed the words away. Let Mrs Hurst think what she would. 'The only hope for us is that we might live far away from Wickenshire, from England, that we might run away and live in France, Italy, Austria, somewhere we would not be found. You have lived like that, I think—'

'Yes,' said Mrs Hurst, 'I have lived like that.' She spoke softly, calmly, and turned towards Amelia as she went on. 'Miss Ashpoint, I told you it was worth it. It was worth it – for me. I think it would be worth it for many people. I love Montgomery. He has been my life. He has been more my husband these ten years than my first husband ever was. But a life like mine – it is not to be chosen lightly. I cannot judge for you. I do not know the magnitude of your love for this man, nor his for you. But to place your trust in someone else so fully – you must be completely sure.

'Miss Ashpoint, your situation is not what mine was. When you choose to snap all bonds with the laws of Society, you leave things behind. My parents were dead. I was an only child. I had no friends to regret. My religion had been weakened already: I did not believe it a sin not to love my husband, so it did not take me long to give up the belief that it was a sin to love another man.' She paused. 'But, Miss Ashpoint – Amelia – you do have a family. You have your father, your siblings, your friends. I am sure Miss McNeil would be devastated if you left Wickenshire.'

Amelia stared down at the grass. It blurred with her tears. She wished with all her heart she could fully explain herself.

'It was worth it for me. I cannot tell whether it would be worth it for you.'

There was a long silence.

Mrs Hurst leant back on the bench, and Amelia turned her eyes to the sky. It was brighter now, as though day had really come. She thought of Clara's familiar smile, the feel of her lips against hers, her tear-stained face last night. Then she thought of Mr and Mrs Hurst, of the talk in the street and on the green, of the day she and Laurie had first seen them, the way the family had seemed to shine. She thought of them hiding at home, packing discreetly, shutting up the house and riding away. Mrs Hurst's kind face. Those sweet children.

'I ought to go back,' said Amelia quietly. 'My family does

not know I am here.' Mrs Hurst nodded, and Amelia moved as if to rise. Then she paused. 'Mrs Hurst – Matilda?'

'Yes?'

'Are you happy?'

Mrs Hurst smiled. 'Yes,' she said. 'It will be sad to leave this place, to be sure, but – well, there are always things to be sad about. I have a full life. I have my husband, our children. We are happy together. That is enough.'

CHAPTER II

In which Mr Ashpoint does his duty

THE BREAKFAST ROOM AT LUDWELL MANOR FELT COLD. IT seemed that autumn had set in with the first day of October. Felicia was in her usual seat, dressed in a fine blue day dress; her mother sat at one end of the table, her father at the other. They all ate in silence. Her father looked thoughtful; her mother looked mutinous. Felicia only felt weary.

Her father put down his newspaper and made a sign for the servants to leave the room – and then, turning to Felicia, said, 'Well, Felicia, have you made up your mind?'

She looked at him, felt the ground shift beneath her feet. 'I—'

'I told the major he might call on Tuesday. In a few more days, I am sure you will be ready.'

She said nothing. She nodded once.

'This is intolerable,' her mother said abruptly. She was glaring at her husband, her lips pressed together, her face red. 'You cannot really intend to marry Felicia to such a man. It will be the ruin of us.'

'On the contrary, Sophronia, for Felicia *not* to marry Major Alderton would be the ruin of us. He is happy to pay all our debts and all of Augustus's. I have mentioned the possibility of future elections and other expenses for Augustus, and I believe we shall not find Major Alderton ungenerous there. Unless you wish ours to be the next bankruptcy and departure, I suggest you hold your tongue.'

Felicia stared down into her cup of tea. She did not know whether to feel offended that Major Alderton had bought her or flattered that he thought her worth the trouble of so expensive a purchase.

'I cannot believe,' said her mother slowly, 'that we live in such times – amongst such sin. To think of a man like that – a – a *bastard* – marrying my daughter! And all this talk of the Hursts. Why, I befriended her, I sought to advise her – and after all my pains and efforts, it turns out that she is – is – the sort of woman who ought not to be spoken of, let alone spoken *to*! I threw a *dinner* for her. I welcomed her into the neighbourhood; I coveted her company. To masquerade as decent people, to live fraudulently amongst respectability – it is simply too horrible. When I think of that abhorrent, wicked woman, I—'

'We do not yet know if it is true,' said Mr Elton.

'I suppose it signifies nothing to *you*,' Mrs Elton retorted, 'when you take Major Alderton's history so lightly.'

Felicia looked up. She thought of Mrs Hurst, her awkward shyness, her words at the gates of Ludwell Manor back in July. What had she said? *If someone should find out—*

And if it were true, what then?

'I do not think she can be very wicked, Mama,' she said – and both her parents looked at her in surprise. 'She seems so harmless. Whatever may be her past, I cannot really think Mrs Hurst *bad*.'

'That is because you know nothing of the world,' declared her mother. 'Sin hides in many shapes. That woman—'

'Be quiet, Sophronia,' said Mr Elton sharply. 'I do not

think it is the *sin* that troubles you so much as the *look* of sin. Would it trouble you, if it were all true but hushed up? Would you tremble so at the thought of Major Alderton's birth were it spoken of less widely?'

'Of course I would,' replied Mrs Elton sharply. 'If I had known what little regard you had for respectability and decency when we were married . . .' She shook her head. 'If my uncle, the Marquis of Denby, were alive to see me brought so low! My cousins will disown us. We shall be shunned in London. When I contemplate the noble blood that runs through my veins . . . And yet still my daughter will wed a nameless, positionless man. She might have been Lady Hammersmith—'

'Mama,' said Felicia, putting her teacup down with a jerk, 'Sir Frederick does not love me. He would never have married me. It was an idle dream. Forget it.' She stood up quickly. 'I am tired of all this fuss. Papa, I shall marry Major Alderton. Mama, let it be.'

She left the room hurriedly. She did not go to her own chamber; she went to the music room, sat down at the piano-forte and made herself play.

~

Mr Ashpoint was riding very slowly towards Radcliffe Park, steeling himself for the hour to come. It seemed impossible, ungentlemanly, that he was on his way to see Mr Hurst with the objective he held. It was intolerable that he was to ask the questions he meditated asking, to receive whatever answers would be given.

He had passed an anxious morning. At breakfast, Amelia had been late and seemed ruffled, and Diggory was clearly nursing a bad headache. Ada and Laurie had been sleepy and silent. He had barely spoken a word to any of them. Instead, he had been thinking of last night, the ball, the rumours, of how somebody must tell Mr Hurst exactly what was being said.

When he finally reached Radcliffe Park, the groom took his horse without a word. The young maid was equally quiet as she led him upstairs to Mr Hurst's study. She left him by the door, and Mr Ashpoint waited, straining to hear the hushed conversation between maid and master inside. Then he was shown in and ushered into a seat opposite Mr Hurst.

The man looked pale, as though he had not slept well. He glanced up with a sort of weary curiosity as Mr Ashpoint sat down. He was dressed lazily: dark trousers, a white shirt, grey waistcoat, no cravat. There was a half-empty teacup on the pedestal desk in front of him, an open book of maps to one side, a few sheets of paper and a quill to the other.

'Well, Mr Ashpoint,' said Mr Hurst, with a pained smile, 'I must confess that this is somewhat of a surprise. It is a pleasure to see you. At least I *think* it is a pleasure. You may very well be about to tell me otherwise.'

This was far worse, far more embarrassing than Mr Ashpoint had imagined. All his rehearsed speeches vanished in an instant. He felt a rush of pity for this man, a rush of anger against Wickenshire and the world.

'Mr Hurst,' said Mr Ashpoint, with a solemn and he hoped sympathetic smile, 'are you quite well? You look pale.'

'I think I have the right to look pale. I dare say you have heard the talk in town.'

That had been Mr Ashpoint's planned opening line. He sighed, stared and cleared his throat very loudly. 'Yes,' he said stiffly. 'Yes, I have. It is about this – this talk, as you say, that I have come. The town – why, the whole county – is full of it. No doubt you have heard the allegations that . . . that your acquaintance with Mrs Hurst is of longer duration than you have said, that the children are—' He broke off, shook his head. 'It is dangerous, surely, my dear sir, to let the people go on like this. It is abominable even for such things to be spoken, let alone to be taken seriously – but there comes a point, I think, when a man must step forwards and publicly deny such things, for the sake of his reputation, for the sake of his family.'

Mr Hurst was looking at him with a curious expression, but Mr Ashpoint only looked down at the desk and spoke faster.

'Mr Hurst, I come to you as a gentleman, because I think I am honour-bound to leave you in no doubt of the serious-ness of these rumours, of the allegations against you and your wife, and I want to suggest, from one gentleman to another, that you make every effort to deny them. If there are any papers you or Mrs Hurst can provide as proofs – the children's birth certificates, perhaps – you ought to produce them. If there are any witnesses who may comment upon Mrs Hurst's previous marriage, bring them forward. It may require some sinking of the pride, but surely, better that than to suffer the talk of the whole county. For myself, of course, I do not believe a word of it. It is scandalous that such rumours have got so far into public discussion. To even think that a gentleman such as yourself – well, it is entirely ridiculous, and—'

'You are quite wrong,' said Mr Hurst.

Mr Ashpoint looked up. He felt himself shrink. There was something in Mr Hurst's tone, as well as in his words, that unsettled him. Mr Hurst sat quite still, his eyes firmly locked on the red-leather insert of his desk, as if he were tracing the scratches in the surface.

'I – I beg your pardon?'

'I said you are mistaken.' Mr Hurst looked up. 'You misunderstand my reasons for not denying this – this *talk*. I do not refuse to deny it because I am insulted, or because I think it beneath me. I refuse to deny it because it is all true.'

CHAPTER III

In which Mr Hurst's tale is told

MR ASHPOINT FELT A KIND OF DREAD RISE WITHIN HIM. He ought not to be here. He ought to have turned back at the gate.

But Mr Ashpoint had always been a curious man. He liked to know things quite as much as he liked to be respectable. And there was something in Mr Hurst's expression that made him feel he could not, would not leave. So he said, very hoarsely, 'I beg your pardon, Mr Hurst?'

'It is all quite true,' said Mr Hurst, in a firm, calm voice. 'John and George are my sons. Eleanor is my daughter. Mr Roberts, when he died last year, had not seen his wife for a decade. Matilda left him long ago, to live with me. In the years I was away from Wickenshire, while my father thought me in Paris, Matilda and I were in fact travelling from place to place under assumed names. After my father died, I was forced to return to Radcliffe; Matilda and the children continued abroad for a little while, but at last the distance was too much for us, and they moved to Richmond. From then until my marriage, I travelled back and forth.

'I am not ashamed of any of it.' Mr Hurst looked steadily at Mr Ashpoint. 'How can I publicly deny what is fact? It would be an insult, to myself, to my wife, to my children.

Oh, I am no fool. It is irritating, infuriating, heartbreaking that it has been discovered, when we have been so careful, when we hoped to live out new lives in this peaceful place. I would not have told the world myself. I would have kept it quiet for as long as I lived. My wife and I have told little lies for months, and we have schooled our children in gentle falsehoods. But I cannot, when faced with such rumours of the truth, deny them. I cannot do it, as a gentleman – no, as a man, as a husband, as a father. My wife and I shall tell anybody our secret if they care to ask us. You are the first to ask me – although, as it happens, your daughter asked my wife this morning, and rather more directly, I gather, than you have asked me. You instinctively doubted the rumours. Miss Ashpoint instinctively suspected them to be true.'

Mr Ashpoint frowned. 'Amelia? This morning?'

'Yes.' Mr Hurst hesitated. 'Miss Ashpoint, you know, has made a friend of my wife. She came here and asked her if the rumours were true. My wife told her, as I have told you, that they are.'

Mr Ashpoint sat for a long time without speaking, without moving. He could not quite fathom why Amelia had done such a thing. When at last his voice returned to him, it sounded as though he had smoked several rich cigars in quick succession. 'I do not understand,' he said, then felt rather stupid, because of course he *did* understand. And yet Mr Hurst was a gentleman. It was madness.

'You are shocked, I see.' Mr Hurst paused. 'But let me ask you a question – a moral dilemma, if you will.'

Mr Ashpoint stared at the table. He heard Mr Hurst breathe slowly in and out.

'Let us say there is a young man – one-and-twenty or thereabouts. Say this young man's mother died when he was a boy. His father is a difficult man; after a decade away at Eton and Cambridge, the son does not know him well. The young man is in possession of nothing but education, money, expectations and time. He must do something. Let us say his father is opposed to the idea of the only son of an old family having a profession. Say, instead, he travels. He moves through Europe – France, Bohemia, Prussia, the Italian Riviera. Say he comes, finally, to Verona.'

Still Mr Hurst kept his gaze on Mr Ashpoint. Mr Ashpoint did not move.

'Our young man walks the streets of Verona, studies art he does not understand and music he is bored by. He reads. He writes. He makes and loses friendships. Let us say, Mr Ashpoint, that our young man is lonely, for I will have no little lies in this story.

'Let us say that something happens on one of his walks. It is very early in the morning, four or five, just light. It is summer. The streets are empty. Our young man reaches the Castelvecchio Bridge and as he crosses it, he sees something. Someone in the water. Someone struggling. Someone drowning. He sees a puff of white linen, a mass of hair – and I ask you, Mr Ashpoint, what does a gentleman do when he sees something like that?'

There was silence. Mr Ashpoint did not speak.

'A gentleman dives,' Mr Hurst told him. 'Well, our young man jumps, swims, carries the struggling figure to the grassy banks. He must realize, as he lifts the figure, that it is a woman. Perhaps he realizes that she is pushing him from her, that she is crying. He thinks that she is affronted, that she does not wish to be touched, so he lets her down gently on the grass and kneels further from her as she cries and splutters.

'By the time the sun has fully risen, the woman is calmer. She is young. She is English, like himself. She is not beautiful – no creature who has been half drowned is beautiful. She is pale and wet and muddy – and she is furious. Our young man tries to take her to a physician, but she refuses. She cries and rages, tells him she meant to do it, that she meant to drown herself in the Adige River, that she has been planning it for weeks.'

Mr Ashpoint shuddered.

'You are with me, Mr Ashpoint? You follow?' Mr Hurst's voice was hoarse. It seemed to stick in his throat. 'She tells our young man that she meant to drown herself. He does not tell her it is a sin. He does not tell her she should not have tried. He only sits beside her and asks why. She shakes her head. She says she should go. When he asks for her name, she says it is Matilda Roberts, and when he asks if he may call to see how she fares, she says her husband will not like it, that he must tell no one what she has tried to do.

'Let us say she tells it all then. Or perhaps it is afterwards, the time she sees him in the street two days later and follows him, then will not speak for an hour for fear of what she has done. Say it is at any time in the weeks that follow, the stolen meetings at coffee houses or in quiet streets, in fields outside the city, two months of confusion and madness and joy. It does not matter when she tells it. So let us say she tells it then.

'Our young woman is the daughter of a poor clergyman. She grows up in a quiet village, has a happy childhood until her mother dies, until her father follows a few years later. At sixteen, the girl is alone and penniless. She has one uncle somewhere whom she barely knows, but he does not want her. Instead, she is taken in by a rich fine lady of the parish, who has taken a fancy to her pretty face.

'But the lady is disappointed with her new ward. She expected a bright young woman to liven her old days, not a bookish, awkward girl with no love of company. They are not suited to one another, and by the time our young woman reaches the age of seventeen, the lady's only wish is to see her married and gone.

'Let us say that there are many men amongst her friends. The lady selects one, a seafaring man, an officer who has just returned from eighteen months at sea. She dresses her ward in the best finery she has and presents her, as a vendor might a rare piece of jewellery. The officer is not, perhaps, a bad man – yet. He has been at sea since he was a boy, was promoted in the Napoleonic Wars over a decade before. In the last year, he has turned thirty-five and has come back to England to seek a wife.

'The fine lady tells him of the sweet nature of her ward. She is pretty. She is young. He does not mind that she is reserved. Let us say he thinks it will suit him. He thinks himself in love, and perhaps he is. He is handsome, cheerful, appears younger than his years. She thinks herself in love, too, and perhaps she is. There should be no mistake here. This is no forced marriage. True, she is keen to leave her guardian's house, but it is a good match, as far as the world is concerned, and as far as they are concerned, too.'

Another pause. Mr Hurst looked at Mr Ashpoint, and Mr Ashpoint looked down at the desk.

'So, our young woman is married. She does not quite know what she is doing, only that she wishes to be happy, that she misses her parents, misses being loved. This is how she tells it, years later, to our young man. Her husband takes her to Portsmouth, then goes to sea two weeks later.

'The first year of her marriage is made up of writing long letters that never seem to reach him, of receiving letters dated months before. She keeps only one maid, a girl her own age, and as there is no one else to talk to, she befriends her. She reads a great deal. She does not often leave the house. In the silence of loneliness, she misses her husband and thinks this must be love.

'When he comes home, he is not the cheerful young fellow she met a year before. He has been passed up for a promotion in favour of a well-bred colleague, a man with better blood. He says he will not stand it. He says he will not sail with that captain again but will find a better, fairer ship to join. He says he has enough money saved up to tide them over. His wife knows nothing of the matter, so of course she agrees.

'They begin their married life as strangers. A year of marriage and barely two months' acquaintance. She is quieter than he thought she would be. He is rougher, more irritable. Says he thinks it degrading for his wife to have befriended a servant. He finds fault with the girl, dismisses her. Perhaps he drinks more than he should, smokes more, gambles. And slowly his wife shrinks from him, and he begins to think that no woman will love a man who cannot get promoted.

'They live for six fraught months in Portsmouth before his savings fall too low. Then he says they must go abroad. France, Italy, Prussia – anywhere they can live cheaply. She does not ask why he is not looking for a ship. She does not ask anything. She thinks that to love is to trust.

'So they travel. She likes to see the world. She wants to

wander new streets and visit museums, see sculptures and paintings, visit old libraries and monasteries and churches. He wants her only to keep house, to keep his wretched company. He tries, intermittently, to get another appointment on a ship, but every time it fails. Their small stock of savings diminishes every month.

'The next few years she tells our young man in a few broken sentences. They move from place to place, with less and less money to their name. What little they have her miserable husband spends on cards. A few years ago, he had fine prospects, but now . . . he tells her it is her fault. He tells her he should not have cared for a promotion had he not a fine lady wife to impress. They live for a year in Nice, then find a new city every week for months. They live in increasing squalor, in disreputable houses with bad landlords. She does not visit monasteries or museums any more. She knits and sews and sells what she makes when he is not looking. She keeps the money for food, and when her husband finds out, he cries that she does not love him. No child comes, and her husband asks what was the good of marrying if he cannot have a son. Then he cries, says he does not want a son, for a son could not be proud of such a father. Let us say she comforts him, at first. She tries to love him.

'But over time it grows worse. He strikes her sometimes, when he is angry. He shouts and worries her until she is afraid, until she cannot lift her eyes to meet his. He plays cards whenever he is able, wastes what little money she can earn. He finds comfort in the brothels of Europe when his wife shrinks from his touch. He uproots her every few weeks or months without a word of warning. He does not let her have friends, is too ashamed of their reduced state to let her speak to ladies of her own class, too proud to let her befriend those as poor as they. He bans her, out of pride, from writing to her uncle.

'By the time our young woman reaches the age of twenty-two, she is thoroughly wretched. She is married to a husband she does not love and who does not love her, who has bullied her into what is scarcely an existence. She is so wretched that she would rather take her own life than stay with such a man.'

There was a long silence in the study. Mr Ashpoint shifted in his seat.

'So here, Mr Ashpoint,' said Mr Hurst, 'we come to our moral dilemma. Our young man meets a married woman in great distress, an intelligent, wise, kind, fascinating, struggling woman whom he cannot help but fall in love with. The woman is determined to leave her husband. She has considered two methods. The first is suicide. The second is to simply leave him, to run away in the dead of night, alone, unprotected, penniless, to try to get work somewhere. In her present state, she does not look respectable enough for teaching or nursing. She has not been brought up for manual work. We all know what the world would drive her to.

'Well then, the dilemma. What is our young man to do?

'His first option is to leave well alone, to go from Verona and abandon her to whatever fate shall bring. Impossible. She will be dead or lost within a year. They both know it.

'The second, then, is to write to England, to restore her to her friends. But her uncle does not care for her, and her old guardian would be concerned only with propriety, with the look of the thing. She would try to persuade her back to her husband.

'The third option, then, is to help the young woman to some place of safety. He has a little money. He could find a

home for her in a nunnery or a house for destitute women.
A possibility, perhaps – but we are forgetting that he loves
her, that he loves her with a passion he did not think possible, that the world beyond her has grown stale and cold.

'His final option, which he feels himself slip towards,
which they discuss in hesitant, fearful tones, each afraid the
other's love might not be strong enough – the final option is
that he will help her leave her husband, that they will fly this
place together and never come back. They cannot return to
England; the risk of discovery would be too great. If he
tried to pass her off as his wife, his father would ask too
many questions, would force them apart. But they could live
a secret life, abroad. They could travel the world as husband
and wife and begin their lives again. She knows that her
husband is sick of her, that he is too indolent, too broken a
man to chase after her.

'It is a great trust for her to put in this young man, a trust
that he will not leave her; and it is a great trust, too, for him,
who could marry a free woman back in England. But to
love is to trust. They have known each other barely a month
by the time the decision is made.'

Mr Hurst paused. His voice cracked. 'A moral dilemma.
This was no common affair, no sordid thing. I have loved
Matilda for more than ten years. I shall love her for another
ten, another twenty, until the day I die. I saved her life, and
she saved mine, too, has saved it every day since I have
known her.

'It has not been easy. I had to lie to my father, to keep his
grandchildren from him. I told him I was living in Paris,
when all the time I was with Matilda, moving from place to
place, living under assumed names, never staying long
enough for our reputation to be questioned. I have had to

lead a double life. I have had to spend wretched months apart from the people I love most on earth to keep up this place and the responsibilities I have here. Matilda and I have pretended in every place we have gone. We have raised our children knowing that life will be difficult for them. We have lived beyond Society.

'Roberts left us alone. How he lived all those years, I hardly know. Whether he thought Matilda had run away or thrown herself into the river, I cannot say. Whether he returned to England or stayed abroad, I do not know. We heard nothing of him for years until last autumn, when we read of his death in a newspaper. Mr Henry Roberts, former second lieutenant, found dead in a tavern in Paris after a fight over a game of cards.

'When we heard – oh, you cannot imagine the release, the sheer joy of it, to at last be free to legally marry the person who has been all to me for so long. I am a blessed man, Mr Ashpoint, though you may not believe it. Our life together may have been a struggle, but I would not change a single day.'

Mr Hurst raised his hands to his eyes. 'Tell me, is it really so very bad that we were married in our own eyes and in the eyes of God – yes, I say in the eyes of *God* – before we were married in the eyes of the law? What is the law? It is mere words. I cannot see that we have done anything but right. You have heard the whole tale, Mr Ashpoint. So tell me, is it really so great a sin?'

CHAPTER IV

In which Miss McNeil decides

As AMELIA WALKED INTO TOWN, JUST BEFORE NOON, EVERY word she heard seemed to be about the Hursts. Lord and Lady Wickford were leaving the country for good in a few weeks, and it seemed nobody cared. Diggory and Lady Rose were going to be married shortly, and no one had a word for them. Lord Salbridge had disgraced himself, and nobody much minded. It was all the Hursts. Every snatch of conversation, every murmur on street corners, outside the milliner's and the public house – the Hursts, the Hursts, the Hursts.

'Oh, Miss Ashpoint,' called Miss Waterson, catching up with her in the street. 'Miss Ashpoint, you are a friend of Mrs Hurst, are you not?'

'What do *you* think of these rumours?' asked Miss Maddon, who had found her way to Amelia's other side. 'I was just saying to Miss Waterson that they are *certain* to be false reports.'

'And I was just saying that they might be true.' Miss Waterson nodded significantly. 'Such things do happen, and rumours do not start themselves.'

'No,' said Amelia, 'but rumours may be started by malicious people who wish to do harm.'

'Well,' said Miss Maddon, 'it does seem a rather bold thing, don't you think, to live so very openly with three natural children at one's feet?'

'I think it is rather impressive,' said Miss Waterson.

Off went the two old ladies, debating the rumours. Amelia frowned as she watched them go. She looked at them, arm in arm, pressed close together, and she wondered if Clara could be right. For a moment, she half thought she might run after them, ask them, as she had asked Mrs Hurst, if they were happy.

Too foolish. Too late. They were already gone. She turned back, began to walk on to Clara's house, moving quickly, head down, trying not to hear the muffled voices coming from Miss Nettlebed's shop, a customer saying something sharp about Mrs Hurst. She went quickly on, turned the corner – and walked straight into Mr Lonsdale.

'Oh, I am sorry, I—'

'It is nothing, Miss Ashpoint.' Still, he looked startled to see her.

'Excuse me, I am just going—'

'Did you read the letter?' He spoke quietly, urgently, and Amelia blinked. She had quite forgotten that Lonsdale had anything to do with the matter, that her novel had any relation to anyone but Clara and herself.

'Oh, yes, I did. Thank you, Mr Lonsdale. You know what it said?'

'I do.'

'I am so happy,' she said. She heard her own voice; she did not sound happy.

'You will – accept? If you write a reply, you can send it through me.'

'Of course. Yes, I must write to the publisher. I may do it myself now, I think.'

Lonsdale nodded, but he looked almost disappointed. 'My friend Browne read it, too,' he said. 'He was most impressed.'

'Thank you.'

There was a moment's pause.

'Did your brother tell you,' Lonsdale began, 'that he has asked me to be the best man at his wedding?'

Amelia smiled. 'He did not, but I am glad of it.' She glanced past him, towards Garrett Lane. She could imagine Clara at her desk by the window, thinking – well, what? How was she ever to know what Clara was thinking when Clara could talk and think as she had yesterday? Impossible. Impossible.

'Are you quite well, Miss Ashpoint?'

'Yes, thank you,' she said, and it sounded too stiff, too formal. She tried to smile.

'You will miss your brother when he marries.'

'Yes.' She was thinking of Clara, and her voice cracked.

'It may seem a loss at first, but he will not be far away.' Lonsdale gave a tight, odd smile. 'You yourself may marry in time.'

She looked up at him: his eager face, the sudden nervousness that seemed to suit him so ill. She thought of that day on the lane, how hurt he had been at the idea that she thought badly of him. Diggory was right, then. Clara was right. Mrs Hurst was right. Even if it were not quite love – even if it were simply that she did not snub him as every other young lady did, even if it were some combination of sincere regard and knowledge of the advantages such a marriage would bring him – well, it hardly mattered. Had she encouraged him? She was not sure. She ought not, perhaps, to have asked him such a favour, to have confided the secret of her writing to someone who stood towards her as he did, though it was hard to regret that now. If she had really thought about his feelings – but then, she never had.

She felt a pang of pain on his behalf now. She liked Lonsdale. Oh, he was proud and ambitious and perhaps a little too aware of his own merits – but in the end, he was simply a man who wished for what he could not have, and there was nothing so very wrong about that. He had been her friend, and she was in need of friends.

'No,' she said softly. 'No, Mr Lonsdale. I shall never marry.'

She saw him swallow. 'Never, Miss Ashpoint?'

'Never. I say it with complete certainty.' She looked at him for a moment. She did not smile. He stared back at her, his cheeks pale. 'I am so very pleased,' she said suddenly, 'that my brother asked you to be his best man. You are just the friend I would choose for Diggory.'

'And I am so very glad about your book.'

'Thank you. Good day, Mr Lonsdale.'

He smiled, a sincere, solemn sort of smile. Then he said, 'Good day, Miss Ashpoint,' in a steady voice, bowed and continued down the street.

～

Amelia walked up Garrett Lane, her heart beating fast. For hours she had been thinking over what she would say to Clara, and it seemed so ridiculous, so atrocious that she should have to plan it out at all, that she should be rehearsing her words to Clara, Clara with whom she had always been so entirely herself.

She reached the house, swallowed hard and knocked.

Hannah opened the door wide for her. 'Miss is upstairs,' she said. 'Master's out on business. I'm going down to the coal cellar, so shout if you'd like some tea.'

Amelia walked softly up the stairs, pausing on each step, her breath hard, her mind a blur. She reached Clara's door, put her hand on the doorknob, then hesitated. She reached up and knocked.

A moment's silence – then, in a low voice, 'Amelia?' and Clara was wrenching open the door before Amelia had the chance to speak.

They stared at one another. Amelia thought about embracing her and did not move. Clara looked blankly back at her. Her eyes were red again, her face pale. And still so beautiful.

'Look at this,' said Amelia. It was not what she had planned, but somehow, she was pulling from her reticule the folded letter, giving it wordlessly to Clara. She stepped inside, closed the door and felt tired relief wash over her.

Clara's eyes skimmed the letter. Then she looked up, a bright smile on her face. 'Oh, Amelia, how wonderful! People will read your book. A. A. Oaksharp shall be famous. What splendid news.'

Yesterday was forgotten. Clara ran forwards and flung her arms around Amelia, kissing her forehead, her cheeks, her mouth.

But Amelia could taste salt on her lips, could feel the ghosts of tears.

'Clara,' she said in a very quiet voice, 'don't you see? This changes everything.'

She felt Clara's hold upon her slip a little.

'Listen,' Amelia went on, speaking quickly, the words tumbling out of her. 'You said yesterday that you were dependent on your father – but you are not any more. A hundred and fifty pounds is a lot of money. And it is money of my own, money I do not have to ask my father for. We could live off it, Clara. We could leave Wickenshire.'

Clara stared at her. 'Leave Wickenshire?' she repeated.

'Yes! You said you were unhappy with our lives here, so let's change them – let's run away. We could go anywhere – London or Paris, Venice or Frankfurt. I can earn more money writing, and you could – well, you could teach sketching or make architectural plans or – you are so clever, we would be bound to find something for you. No one would know us. We could live together, pretend to be sisters or friends. Who would question it for a second? We could build a different life together, and if you want opportunities, well, there is a whole world out there for us to explore. And—'

'What of our families?' asked Clara gently. 'Amelia, it is impossible.'

'It is *not* impossible,' she replied. She knew she sounded desperate, that her words were fast, her voice too shaky. She went quickly on. 'Listen – Clara, I spoke to Mrs Hurst. Don't worry, I didn't – I didn't say anything about you. She thinks I am in love with some married man and deciding whether to run away with him. But the rumours are true. She left her husband to live with Mr Hurst a long time ago. She told me as much herself.'

Clara frowned. 'She did?'

'Yes, but listen, that is not what matters. What matters is that she and Mr Hurst have spent ten years living apart from the world, struggling to keep their past a secret, moving from place to place. They have done that – and they are happy. She told me that it was worth it – hard, yes, but worth all the trouble and danger in the world, because they love each other. And why shouldn't we? Let's live as they have done. Let's travel – let's explore. We have always wanted to see the world.'

Clara's arms had fallen from her side. She was staring at Amelia. 'Did Mrs Hurst say it was hard to – to leave her family?'

'Well, she was an orphan – but—'

'Amelia—'

'No, *listen*. We could. It is possible. If they did it, why not us?'

'You know it is not the same.'

'No, it is *easier*. If a man and woman live together, people will assume they are married or ask questions. Two women – well, who would suspect a thing?'

'But, Amelia—'

'*Why not?*' cried Amelia. Her breathing was unsteady. She grasped Clara's arms, almost shook her. 'Tell me why not, Clara! I know you are saying no. I have known you long enough to know when you are saying no – but I don't understand. Tell me why not.'

'Because it is too much!' Clara stepped back, shook her head. She sat, almost fell to the floor, leant back against the bed, her arms around her legs. 'Because it is too much to ask – because I am not brave enough – because I cannot bear to leave my father and my life behind – because I cannot bear that you should leave your family – because I love Melford and I am afraid to leave it – because I don't think it practical – because I think we will run out of money – because you have never been frowned at or scorned in your life, but I have, and I know what it is to not be respected, and I do not want that to be our lives – because, Amelia, this is not one of your adventure stories!'

Amelia sat down slowly at her side. There was a long pause, and at last she said, in a muffled voice, 'What is it then?'

'I don't know.' Clara's voice was weak now, trembling. 'A very sad sort of love story, I suppose.'

Amelia slotted her fingers through Clara's, and for a long time they sat, leaning back against the bed, hands pressed together. Through the window, they could hear voices and birdsong from the street.

At last, Amelia said, 'What do we do now?'

Clara shifted. Her voice was barely a murmur. 'I suppose I shall marry Sir Frederick and buy respect and children, and I shall be half ashamed and half happy. He is a good man, Amelia. I care dearly for his mother, and she is fond of me. And you will be a maiden aunt to a dozen nieces and nephews. You will write your novels. You and I shall go for walks and take tea in locked rooms at each other's houses. We have never been ourselves to the world before. We can go on as we are.'

There was a long pause. Amelia turned her face away.

'Amelia?'

'Clara,' she said, in a low voice, 'you must know that I cannot do that.'

'Why not?'

Amelia swallowed hard. 'Do you think I could bear it, Clara, to part with you each time we meet and know you are returning to him? That I could bear to feel you slip from me into your new life? How can you say that nothing would change when *everything* would change?' She shook her head.

'Who do we harm now? No one knows and no one cares. Oh, I know, our families and the world might be horrified if they knew, but that is their error, not ours.' She heard her voice crack. 'A husband is different. You must see that.'

'But—' Clara stared at her, her voice trembling, her eyes brimming with tears. 'But, Amelia, I cannot lose you.'

Amelia turned and clasped Clara to her, wrapped her arms around her warm frame, buried her face in her hair. 'Clara, I think you already have.'

'Is it because I have betrayed you?' breathed Clara, and Amelia could feel her tears on her cheek. 'Is it because—'

'No,' said Amelia. 'No. It is just as you said. It would be too much. It is too much for you to ask.'

They sat in silence for a long, long time, arms tight around each other, eyes closed, each praying for the minutes to slow, for the future to never come.

CHAPTER V

In which Mr Ashpoint finds his answer

Mr ashpoint left radcliffe park in a daze. he got onto his horse with his head swimming, rode home with a thousand contradictions and confusions running through his mind. He was halfway to the brewery when he decided against it. It was almost three o'clock, and he was in no state of mind to work. Instead, he turned towards his own stables and dismounted, lost in thought. He walked up the steps and slowly, confusedly, into the morning room.

Diggory was at work at the brewery and his two youngest children were at their lessons upstairs, so he found only Amelia, sat on the settee at the far side of the room, her legs up on the cushions, her skirts piled around her, a novel in her hand. He watched her for a moment from the doorway. She looked different, somehow – tired, upset. Her face was pale, but her eyes looked a little red. He wondered what had possessed her to go and ask Mrs Hurst if it were all true this morning – and yet, somehow, he was glad that she had.

She looked up. 'Papa?' Her voice sounded uneven.

'Are you – all right, my dear?'

'Of course,' she said, with a smile that was not quite a smile. 'I was not expecting you until five.'

He nodded slowly as he came into the room and sat down

heavily upon a chair. 'I have not been to the brewery today,' he said.

'Oh?'

'I have been to Radcliffe Park.'

Amelia closed her book and sat up properly. 'To Radcliffe Park?' she repeated.

'Yes. I went to see Mr Hurst. It occurred to me, yesterday, at the Harvest Ball, that perhaps someone ought to speak to him, advise him to contradict all the talk before it goes too far.'

Amelia was staring at him. 'What did Mr Hurst say?'

'Well, he . . . told me the truth.' He glanced across at Amelia. 'I am given to understand that you paid Mrs Hurst a visit this morning, too, Amelia, that you – asked her.'

Amelia's cheeks went a little pink. 'I – I did,' she replied, in some confusion.

'Did she mention to you that they are planning to leave Wickenshire, maybe even England?'

'She said it was likely.'

They sat in silence for what felt like a long time. Amelia glanced at her book, then back at him. He still thought she looked pale, uncertain – unhappy, almost. He was trying to think of the last time he had seen Amelia unhappy. Cross, yes; furious, to be sure – but unhappy?

'Are you certain you are quite well, Amelia?'

'Oh yes,' she said, in a voice a little more like her usual tone. 'I am only tired. Balls are always exhausting, and I slept poorly.'

Well, he would not press it. He looked across at her, and his mind fell back upon the Hursts. He said slowly, 'Amelia, I want to ask your advice on a little matter.'

'My advice? Of course, Papa, if I can give it.'

'What should you think,' he said, his voice hesitant, 'if I were to take out my pen and a few sheets of paper and write some notes to our neighbours?'

Amelia frowned. 'I am not sure I follow.'

'What if I were to write a few notes, saying that I had been to see Mr Hurst, that the whole matter was resolved, that all the talk in town was worth so much dust and little more, that I had conversed at length with Mr Hurst and could stake my word as a gentleman on his innocence of any wrongdoing? I might even go so far as to say that I believed it the duty of Society to deny these rumours wherever possible. I might add that Mr and Mrs Hurst were invited to Diggory and Lady Rose's wedding, and that I was also inviting the family to dinner very soon.'

Amelia stared. 'You say Mr Hurst told you the *whole* truth?'

'Yes,' said her father. 'As Mrs Hurst told you. Have you told anyone?'

'Only Clara,' she said very quietly.

'I think Clara may safely be relied upon, don't you? I believe I shall write those notes. What do you think, Amelia?'

Amelia looked amazed, even impressed. There was a moment's pause, and then she smiled – a very bright smile, the kind that seemed to dispel all the shadows. 'Papa, I think you ought to write them at once.'

'To whom, do we think? Lord Wickford, of course – he will have to listen to me, in consideration of our new relationship. Mr Elton, I am sure, could be persuaded to hear reason, especially if I remind him that my support might be of use in his son's next election. And Mr Crayton, perhaps – I need to open a new account with him for Diggory anyhow, and Captain Palmer—'

'And Mr Duckfield,' said Amelia, with a smile. 'He has been asking for weeks for contributions to repair the stained-glass window at St Matthew's, so—'

'Precisely,' said Mr Ashpoint. 'And perhaps I might mention the matter to Lonsdale, just in passing, tell him that I have spoken to Mr Hurst himself and that I know it all to be poppycock. I shall have a word with the servants here, too.'

'Perhaps, Papa, I might call upon Miss Waterson and Miss Maddon tomorrow morning. And I could mention it at the bookseller's and the dressmaker's while I am in Melford.'

'A marvellous idea. Visit as many shops as possible – and best to make a few purchases while you are there. That should do the job well, don't you think, Amelia?'

'It will certainly be a start.' She seemed to hesitate. 'Papa, are you quite certain Mr Hurst told you *everything*?'

'He certainly did.' Mr Ashpoint turned towards her. He wondered if there were a particular reason his daughter had asked Mrs Hurst for the truth, or if she had simply asked out of sympathy, out of a desire to help her new friend. He reached out his hand, laid it on her arm. 'It is not that I dislike truths,' he said slowly, 'or that I am not averse to falsehoods. It is only that I like Mr Hurst. I have known him since he was a boy and should hate to see him leave the neighbourhood. And I like Mrs Hurst. She seems a good sort of lady. I like the children. I should think any parent would wish any child, even if not their own, a pleasant, carefree life. We all have our sins, I suppose, and the world is rather a shocking place, but I see no reason not to avoid unpleasantness. If I must part with a little money for the sake of a good cause – well, I am spending enough on Diggory's wedding as it is, and what is a little more? Mr

Hurst may object to flat untruths, but I do not think he would object to us saying one or two on his behalf. Do you agree?'

Amelia smiled. 'I certainly do.'

'Well then,' said Mr Ashpoint, rising from his seat, 'will you pass me the ink, my dear?'

CHAPTER VI

In which Miss Elton's fate is sealed

TUESDAY HAD COME, AND FELICIA ELTON WAS IN THE music room at Ludwell Manor. Major Alderton was sitting on one of the open armchairs beside the settee, holding a copy of the *Quarterly Review*.

He was early. He usually came towards the end of her piano lesson, not before it. He had interrupted her while she was practising Carl Czerny's Sonata No.11 in D flat major, and all she could think, at this pivotal moment of her life, was that she would not be able to play the piece as well as she ought when Monsieur Brisset arrived.

Major Alderton folded the newspaper on his lap and looked at her. His smile was too bright, too cheerful. She turned away.

'You know I have called for your answer,' he said, with every appearance of calm. 'I hope I have given you sufficient time to decide. As it happens, it has been time enough for others to make up their minds, too. I was rather surprised to hear the news of Sir Frederick's coming marriage to Miss McNeil, although perhaps this engagement is not such a surprise to you.'

He looked across at her, and when she said nothing, he continued. 'Miss Elton, you know what I am. You know there is a shadow over my life that I cannot ignore. But I think you also know that, with me, you would never need to worry. Money will never be a concern, neither for you, as my wife, nor for your family. I have told your father that I am very willing to smooth over any difficulties he may encounter, both now and in the future. Even taking into account the one less favourable circumstance of my life, I believe – I hope – that I am a worthy match for you.' He smiled, all frankness and affability. 'Well, what is it to be, Miss Elton? Will you have me?'

It pained her a little, his measured, reasonable speech. She would have preferred passionate cries of love – such things were vexing, to be sure, but she would have felt certain of her power. As it was, she felt as though it were she not he who was waiting to hear their fate.

She swallowed. She set her teacup down. She was nineteen years old, and her whole life had been building to this. All her talents, her accomplishments, her music – designed to win her a husband. All her natural beauty, all the finery, the prettiness, the perfection her mother had cultivated – all for this moment, sat in the music room with this man she did not really know.

Still, it must be done. Sir Frederick's engagement to Clara McNeil had been announced. Lord Salbridge would soon be gone. Her reign was over. The family's fortunes were thinning. If Felicia did not marry money, they would follow the Wickfords into ruin soon enough. It would be preposterous to say no.

Felicia looked up at him. She folded her hands in her lap. 'Major Alderton—'

'Charles, please.'

'Charles, then,' she said, with an attempt at a smile, 'I shall give you your answer, but there is something I must say with it, and I should not like you to interrupt me until I am finished. Will you agree?'

'With pleasure.'

'Thank you.' She swallowed hard. 'I shall marry you.' He sat up, the closest to animated she had ever seen him, and it almost startled her. She hurried on at once. 'But you must know – it is important you know – that I do not love you. I think well of you, and the shadow you spoke of does not trouble me. You are an agreeable, sensible man, and I see your worth. I am sure I will grow to like you in time. But I do not love you. If you wish to marry me, you must not ask it of me. I have never been romantic. In truth, I do not think I have very much of a heart. I shall be true to you, and I shall do my best to make you happy, but you must never ask me to love you.'

There was a moment's pause. Then, to her astonishment, Major Alderton smiled. She felt herself shrink as he let out a single, loud laugh.

'Oh, Miss Elton – Felicia, my dearest, as you are, and shall be – give me your hand.'

She did so, hesitantly. His hands were large and warm, and when he held her one in both of his she knew she could not pull back if she tried.

'Is this all that has caused your delay? What a thing to worry over – my dearest girl, if I had known you had such thoughts in your mind, I might have spoken more plainly before.' He smiled. 'Felicia, I am very fond of you. You are beautiful. You have many talents.' He nodded vaguely towards the pianoforte. 'But if you think I am dying for love, you are mistaken. Indeed, part of the reason for my choice has been your lack of romantic tendencies. I have never seen any synonym of love in you. You know your own worth. I respect that. I am sure you have crushed and will crush hearts in your time, but I am not a man to be crushed.

'This is a practical step for both of us. I have money. Your family, I know, need money. You have high blood, respect-ability, a position in Society. I need respectability. All my life, I have been shunned or whispered about. But say I marry a young lady from one of the oldest and grandest families in Wickenshire, why, who will sneer at my background then? The shadow will lift. The world will think, if he is good enough for the Eltons, he is quite good enough for us.' He smiled. 'People like us have other things to think of besides love, Felicia. That is why we shall suit each other well.'

Felicia felt a wave of sickness come over her. All her beauty, all her attractions, her accomplishments – and not even the man she was to marry loved her. She had worked all her life for perfection, and he married her only for her respectability.

Still, her hand was in his. He said, 'Felicia, are you well?'

'Yes.' She spoke almost mechanically. 'Quite well.'

'And quite happy?'

'Of course. You are right. We shall suit each other, I think.'

'Yes, indeed.' He sat forwards. 'Should you like a house in town for the Season?'

The sickness subsided a little. 'Oh yes. Very much.'

'Then we shall select one together. I defy the man who will not respect me when he sees the bride I have won.'

He leant forwards and, to Felicia's confusion, kissed her on the mouth. She rather wished he wouldn't. It seemed a silly sham after what they had just discussed, and his whisk-ers felt sharp, strange against her skin. Still, she supposed such things were necessary. No doubt he would expect her to produce a troop of respectable little ladies and gentle-men, which would involve various inconveniences.

So she let him kiss her, and just as he was pulling back, his face close to hers, her hand still encased in his, she heard a noise behind them – and turned to see Monsieur Brisset standing in the doorway.

There was a long moment of confusion, in which Monsieur Brisset stared; in which Major Alderton moved away from her with a hesitant laugh; in which Felicia looked up and saw the expression on her music master's face.

It would have been better if he had looked angry, better if he had looked disgusted, better if his expression had turned harsh and hard as it did when she played below her best. But he looked only solemn and grave, staring at her and the man who was to be her husband. For a strange second, Felicia thought she might cry.

Then Monsieur Brisset said, 'I am sorry – I am early,' and backed quickly out of the door.

Felicia felt her colour rise, felt her throat stick.

'Come, dearest, you needn't look embarrassed,' said Major Alderton. 'We are to be married, after all. Why don't you cancel your lesson today? We ought to celebrate, you and I, and of course I must talk to your father.'

'No,' said Felicia, more firmly than she expected.

Major Alderton frowned. 'Felicia?'

'Oh, of course you must speak to Papa. I only meant that I must have my lesson, as Monsieur Brisset has come to give it. I shall let him know that it will be the last.' She paused. 'You can see Papa while I am with Monsieur Brisset.'

'Certainly,' Major Alderton replied. 'Perhaps make your lesson a short one today. I am sure Brisset will understand;

he is an excellent fellow – I often see him at the Lantern. And you and I have so much to discuss. Indeed, we have not set the day. I think the sooner the better, though of course you will have your trousseau to arrange, and I shall need to inform a' – he coughed – 'certain friend of mine. Shall we say before Christmas?'

By a certain friend, Felicia supposed he meant his natural father – the duke or viscount or whatever he might be. She wondered if Major Alderton ever saw the man or if he only provided money from afar. She merely said, 'Just as you please.'

'Very good.' He rose from his seat, then paused. Perhaps he caught her grave expression, for he said, 'When we are married, we must buy you a pianoforte for Netherworth – the finest we can get. You may play every day if you wish to. You have made me very happy, Felicia, and I shall do everything in my power to make you so, too.'

They were both quiet for the first half hour of the lesson. Monsieur Brisset sat beside her at the pianoforte as always, turning the pages, watching her hands on the notes, correcting her when she made mistakes. That was all. They did not mention what had happened before the lesson, did not talk about the music as they normally did. They only sat stiffly together while she played far worse than usual. Even Sarah, sat in the corner as chaperone, kept looking up in surprise at all the wrong notes. Felicia could not help it. She kept thinking of Major Alderton. She kept thinking of Monsieur Brisset. She kept thinking of Clara McNeil and Sir Frederick and how they must love each other, of Diggory and Lady

Rose, of what that might be like, to marry a man you loved, a man who loved you. She played one wrong note, two, three, four. Her timing was unsteady. She missed whole bars of the music.

At last, Monsieur Brisset said, 'You play poorly today, Miss Elton. You are distracted.'

She stopped mid-bar, lifted her hands from the piano and stared down at her skirts. Beside her, the music master sat motionless.

'Sarah,' said Felicia, glancing across at her maid, 'I am cold – would you fetch my shawl? The green one, if you please. I think it is upstairs.'

It was not upstairs – she had left it in the carriage – but the search for it would surely keep Sarah for five minutes at least.

Sarah hesitated, glanced between Felicia and Monsieur Brisset, then nodded and rose to her feet. Felicia knew Sarah was too clever not to see why she was being sent away, but at this moment she did not care.

Once Sarah had left the room, Felicia said slowly, 'I am to be married – to Major Alderton.'

Monsieur Brisset did not look at her. 'I gathered as much,' he said quietly.

'I think perhaps this ought to be our last lesson.'

There was a long pause. She heard him breathe in and out.

'I see,' he said at last, and there was something so choked in his voice that she thought what little heart she had might break.

She rested her hands on the keys, so lightly they made no sound. She closed her eyes, listened to the sound of his breathing and hers. For a moment, she almost let herself imagine another possibility, another life, another path. Then, at last, knowing it was unwise, knowing it would only make it worse for them both, she said softly, 'It is all a business deal. I do not love him. He does not love me. He will make me rich, and I will make him respectable. I suppose he admires me a little, but then what does that matter? I am no more than a china doll to any of them.'

'You are not a china doll to me, Felicia.'

He had never called her by her Christian name before. Over their last two years of lessons together, he must have heard it a thousand times from the lips of her mother and father. She wondered if that was how he thought of her, if she were Felicia and not Miss Elton in his mind, and it made her inexplicably happy and made her want to cry. It was enough, she thought, for him to call her Felicia. It was enough for her to know.

She spoke without looking at him. She kept her eyes on the piano. 'You are the only man I have ever – respected. You are the only man who has ever respected me.'

A pause. He said, his voice shaking, 'I hope you will be happy with Major Alderton.'

'I am sure we shall do well enough together.'

'You would not be happy, I think, as the wife of a poor man.'

'No,' she said gently, because it was almost – almost – a question. 'No, I do not think I would.'

He said, so quietly she barely heard the words, 'I wish I had ten thousand pounds.'

She stared at the pianoforte and blinked back tears.

Beside her, Monsieur Brisset cleared his throat. 'Beethoven Sonata No. 4,' he said.

It was the longest piece she could play, as he knew well.

She nodded stiffly, wiped her eyes with her hands before she reached for the music. She glanced for a moment at the man beside her. His eyes were red and his face was pale, and for the first time in a long time, Felicia remembered how young he was. Her music master, who always seemed to much older and wiser than her; after all, he could scarcely be much above three-and-twenty.

She raised her hands and began to play. They sat together, she and Monsieur Brisset, as they had done a hundred times before. She played softly, so that she could hear the sound of his breathing over the music. She played slowly, as though by sheer effort she could make this moment last an eternity.

CHAPTER VII

In which the tide of gossip changes course

WORD OF MR HURST'S REPRIEVE SPREAD FAST THROUGH Wickenshire.

Everyone was soon saying that Mr Hurst had been maligned. Mrs Hurst had been slandered. Those poor children had been unfairly defamed. Every house, shop and street whispered about the couple. Everyone knew someone who knew someone else who had full and complete proof that it was all nonsense. Every servant and every master nodded sagely and said that they themselves had never believed it, not for one moment.

Mr Elton told his wife that he knew without a doubt it was all slander, that the talk was so much dust in the air. Mrs Elton frowned and said that, whether it was all *so much dust* or not, she would rather not see such an infamous pair at *her* dinner table.

'Well, you will have to,' said Mr Elton, 'for I have invited them to dine with us in a fortnight. Alderton will come along, of course, and the Ashpoints, too. Don't scowl so, Sophronia – we shall need Mr Ashpoint's support in Melford when Augustus runs for re-election. He has sway with all the shopkeepers.'

Miss Nettlebed told every customer in the dressmaker's

that the Hursts had been slandered. She was under the vague impression that Mr and Mrs Hurst had shown Amelia Ashpoint some proof, but she did not much mind either way, for the Ashpoints' order for Lady Rose's trousseau was quite large enough for her to repeat anything they said. She told the Palmers, the Craytons, the farmers' daughters and the tradesmen's wives. She discussed the matter at length with Miss Waterson and Miss Maddon. She told every other shopkeeper on Grange Street.

It was all rubbish, Lonsdale told every man who worked at the brewery. Mr Ashpoint had told him as much himself, and Mr Ashpoint was a gentleman. They all knew Mr Ashpoint to be a proud man (the men nodded in agreement), and he was not one to allow Mr and Mrs Hurst to attend his son's wedding without some proof of their virtue.

After days of silence, of quiet packing and planning, the Hursts found themselves suddenly in demand. A friendly visit from the doctor. A summons to tea with Miss Waterson and Miss Maddon. A note from the bookseller informing them that a few books Mrs Hurst had enquired for had arrived. Everyone was keen to prove they were not the followers of deceit and lies that Mr Duckfield had so railed against in Sunday's sermon.

On market day, the Hursts ventured cautiously into Melford, leaving the children behind at home. They were stopped with cheerful greetings in the street, welcomed kindly into the stationer's and the dressmaker's. Anne Palmer smiled at them in the bookseller's, and Miss Waterson curtseyed to them in the milliner's. The baker's wife felt so guilty for speaking ill of them at the Harvest Ball that she gave Mrs Hurst a large quantity of cakes and biscuits for free.

Amelia Ashpoint watched from across the street as her

friend came out of the bakery, her basket full. Mrs Hurst met her eye and smiled.

~

All in all, it was rather a splendid week for Wickenshire. Mr and Mrs Hurst had more or less been cleared. The remaining wisps of scandal were submerged beneath the hum of approval. And if Wickenshire grew tired of discussing the innocence of the Hursts, there was still much to talk of. The county was on the brink of one important wedding, with two more promised before Christmas.

The two most recent engagements had quite shocked Wickenshire. The county felt smug with romance – for what but love could have brought two such unlikely pairs together? Sir Frederick Hammersmith was so very much above Miss McNeil that the pair must really be very attached to one another. Everyone had expected him to wed Miss Elton – who, in another shocking turn of events, was now announced betrothed to Major Alderton. Another love match, whispered Wickenshire, for what else could possess the beautiful, talented, wealthy Miss Elton to marry Major Alderton, who came from nowhere, whose very name he had no right to?

Although, really, whispered the town gossips, on staircases, on street corners – what proof did they have of any scandal around Major Alderton's birth? Was it possible that this story, too, might be a concoction, the idle talk of wicked tongues? After all, it was unthinkable that so proud a family as the Eltons would unite themselves to sin. Perhaps Major Alderton was more respectable than everyone had always thought.

~

Miss Waterson and Miss Maddon brought out the old Sunday school blackboard and examined the rows of Wickenshire's bachelors and maidens. They rubbed out lines and drew new connections, considering possible matches. Why not a fourth wedding before next spring? There were plenty of unwed young folk still in Wickenshire. And there would be a new owner at Wickford Towers soon enough – he might be a bachelor, too.

'I do worry about Miss Ashpoint,' said Miss Maddon, as she rubbed out the line between Amelia Ashpoint and Clara McNeil, and joined Clara to Sir Frederick instead.

'Yes,' said Miss Waterson gravely. 'That is a sad matter. Do you think she is – well, do you think she is all right?'

'I should say probably not,' said Miss Maddon. 'But she will be, in time. I told you about my difficulties with Miss Letitia Lavender, did I not?'

'Oh, a dozen times.'

'Surely not as many as that,' said Miss Maddon, a sly smile creeping over her features. 'I should have said about ten.'

'At least eleven.' Miss Waterson looked at her, and the two of them burst out laughing.

They had, over the years, developed a habit of quibbling over details in front of their neighbours. It was useful, for nobody considered *silly* was ever thought to have secrets, and it had become a great source of amusement to them both. It was delightful, Miss Maddon always declared, to laugh at the expense of those who thought they were laughing at you.

When the laughter died down, Miss Maddon turned back to the blackboard. 'I wonder . . .' She hesitated, then raised the chalk in her hand and drew a new line for Anne Palmer.

'Do you really think so?' asked Miss Waterson. 'You are so terribly clever about these things.'

'It is only an idea. And not yet, of course.'

'No, not yet.'

The two of them looked at the blackboard, deep in contemplation.

'In the meantime, perhaps we ought to take Miss Ashpoint under our wing,' said Miss Waterson.

'Yes, she may need it.'

Miss Waterson nodded. She smiled at Miss Maddon and put her arm around her waist. 'A good evening's work, I think,' she said, and kissed her. 'Now, how about a cup of tea?'

CHAPTER VIII

In which the sun shines for Diggory Ashpoint

DIGGORY WAS CONTEMPLATING HIMSELF IN THE SITTING-ROOM mirror. He thought he looked all right, really, although he would look far more charming with Rose beside him. He had combed his hair very hard, until it was sticking up pleasingly above his head. His grey morning suit was stiff and perfect, his cravat a pale yellow to compliment Rose's dress, his buttonhole bright orange. His shoes were very shiny. He was ready, in short, to get married.

It was to be a large wedding – larger, perhaps, than someone like Mrs Elton might consider truly genteel – but Lord and Lady Wickford had wanted to combine the wedding breakfast with a going-away feast for themselves, with a little dancing in the afternoon. The family were leaving tomorrow, and it was the last time the earl and countess would see their neighbours and friends for what might be many years.

'You look like a little boy at play,' said Amelia, coming into the room. She looked rather smart in her bridesmaid's dress. 'But I am sure Lady Rose will like you, and that is probably your greatest concern. The carriage will be here soon to collect me and Ada – should you not be getting to the church? It would make rather a poor impression if you

were late, you know, when Papa has been telling everybody
how very trustworthy you are these days.'

Diggory pulled a face at her. 'I *am* very trustworthy.'

Amelia's reply was lost in noise as Ada and Laurie
bounded into the room, dressed in their finest. They were
followed by Mr Ashpoint, in a grey frock coat with a blue
buttonhole. He smiled around at his family, and they smiled
back – until Diggory noticed the tears in his father's eyes.

'Oh, calm yourself, Papa. I am only getting married. I
shall be barely a half hour's walk away in Lowick Terrace.
You may call upon me as often as you like, and we shall
meet at the brewery every day.'

Mr Ashpoint sniffed and smiled. His eyes were very wet.
He rummaged in his pockets, and in the absence of a hand-
kerchief wiped his eyes on the cravat he was supposed to
give to Laurie. 'It is only,' he said, laying a damp hand on
Diggory's shoulder, 'that I wish your mother could see you.
And then I am so very happy for you. It quite unmans me.'

Amelia put a hand on her father's arm. It was the gesture
of a moment, but Diggory did not think she would have
made it a month ago.

Mr Ashpoint looked round at her, smiled a little, and then
turned back to Diggory. 'Well, my boy,' he said, making an
effort to sniff back his emotions, 'shall we go?'

By half past ten, Diggory was standing at the altar of St
Matthew's. He was smoothing his warm, shaking hands on
his trousers, putting them into his pockets, removing them,
frowning, smiling, stepping one pace to the right, one to the
left, checking every three minutes that Lonsdale had the

ring, and being altogether as thoroughly nervous as any young bridegroom might be.

He glanced out at the crowd already gathering in the pews. At the back of the church sat the Eltons, with Major Alderton beside Felicia. His eyes ran over Mr McNeil and Clara, sat with Sir Frederick, Mr and Mrs Hurst on their other side. The Palmers were coming in now, giving a cheerful greeting to the Hursts, taking their seats next to the Craytons, Louisa and Cassandra debating the likelihood of Lady Rose coming in in a white dress like the Queen had worn at her wedding. In front of them sat Miss Maddon and Miss Waterson, beaming encouraging smiles at Diggory.

Diggory looked down at his shoes. He could see the church ceiling reflected in them, and this gave him comfort. There were too many people watching him and he was, at this moment, feeling a little unwell. He loved Rose so very much. It had stolen upon him slowly, and he could not quite say when it was that she had suddenly, startlingly, become the single most important thing in his entire world. The idea of life without Rose was impossible. The idea of a life with Rose was bright and beautiful and altogether so wonderfully grown-up and serious that he felt it perfectly natural that he was sweating.

Diggory put his hands in his pockets. He needed Amelia badly. He needed his sister to tease him and give one of her knowing smiles. He needed Rose, too. One look would be enough to show him that she took him seriously, that she knew he could be so much more than the gloomy young man slouched at the back of the ball with a glass of punch.

'Are you quite well, Ashpoint?'

He turned to see Lonsdale looking at him, and his calm smile helped.

'Quite well, thank you.' He paused. 'Lonsdale?'

'Yes?'

'If you were me,' he began, in a low voice, 'would you be nervous?'

Lonsdale smiled. 'I expect so.'

'You think it perfectly ordinary?'

'Perfectly.'

The doors opened again, and Diggory felt his stomach lurch. Standing in the entranceway, dressed in fine red silk, was Lady Wickford. By her side stood Lord Salbridge.

Salbridge.

Salbridge who had shown Diggory how to smoke a pipe and drink whisky. Salbridge who had spent years teaching him to be sarcastic and sullen, telling him that a young man could make the world care for him by caring for nothing. Salbridge who had said he was not worthy of Rose.

Diggory had hoped that Salbridge would not be allowed to attend the wedding, but Rose's parents had decided that it was proper for him to come. He thought of Salbridge's words at Mrs Elton's dinner, of Grace Abbott standing before him on the road. And then he thought of Rose, and he grew calmer. He swallowed hard, looked up and met Salbridge's eye.

For a moment, he thought Salbridge might speak to him, but he only filed into a pew beside his mother and stared at the floor with settled fury on his face.

Diggory did not have time to think of Salbridge's anger, because at that moment Mr Duckfield was emerging from the vestry and the organ was beginning to play, and Diggory glanced at Lonsdale for a smile of encouragement as his heart pounded and his throat went dry – and then the church doors opened and his bride walked in.

Rose was astounding.

Of course Diggory had long thought her beautiful. But he had never stared at her for quite this length of time before, had never been about to marry her. He watched her walk, slowly, brightly, up the aisle. He took her in, her curling dark hair, the orange flowers pinned within it, the grace with which she held her small frame, her quiet smile as she looked from him to her bouquet, as her eyes glanced around the church, at the friends and acquaintances who all stood for her.

Beside her was her father, and behind them came Amelia. He saw her glance around the church, eyes resting on Clara, on Sir Frederick, on the Hursts and finally on her brother. Amelia smiled at him with the sort of sincerity he had only seen from her a handful of times. Behind Amelia came Ada, grinning hard. Diggory breathed in. His eyes met Rose's, and his hands stopped shaking.

'Ladies and gentlemen,' Mr Duckfield was saying, but Diggory was not listening. He was looking at Rose and thinking what a world it was. He felt that at this moment he could do anything, achieve anything, bear anything, so long as there were moments in life like this, caught in the light, Rose beside him, her warm hand clasped in his own as if they could live for centuries, as if the world was theirs to claim and conquer, as if the sun shone for them alone.

CHAPTER IX

In which the toasts are made

A FEW HOURS LATER, THE CELEBRATIONS AT ASHPOINT Hall were well under way. In the dining room, three rows of tables were awash with empty wine glasses, scraped plates and bowls, flowers and favours, displaced decorations – and smiling faces. Amelia had had no appetite for days, but even she could not deny that the wedding breakfast had been a great success: lamb and veal pie, partridges and chicken, white grapes and mock turtle soup, cold salmon and French beans à la crème, pigeons in jelly, lobster and peaches, blackberries and pears, sponge cakes and wine jelly and Savoy cake and truffles and three wedding cakes piled high with orange flowers.

A pianoforte, cornet, violin and violoncello were playing loudly at one end of the room, but even their cheerful songs were lost amongst the sounds of talking, laughing, eating. Diggory and Rose seemed unable to stop smiling. All throughout the meal, they'd beamed at each other, held each other's hands, taken sips from each other's glasses and barely spoken to anyone else.

The sound of a fork tapped against a glass came from the top of the hall. Mr Ashpoint was standing up, the hall quietening as he raised his hand. The musicians stopped playing.

'Ladies and gentlemen, friends and family – it is my great honour to be present before you all today at the marriage of my son, Mr Diggory Ashpoint, to Lady Rose Ravensdale, daughter of the Earl and Countess of Wickford. Lady Rose is one of the most charming young ladies I have ever had the pleasure to know. I have seen them both grow from boy and girl into man and woman – and now, into man and wife. I wish them every happiness.' He raised his glass, and the rest of the assembly followed suit. A murmur of congratulations ran round the tables, and when Mr Ashpoint sat down, Lord Wickford rose to his feet.

'Before I announce the dance open, I, too, would like to say a few words. Firstly, I am grateful to Mr Ashpoint, not only for bringing such a young man as Diggory into the world but for providing such pleasant celebrations today. The honour ought to have rested with me, but . . .' Lord Wickford's voice faltered. 'As you all know, my wife, my son and I are leaving Wickenshire tomorrow for the Continent. It is with great regret that we leave the home of my ancestors. We have so many dear friends here. You will all be missed. I can only hope we shall be missed, too.' A few heads nodded solemnly, and Amelia shifted in her seat. 'But on to happier matters. I trust you are all prepared to dance your best in honour of my daughter and my new son. If you would like to make your way down the corridor, dancing will begin in the ballroom very shortly.'

Lord Wickford reclaimed his seat, but before even the most eager individuals could rise from their chairs, there came the sound of another fork tapped against another glass, and the room watched in astonishment as Lord Salbridge rose to his feet.

'I would like to say something,' he began.

Sitting beside him, Lonsdale looked up with wary surprise. Lord Wickford stared. Lady Wickford looked away. A murmur ran around the room. Diggory looked at Rose, and Rose looked at him, their smiles gone.

Lord Salbridge stood resolutely above the rest of them, a glass of wine in his hand, and said, 'I do not approve of this marriage.'

His voice was clear and slow. Amelia could not tell whether he was drunk or not – perhaps a little: not so drunk as to not know what he was doing, just drunk enough to dare to do it. A dreadful whisper started up, and Lord Wickford cried out, 'Alexander, be quiet—'

'Hold your tongue, Father! I shall be heard. This marriage is a *disgrace*. You are all very much mistaken if you think my being here today is any sign of approval or forgiveness.' He glanced at Diggory, and the room held its breath. 'It does not matter how much my parents claim to approve of you. It does not matter how much money you have. It does not matter how many miles will soon be between us. You will always be the grandson of a shopkeeper and the son of a brewer – and nothing more.'

Diggory made an angry start, but Rose laid a hand on his arm to steady him.

Salbridge laughed harshly and glanced back at the rest of the room. They watched him in awed, silent horror. 'My family have lived at Wickford Towers for centuries,' he said. 'The blood in my veins has ruled this county for generation upon generation. No rumour can take away my title. No debt can take away my birth. What are a few little indiscretions in comparison to *that*? I suppose you have all heard the rumours, the talk that I have ruined our family. But I tell you, it is *Rose* who has ruined us, not me.

'I suppose you all think I'm very wicked, don't you?' he said, quite coolly, quite calmly. 'Well, I do not give a damn what you think. I am tired of everyone pretending I am so much very worse than them. I know better. I know things about the people in this room that would horrify you all.'

A sort of nervousness spread down the tables. Miss Waterson and Miss Maddon exchanged glances. Anne Palmer shrank a little in her seat. The Hursts turned pale. Amelia looked at Clara, and Clara looked back.

'Everyone has secrets,' said Lord Salbridge. 'Everyone sins. Everyone pretends to be something they are not. We are all rotten, every last one of us, down to the core. Why, look at the Hursts – you have all been so eager to discuss and dismiss any possibility of wrongdoing there, though *my* faults are not to be questioned. Where is the logic there? Have any of you actually any proof of their innocence? And even here at Ashpoint Hall – why, I could tell you things about Miss Amelia Ashpoint and—'

'That's enough.' Lonsdale was on his feet, and his hand closed tightly around Salbridge's arm. Salbridge seemed to shrink beside Lonsdale's tall, powerful presence.

'What are you doing? Take your hands off me!'

'I will not,' said Lonsdale. He grabbed Salbridge's other arm and pulled him roughly back from the table with a strength Salbridge could not fight. 'You have said quite enough. You are no longer welcome here.'

Salbridge was red with fury. 'What right—?'

'I am Diggory's best man. I have every right to prevent his wedding being disturbed.'

Salbridge gave a cold laugh – cut short a moment later as Lonsdale forced him further from the table, pinning his arms back, pushing him forwards, his grip never slackening.

'Unhand me!' cried Salbridge. And then, with a glance behind him at the awestruck room, 'Stop him! Mother, Father—'

Lady Wickford would not look at him. Lord Wickford put his head in his hands.

He turned, appealing to the onlookers, but nobody would meet his eyes. Even Edmund Crayton looked away.

'I shan't leave,' said Salbridge, trying to free himself from Lonsdale's grip. 'What are you going to do, drag me out the room?'

Lonsdale only pulled Salbridge further towards the doors.

'You wouldn't,' stammered Salbridge, as Lonsdale pulled him roughly on. A note of panic, of humiliation, crept into his voice. 'And this is the fellow chosen as best man at my sister's wedding!' he said with a sneer. 'A real gentleman would never—'

'And what would *you* know,' said Lonsdale, forcing him through the doors, 'about being a gentleman?'

CHAPTER X

In which Miss Elton acts for herself

AN AWED HUSH SPREAD OVER THE GUESTS. SALBRIDGE'S words hung heavily in the air. Everybody looked warily at their neighbours. Nobody dared to speak.

Amelia sat in horror, thinking, he knew – after all, he really knew. A sentence more, a word more, and her life would have slipped from under her.

Across the room, Clara looked very pale. Sir Frederick was talking softly to her, and it hurt, that he was the one to comfort her. Amelia felt Diggory's hand on her arm and looked round at her brother's concerned face. She tried to smile back.

The Hursts sat in silence, as one or two wary glances were cast in their direction. The rumours of a fortnight earlier were fresh in people's minds. Wickenshire had welcomed the Hursts back into Society, but now there was a moment's pause, a hesitation. What if Lord Salbridge was right? What if they had all been too keen to dismiss the rumours?

And then—

'Really, Lord Wickford,' said Mr Ashpoint, very loudly, 'your son does talk rather a lot of nonsense.'

A murmur spread through the room, and then it became a nervous laugh. Lord Wickford and his wife looked at one another and made themselves laugh, too, though Amelia thought they looked like they would rather cry.

Lord Wickford finally rose to his feet. He spoke with some apparent effort to keep his voice steady. 'After that . . . interruption, I think perhaps we ought to go on with the festivities. We shall open the dance in the ballroom in ten minutes.'

$\approx$

The music was nearly loud enough to drown out the whispers as the dancing began. Lady Rose and Diggory were the top couple; Lonsdale and Amelia, as best man and chief bridesmaid, came next, followed by Sir Frederick and Clara – oh, why did they have to stand so nearby? – and after them, Miss Elton and Major Alderton. Amelia tried to look at Lonsdale, not at Clara, as the dance began.

'Thank you,' Amelia said to him in a low voice, 'for interrupting Lord Salbridge, for—'

'It was about time somebody put him down.'

Then the dance turned her away from him for a moment, and she found herself, horribly, bewilderingly, between Sir Frederick and Clara. Clara tried to meet her gaze, and she looked away. Another turn and shift of movement, and she was back at Lonsdale's side, flushed despite herself.

'I do not like people to speak ill of my friends,' he said.

Amelia smiled. 'Do you know, Mr Lonsdale,' she said, after a moment's pause, 'I am very glad you are my friend.'

'Good,' he replied, and his manner seemed more natural than it had in recent months, calmer than that day she'd met him in the street on her way to see Clara. He said, 'I am very glad, too.'

The dance ended. Amelia found a seat in a corner of the

hall, watched as partners were swapped and traded, as Clara remained at Sir Frederick's side. Felicia Elton was dancing with Major Alderton again. Anne Palmer was dancing with Monsieur Brisset, but Amelia saw her look over her shoulder, saw her gaze run around the room, as though she were looking for someone else. She gave Amelia a slight smile before turning back to her partner.

Amelia looked at the Hursts, sat alone together in another corner of the ballroom, talking in quick whispers. Society was giving them a wide berth now, glancing with caution as they passed their table. Surely all her and her father's work could not have been for nothing. Amelia was about to cross the room to speak to them when she saw Diggory approaching her. He pulled up a chair and sat down at her side.

'Are you all right, Amy?' he asked.

It was such a simple question, and it somehow made her want to cry. 'Yes, I'm all right,' she said, with an attempt at a smile.

'I am glad Lonsdale acted as he did – he is a very fine fellow. I am afraid I shall never be as brave as him.' Diggory sighed. 'What a devil Salbridge is. But he was only talking rot, you know – everybody ignored him.'

'What if he wasn't?' she murmured. 'What if it wasn't rot? You know about the book – you know I have kept secrets before.'

Diggory shrugged. 'I know nothing about secrets,' he said quietly, 'but I know it was rot to suggest you might have ever done anything really wrong.'

He turned to look at her. She could not quite meet his gaze. She was caught by the movements of the dancers, by the way Sir Frederick held Clara, by the sight of a laugh, a smile on Clara's lips. Intolerable. Impossible.

Diggory followed her gaze.

'Amy,' he said slowly, almost carefully, 'you are rather cut up about Clara's marriage, aren't you?'

She nodded. There was something new in Diggory's tone, and she did not trust herself to speak.

'*Very* cut up?'

Another nod.

'I am sorry that you are unhappy.' Her brother's voice was gentle, soft. 'Listen, Amy,' he said, 'I do not know very much about heartbreak.'

Amelia felt herself start at the word. She looked at Diggory, and he looked back at her, and she knew that he had worked it out at last.

'But,' Diggory went on, putting his hand on her arm, 'I do know quite a lot about you, and I think you are rather tough – don't you agree?'

Amelia laughed. It was a very shaky laugh. 'Oh, terribly tough.'

'And you know, Amy, that you can always talk to me. About anything.'

She felt as though the world were spinning. She wanted to laugh, and she wanted to cry, and she wanted to hug her brother tight. She was so unhappy and so very, very glad.

'And you know, Amy,' said Diggory, 'if you ever get bored of Papa, you can always come and live with me and Rose.'

'Thank you,' she said, and she did not know what more to say. Too many words stuck in her throat. She squeezed her brother's arm. 'Go and dance,' she said gently. 'It is your wedding day. Enjoy it. Be happy for me.'

He looked at her, grinned and was gone.

∾

Felicia was dancing with Major Alderton. It felt strange to appear with him in public, to know the world was talking of them, that everybody knew she was to be his bride. It had unnerved her this morning at St Matthew's, watching Lady Rose and Diggory Ashpoint get married, knowing that she would be making the same promises in a matter of weeks.

The dance ended, and Major Alderton went to fetch them both a glass of wine. She really could not get used to thinking of him as Charles. She would have to school herself to it soon.

She stood for a moment at the edge of the ballroom, watching the moving figures before her. There was her mother, talking solemnly to Lady Wickford – her mother, so defeated, so outmanoeuvred, forced to make the best of her daughter's disappointing marriage. There were Sir Frederick and Clara McNeil, still dancing. And there was Monsieur Brisset, standing with Mr Lonsdale. Her music master glanced at her, smiled faintly, then looked away. She tried very hard not to look at him.

And there were the Hursts and the Robertses, sitting in one corner of the ballroom, looking so very alone. Felicia thought of all the rumours, of Lord Salbridge's spiteful words after dinner. She wondered how she had ever found him amusing. She looked at Mr Hurst, his kind face turned so weary; she looked at Mrs Hurst, so pale – at the children, chattering amongst themselves because the other children at the wedding would not play with them. She thought again of the words she had overheard between Mr and Mrs Hurst after the dinner all those months ago, the painful anxiety in their voices. She thought of all the lonely years of her own childhood, how often she had wished for a friend.

Major Alderton was back at her side now, handing her a glass of wine.

'Charles,' said Felicia slowly, 'should we go and speak to them?'

He followed her gaze towards the Hursts, then turned back to her. He observed her steadily for a moment, as though she had taken him by surprise, then nodded. If the rumours about the Hursts were really true, thought Felicia, then the Roberts children were not so very different from Major Alderton, and that must mean something to him. And if they were not true – well, he knew what it was to be talked of.

'We ought to – to make a show of it,' she said. 'You understand what I mean?'

Major Alderton laughed. 'You mean that you have made me respectable, and now you will make them so, too?'

Felicia smiled. It was, she thought, the first time he had made her smile.

She put her arm through his, because after all, he was to be her husband, and together they crossed the room, calmly, steadily – slowly enough to gain the attention of half the guests. Then they sat down in the seats beside Mr and Mrs Hurst and struck up an animated conversation.

Society watched. Society murmured. Nobody had wanted to believe Lord Salbridge, of course – everybody had been happier to think well of the Hursts, to dismiss all that scandalous talk. But nor had anybody wanted to make the first move. To have their logic questioned so openly, to have the Hursts dragged back into the shade – it had caused a ripple of apprehension, a fresh seed of doubt.

But here was Miss Elton – irreproachable, perfect Miss Elton – sitting down with the Hursts, quite content. *She*, certainly, believed no ill of them. And who possibly could after that?

Amelia Ashpoint looked on in surprise from across the ballroom. She watched the guests visibly relax as the next dance began. She watched Anne Palmer approach the table, saw Mrs Crayton hurry over to pay her respects to the Hursts. Mr Elton was coming to join his daughter, and the youngest of the Palmer girls went up to Eleanor Roberts to introduce herself.

Amelia smiled.

If her father's money and stratagems had not been enough to withstand Lord Salbridge's words – well, the perfection of Miss Felicia Elton was unshakable.

Of all the unlikely allies.

Across the room, Felicia glanced up from her conversation with Mrs Hurst. She met Amelia's gaze and gave her a faint smile.

CHAPTER XI

In which Lord Salbridge miscalculates

MEANWHILE, FOUR MILES AWAY FROM ASHPOINT HALL, Lord Salbridge was walking through Wickford village. He had been packed up in the carriage and sent home from the wedding in disgrace, but it had not been hard to escape Wickford Towers tonight. Most of the staff had left already, and though the front doors were locked, nobody had thought to secure the servants' entrance.

So here he was, walking through the village in the cool evening air, out into the fields, in the familiar direction of Grace Abbott's house.

He was shaken by the events of the day, by that dreadful scandal of a wedding, by that upstart Lonsdale's behaviour. He needed comfort. He needed something, someone.

Grace's home was much like all the other cottages – thatched roof, cobbled walls, a little damp, a little rough – but something had changed since he was last here. One of the windows was broken and boarded up, and there was a gaping hole in one side of the thatch. He wondered for a moment if Grace had left the village, but then he heard a child's voice inside.

He did not hesitate. He had enough confidence in his charm and manner to feel secure. She would let him in, and they would sit at the old table, and he would talk to her. She would take him back, of course. He would make her forgive him, make her see the damage she had done. He would ask her to go to his mother tomorrow morning before they left, confess that it was all nonsense, deny the affair, admit that she had lied about being with child. It might make his parents keep him on a looser leash on the Continent.

He walked up to the door and knocked.

There was a moment's pause, a sound of panic and a short hurry of steps – and then the door opened and Grace stood before him.

He stared. All words left him in an instant. He was looking at her face, angry and careworn as he had never seen it. She had never looked at him like this before, with astonishment and hatred in her eyes. Then he looked at her figure, the slight but clear swell of her belly, and he simply could not move.

He had never believed in the child. He had thought it a lie to get his mother's sympathy, to petition for money, to make the scandal worse than it might have been. And now he reeled at the unmistakable truth. She was with child. And of course the child must be his. He could see it in her eyes: the anger, the fury.

'What in God's name are you doing here?' she said, in a low, burning tone.

All his old charm, his careless manners deserted him. He could not reply.

'Do you think you're welcome here, after everything? You are not a part of my life – you are not worthy to stand on my doorstep.' She seemed to be trying to control her voice, but he still heard it, the sting of the sheer loathing. 'Do you know what they call me now? The other folk round here – they call me the young lord's whore. Someone threw a brick through my window, hit Janey on the arm. The milkmaids tried to burn us out last week and would've, too, if I hadn't been quick to stop the fire. Do you have any idea of the mess you've left me in? Damn you to hell. Get away from here – I've nothing to say to you!'

'Grace—' he began, but before he could get any further, she spat at his feet and slammed the door in his face.

~

'I am glad you threw that fellow out,' Brisset said to Lonsdale as they stood together at the edge of the ballroom. 'I shall be glad to see the back of him.'

Lonsdale smiled. 'He will be spreading no more rumours here.'

They both glanced to where the Hursts sat. Felicia Elton was talking to the two eldest children, while Major Alderton was conversing with their mother. His eyes remained on Felicia Elton as Captain and Mrs Palmer came up to the table to speak to Mr Hurst.

'I am pleased she did that,' said Brisset softly, and Lonsdale did not need to ask whom he meant.

'You are losing your best pupil, Brisset.'

'It happens.'

He gave a solemn shrug, but Lonsdale could see in his face that Miss Elton's marriage hit him harder than he would like to admit. Lonsdale said nothing, but he put his hand for a moment on his friend's arm.

Brisset shook him off with a faint smile. 'I am all right,' he said. 'Go and dance.' And he inclined his head towards Amelia Ashpoint, who was talking to her younger siblings.

Lonsdale shook his head. 'No,' he said softly, 'I think not.'

'No?' Brisset frowned. He studied Lonsdale's face. 'You have lost, too, eh?'

'I have lost nothing.' Lonsdale smiled, felt lighter than he thought Brisset did. 'She is a true friend, and so is her brother. That is all.'

'Yes, I do like Mr Diggory,' said Brisset. 'It was kind of him to invite me today.'

'Didn't I tell you that we half-gentlemen would win in the end?' Lonsdale nudged his glass of champagne towards his friend's. 'Come, you are not still thinking of leaving Wickenshire?'

Brisset turned to him with a smile. 'Well,' he said, 'perhaps I shall stay a little longer.'

~

At the end of yet another dance, Diggory sat down, exhausted, at one of the side tables, and was drinking his wine very thankfully when his new wife appeared at his side. He reached for her hand.

'What a day it has been!' she said.

Diggory was too tired and too happy to think of a sensible reply. He began to laugh. He pulled Rose down to sit beside him, put his arm around her waist and leant his head on her shoulder.

'Diggory,' she said, her smile faltering a little, 'Diggory – there is something I wanted to talk to you about, about Salbridge.'

'What is it?'

She lowered her voice, glanced around. 'You do not think anyone can hear us?'

Diggory sat up straighter. 'No, no. Whatever is the matter?'

'Only – well, with my family going away, and – Diggory, there is something I overheard at home, something about Salbridge that is very dreadful, and I should like to help and – oh, I could not have spoken to you about such things before we were married, but *now*—' She took a deep breath, then went on in a low, eager voice, 'There is a woman named Grace Abbott, who—'

'You know?' exclaimed Diggory.

She stared at him. '*You* know?'

'Well, yes, I—'

'That makes things easier.' Rose paused, and then, placing her hand in Diggory's, she said, 'I know she came to ask Mama for money, for the – the child, and for her daughter, too, who she is keen to see educated. Mama gave her a little, but there was hardly anything left, and – well, I overheard it all, and I thought, perhaps, *we* could do what Mama could not. I should like to meet her – and the child, when it comes. I should like to help her, if we can, if she will let us. Would you – well, would you come with me to see her?'

'Rose,' he began slowly, 'is that—'

'The child will be my niece or nephew, you know, in blood if not in law. Salbridge may not care about such things, but I should hope *I* do.'

Diggory looked at her, his brilliant, kind, perfect wife. He raised her hand to his lips. 'Of course I shall come with you,' he said. 'Of course we shall help her any way we can.'

Rose put her head on his shoulder, wound her hands into his. Then, as her eyes passed over Mr and Mrs Hurst, dancing with the rest of them now, nobody giving them a second glance, she said softly, 'Do you think it is really nonsense about the Hursts?'

'Rose! You know it is all slander of your brother's.'

'I suppose so,' said Rose. She ran her thumb over Diggory's palm. 'Do you think you would still love me, if I were married to somebody else?'

Diggory frowned. 'Would you still want me to?'

'Well, say I was unhappily married. Say I had been forced or deceived or something like that. Do you think you would still love me?'

Diggory looked round at her. He thought of this morning, Rose's shining smile as she moved down the aisle. 'Yes,' he said gently. 'Yes, I think I would.'

CHAPTER XII

In which the dance goes on

AMELIA HAD BEEN TUCKED AWAY IN ONE OF THE SIDE rooms for half an hour. Hardly anybody seemed to notice. Anne Palmer had passed by and looked in at her curiously, but no one had yet disturbed her.

She was watching the ball through the open door. Diggory and Rose were up again. Her father was waltzing with Lady Wickford. Laurie was dancing with Eleanor Roberts, and Ada was helping little Georgy toddle around the ballroom. Major Alderton and Felicia made up another couple. Clara was dancing with Lonsdale now. Amelia had lost sight of Sir Frederick.

It seemed almost impossible that Clara was really lost to her. It was a deep, unruly sort of pain, the knowledge of their split future, the thought that she and Clara would meet at parties as half-indifferent acquaintances, that the new Lady Hammersmith would pay her stately calls and send her invitations to dinners she did not wish to attend. They would never talk as they used to. She would never tell Clara stories again.

'Miss Ashpoint?'

She found to her dismay that Sir Frederick was standing

in the doorway of her solitary retreat. He hesitated, then walked forwards, pulled a chair close to hers and sat down.

'What a pleasant party this is.' When she did not reply, he said, 'I wanted to talk to you, Miss Ashpoint.'

'Very well,' she replied stiffly.

'Look,' he said, after a moment's awkward silence, 'Miss Ashpoint, I know you do not like me.'

She flinched. Of course it was true, but it was so dreadful to know that he knew, to know that he must think her a friend who deemed him unworthy, that he was so far from the mark as that. She thought of that day at Clara's house when she had goaded him about Miss Elton and about his clothes, when he had not known how to respond. She had always prided herself on being witty, sharp, clever – but what must Sir Frederick have thought of her then? She would simply have been the unkind friend of the girl he was falling in love with.

'It is a shame,' he was saying now, 'for I like you, but I suppose there is – well, not much to be done about it. Nonetheless, I should like us to get along, for Clara's sake – and surely you must, too. You are very important to Clara, I know, and that you should consider cutting her because she makes a marriage you disapprove of—'

'Oh, it is not that.' Amelia really thought that she might cry. It was unbearable to hear him call her Clara. 'I am sorry, Sir Frederick, if I have offended you. I know I am sometimes a little—' She broke off. What was she to say? That she was aware she could be unfair, that she had laughed at him because it had pleased her to do so, because it had been easier to think him silly than to let herself see that he admired Clara?

Instead she said, 'Clara's marriage makes a change in the friendship we have shared.'

Sir Frederick nodded. 'I won't pretend that I quite understand,' he said slowly, 'but, Miss Ashpoint, you must believe that I love your friend very dearly. I know I am not as clever as her, and I know that I am considered a little . . . eccentric, but – well, I promise that I shall do everything in my power to make Clara happy.'

Amelia looked at him. Even in purple and stripes he looked earnest. She had misjudged him – and really, who had she not misjudged? Even Felicia Elton had surprised her today.

'I believe you,' she murmured, and it hurt to speak the words.

'I'm glad of it.' He paused. Through the open door, the music slowed and started once more. 'That is not, however, what I wanted to say.' Sir Frederick cleared his throat and lowered his voice. 'In fact, I wanted to say a word to you about the Hursts.'

Amelia frowned in surprise. 'The Hursts?'

'Yes.' His voice was very quiet. 'I know what you and your father have done, these last few weeks, to ensure that Wickenshire believes the rumour to be a lie. And I know, as you and your father do, that it is not.'

Amelia started. '*You* know?'

'Of course. Mr Hurst is my greatest friend.'

'But – but you didn't – well, judge him for it? I always thought you were—' She broke off, aware that to go on would be an affront.

'Stiff?' suggested Sir Frederick. 'Conservative, old-fashioned?' He shrugged, smiled. 'I know my father's mistakes have made me judge certain pleasures rather harshly – I do not gamble or drink or go to the Lantern – but the situation with Montgomery is something entirely different. His has not been an easy life, as you can imagine. He wrote to me when first he met Matilda, and I have known her these ten years. I used to visit them on the Continent. She is as dear a friend to me as he is. I am god-father to all three of the children – not, of course, that that can ever be known here.'

Amelia stared. She almost softened towards him, but then she spotted Clara dancing out in the ballroom, and she felt her heart harden. 'I did not know.'

'Well, I wanted to thank you – and your father, too. Montgomery and Matilda are now content to stay in Wickenshire – they have said so to me this very night. They hope to live here in peace. What you and your father have done – they are truly grateful for it. *I* am truly grateful. I could not have lost my best friends without much regret.' He hesitated. 'I wanted to ask you if – well, have you ever mentioned the circumstances to Clara? I thought perhaps you might have done, and if she knows, I should like for us both to be aware that the other knows the truth. I should hate to have any secrets from Clara. And of course, our marriage will bring her into intimacy with the Hursts and—'

'She knows,' said Amelia. She spoke very quietly.

'Ah. Good.' Sir Frederick smiled. 'I am glad to hear it. She does not think the worse of them? I hope – I trust – I am sure she does not.'

'She does not.'

'Then that confirms my opinion of her. Thank you.' He hesitated, rose awkwardly, glanced at the open door, then looked round at Amelia. 'I have a proposition for you,' he said. 'If I – well, if I pretend to be unaware that you dislike me, will you pretend not to dislike me quite as much as you do? I think it would spare Clara some pain.'

It was worse, she thought, that he must be good, worse that he must be kind and unaware, worse that she had misjudged him. It made him so much harder for her to hate and so much easier, perhaps, for Clara to love – not quite as she had loved Amelia, but enough to get by, enough for her not to long for Amelia as much as Amelia would long for her.

'I think you will make Clara happy,' said Amelia stiffly. 'Clara's happiness is important to me.'

'Then you agree to my proposition?'

He held out his hand for her to shake, and she took it reluctantly.

'I agree,' she said. 'I agree to try.'

~

Mr Ashpoint was pleased when Amelia emerged from the side room. He had not wanted to disturb her in her solitude, but he was glad to see her joining the ball once more. He glanced around at the rest of his family – Laurie and Ada dancing their best with the little Robertses, wide-eyed and beaming; Diggory waltzing round and round with Rose.

He would miss Diggory. Of course, he would not be far away, but it was not quite the same thing. He would miss having him at Ashpoint Hall. He would miss the way he rolled his eyes, how he was always late down for breakfast. Diggory was the first of the family to leave home, and perhaps they all would be at it soon. When Laurie got older, he might be off to some profession or other, even to a university if he were so inclined. Ada would be out in a year or two, and within a few years she would probably be married. And Amelia – no, Mr Ashpoint did not think Amelia would marry. He could not say quite why he believed this, why the feeling had stolen upon him these last few weeks, why it troubled him less than it used to – but there it was. She was such a dear girl. Let her live as she chose.

How strange it was, for one's children to be suddenly grown-up, to realize within a moment that one was getting old.

He watched Diggory and Rose dancing and thought of his own wedding day, how very long ago it had been. He missed Charlotte dreadfully sometimes. He wished she could have been here today, seen how their son had shone with happiness. He wished he could show her how kind and strange and wonderful all four of their children were. He was very lucky, he thought, to have such a family. He was very lucky indeed.

~

'May we join you, Miss Ashpoint?'

Amelia looked up to see Miss Waterson and Miss Maddon. They did not wait for her reply, but each pulled up a chair at her table and sat down across from her. She made herself smile.

'If you are not engaged next Tuesday, Miss Ashpoint,' said Miss Waterson, 'won't you come and take tea with us?'

'We thought we might ask some of the Palmer girls, too,' added Miss Maddon.

Amelia smiled. 'I should like that very much,' she replied.

She looked beyond them, towards the dance, and she caught sight of her father, watching her from across the room. He raised his hand in salutation, and Amelia nodded back. Six months ago, her father would have frowned to see her sitting down without a partner. But perhaps he understood her a little better these days.

In the last fortnight, Amelia had sometimes considered running away on her own. The coming weddings depressed her. The idea that she and Clara could never be what they once were to one another crushed her spirits, dampened her enthusiasm for everything save writing. She could do it alone. She could leave Wickenshire and go to the Continent, visit all the places Mrs Hurst had mentioned, style herself as a widow and earn bread from her books, leave everyone behind. She was intelligent. She was resourceful. She would find a way.

But then she looked at Diggory, her charming, funny brother with his shiny shoes and his sloppy manners. She thought of his words earlier, the warmth it had brought her to know that he *knew*, that he understood. She looked at Lady Rose, her new sister-in-law with her dimpled happiness and her bright, eager smile. At the edge of the ballroom, Laurie and Ada were dancing together – and look at them, so young and sweet, so preposterous and pretty. She would not like to miss their strange conversations, to live without Laurie's shyness and Ada's sighs over romantic novels. She had a notion that Ada would rather like the work of A. A. Oaksharp. Amelia glanced at her father, her father who loved gossip and news, her father whom she had once believed so proud, so closed in his views; her father, with whom she kept the secret of the Hursts, who had been amongst the first to shout Lord Salbridge down; her father, whom she knew so much better now.

And she thought of Clara, those long years of love. She

thought of the touch of Clara's hand, the pressure of Clara's lips on hers. She thought of Clara's intelligence, her simple kindness, her small smile. It was an aching, dreadful pain to see her dance with Sir Frederick, to know that they would marry, have children, lead a life together and apart from her. But it would be even more unbearable to leave and not look back, to know that she would never see Clara again.

As the music slowed and the dancers came to a stop, Amelia knew how it would be. She would stay in Wickenshire, for now, at least. It was her home, and she loved it, in her way. The thought of running away was an adventure story – and she was done with adventure stories for a while. Perhaps her next novel would be about a small town instead.

Yes, she would stay to see the Hursts happy and respected. She would take tea occasionally with the new Aldertons, talk literature with Lonsdale, dine awkwardly with Sir Frederick and Lady Clara Hammersmith, lunch with the Palmer sisters, play cards with her siblings. She would make more effort with Miss Waterson and Miss Maddon. She would try to laugh at her neighbours a little less. She would attend weddings, christenings and funerals, card parties, dinners and balls. In the long evenings at home, she would sit with her father. One day, she would tell him about her book.

And who knew what the years would bring? She might go to London for the Season with Diggory and Rose, meet her publishers, attend the kind of literary dinners she read of in books. There were ways to travel without running away. And perhaps, in time, she might find someone else, a woman a little – but not too much – like Clara. Someone to tell stories with, to write letters to, to hold in secret. Someone – she would not say braver than Clara, but someone with different wishes, different plans. Amelia was still young. But she knew it would be a long time before the ache of losing Clara took up less space in her heart.

For now, she would watch it all. She would listen to the waves of gossip that flooded through Wickenshire, hear the farmhands and servants whisper, the ladies and gentlemen spread their secrets. She would write her stories.

It would not, all in all, be so very bad a life.

Acknowledgements

The Trouble with Mrs Montgomery Hurst has been living in my head for nearly a decade. It is a much older idea than my first novel, *The Secrets of Hartwood Hall*, and it has been through dozens of iterations. If *The Secrets of Hartwood Hall* is a love letter to the Brontës, then *The Trouble with Mrs Montgomery Hurst* is a love letter to Anthony Trollope, Jane Austen and Elizabeth Gaskell. It owes a particular debt to *Pride and Prejudice*, *Emma*, *Cranford*, *Wives and Daughters* and *The Chronicles of Barsetshire*. If *The Secrets of Hartwood Hall* is about escaping nineteenth-century society, then *The Trouble with Mrs Montgomery Hurst* is about the people who were left to live in it.

I owe a lot to all the individuals, places and books that assisted me with my research. The nineteenth-century diaries, accounts and advice books – especially on brewing and etiquette – that I was able to read through the British Library were hugely helpful. This novel would not be what it is without *The Secret Diaries of Anne Lister*, edited by Helena Whitbread, or Mallory James's wonderful work of non-fiction, *Elegant Etiquette in the Nineteenth Century*. My thanks go to Hook Norton Brewery, especially to David, the brewery tour guide, and Sean, the walking tour guide, both of whom gave me such useful information on my visit. Thanks also to Claudia for her invaluable knowledge of early nineteenth-century music. I am also very grateful to the late Judith Miller for everything she taught me about history and antiques while I was working with her on the *Miller's Antiques Price Guides* back in 2017 and 2018, while writing the earliest versions of *The Trouble with Mrs Montgomery Hurst*.

This novel owes so much to two amazing editors: Emma Plater and Jessica Leeke. Thank you both for your sound advice and for your total understanding of this slightly odd novel. Thank you also to everyone else at Penguin Michael Joseph: Nina Elstad for the amazing cover; Kallie Townsend and Ciara Berry for fantastic publicity work; Courtney Barclay, Steph Biddle and Jessie Beswick for marketing magic; Maxine Hitchcock for all her support; Nick Lowndes for desk editing; Serena Nazareth in production; Christina Ellicott, Laura Garrod, Kelly Mason, Sophie Marston and Hannah Padgham in the sales team; and Anna Curvis and Akua Akowuah in the international team.

Thank you to my fantastic sensitivity reader, Reina Gattuso, for all your insight, help and encouragement. Clare Bowron, thank you for your editorial advice. Thank you, too, to my copy editor, Emma Horton, for helping me to sort out impossible locations and reminding me how frowning works, and thanks also to my eagle-eyed proof-reader, Liz Cowen. Huge thanks also to Neil Gower, for taking my initial poorly drawn map of Wickenshire and turning it into a real and beautiful place.

A huge thank you as ever to my agent, Karolina Sutton, for all her support, understanding and encouragement. Thanks also to Izzy Redfern and Sarah Harvey and the rest of the team at CAA.

I also wanted to thank the BookTube community and the wider online bookish community for all its support with my first novel, *The Secrets of Hartwood Hall*. Every positive review and every tag on Instagram of my book in an actual bookshop brings me so much joy. I'm really grateful to all my fellow BookTubers for their support.

Thank you to my amazing writing group, who, over the years, have read so many extracts from so many different versions of *The Trouble with Mrs Montgomery Hurst*. It would not be the book it is without your encouragement and feedback. Special thanks go to George, for running the group, and to Hannah, Andrew, Will and Natalie, for being amongst the novel's earliest readers. Without them, Mrs Ashpoint would still be alive and Amelia's character arc would be much less strong. Hannah, I can only apologize for the lack of attractive gardeners in this novel, and I'll try to do better next time.

Thank you to all my friends for their support and enthusiasm about my books, especially to: Jess, Céline, Molly, Steph, Jenny, Sarah, Sophie, Jenny, Marissa, Elli – and Lexy, who read a very early version of this novel many years ago.

Thank you to all my family, near and far, especially to Granny and Auntie Lou, whose encouragement and support meant so much to me over the years.

I am so grateful to both my parents for their continued support and enthusiasm – and for their ability to sell *The Secrets of Hartwood Hall* to everybody they work with. Thank you, as always, to my brother, Jim, who has been reading my writing since we were very young children. I am nothing like Amelia, and you are not much like Diggory, but I am glad to know we have a friendship as strong as theirs.

Thank you to my husband, Nick: for always understanding and loving my writing; for maintaining excitement about Wickenshire and its residents for nearly a decade; for naming the county of Wickenshire; for reading and commenting on version after version of this book; and for helping me with Amelia's wit when I failed to be 'mean enough'. Amelia owes some of her funniest moments to you.

Finally, I want to thank Mary Rose, who shared my love of books and to whom this novel is dedicated. The thing about family friends is that they are both family and friends, and no one could have asked for a greater friend than you. You are, and will always be, sorely missed.